GRASS ROOTS

STUART WOODS

G. P. PUTNAM'S SONS
NEW YORK

PUTNAM

G. P. PUTNAM'S SONS
Publishers Since 1838
An imprint of Penguin Random House LLC
375 Hudson Street
New York, New York 10014

First Simon and Schuster hardcover edition / July 1989
First Signet premium edition / August 2011
First G. P. Putnam's Sons premium edition / May 2017
G. P. Putnam's Sons premium edition ISBN: 9780451234308

Printed in the United States of America
5   7   9   10   8   6

This book is for Dot,
with love.

BOOKS BY STUART WOODS

FICTION

Fast & Loose[†]
Below the Belt[†]
Sex, Lies & Serious Money[†]
Dishonorable Intentions[†]
Family Jewels[†]
Scandalous Behavior[†]
Foreign Affairs[†]
Naked Greed[†]
Hot Pursuit[†]
Insatiable Appetites[†]
Paris Match[†]
Cut and Thrust[†]
Carnal Curiosity[†]
Standup Guy[†]
Doing Hard Time[†]
Unintended Consequences[†]
Collateral Damage[†]
Severe Clear[†]
Unnatural Acts[†]
D.C. Dead[†]
Son of Stone[†]

Bel-Air Dead[†]
Strategic Moves[†]
Santa Fe Edge[§]
Lucid Intervals[†]
Kisser[†]
Hothouse Orchid[*]
Loitering with Intent[†]
Mounting Fears[‡]
Hot Mahogany[†]
Santa Fe Dead[§]
Beverly Hills Dead
Shoot Him If He Runs[†]
Fresh Disasters[†]
Short Straw[§]
Dark Harbor[†]
Iron Orchid[*]
Two-Dollar Bill[†]
The Prince of Beverly Hills
Reckless Abandon[†]
Capital Crimes[‡]
Dirty Work[†]
Blood Orchid[*]
The Short Forever[†]

Orchid Blues[*]
Cold Paradise[†]
L.A. Dead[†]
The Run[‡]
Worst Fears Realized[†]
Orchid Beach[*]
Swimming to Catalina[†]
Dead in the Water[†]
Dirt[†]
Choke
Imperfect Strangers
Heat
Dead Eyes
L.A. Times
Santa Fe Rules[§]
New York Dead[†]
Palindrome
Grass Roots[‡]
White Cargo
Deep Lie[‡]
Under the Lake
Run Before the Wind[‡]
Chiefs[‡]

COAUTHORED BOOKS
Smooth Operator[**]
(with Parnell Hall)

TRAVEL
A Romantic's Guide to the Country Inns of Britain and Ireland (1979)

MEMOIR
Blue Water, Green Skipper

[*]A Holly Barker Novel
[†]A Stone Barrington Novel
[‡]A Will Lee Novel
[§]An Ed Eagle Novel
[**]A Teddy Fay Novel

Praise for Stuart Woods
and *Grass Roots*

"A dandy story . . . sensational. . . . Woods keeps the pages turning briskly." —*The Dallas Morning News*

"Superbly plotted, its dramatic events coming at break-neck speed and its momentum hurling the reader toward the toe-curling conclusion."
—*The Atlanta Journal-Constitution*

"Woods . . . is one of the best around at tense, fast-paced plotting." —*St. Petersburg Times*

"Grabs you and jerks you forward at a rapid pace, making it hard to catch your breath . . . there are enough surprises along the way to keep you guessing until the very end. . . . A finely crafted novel that is full of enjoyment."
—*The Chattanooga Times*

"An excellent piece of writing." —*Pasadena Star-News*

"The story holds magic." —*St. Louis Post-Dispatch*

"Woods effectively mixes suspense, politics, and murder in the rural South." —*The Orlando Sentinel*

"This time he's so good he cost me several sleepless nights. . . . A wonderful book, rich and full and fast-moving and horrifyingly timely." —Anne Rivers Siddons

"Woods is a world-class mystery writer. And he's getting better and better. . . . I try to put Woods's books down, and I can't. The pace is terrific without being breathless. His prose style is fluid, his dialogue plentiful and excel-lent." —*Houston Chronicle*

A senator's sudden illness . . .
A trial that fans the flames of racism . . .
A political future on the line . . .

"Woods is a no-nonsense, slam-bang storyteller."
—*Chicago Tribune*

As a Georgia senator's chief of staff, attorney Will Lee knows what it takes to run a successful political campaign. With his sights on his own senate run in two years' time, he heads to Delano, Georgia—and back to his family's law practice—hoping to establish a presence in his home state. But his first case, defending a white man accused of murdering a black woman, puts Will on shaky ground. And when his boss is struck down and Will decides to run for his vacant seat, he's catapulted into the spotlight—and becomes a target for shadowy forces who will stop at nothing to keep him out of office. . . .

"[Woods] tells a terrific yarn."
—*The Boston Globe*

"A twisting, turning tide of action and circumstance . . . there isn't a dead moment or a wasted scene."
—*Houston Chronicle*

"Stuart Woods is a wonderful storyteller who could teach Robert Ludlum and Tom Clancy a thing or two."
—*The State* (Columbia, SC)

continued . . .

PROLOGUE

"One full clip, lock and load."

Four loud clicks sounded, as one.

"Arm your weapon."

Four bolts slid back, as one.

"Ready on the right; ready on the left; ready on the firing line. In short bursts, fire at will."

Perkerson blinked involuntarily, as he always did when the weapons were fired without suppressors. The second burst came in unison, then the pattern broke up as his four students placed their bursts. When the firing was over, and the weapons were at port arms again, there was no need to bring the targets back. Each of them was shredded at the center of the chest of the figure drawn on the target. No group was greater in diameter than ten inches. Damn fine shooting, for automatic weapons, Perkerson thought.

Automatically, his eyes shifted to the catwalk in the shadows above and behind the range. Perkerson jumped. He was there. No one had known he was coming; he was just suddenly there.

"Blindfolds."

The four men let their weapons hang and tied bandanas about their eyes.

"About-face. Kneel. Fieldstrip and reassemble your weapons." Perkerson watched, a little anxiously, as four pairs of hands quickly dismantled the submachine pistols. He tried not to look up at the catwalk as his students deftly did as they had been taught. The first finished in record time; none of the others was more than a few seconds behind.

"Atten-shun! At ease! Number four, nobody told you to remove your blindfold." Perkerson looked up at the catwalk, waiting. The man moved his eyes from the four students to Perkerson and nodded.

Perkerson found he had been holding his breath. He released it and turned toward the four trainees. "Men," he said, keeping his voice steady, "tonight, you have the honor to be addressed directly by the Archon."

In spite of the blindfolds, surprise and pleasure showed on the men's faces. When the voice came, they jerked as if experiencing an electric shock.

"Good evening, gentlemen," the Archon said. He did not need to raise his voice; it was rich and resonant. "Tonight you are admitted."

One of the students released a nervous giggle.

"Tonight, there are four fewer Americans wandering, lost, in their own land. Tonight, you join a company which, for a little while longer, must remain secret. You pledge with your blood, with your very life, to protect that secret. There is no oath to take. The oath is in your hearts, in that place where every man knows the truth, where love and hate reside—love for your country as it should be;

hatred for those who would weaken it, the mongrel rabble that sucks its lifeblood while poisoning the minds of its children."

The Archon paused for effect. "Congratulations to you all. Tonight, you are . . . The Elect."

Perkerson watched as the figure receded into the darkness. There was the sound of a door opening and softly closing. "All right," Perkerson said to his charges. "You may remove your blindfolds."

The four men pulled away the bandanas and blinked in the bright lights of the shooting range. "Jesus," one of them said. "That wasn't no tape, was it?"

"That," Perkerson said, "was the real thing. You've met the Man, the Archon himself."

"Shit," the man said. "I never thought I'd meet him this soon."

"It might be a long time before you meet him again," Perkerson said to all of them, "but meet him you will, on The Day."

One of the men raised a fist. "On The Day," he said.

"On The Day," the others repeated.

BOOK ONE

BOOK ONE

I

Will Lee flashed his identification at the guard and nodded toward the car. "Can I park out front for just a few minutes? I've got to pick up some stuff from the office."

The guard came down the steps and walked around the Porsche—not new, not clean—and carefully inspected the parking sticker on the windshield. Taking his time, he walked back to where Will shivered. "Ten minutes," the man said. "No more."

Everybody in Washington loved power, Will reflected as he got out of the car and slammed the door. Not least, Capitol guards. Seven-thirty on a Saturday morning in December, Congress having recessed the day before, and the man was worried about traffic. Will raced into the Russell Building, under low, leaden skies, the cold nipping at his neck. He paused to sign in at the inside guard's desk, then entered the building, his steps echoing off the marble floor as he headed toward the elevators. In a hurry and almost without thinking, he did something he had never done before: he pushed the members' button, guaranteeing express service. He leaned against the paneling as the car rose, taking in a faint odor of varnish and cigars, and allowed himself a ten-second reverie: he was not an interloper in this car, but an elected member, leaving the press gathered at the elevator door as he rose to his suite of offices to take a phone call from a worried President. It made him laugh that he was no more immune to the lure of power than the building guard. The car eased to a stop, and Will walked quickly down the hallway to the office. To his surprise, the door swung open before he could turn the key.

Will dismissed the thought of anything sinister; the cleaners must have forgotten to lock it. He strode quickly through the small reception area and past the staff desks that crowded the main room of the suite, then turned right past the Senator's closed door to his own small office. Even a senator's chief of staff did not rate much space in the crowded Russell Building. He had got behind his desk and was opening a drawer before he noticed the light coming from under the other door, the one that opened into his boss's room. Someone was in Benjamin Carr's office.

Will hesitated, then put aside his caution. He walked to the door and opened it, prepared to accost an intruder with righteous indignation, at the very least. His eye fell first on the collection of photographs of Ben Carr with each of the last nine Presidents of the United States, starting with an ill-looking Franklin Roosevelt, on the front porch of the Little White House, in Warm Springs, Georgia. Then his attention went to the figure hunched over the Senator's desk.

Ben Carr looked up, surprised. "What're you doing in here this time of day, boy?" he asked in his gravelly voice.

"Morning, Senator," Will replied, surprised himself. "I was on my way to the airport. I forgot something." He frowned. "What on earth are *you* doing in here at this hour on a Saturday?"

The Senator looked sly. "How do you know I'm not here *every* Saturday morning?" He waved a hand. "I know, I know, because you're here yourself. Naw, I'm here for the same reason as you. I've got a nine-o'clock plane to Atlanta; Jasper's waiting in the garage."

"How'd the physical go?" Will asked. He had not seen his boss for two days, since the Senator had spent Friday at Walter Reed Hospital.

"Sound as a—yen," the Senator replied, chuckling at his own joke. "They say I'm fighting fit."

"Now is that a fact, sir?" Will asked. "You know I'll find out if it isn't." Ben Carr was seventy-eight, and he had been looking tired lately.

"Hell, you sure will," Carr laughed. "Can't keep a secret anymore in this town. Used to be, a member of Congress could keep a girl in Georgetown or screw a colleague's wife, and the press didn't write about it. Not anymore, though." He raised a calming hand. "Don't get worried, now; my blood pressure's up a little, that's all. They gave me some pills; I might even take 'em."

"You're sure that's all?"

"That's all. They tell me I'll live through another term. We'll announce right after Christmas, I think. We don't want the Republicans to have too much time to get excited, do we?"

Will grinned. "No, sir. We'll let 'em down early."

Ben Carr placed his palms on his desk and pushed himself to his feet. Tall, bald, a little stooped, he walked around the desk. "I'm glad you came by this morning, Will. Sit down for a minute; I want to talk to you."

Will took a seat at one end of the leather sofa, and the Senator arranged his lanky frame at the other end, drawing a knee up beside him.

"Will, we've never really talked about this—I mean, right out in the open—but you want this job, don't you?"

"Not *your* job, sir," Will replied honestly.

"I know, I know," Carr said. "But you'd like Jim Barnett's seat next time, wouldn't you?" James J. Barnett was the lackluster Republican who had become the junior senator from Georgia two years before.

"Yes, sir, I think I would," Will said, grinning.

"Good, good," Carr said, slapping the back of the sofa. "You'll do it damned well, too."

"Thank you, sir." Will tried to meet the Senator's gaze and failed. "I thought I'd . . . after you're reelected, of course, I thought I'd better go home and get some red mud on my shoes." It was Ben Carr's own phrase for moving among the Georgia electorate, and Will had chosen it deliberately. "I've been in Washington nearly eight years now, and I'm a little out of touch."

Carr nodded. "You're right to want to do that, Will. I don't know about New York and California, but in Georgia, you win elections at the grass roots. Remember that and live by it, and you're halfway to elected office." He fell silent.

Will did not step into the breach; he knew what was

coming. He didn't want to do it, and he wasn't going to volunteer.

Ben Carr gathered his considerable presence and directed it at Will. "Will, son, I'll come right out with this. I don't want you to leave me just yet. Stay with me for two more years after the election, and I'll do everything I can to help you take Barnett's seat. I'll support you publicly from the day you announce; I'll go on television for you; I'll call in every debt owed me; every time I get a speaking request in the state, I'll send you instead." The Senator stopped and waited for a reply.

Will was staring at the carpet. This was astonishing. Ben Carr was well-known for not supporting candidates in primaries.

"I'll raise two million dollars for you," Carr said.

Will looked at him, amazed, but still said nothing.

The Senator bored into him. "Listen to me, son. I'll let it be known in the right quarters that if I die in office, I want you to be appointed to succeed me. I know that's no guarantee, but the Governor owes me more than a few favors, and I think he might just abide by my wishes in such an event."

Will took a deep breath and started to speak, but the Senator interrupted him.

"Oh, hell, you know damn good and well that I'd do all that for you anyway, whether you stay on with me or not, but goddammit, boy, I need you." He stopped talking, finally, and waited.

Will looked at the old man, who had become a second father to him during the past eight years. Ben Carr was a lifelong bachelor, and Will knew as well as he knew anything that he was the closest thing to a son the man would ever have. Their relationship was like that of many Southern men—even father and son: open affection was an embarrassment, to be shown only in a word, a gesture, a warm handshake. It was taken for granted that each of them knew how the other felt, and in this case, neither man was wrong.

He had joined the Senator's staff as a junior administrative assistant, had progressed quickly to chief legislative assistant, then chief administrative assistant, and, finally, to what amounted to chief of staff. During the first four years, he had reorganized the office, vastly improving constituent services. For two years after that, as a legislative assistant, he had expanded the Senator's research network and had personally written every formal statement Carr had made in committee or to the press. As counsel to the Senate Select Committee on Intelligence, which Carr chaired, Will had become an acknowledged expert on the United States intelligence community, with an intimate working knowledge of budgets and operations. And, finally, in the past two years, as chief of staff, he had devoted himself to assembling for the Senator what knowledgeable members of the press called the best staff on the Hill. He had thought his work was done, but now he knew it was not.

"Of course I'll stay on, Senator," Will said, then smiled. "And thank you for making it so easy for me."

Ben Carr stood up and offered his hand. "Thank you, Will. I'll do my best to see you don't regret it." He placed a hand on the younger man's shoulder and guided him to the door. "I don't think it's too early for you to start planning your campaign, and you surely ought to be seen a lot at home. You can have as much time off as you want to dig in down there."

Will stopped at his office door. "Thank you, sir, I appreciate that." He cocked his head to one side. "Can I give you a lift to Atlanta? It's right on my way. No trouble at all."

Carr grabbed Will's shoulder and shook him slightly. "Oh, no, you don't. You're not getting me in one of those little airplanes. I'll stick to the airlines. If I die on one, at least I'll have a lot of company on the way down."

"You don't seem to mind a chopper ride every now and then." Will grinned. He knew the Senator would be met by a wealthy friend's helicopter at the Atlanta airport and flown to his farm in south Georgia.

"That's different," the Senator replied gravely. "That has a bar on it."

"Whatever you say," Will laughed.

But Ben Carr had not let go of Will's shoulder. He squeezed it again, and for a moment Will thought the Senator, normally undemonstrative, was going to embrace him. Instead, Carr gave him a crooked smile, pushed him through the door, and closed it behind him.

Will drove the Porsche down Capitol Hill and, instead of heading for the airport at College Park, Maryland, turned back toward Georgetown. He felt a little numb, but elated. First of all, he had not been looking forward all that much to returning to Delano, Georgia, to a country law practice, to the hard work of assembling a political campaign against formidable odds. His father, who had been a governor, would help, of course, but it was hard for someone who had never run for office to put together a credible candidacy for the United States Senate. Now he wouldn't have to do that, not yet, anyway, and when he did, he'd have Ben Carr paving the way.

In Georgetown, he turned into P Street with the assurance of a man who had just had the course of his life plotted and ensured. He was going to get everything he wanted, and part of what he wanted was in P Street, a couple of blocks past his own town house. He found a parking place, got out, and raced up the steps, quietly letting himself in with his key. Before he closed the front door, he rang the bell three times, their usual signal; then he punched in the alarm code and trotted up the stairs to her bedroom.

Katharine Rule turned over, brushing the auburn hair from her sleepy eyes. "What are you doing back?" she mumbled. "You just left, didn't you?" She smiled as he sat on the bed.

He bent over and nuzzled the warm-with-sleep hollow of her neck. "I had to come back and tell you what's happened."

"What could happen at this hour on a Saturday morning?" she asked, puzzled. She was awake now.

"The Senator was in his office when I got there." He related their conversation.

She placed a hand on his cheek. "You'll be here, then, where I can get my hands on you."

"You betcha," he said. "I'll have to go back to Georgia, of course, just like I'd planned, but not for another couple of years."

She pulled his head down to her and kissed him. "So I don't have to come to Georgia as the candidate's wife yet? I've got a reprieve?"

"Not unless you want a reprieve. I'll marry you today, if you like."

She kissed him again. "Listen, sport, there's plenty of time for that." She looked a little embarrassed. "I didn't want to tell you just yet, but Beken took me aside yesterday and told me he's behind me for ADDI. He's willing to recommend me. That means, if I want it, it's mine." The look she gave him now begged for his indulgence.

"Assistant Deputy Director for Intelligence?"

"Right. I was going to pass, but if I've got another couple of years, well . . ."

"The first woman in the job?"

A smile spread across her face. "The very first." Now her guard was down. "Oh, Will, I've dreamed about having a shot at this. I've wanted it so much, and I had begun to think I'd never get it."

"I'm glad there's time for you to have a shot at it."

"We'll have to keep things as they are, though," she said. It was a question; she was looking at him worriedly. "You do understand? If Beken or the Director got wind of our relationship, it could cut the ground right from under me at a time when I'm about to get everything I really want at the Agency."

He grinned. "Things are pretty good. I'm satisfied. Two years from next November, though, and we're off to Georgia?"

"You've got a deal."

He kissed her. "Did I ever mention that I like kissing you when you've been asleep? Your mouth is so warm."

"Mmmmm," she said. "Come back to bed."

*   *   *

As he left the house and got back into the Porsche, Will was glad he'd come back to tell Kate the news. Still, he was a little apprehensive about her promotion. She liked her work, and she was brilliant at it. She had been head of the Soviet Office at the Central Intelligence Agency, but two years before, in what seemed to be a lateral move, after most of the hierarchy had resigned after a scandal, she had been shuffled into a special assistant's job, Liaison to the Operations Directorate, with no real authority. Seemingly at a dead end, her enthusiasm had waned to the point where she had promised to leave the Agency and marry him when he returned to Georgia to prepare his campaign for the Senate.

Now, she was up for an important promotion, to one of the top half-dozen jobs in the Agency. He wondered whether, in only a couple of years' time, she would be ready to leave it.

He turned up the car's heater. It had suddenly become colder.

2

Will drove to the little airport at College Park, Maryland. It was the only general aviation airport in the Washington, D.C., area, founded by the Wright Brothers. He drove the car out to the tie-down and loaded his luggage and two briefcases into the Cessna 182RG, then parked the car in the lot and left the keys at the office. The car would be collected and garaged at a local gas station.

After a thorough pre-flight inspection of the single-engine airplane, he phoned air-traffic control for his clearance, then took off, following the airport's mandated departure procedure. The little field was surrounded by the University of Maryland and a heavily built-up area that was allergic to aircraft noise. He contacted Washington Departure and was cleared to ascend to his cruising altitude of eight thousand feet.

In a moment, he was into the two-thousand-foot overcast, and at four thousand feet, he broke out into sunshine and clear skies. He had picked up a little ice in the clouds, but now the sun melted it away. Shortly, he was over

Virginia and headed south by southwest. The sun streamed
into the airplane, warming the air and washing away the
cares of the capital city, and he began to unwind as he
could only at the end of a congressional session. He felt a
tug of regret at leaving Kate behind, but she was spending
Christmas with her son and her parents.

As he flew on toward Georgia, the clouds beneath him
became broken, then scattered, then gave way entirely to
give the earthbound a sparkling day. The green fields of
North Carolina rolled out before him, and the blue of the
Appalachian chain rose to his right. Again, he allowed
himself to feel the wave of satisfaction that had come with
Benjamin Carr's promise to help him be elected to the
Senate. There was a long road yet to travel, of course, but
he already had the most important vote of all. The Senator's stature was such that he had not even run a reelection
campaign for the past three terms. He had simply sat on
his south Georgia front porch and made a few dozen telephone calls to the faithful around the state. Now the Senator was going to be making those calls for Will Lee.

How many of the faithful would Carr be able to move
behind Will? Not all of them, he thought; some would
have their own favorite for the seat. But most of them
would do as they were asked. Few Georgia Democrats
could hold out against the persuasive powers of Ben Carr.
His friends were everywhere in the state, from the capitol
to the smallest farm, and his enemies had long since run
for cover.

As the airplane crossed the South Carolina border into
Georgia, Will reflected that, after the Senator was reelected
to a sixth term, he would have to start putting out feelers

to some other Capitol Hill staffers, to form the nucleus of, first, a campaign organization, and, later, a senator's staff. But, more important, Will thought, he had to start being a Georgian again.

After law school, he had joined his father in the firm of Lee & Lee, and, with his father's connections from his days as governor, they had built a solid practice, both in their home town of Delano and in Atlanta. Will had become known around the state as a good lawyer and the bearer of an important political name. But in the eight years since he had joined Ben Carr's staff, his practice of law in Georgia had been desultory, squeezed in between congressional sessions, while his father and a few associates had maintained the practice. Billy Lee had had a heart attack the previous year, and though it had not been a bad one, he had slowed down somewhat, hanging on to the practice for a time when Will might want to return to it.

The airplane flew directly over downtown Atlanta now, and then over Hartsfield International Airport. The Senator would have already landed and taken off again in the helicopter. Air Traffic Control cleared Will directly to Roosevelt Memorial Field, at Warm Springs, a few miles from his home town of Delano, in Meriwether County. He began his descent from eight thousand feet.

He would have to sit down with his father and talk about spending larger chunks of time at home over the next couple of years. The Senator had promised him time off, and Will would want to choose the work from their caseload that would give him some exposure, both locally and statewide.

Soon, Will had the airfield in sight, a three-thousand-foot strip of asphalt with half a dozen light airplanes tied down on a paved ramp next to it. Will canceled his instrument flight plan, changed to the local Common Traffic Advisory Frequency, and announced his position and intentions to traffic in the Warm Springs airport area. Then he turned into a standard left traffic pattern and set the airplane down gently on the tarmac. As he taxied to the ramp, he saw that the Wagoneer had been left in the carpark for him.

The airplane secured and refueled and his luggage in the back of the car, Will unlocked the door and started to get in. He was stopped by the sight of a note on the driver's seat. He tore open the envelope and read:

Dear Will,

Judge Boggs called at lunchtime to inquire when you would be home. I told him you were expected in the early afternoon, and he asked that you come to see him at the courthouse, directly from the airport, on "a matter of some importance," as he put it. He wanted you, specifically, not your father. I told him you would come. I hope you don't mind.

We'll all be out Christmas shopping this afternoon, so we'll see you at the big house around seven for drinks and dinner.

Love,
Your Ma

What would the Judge want with him on a Saturday afternoon? He hadn't seen the old man for more than a year, when he tried a personal-injury case in his court. Will sighed and turned the car away from Delano toward Greenville, the seat of Meriwether County.

He drove slowly into the quiet antebellum town, remembering that the sheriff didn't like speeders. He parked in the courthouse square, in a space reserved for lawyers, and another car pulled into the spot next to him. As he got out of the Wagoneer, someone called out to him.

"Hello, Will, it's Elton Hunter," the man said, sticking out his hand.

Will took the hand. Hunter was dressed in a dark business suit, severe for a Saturday afternoon, Will thought. "Hello, Elton, how are you?" He didn't know the young lawyer well. Hunter was from Columbus, had married the banker's daughter in Greenville, and set up a practice four or five years before, with the bank as his first client. He was prospering, from all accounts. The two men exchanged small talk as they entered the courthouse together. The old courthouse, built in the 1840s, looked fresh and new, having recently been restored after a disastrous fire.

Inside the door, Will stopped. "Well, if you'll excuse me, I've got to see Judge Boggs," he said.

"Yeah? Me, too," Hunter said, frowning. "What could he want with both of us?"

"Let's find out," Will said, steering him through the courtroom and to the door of the Judge's chambers.

"Come in!" a voice rumbled.

Will ushered Hunter ahead of him into the office, which had been restored to its original condition after the fire. Dark oak paneling and bookcases rose to a considerable height above the massive desk. The Judge, a short, stout man in his late sixties, with thick, white hair and a florid complexion, stood to meet them. He beamed at the two younger men. "Elton, how's Ginny? The children? Good." He turned to Will. "How's the view from the Hill these days, boy?"

Will grinned. "Pretty murky, as usual. The Senator's humming on all cylinders, got a clean bill of health from Walter Reed yesterday, looking forward to running again."

"I know," the Judge said, sinking into an enormous leather chair that nearly swallowed him. "I just talked to him."

"Where?" Will asked, surprised.

"I reached him at home, down at Flat Rock Farm, fresh from the airport."

Will took a chair, wondering what was going on, but not asking.

Judge Boggs brushed aside a strand of snowy hair and looked at the two younger men for a moment. "Gentlemen," he said finally, "I need your help."

"Of course, Judge," Will said.

"Surely," Hunter replied.

"We had a pretty bad murder around here this past week."

"The Cole girl?" Hunter asked.

"Yes."

"I haven't heard about it," Will said.

"No, you wouldn't have," the Judge replied. "Bad one. Rape, strangulation. Her daddy's a farmer, right prosperous." He paused. "Colored fellow."

"I know him," Hunter said. "Drew his will. I've seen her around the square."

"I don't know them," Will said. He waited to find out why he was here.

"Sheriff made an arrest this morning," the Judge said. "One Larry Eugene Moody, fixes furnaces for a living. Works for Morgan and Morgan, over in La Grange."

"They do my work," Hunter said. "Don't know whether this Moody was ever at the house, though."

"Just as well you don't know him," the Judge said. "Will?"

"Nope. Manchester Heating Supply does our work."

"Larry Eugene Moody is white," the Judge said, rather suddenly.

Neither Will nor Hunter said anything. Everyone seemed to have stopped breathing.

"He's asked for a public defender," the Judge said.

Will started to breathe again. He glanced at Hunter, who seemed to be thinking very hard.

"That's one of my problems," the Judge said. "The other one is, J. C. Roberts had prostate surgery yesterday over at Callaway Hospital in La Grange." J. C. Roberts was the county prosecutor. "J. C.'s only got one assistant, and with his boss flat on his back, the fellow's got his hands full."

Hunter exhaled.

"Now this case is going to get a lot of attention around the state, maybe beyond," the Judge said, "and I want it tried well. I don't want the goddamned Atlanta newspapers and TV talking about us down here like we're a bunch of rednecks. That's why I wouldn't want J. C.'s assistant to prosecute, even if he had the time, and I wouldn't want most of the lawyers in the county to defend it. What I want is two first-class lawyers, one to prosecute, one to defend."

"Isn't the procedure to bring in a prosecutor from another county?" Elton Hunter asked.

"That's true," the Judge replied, "but I'm damned if I want a prosecutor from the next circuit, or some greenhorn down from Atlanta, which is what they'd send us. So I asked the Governor to appoint a special prosecutor, and I told him I want to pick the man. Either of you fellows ever tried a murder?"

"Once," said Hunter.

The Judge permitted himself a small smile. "That the fellow Higgins, that's on death row now?"

"Right," Hunter said, embarrassed. "I tried to get him to plead; he wouldn't."

"I remember," the Judge said. "You did as well as anybody could have, under the circumstances." He turned to Will.

"Never," Will said. "I guess I've defended in a couple of dozen criminal cases; biggest one was armed robbery." He was thinking fast now. This case might be just the right thing to get him in the public eye. "White Man Charged with Sex Murder of Black Girl." That would make the Atlanta papers day after day.

"I'm satisfied with your abilities," the Judge said. "Both of you." He looked from Will to Hunter. "How about it, gentlemen?"

"All right," Hunter said immediately.

"Who's prosecuting and who's defending?" Will asked. He didn't want to defend.

The Judge opened his desk drawer and produced a half-dollar. He flipped it, caught it, and slapped it down on his desk blotter, covering it with his hand.

"Hang on," Will said. "I'll have to talk with the Senator about this." He needed time to think before committing himself.

"I told you," the Judge said, "I already talked to him." He smiled. "The Senator says you can have as much time as it takes."

Will sank back into his chair. Prosecute, he thought, I want to prosecute.

"Heads, you prosecute, Elton," the Judge said. "Tails, Will prosecutes." He lifted his hand.

Involuntarily, Will leaned forward to see. So did Elton Hunter.

The Judge peered at the half-dollar. "Heads!" he cried, sweeping the coin back into his desk drawer and closing it.

Will tried hard not to wince. Hunter was unable to suppress a broad smile.

The Judge looked at them, his eyebrows up. "You're in, then—both of you?"

Hunter nodded eagerly.

Will looked at the Judge. "You talked to the Senator?"

"I did. I already told you."

"And he said I could take the time."

"He did. Now are you in, or have I been wasting my time?"

"All right," Will said resignedly, "I'm in."

"Good," the Judge said, getting to his feet. "Now, I've got to get home and clean my shotguns. I'm going dove hunting tomorrow."

Will and Elton Hunter rose with him, and he shooed them toward the door like a pair of chicks. When they were in the hall, the Judge leaned against the doorjamb.

"Go see your client, Will. I'll hold a preliminary hearing Monday morning at ten."

"Yes, sir," both lawyers said in unison.

"One more thing," the Judge said. "Now that you're on this case, don't either one of you ever come to me and ask out of it. You're in this for the duration." He walked back into his office and closed the door behind him.

3

Will stood in the little room and waited. The jail was new, but it was aging fast. Paint was already peeling from the windowless walls, and the asphalt-tile floors looked scuffed and worn. There were two doors in the room, one leading from the lockup, one from the outside world. There was some steel furniture, a table and four chairs, bolted to the floor.

A muffled clang from somewhere else, then another, then the door opened. A deputy sheriff stepped into the room, followed by Larry Eugene Moody.

"He's all yours, Counselor," the deputy said. "Take as long as you like; ring the bell, here, when you're all finished." He pointed to a button beside the door, then disappeared, locking the door behind him.

"Hi," the young man said uncertainly. He was five-eight or so, well built. His yellow-blond hair was well groomed, parted in the middle, not too long, blown-dry and neatly combed. A wispy attempt at a mustache adorned his upper lip. He was dressed in jeans and a short-sleeved polo shirt with an indecipherable emblem at the left breast. Larry Eugene Moody couldn't have been more than twenty-five. He managed a small smile and stuck out a hand. "I'm Larry Moody," he said.

Will shook the hand. "My name is Will Lee, Larry," he said. "The court has appointed me to represent you in this matter. Have a seat, and let's talk."

"Boy, am I glad to see you!" Moody said, sliding into a chair. "I've been here since ten o'clock this morning, and I haven't seen anybody but deputies and jailbirds. Can you get me out of here?"

He looked worried and a little scared, Will thought. A proper reaction to being arrested. "I don't know yet. First, let's talk for a few minutes, then we'll see where we stand."

"Okay, I'll tell you anything you want to know," Moody said earnestly.

Will leaned forward and rested his elbows on the table, watching Moody carefully for his reactions. "First of all, is it all right with you if I represent you? Do you have any objections to that?"

"Sure, no. I mean, it's okay with me."

"Good. Now, from now on, anything you say to me is in absolute confidence. I can never repeat anything you say to me without your permission, and nobody can legally require me to reveal any information I get from you. Do you understand that?"

"You mean, like between somebody and a Catholic priest?"

"Exactly like that. Even if you told me that you had committed a crime, I would be bound not to tell anyone else, and no one could force me to tell. If I did tell, you couldn't be prosecuted for the crime on the evidence of my testimony."

"Okay, I understand."

"It's important that you do, because I want you to feel that you can trust me, tell me anything you want to, without fear of being punished for it."

"I got it."

"And, Larry, it is very important that you tell me the truth. The dumbest thing you can do is to lie to your lawyer."

"No sweat; I'll tell you the truth."

"Good." Will reached into his jacket pocket and produced a paper. "This is a copy of a warrant for your arrest on a charge of murder in the first degree. Murder is when you willfully kill somebody. This warrant means the sheriff thinks you killed somebody. First degree means 'with malice aforethought,' that the sheriff thinks you knew what you were doing, that you meant to do it, that you had time to consider whether or not you should have done it. It also assumes that you are of legal age, that you have the capacity to know right from wrong, and that you were in your right mind at the time."

Moody nodded, looking intently at Will.

"Now," Will continued, "just because the sheriff swore out a warrant doesn't mean you're guilty of anything. Under our system of justice, you are presumed to be innocent, and before you can be found guilty of anything, the state has to prove your guilt beyond a reasonable doubt. Do you understand?"

Larry nodded. "Sure, we had all that in high school, and you see it on TV all the time, but boy, I never thought somebody would be saying it to me."

"I understand how you feel," Will said. "You have other rights, too. Has anybody, since you were arrested this morning, said anything to you about your rights?"

"Yeah, the sheriff told me about my rights when I got to the jail."

"Did the sheriff or anybody else ask you to sign anything?"

"Yeah, they asked me to sign a paper saying they had told me my rights."

"Did they ask you to do anything else?"

"Oh, yeah, they asked if they could look at my van. There was something in the paper about that."

"Did you give them permission to look at your van?"

"Yeah, I didn't mind."

Will took another piece of paper from his pocket and handed it to Larry. "Is this a correct copy of what you signed?"

Larry read the paper. "Yeah, that's my signature."

"Okay, then." Will got a legal pad from his briefcase. "Now, I want you to tell me everything that happened from the time you first saw the police—the sheriff or his deputies—this morning."

Moody leaned back and seemed to concentrate. "Well, I was just finishing my second cup of coffee . . ."

"What time?"

"Ten, maybe a little after. Then Kenny Eberhart rang the doorbell and said would I come down to the office and talk to the sheriff."

"Who's Kenny Eberhart?"

"He's a deputy. I know him from around town."

"Did he say you were under arrest?"

"No, he said it wouldn't take long, could I just come on down to the office. Then he said would I mind bringing my car, because he had to make rounds and wouldn't be able to bring me back. I thought it was kind of funny—when I was about halfway down here, I looked in the mirror and saw him about a block back, and I wondered if he was following me."

"Then what happened?"

"I got here, and I asked for the sheriff, and he took me in his office and sat me down. There was another deputy there, too, leaning against the wall. The sheriff was real friendly and all, and he asked me what I was doing on Thursday night."

"Did he tell you that you were under arrest at that time?"

"No, but he did tell me about my rights."

"What did he tell you about your rights, and how did he do it?"

"He said, 'I just want to ask you some questions, Larry, and you know, you don't have to answer them, and if you want a lawyer, you can have one.'"

"Did he say that what you said could be used against you?"

"Yeah, kind of as an afterthought. He said, 'Oh, yeah, I'll use what you say against you, if I feel like it.' He sort of made it a joke. Then he said, 'You mind if we take a look at your van?' And I said no, and I gave him the keys. That's when he asked me to sign the paper."

"Did he ask you to read it first?"

"Yeah. He said, 'Oh, by the way, read this and sign it if what it says is true.' And it was, so I signed it."

"All right, Thursday night. He asked you your whereabouts on Thursday night. How did you answer?"

"I said I worked until nearly six."

"Do you often work past five?"

"Sometimes, if we get a call, somebody's heating or hot water or something is out. I had one of those."

"Where was the call?"

"At Mr. Hunter's house, the lawyer."

"Elton Hunter?"

"Yeah. I'd been out there before, replaced the heat exchangers in his furnace last year."

Will suppressed a laugh. "Was Mr. Hunter there?"

"His wife made the call. He came home about the time I finished. He signed for the work."

"Good. Then where did you go?"

"I went home."

"In your van?"

"Yeah."

"Is that your only car?"

"Yeah. Charlene was getting a ride home from work, so I went straight home."

"Who's Charlene?"

"She's my girlfriend. Charlene Joiner. She lives with me."

"What about the rest of your evening?"

"Well, I had a beer, and Charlene came in, I guess, a little after six. She gets off at six. She brought a chicken home, and we ate that. Then we watched a video. Charlene brought that, too."

"Where does Charlene work?"

"At the MagiMart. That's a convenience store out on the La Grange highway. They have a video-rental thing, and they let her bring them home overnight. She takes them back the next morning."

"What did you watch?"

"*Beverly Hills Cop,* with Eddie Murphy."

"Then what?"

Larry looked embarrassed. "Then we . . . well, we went to bed."

"Did you make love?"

"Sir?"

"I'm not prying, Larry. This might be important later."

"Yes, sir, we sure did. Charlene's sort of . . ."

"Sort of what?"

"Well, sort of horny."

"That night?"

"Every night." Larry frowned a little. "Are you sure this is important?"

"Yes."

"Well, to tell you the truth, Charlene is horny *all the time*. I mean, she wants to do it anytime, day or night, wherever we can get away with it."

"You mean, outside the house?"

"I mean *anywhere*. I had to stop taking her to the movies, at the movie theater. She'd be all over me. Now we stay home and watch videos or go to the drive-in out on the highway. We were out there . . . let's see, Wednesday night, and we ended up doing it on the floor of the van. I'm lucky I'm in good shape, or she'd kill me."

"So, on Thursday night, after the video, you and Charlene were . . . occupied with each other, for how long?"

"I don't know. You kind of lose track of time, you know?"

"How long have you known Charlene?"

"About . . . let's see, we met in June, over at Callaway Gardens, at the beach."

"And when did she move in?"

"In June. The same day. She's from Newnan, but she moved in with me and got the job at the MagiMart."

"And it's been like this with Charlene all the time, since June?"

"Yes, sir, all the time. I don't reckon we've missed a day."

"You didn't leave the house again on Thursday night? Didn't drive the van again?"

"No, sir. After Charlene and I have been at it, well, I don't feel much like doing anything but sleeping."

"That's it, then. That's your whole Thursday night?"

"That's it."

"And you told the sheriff that?"

"Well, I didn't tell him about Charlene and me. I mean, you said you couldn't tell anybody what I told you. I reckon the sheriff would tell everybody."

Will laughed in spite of himself. "What else did the sheriff ask you?"

"He asked me if I knew Sarah Cole. I said, 'Yeah, I fixed the furnace at that place she works.'"

"When did you fix it?"

"It was Thursday afternoon."

"Had you met her before?"

"No, sir. I went over there on a call, and I talked to a receptionist, I guess she was, and I fixed the furnace—it was just a bad thermostat, and I replaced it—and then this Sarah Cole came out of an office and signed the ticket and gave me a check."

"And that was the first time you had seen her?"

"No, I guess I'd seen her around town, but I didn't *know* her."

"Ever spoken to her before?"

"No, sir."

"When you spoke to her at her office, did you have any sort of disagreement or argument?"

"No, sir. Well, she said she thought the thermostat was too expensive. I told her it was the cheapest one we carry, and she was welcome to shop around, but she gave me the check. I don't guess we spoke more than ten words."

"Was anybody else present when you spoke to her?"

"The receptionist was there."

"What else did the sheriff ask you?"

"He asked me if I knew where the city dump was, and I said I did. He asked me if I was out at the city dump on Thursday night, and I said, 'No, I told you, I was home with Charlene.'"

"What else?"

"That was about it, I guess. He left me in the office with the deputy while he went to look at the van. I guess he was gone about twenty minutes, and I read a magazine. Then he came back and told me I was under arrest for murder, and he showed me the warrant, and he read me my rights again, that time from a card. Then they made me empty my pockets, and they put me in a cell."

"Did he tell you that you could make a phone call?"

"Oh, yeah. I called out to the MagiMart a couple times, but the line was busy. Charlene is working today. I didn't know who else to call. I could have called my boss, I guess, but I didn't want him to know I was in jail. I said I didn't know a lawyer and couldn't afford one, and the sheriff said they'd get one for me."

Will took the young man through his life story, making notes. Larry Moody was twenty-four; born and raised in La Grange, twenty miles away; finished high school, made Bs and Cs; father died when he was six, mother worked in a mill, died when he was nineteen; played center on the football team; went to work for Morgan & Morgan after high school—they taught him about furnaces and air conditioners; had lived in Greenville, where his company had a branch, for just over a year.

"Good," Will said. "Now, there's something I have to know, and I want you to tell me the absolute truth. Have you ever been in any kind of trouble? Have you ever been arrested? For anything? I'll tell you right now, Larry, if you have, it'll come out. You'd best tell me now. Have you *ever* been in trouble?"

Larry, for the first time, looked away from him. "Yes, sir," he said quietly.

"Tell me about it," Will said, "and don't leave anything out."

"Well, when I was twenty, I had three speeding tickets in a row, over about four months. They took my license away from me, except for work. After I got it back, I bought the van. The van is pretty slow."

"That's it?" Will asked, afraid to be relieved. "That's all the trouble you were ever in?"

"Yes, sir, that's it."

"Was any of them a DUI? Were you drinking?"

"No, sir."

Will took a deep breath and let it out. "All right, if you

think of anything else, you can tell me later. Now, I want you to give me the names and addresses of three or four people who you think might have a good opinion of you."

Larry gave him the names of a high school teacher, his football coach, and his boss.

"Now, I want you to give me some names of people you don't get along with, who dislike you."

Larry looked puzzled, then stared at the ceiling for a moment. "I can't think of anybody," he said finally.

"You don't have any enemies at all?"

Larry shook his head. "Not that I know of," he said.

"Okay, Larry, if you say so. Do you go to church in Greenville? Do you have a minister?"

"No, sir. I'm not very religious, I guess."

Will put his legal pad away. "Now, here's what's going to happen next: you're going to have to spend the week-end here; you'll have a preliminary hearing on Monday morning, at ten. At that time, Judge Boggs will hear from the prosecution about their case, and he'll decide if there's a case to answer. The prosecution will present witnesses, but maybe not all they've got, and we'll start to have an idea of what they think they've got on you. If the Judge decides they have a good-enough case, he'll send your case to a grand jury, and if they think there's enough evidence against you to warrant a trial, they'll indict you, and then you'll be tried."

"How long will all this take?" Larry asked. "Am I going to be stuck in here?"

"We can try for bail at the preliminary hearing. Do you have any property?"

"Just the van, and it won't be paid up for another three years."

"Do you own your house or apartment?"

"No, sir, I rent a house."

"Do you know anybody who might put up some property?"

"Maybe my boss, Mr. Morgan. I wouldn't want to ask him, though."

"I'll talk to him. He'll need to know that you won't be at work on Monday, anyway."

Larry slapped his forehead. "Geez, I forgot to tell you about the lineup. I just remembered."

"The sheriff put you in a lineup?"

"Yeah, with four other guys."

"Were they about your size and general description?"

"More or less. It's funny, though. They made us stand with our faces to the wall."

"You mean the witness was looking at your backs?"

"At first. After a couple of minutes, they told us to turn around."

"Did you see the witness, the person who was looking at you?"

"No, there was a mirror. I guess there was somebody behind it, one of those two-way things."

"That's the way it's usually done." Will snapped his briefcase shut.

"Mr. Lee, how much trouble am I in?" Moody looked more than just worried now.

"I don't know yet, Larry. We won't know that until we hear more about the prosecution's case. I'd better tell you what your options are. On Monday morning at the preliminary hearing, you're going to have to enter a plea. That means you'll plead either guilty or not guilty. If you plead not guilty and go to trial and are convicted of first-degree murder, then you might very well get the death penalty, but you might get life, depending on the circumstances.

"But"—Will leaned forward on his elbows—"you have the option of pleading guilty. If you are guilty. If you decide to do that, I can go to the prosecution and maybe make a deal, let you plead to a lesser charge, maybe voluntary manslaughter, depending on the circumstances. In that case, you'd probably get a shorter sentence, be out in a few years. It boils down to this, Larry. Plead guilty and do, maybe, five to ten years in jail; or plead not guilty, in which case you might go free or you might die. You think about it over the weekend, and we'll talk before your hearing on Monday. If you want me to, I can feel out the prosecutor and see what sort of a plea bargain might be available. You can let me know what you want to do then."

"Oh, I already know," Larry said, sitting up. "I want to plead not guilty."

"You're sure," Will said.

"I'm absolutely sure."

"Fine." Will rose. "I've got to go now. Is there anything I can do for you before Monday, besides call your boss?"

"Yes, sir. You can bring me some shaving stuff and a change of clothes from the house, and let Charlene know where I am." He wrote down the address and gave Will directions. "There's a key under the flowerpot. And you could give Charlene the keys to the van, so she can use it. She doesn't have a car."

"That may not be possible. The sheriff may hold the van as evidence, but I'll try. Anything else?"

Moody looked away from him. "Something's bothering me," he said.

"What is it?"

Moody turned to face him again. "You never asked me if I murdered that woman."

It was Will's turn to look away. "Well, Larry, that's a question a lawyer sometimes doesn't want to ask his client."

"Well, you don't have to ask. I'll tell you," Moody said.

Will held his breath. If this boy was guilty, he didn't want to know it.

"I did not kill her," Larry said with conviction. "I swear to God, I didn't. Everything I've told you today is the gospel truth."

Will smiled. "In that case, Larry," he said with more certainty than he felt, "you don't have anything to worry about."

Larry grabbed Will's hand and pumped it, smiling as though he had just been acquitted.

4

Will rapped on the glass partition that separated the sheriff's office from the squad room. "Morning, Dan. How you doing?"

Sheriff Cox lifted his head from the paperwork before him, got up, and shook Will's hand. "Pretty fair, Will. How 'bout you?"

Will knew the sheriff as well as most lawyers in small counties knew sheriffs. "Can't complain. Course, I'm not too happy about you putting my innocent client in jail."

The sheriff grinned. "I reckon I can make it stick."

"He'd like to have his van back for his girlfriend to use. Can I have the keys?"

Cox shook his head. "Nope, it's impounded as evidence."

"Can I have a look at it?"

"Nope. Investigation is still in progress."

Will hadn't expected to get to see the van. "You'll send me the crime lab report, though, won't you?" He was entitled to see all the lab results. "And the autopsy report on the victim?"

"Oh, sure. Don't think I'll have anything for you before the middle of next week, though. These folks take their time."

"That'll be okay. Listen, when you're finished with the van, can Moody's girl have it? No point in hanging on to it until the trial, is there?"

"We'll see," the sheriff said cagily.

Will left the jail, got into his car, and followed Larry Moody's directions to his house. It turned out to be a shell home, one of those bought as nothing more than four walls and a roof, then finished by the owner. The little place sat on a lot bare of grass, separated from the road by a deep drainage ditch. Will pulled his car onto the wide shoulder of the road, got out and crossed a crude footbridge over the ditch. He found the flowerpot, which contained the remnants of some dead plant, and the key, and let himself into the house.

There was a surprising amount of furniture, most of it inexpensive and new-looking, packed into the small living room. There was a stacked stereo system in a rack against the wall, next to a large color television set and an expensive videotape recorder. The tiny dining room was given over to an elaborate weight-lifting system. Judging from the amount of stuff in the house, and guessing at what the income of a furnace repairman must be, Will could see why Larry Moody couldn't afford a lawyer. He must be in hock up to his ears, what with all this stuff and the van.

Will stood for a moment, taking it all in. He was about to move toward the bedroom to collect Larry's gear, when the front door suddenly opened, and he found himself facing a young woman.

She stood stock-still, staring at him, surprised.

Will was struck by how pretty—almost beautiful—she was. Her hair was even blonder than Larry's, and he thought it must be her own color; her eyes were large and vividly blue; her nose was slight; and her lips were full and wide. She was no more than five feet four, but so well proportioned that she seemed taller. She was the first to speak.

"Who are you?" she asked, her brow wrinkling. Her speech was firm and broadly accented, much like her boyfriend's.

"My name is Will Lee. I'm a lawyer, representing Larry Moody. I'm sorry if I startled you; Larry asked me to come here and pick up some things for him." He stopped talking for a moment, but she didn't speak. They stood, looking at each other. "You must be Charlene Joiner," he said finally.

"Yes," she said. "Somebody came in the store a few minutes ago and said they'd heard Larry was in some kind of trouble. I got a ride home."

"Yes, I'm afraid he is. I've just come from the jail; the court has appointed me to represent him." He stopped, unwilling to break the news to her.

"Well," she said, her voice rising slightly, "are you going to tell me what's happened?"

"I'm sorry," Will stammered. "Look, you'd better come sit down for a minute."

She sat next to him on the sofa, facing him, clear-eyed, expressionless, as he told her about the charges against Larry. When he had finished, she stood up and shrugged off the parka she had been wearing. Beneath it was a yellow nylon smock with the MagiMart logo emblazoned upon it. "That's crazy," she said. "Larry wouldn't kill anybody. What the hell is going on?" She unzipped the smock and threw it at a chair. When she turned back toward him she was wearing only a thin T-shirt, the bottom of which missed meeting her low-cut jeans by a good six inches, leaving an expanse of silky, lightly browned skin.

Will was slightly rocked by the sight. Her breasts were full, and the nipples were hard, thrust lightly against the T-shirt. "Well, uh, we won't know much more about the case until Monday morning, when the preliminary hearing will be held. I'd like you to come to that." He tried to keep his breathing slow and steady.

"Sure I will," she said, sitting next to him on the sofa again.

Involuntarily, he inched away from her. "As long as I'm here, I need to ask you some questions," he said.

"Okay," she said. "Whatever will help Larry."

"I should tell you that anything you say to me will be in confidence and can't be used against Larry. Our conversation is privileged."

"Right," she said, moving her tongue over her lower lip, in a motion that seemed astonishingly sensual to Will.

He coughed into his fist and made an effort to compose himself. This girl's presence was having the most unsettling effect on him. He crossed his legs and realized that he was becoming tumescent. He coughed again, then began questioning her about her movements on Thursday night.

Her account of the evening matched Larry's in every respect, except she said they had eaten ribs, instead of chicken. She did not, however, share Larry's initial reticence in describing the later part of their evening. "After the movie," she said, "we fucked." She wrinkled her brow as if trying to be precise. "Two or three times."

Will nodded and swallowed. "I don't want you to think I'm prying," he said, "but is that something you and Larry do a lot of?"

Her eyebrows went up. "Fucking? Oh, yeah. We like it. We're good together." She looked at him and smiled. "Why, Counselor, I'm embarrassing you."

"Not at all," Will lied. "Ah, is there anything else you want to know about Larry's case?"

She questioned him briskly about the charges against Larry and what might happen to him. There was none of the deference that Larry had shown; she addressed Will as an equal, and her questions were intelligent and to the point. She seemed somehow older, more mature than Larry.

When he had answered her, Will stood. "Well, I'd better get going. If you'll put together a couple of changes of clothes and some shaving gear for Larry, I'll drop them off at the jail."

"I'll take it myself. I want to see him."

Will glanced at his watch. "It's after visiting hours, I'm afraid. You can go by tomorrow, though, between two and five."

She disappeared into a bedroom, came back with a packed nylon duffel, and handed it to him.

"They'll search it," Will said to her. "If there's anything in here you don't want them to see . . ."

"No," she said, then stuck out her hand. "Thank you, Will, for what you're doing for Larry. Can I call you Will?"

"Sure," he said, taking her hand. It was warm and soft;

her fingers were long and her grip firm. "The sheriff is holding Larry's van for the moment. I may be able to get it released late next week. Larry wanted you to be able to use it. Call me if you have any other questions; I'm in the Delano phone book—the office is Lee and Lee. Home is W. H. Lee the Fourth."

She frowned, not letting go of his hand. "Is your father Billy Lee? The one who was governor?"

"That's right." He took his hand back and put it in his pocket. It was damp.

"Good-bye," she said.

Will left the house and got into his car with the duffel. "Jesus Christ!" he said aloud to himself. "No wonder Larry wants to get out of jail!" He drove off toward the square, trying not to think about Charlene Joiner.

5

Will entertained himself by driving back-country to the family farm, testing his memory on the network of little roads, most of them without signposts. Twenty minutes later, he turned onto the Raleigh road, and a moment later, the main house came into view. It was on the site where his great-great-grandfather had built, but the original frame farmhouse had burned in the 1930s.

His father had returned in 1945 from service in the Army Air Corps, flying bombers out of England, and had brought back with him an Anglo-Irish bride. Patricia Worth-Newenam Lee had carried with her the original drawings of her Georgian family home in County Cork, and she had overseen the construction of a more than reasonable facsimile in the Southern countryside, built of brick, rather than the stone of the Irish house. The house was of a comfortable size, not quite grand, and it seemed as much at home on the red clay of Georgia as the original had on the green fields of Ireland.

Will turned into the semicircular driveway, and, instead

of continuing to the front door, went straight on toward a grove of trees on a little lake a couple of hundred yards behind the house. As he passed the house, a dog—a golden Labrador retriever—leapt from the back porch and tore after the car. Will slowed until the dog caught up with him, then laughed as the handsome animal raced alongside the car toward the trees.

Will turned into a well-kept dirt track through the trees and came to his own house, a small, neat, angular cottage of stone and cedar. He had built it, with the help of two farmhands, the year he had joined his father in the law practice, when he was twenty-five. It sat in the copse, elevated a few feet from the ten-acre lake that his mother had designed and had constructed during the 1950s. Now the lake looked as though it had always been there.

He got out of the car and was nearly knocked down by the flying dog. "Hey, Fred! How are you, old sport?" He knelt and let the animal lick his face and, gradually, calmed him. He got the luggage out of the back of the Wagoneer and gave Fred a briefcase to carry. The dog pranced about, proud of himself, and tried to bark, in spite of the handle in his mouth.

Will trotted up the steps to the porch with the rest of his luggage, went into the house, and dumped everything on the bed. Fred came and put the briefcase carefully on the bed, too. "What a good boy!" He scratched the dog behind the ears and sniffed the air; Marie, half of the black couple who took care of his parents, had left something good in the house. He wandered through the book-cluttered living room to the kitchen, found a plate of fresh chocolate-chip cookies, helped himself, then went back to the bedroom, munching, and unpacked. After a hot shower, he threw himself on the bed and dozed fitfully, stirring now and then to glimpse the sun sink into the lake.

When he woke, he got into some clothes. The main house was run his mother's way, and that meant a jacket and tie at dinner. Under a rising moon, with Fred running ahead, he walked through the trees and over the grassy expanse that separated the cottage from the main house. It was chilly, but not cold, an improvement over Washington, he thought.

He entered the house and immediately ran into his father's younger sister, Eloise, coming out of the kitchen. They embraced warmly.

"You've lost some weight," Ellie said. She had been widowed in World War II and had never remarried, still operating the ladies' clothing store that her mother had started when Will's grandfather had died. Now in her early seventies, she lived alone in Delano, but often came to dinner.

"I've needed to." Will laughed. "Anyway, they'll put it back on me over Christmas, and if I know you, you'll help."

Patricia Lee met her son at the library door and hugged him. At seventy, she was still a beautiful woman—tall, slender, and erect, though her auburn hair had mostly faded to white. She stood back and held Will's face in her hands. "You look tired," she said. "But then you always do when you come home from Washington." Her accent had softened a bit over the past forty years, but there was still a distinct west British edge to it. When she was joking or angry, she lapsed into a County Cork brogue.

Will's father, Billy Lee, turned from his work at the cocktail cabinet concealed behind rows of leather book spines. "Hello, there, boy!" he half shouted. He came and embraced his son. Billy Lee was in his late seventies now, and in spite of a heart attack a year before, he looked and sounded ten years younger. His thick hair had gone entirely white, and Will reflected, not for the first time, that his father looked much more the part of senator than did Benjamin Carr. "Can I interest you in some bourbon whiskey?" he asked.

"You betcha," Will said. He took the drink and sank into the sofa, opposite his parents' matching chairs, before the hearth, where a cheerful fire was crackling away. He loved this room.

"Good flight down?" his father asked.

"Real good. It was pretty murky in the D.C. area, but it cleared up as I came south."

"That's as good a metaphor for the state of the union as I've heard." His father laughed.

"What did Judge Boggs want?" his mother demanded. "I expect he's stuck you with some case nobody else would take."

"Probably," Will said, "but he made it sound like he wouldn't trust it to anybody else. He roped in Elton Hunter, the Greenville lawyer, too. He's prosecuting." He gave them an account of his meeting with Judge Boggs. "The cagey old reprobate had already spoken with the Senator about my time. There was no way out."

"You think this Moody fellow did it?" his mother asked.

"Hard to say," Will replied. "The boy comes off well; he'll be good on the stand, if I use him. I don't really know what sort of a case they've got yet, but they have some sort of a witness—to what, I don't know. Still, there's something about Moody that makes me want to believe him—a sort of sweetness. The women on the jury will want to mother him."

"Has he got an alibi?" Billy Lee asked.

"Has he? Wow! He's got a girlfriend, who, when she gets on the stand, will make everybody doubt that he would have the energy to rape somebody else."

"Do you know anything about Sarah Cole?" his father asked.

"Just that she's black and a farmer's daughter from up around Luthersville."

"There's a lot more to her than that," Billy said. "She's—she was—smart as a whip. She graduated from high school in Greenville, but she got a scholarship to Bennington, in Vermont, and she apparently excelled there."

"You knew her?"

"No, this has all been in the papers. There's more, too. She got some sort of foundation grant and was running a counseling service for pregnant teenagers—the only thing like it around here."

"Sounds good," Will said. "There's a need for that."

"Yes, but Sarah Cole wasn't making any friends in the county, not any white ones, anyway. She was a militant feminist, an avowed atheist, and a general all-round pain in the ass, or so I hear around the courthouse." Billy got up and retrieved a newspaper from a table and handed it to Will. "She was also real good-looking."

Will stared into a strikingly beautiful face: café-au-lait

skin, the features perfectly arranged, the hair in a short Afro cut, the eyes intelligent and, he thought, a little angry.

"She's said to have had a couple of white grandparents," Billy said. "I think it annoyed a lot of people that she could be so objectionable and still be so attractive. She didn't sound black, either. That always drives the white trash nuts."

"Well, this case obviously has all sorts of facets that will affect the trial," Will said. He didn't like them much, either.

"It's that way with every case," his father replied. "You never know what you're getting into. Tell me, did Judge Boggs flip a coin to decide who'd prosecute and who'd defend?"

"Yes. How did you know?"

"He's had that fifty-cent piece for thirty years. It's got heads on both sides."

Will winced.

Billy laughed. "He had already decided he wanted you to defend. No lawyer in the tri-county area would have defended that boy, so the Judge just picked one. You. Take it as a compliment."

Henry, Marie's husband and the Lees' houseman and factotum, stepped into the library, dressed in his usual uniform of black trousers, white shirt, and black bow tie. "It's on the table, Miz Lee," he said to Will's mother.

Patricia sighed. "In twenty years, I've never been able to get Henry to say, 'Dinner is served.'" They all got to their feet and moved toward the dining room.

When they were seated and the wine had been poured, Will cleared his throat. "I've got some news," he said.

His parents and aunt looked at him expectantly.

"Senator Carr and I had a little talk this morning," he said. "I've agreed to stay on with him through the election and for two years after that."

There was silence around the table. Both his parents looked slightly disappointed. His father started to speak, but Will held up a hand.

"There's more," he said. "In exchange for the two years, he's offered to back me to the hilt against Jim Barnett in four years' time.

"What does that mean, 'to the hilt'?" his father asked.

"It means he'll support me publicly; he'll call in every political debt owed him." Will grinned. "And he'll raise two million dollars for me."

"Hurrah!" his mother shouted.

"You're damn right, hurrah!" his father said. "If Ben Carr will really get behind you, you're as good as elected!"

"That's wonderful, Will," his aunt Ellie said. "I really didn't think Ben Carr would ever commit himself like that. He's always just stood aside and smiled a secret smile in every campaign I can remember."

Will's father slapped his palm on the table and drew himself up into a semblance of Benjamin Carr's posture. "I will vote for the nominee of my party!" he aped. "That's the only endorsement I've heard him give since he campaigned for Franklin Roosevelt!" Billy picked up his glass. "I propose a toast," he said. "To the future junior senator from Georgia!" They all drank to Will.

Out in the hall, the telephone rang. Henry could be heard clomping toward it.

"Well, that might be just a little premature," Will said. "I mean, anything could happen in four years."

Henry stepped through the door from the hall. "Mr. Will," he said. "Telephone for you."

"Henry," Patricia said, "I've told you a hundred times that nobody in this family takes a phone call during dinner. Take a message."

"Yes'm," Henry said, and retreated to the hall. A moment later, he was back. "It's a Mr. Wendell from the *Atlanta Constitution*. He says it's real important."

"Henry!" Patricia Lee growled.

"No, it's all right, Mother," Will said. "Dudley Wendell is the assistant managing editor for news. He wouldn't normally call; a reporter would. I'd better talk to him." Will got up and followed Henry into the hall. He picked up the phone. "Hello, Dudley?"

"Hey, Will. I'm sorry to bother you this time of night, but I need a comment on this story." He stopped talking and waited.

Will was baffled. Could the paper have already heard that he was defending Larry Moody? And was it important enough for an editor to call, instead of a reporter? "What story is that?" Will asked.

Wendell still didn't speak for a moment. "Do you mean you haven't heard?" He sounded incredulous.

"Heard what?"

"Jesus, Will, I'm sorry to be the one to break this to you."

"Break what, Dudley? What the hell are you talking about?"

Wendell could be heard drawing a deep breath. "Ben Carr has had a stroke. A bad one."

6

Will switched on the autopilot, poured himself a cup of coffee from the thermos, and opened the roast-beef sandwich Marie had made for him. He managed a few bites, but his appetite had left him. He put the sandwich aside and contented himself with the coffee as he stared out into the night around him. The lights of small towns and occasional farmhouses passed beneath him, pinpoints in the darkness. He felt hollow. He was afraid.

He was forty-one years old, and the past eight years of his life had revolved around the career of Ben Carr; now the man might be dying. The doctor Will had spoken to at the hospital in Newport, Georgia, the nearest to the Senator's Flat Rock Farm, had not been optimistic. It was a bad stroke, as the newspaper editor had said, and the outcome was in doubt.

Normally, in an emergency, Will's mind would focus on what had to be done to fix things or minimize the damage—what to say to the press. Now all he could do was think about his first meeting with Benjamin Carr.

*   *   *

"Your daddy says you need a job," the Senator said dryly.

"I guess that's right," Will admitted. He was tired of practicing law. The idea of working for a powerful senator appealed to him.

Carr clasped his hands behind his head and leaned back in his chair. "What can you do?" he asked, as if he didn't expect much of an answer.

"Let's see," Will said, trying to think of a clever answer and failing. "I can draw a will; I can write a pretty good final-demand letter; I can defend a felon, or at least plea-bargain for him. I can negotiate a settlement, if the parties aren't too far apart. I can build a boat and sail it; I can fly an airplane, as long as it doesn't have more than one engine."

The Senator remained expressionless. "Are you any good at detail?" he asked. "I mean petty, boring detail."

Will nodded. "Pretty good, as long as it's not all I have to do, or if I don't have to do it for too long."

The Senator nodded back, the first encouragement he had given Will. "Can you hold your liquor?"

"I'm better at not drinking too much of it than I am at holding it," Will replied honestly.

The Senator nodded again. "Can you keep your mouth shut?"

"Yes, sir."

"You'd be surprised how hard it is to find young fellows who can do that." The Senator leaned forward, placed his elbows on his desk, and cradled his chin in his hands. "You ever draw any legislation?"

"Yes, sir, twice, both times for clients who wanted something done in the state legislature."

"Were they signed into law?"

"The first one didn't make it out of committee; the second passed with enough amendments to make it ineffective."

The Senator grinned. "You were learning, anyhow," he said. "You got any money of your own?"

"Yes, sir."

"How much?"

Will started to tell him it was none of his business, then checked himself. Instead, he said nothing, just returned the Senator's gaze.

"Let me put it this way," the Senator said. "Can you get by on fifteen thousand dollars a year? That's what I'm paying."

"Yes, sir," Will replied without hesitation.

The Senator fished a gold watch out of his vest pocket and consulted it. "Well, I've got a committee meeting in three minutes." He stood up. "Come on, you might as well see what we're up against around here." He strode from the office with Will at his heels.

In the hallway, Will caught up with him. "Excuse me, Senator," he panted. "Am I hired?"

"Son," the Senator replied without looking at him, "you've already started."

The wink of an airport beacon interrupted Will's reverie, first white, then green. He reduced power and began his descent. On the ground, he spun the airplane around at a tie-down and cut the engine. As he did so, another racket filled his ears, and, fifty feet in front of him, a helicopter descended, its landing lights blinding him. As he got out of the airplane, he saw a Georgia State Patrol car speeding across the tarmac toward the copter, blue lights flashing. As Will watched, the Governor of Georgia, Mack Dean, hopped out of the helicopter and strode toward the waiting car, followed by a younger man and a state patrolman. Dean caught sight of Will and shouted over the whine of the dying copter engine, "Come on, Will, I'll give you a lift!"

Will piled into the state patrol car and found himself sandwiched between the Governor and the younger man.

"You know Rob Cutts from the *Constitution*?" the Governor asked.

Will shook the young man's hand.

"How is the Senator?" Cutts asked.

"Now, Rob," the Governor interjected. "Will can't know any more than we do. He just got here, too. We'll be at the hospital in a minute." He turned to Will. "I just talked to him late this afternoon. He sounded fine."

Will nodded. "I know."

"He's always been strong as a mule," the Governor said. "You know, all he talked about this afternoon was you."

Will froze, remembering the Senator's promise that morning to recommend to the Governor that he be appointed to succeed his boss if he died in office. He hadn't wasted any time. They all sat quietly until the patrol car pulled up at the emergency entrance to the small hospital.

The Governor led the way in, speaking or waving to the nurses and every other person he passed. He seemed disappointed that at this time of the night there weren't more people to charm. A state patrolman stood guard outside the Senator's room, and as they approached, a doctor came out of the room.

"Governor," he said, extending his hand, "I'm Ralph Daniels."

"Hey, Ralph," the Governor replied, pumping the man's hand, "how you doing? Or, more important, how's the Senator doing?"

The doctor shook his head. "It doesn't look good, I'm afraid. I can't guarantee he'll make it through the night."

Rob Cutts, the reporter, trotted off in search of a phone.

Will spoke up. "Dr. Daniels, I'm Will Lee, the Senator's chief assistant."

"Oh, we've been waiting for you," the doctor replied. "Miss Emmy wants to see you. She's with the Senator."

"Just a minute," Will said. "First, please tell me exactly what happened and what treatment he's had."

"Oh, of course," the doctor said. "His driver and his sister brought him in about six. He had been vomiting and had had numbness in his arms and legs, classic stroke symptoms. We got him started on IV fluids and oxygen; then I ordered a CAT scan—fortunately, we have the equipment; not many small-town hospitals do."

Will remembered pushing through the grant for the CAT scanner, at the Senator's behest.

"He became aphasic and more and more lethargic, and by the time we got him into bed, he was unconscious."

"What's aphasic?" the Governor asked.

"Unable to respond or communicate," the doctor replied.

"What did the CAT scan show?" Will asked.

"He's got a massive clot in what's called Broca's area of the brain, the part that controls speech and communication."

"Thank you," Will said. "Let's go in now." He followed the doctor into the Senator's room, with the Governor bringing up the rear. Benjamin Carr lay in bed, unconscious and breathing rapidly, attached to a container of clear fluid and to nasal cannulae for oxygen. The sight of him struck Will like a physical blow. Less than twenty-four hours before, the Senator had been his usual, strong self; now, instead of exuding vitality, the stuff of life came from bottles, dripping from tubes, seeping from hoses into his helpless body. Will was suddenly numb with pity and grief.

Emma Carr, the Senator's sister and only living relative, sat by the bed, holding his hand. She looked up and saw Will, and her face contorted. "You!" she spat. "You did this to him, him working the way he did. I guess you're glad now, doing this to him! I wanted to see you so I could tell you to your face!"

Will stood speechless, staring at the tiny bird-like creature, her hair white and her skin wrinkled and leathered from the south Georgia sun. What the hell was she talking about? The woman had always been something of an eccentric, and it had often occurred to Will that her presence in Ben Carr's house was as much for him to keep an eye on her as for her to keep house for him. The black servants ran the place, anyway, with little help but much interference from Miss Emmy, as everyone called her.

The doctor went to her side. "Please, Miss Emmy," he said firmly, "we must keep it quiet in here."

Ben Carr suddenly drew a deep and noisy breath, then

let it out. Everyone turned and looked at him. Will waited for him to inhale again, but he did not. The seconds ticked away, and Ben Carr lay perfectly still, not breathing.

"Doctor?" Will managed to say, "Is he . . ."

The doctor was about to speak when he was interrupted by another sudden, loud inhaling from Ben Carr.

"He's in Cheyne-Stokes syndrome," the doctor said. "I know it's disturbing, but he's breathing. Don't worry, he won't die of that."

Will became aware that Jasper, the Senator's driver and factotum, was sitting quietly in a corner, crying softly. He went to the man. "Jasper," he said. "Try not to worry. He's doing all right."

Jasper looked up at him with wide, shining eyes. "I done what I could, Mr. Will," he said. "I got him down here just as fast as the car would take me."

"I know you did," Will replied soothingly. "You did exactly right. You probably saved his life."

"Oh, I hope so," Jasper said. "I'm not ready to let go of that man."

The group stood silently for another ten minutes as Ben Carr struggled on. Once, Will counted thirty seconds after the Senator exhaled before he inhaled again. Miss Emmy still sat, holding her brother's hand, now oblivious to the others.

Finally, the doctor motioned Will and the Governor from the room. In the hallway he turned to Will. "She's a handful, you know." He nodded toward the room.

"I know," Will said.

"Don't you pay no attention to that old woman," the Governor said. "She's crazy as a bat."

"I'm not sure she's competent to make judgments about his treatment," the doctor said.

"I don't think she is," Will agreed. "Humor her as best you can, but please consult me if any decisions have to be made."

"I've never treated the Senator," the doctor said, "so, of course, I haven't been able to get a history. Who is his regular physician?"

"The Senate doctor and Walter Reed Hospital have taken care of him for years," Will said. "He had a physical only yesterday, so you can get an up-to-date history from the hospital. I know that his blood pressure was up, but I don't know how much. They had prescribed some medication, but I don't think he would even have had time to have the prescription filled."

"I'll check with them immediately," the doctor said. He frowned at Will. "You look pretty tired. Will you be staying at the hospital?"

"Yes."

The doctor nodded at a room next door to the Senator's. "The other state patrolman is sleeping in there. There's another bed, so why don't you get some rest. I'll call you if anything changes. There's really nothing you can do right now."

Will nodded. "Thank you. I'd appreciate it if you could find someplace for the Senator's driver to rest, too. He won't leave the hospital while the Senator is in danger."

"Of course; I'll have a nurse attend to it." The doctor left to call Walter Reed, and the Governor stuck his arm in Will's and walked him down the hall toward where the patrol car waited. "I don't think there's anything I can do here," he said, "so I'm going on back to Atlanta. I've got a full schedule tomorrow morning."

"Of course, Mack," Will said. "I'll call you if there's any change."

They passed through the emergency-room door, and the Governor stopped on the sidewalk outside. "Will," he said, "about my conversation with the Senator this afternoon." He looked around him and sniffed the chill night air. "I don't want you to have any false hopes, so I'd better tell you now that I intend to appoint myself to the vacant seat." He stopped and waited for Will to reply.

Will said nothing.

"I'd like you to stay on in your job," Mack Dean said. "I know you're good at it, and I'm going to need you." He waited again for Will to reply. "Well?" he asked finally.

Will gazed into the pale, puffy face. He wanted to hit the man, not because Dean preferred himself to Will as an appointee, but because he was already trading for Ben Carr's position and staff and, most of all, power. Will turned and walked back into the hospital.

7

It was ten o'clock on Sunday evening before Will remembered that he had a preliminary hearing to attend the following morning. He had spent the day fielding telephone calls from everybody from the *New York Times* to the President of the United States and trying to deal with Miss Emmy. At midafternoon, he and Dr. Daniels had visited the probate judge, who knew Emma Carr well, and obtained a temporary order placing the Senator's affairs in Will's hands.

Now he had to turn his attention to the defense of Larry Moody, at least until he could talk to Judge Boggs, who, under the circumstances, would assign another lawyer. Checking his notes, he called Larry Moody's boss, John Morgan, of Morgan & Morgan Heating and Air-Conditioning, in La Grange. Morgan had already heard about the arrest and had been to see Moody in jail.

"You just tell me what I can do, Mr. Lee," Morgan said. "That boy is the best man I've got—that's why I sent him over there to handle Greenville."

"Well, I can try to get him out on bail," Will said, "but he doesn't have any money or property to speak of."

"What would you need?" Morgan asked.

"I expect the Judge would want at least fifty thousand dollars, maybe a hundred, if he'll set bail at all."

"I've got property worth a lot more than that," Morgan said.

"Then be at the Meriwether County Courthouse tomorrow morning at ten," Will said, "and bring a deed."

"I'll be there," Morgan said.

"You have to realize, Mr. Morgan, that even if Larry is out of jail, a lot of people won't want a man accused of murder in their houses fixing their furnaces."

"I'm not worried about that," Morgan said. "I'll see you in the morning."

Will hung up. If Larry Moody's boss would do that for him, it made him feel better about his client. He began to regret having to give up the case. He'd try to help find somebody good to replace him. He looked up to see the doctor coming toward him.

"I've just checked him again," Daniels said. "His breathing is normal now; he's out of Cheyne-Stokes, and that's good. He's still in critical condition, but he seems a little more stable."

"That's good," Will said, scribbling his telephone numbers on a card. "I've got to be in court tomorrow morning. I'll be reachable for the most part, but if for any reason you can't find me, rely on Jasper's judgment. He's been taking care of the Senator for a long time."

"All right," the doctor replied.

"I'll be back tomorrow afternoon," Will said.

*   *   *

It was after two in the morning before Will was in his own
bed, and it took him a while to wind down. In spite of his
lack of sleep, he woke at his usual six-thirty A.M., made himself some breakfast, watched reports of the Senator's illness
on the morning network shows, and gave some thought to
Larry Moody's preliminary hearing. Before heading for
Greenville and the courthouse, he drove into Delano and
stopped by the law offices of Lee & Lee on Main Street.
Some years before, he and his father had designed and constructed a freestanding building in the Williamsburg style to
contain their practice. He exchanged greetings with Kathy,
the receptionist, and with the formidable Maxine Morris,
secretary to his father and, when he was in town, himself.
Maxine was sixtyish, tall, stout, and smart as a whip. She ran
the office, and sometimes her bosses, with an iron hand.

"There's no mail for you, but somebody put this through
the letter slot," she said, placing a padded brown envelope,
the sort for mailing books, on his desk. It was addressed to
him in heavy marking pen.

"Thanks, Maxine," Will said. "I just wanted to check
in. I've got a hearing at ten."

"I know," Maxine replied. "I was sorry to hear about
the Senator," she said. "How's he doing?"

"Hanging on," Will said. "If a Dr. Daniels tries to reach
me here, get hold of me at the courthouse, all right?"

"Sure. You want coffee?"

"I think I could use an extra cup."

Maxine left, and Will plucked at the staples on the padded envelope, then shook the contents out onto his desk.
The sight froze him for a moment. Piled on the green

blotter were a dozen bundles of bills—hundreds, twenties, and fifties, bound with rubber bands. He heard Maxine's voice in the hallway and quickly opened the center drawer of his desk and swept the money into it. It surprised him that he didn't want her to see it, but there was something vaguely illicit about that much cash. When she had gone, he opened the drawer and counted the money. Exactly twenty-five thousand dollars.

He looked into the padded envelope and fished out a single folded sheet of paper. Written upon it, also in marking pen and in block letters, was the message FOR THE DEFENSE OF LARRY EUGENE MOODY. When he thought about it, it was easy to see why Larry's benefactor would not want to be publicly associated with him, why this person or persons would send untraceable cash. Well, he thought, that was all right with him.

Will put the money and the note back into the envelope and tossed it into his briefcase. Larry Moody had more friends than he knew. Will wondered why the person wanted to remain anonymous. Probably because of the nature of the crime. Greenville was a small town, after all.

At nine-thirty, Will knocked on the door of Judge Boggs's chambers.

"Come in!" The Judge waved him to a chair. "What can I do for you, Counselor?"

"Judge, I expect you've heard about the Senator's stroke."

"I sure have. How's he doing?" Before Will could reply, the phone on the Judge's desk rang, and he picked it up. "Hello?" He handed the receiver to Will. "It's for you."

"This is Dr. Daniels," a voice said.

A stab of anxiety passed through Will's innards. "Yes, Doctor, what's happening?"

"The Senator is conscious," the doctor said. "I'm surprised, I'll admit it; he's still aphasic, not responding to anything, but he seems aware; his vital signs are stable. He's by no means out of the woods, but I'm more optimistic."

"That's good news, Doctor," Will said.

"Do you want me to tell anybody?"

"Is that reporter from the *Constitution* still there?"

"Yes, and a television crew from the Atlanta station, too."

"All right, why don't you hold a little press conference and tell them what you've told me. Keep it brief; say you have an announcement, but you won't take questions; got that?"

"All right."

"Just don't let them press you into speculating about anything."

"I understand."

Will thanked him and hung up. He reported the news to the Judge.

"I'm glad to hear it," Boggs said. "He's a good man, and I hope he makes it. Now, what can I do for you?"

"Judge, as you can understand, the Senator's illness places me in a difficult position with regard to the defense of Larry Moody. I'm afraid that, under the circumstances, I'll have to ask to be excused from the case."

The Judge shook his head. "Nope. I told you and Elton both that you're in for the duration. I'll give you all the leeway I can to handle the Senator's affairs, but you are defending Moody, and you'd better get used to the idea."

Will tried not to seem angry. "Judge, that's unreasonable, in this situation. Let me handle the preliminary hearing, then hand off to somebody else. You'd hardly be prejudicing the defendant's chances. I've only seen him once."

"Will, I know you've got problems, and I'll help if I can, but I've got a problem, too, and we're going to solve my problem first. I'm real happy with the way this is shaping up, and I'm not changing a thing." He looked at his watch. "I'll see you in court in twenty minutes."

Will stood up and started for the door. "As you wish," he said, sounding less annoyed than he felt. He stopped at the door. "Oh, by the way, Moody is no longer an indigent defendant. I've been contacted by a party who is offering a retainer for his defense."

"Oh?" The Judge's eyebrows went up. "Who?"

"The party would prefer to remain anonymous."

"How much?"

"An adequate retainer." There didn't seem any reason for the Judge to know the amount.

"Well, that's very interesting, Will. Glad to hear it. Now get out of here."

At ten minutes before ten, a deputy brought Larry Moody into the courtroom. Will waited until the handcuffs had been removed, then shook his hand. "Have they been treating you all right, Larry?" he asked.

"Yes, sir," Moody replied. "I'm sure tired of being in there, though."

Will saw John Morgan enter the courtroom and waved him over. The deputy did not object when Morgan and Moody shook hands over the rail. "Larry," Will said, "Mr. Morgan has offered to go bail for you—if we can get bail—and we're going to try."

"Thank you, sir," Moody said.

"That's all right, son," Morgan replied. "We know you didn't have anything to do with all this. We're behind you; know that."

"Mr. Morgan," Will said, "I'd like to call you as a character witness, if that's all right."

"Be glad to," Morgan said. He took a seat in the front row of the courtroom.

Will motioned for Moody to sit next to him at the defense table. "Now, what we're going to see this morning is not a trial, but we'll get to see what sort of case the prosecution has," Will said. "I'll . . ." He stopped when a hand appeared on Moody's shoulder. He looked around to find Charlene Joiner smiling at them. Even in the simple, rather prim dress, she still had an unsettling effect on Will.

"Hey," she said to Moody. "Boy, do I miss you!"

Moody smiled back at her. "Me, too. Mr. Lee says I might get out on bail, though."

"Good morning," she said, turning her gaze to Will.

"Good morning, Miss Joiner," Will replied. "I'm not at all sure we can get bail, but we're going to try."

"I know you'll do the best you can," she said. She took a seat next to John Morgan, and they exchanged a friendly greeting.

Will turned back to Moody. "Listen, I think you ought

to know that, this morning, I asked the Judge to excuse me from representing you."

Alarm crossed Moody's face. "But why?"

"It's nothing to do with you or your case, Larry. It's just that, besides practicing law, I work in Washington for Senator Benjamin Carr—in fact, that's my main job—and the Senator had a stroke last Saturday. It's going to take a lot of time for me to keep the Senator's affairs in order while he's sick, and I told the Judge that, but he won't release me."

Moody let out a sigh of relief. "Boy, I'm glad to hear that," he said. "I want you to represent me."

"I appreciate that, Larry, but you have to understand that another lawyer might do a better job for you in the present circumstances. At the very least, there are going to be delays associated with my situation, and that might mean taking longer to come to trial. If we can't get you out on bail, you'd have to wait in jail all that time." Will took a deep breath and played his last card in getting out of the case. "Now, if you tell the Judge this morning that you want another lawyer, well, he'll have to grant your request. And I have to tell you, I think you'd be better off with somebody else. What do you say?"

"No, sir, I want you," Moody said emphatically. "I think you're smart, and you'll do a good job. Charlene thinks so, too."

Will glanced over his shoulder to Charlene, who looked back at him and smiled slightly. "Larry, this morning, somebody left twenty-five thousand dollars in cash at my office for your defense. With that sort of money available, I might even be able to get a top Atlanta criminal lawyer to take your case—somebody who's got a real track record in murder trials."

Larry shook his head. "No, sir, I want you. So does Charlene," he repeated.

Will was stuck now, and he knew it. "All right, then, I guess I'm your lawyer," he said. "By the way, do you have any idea who might have put up the money for your defense?"

Larry shook his head. "No."

"All rise!" the bailiff said loudly.

Judge Boggs walked briskly into the courtroom, robes flowing, sat down, and called his court to order. "Mr. Hunter?" he said, looking at the prosecutor.

Elton Hunter rose. "Your Honor, this is a preliminary hearing in the matter of the State of Georgia versus Larry Eugene Moody, on a charge of murder in the first degree. I will call only one witness."

"Call your witness."

"The state calls Sheriff Dan Cox." The sheriff rose from his seat, took the stand, and was sworn.

Will leaned over and whispered to Larry Moody, "The prosecution is playing it cagey by calling just the sheriff. They don't want us to know any more than we have to."

Elton Hunter addressed his witness. "Mr. Cox, you are the sheriff of Meriwether County, are you not?"

"I am."

"And you arrested the accused, Larry Eugene Moody, on Thursday last?"

"I did."

"What cause did you have to request a warrant for his arrest?"

"I have a witness who can place the accused at the scene of the crime. The witness has identified the accused at a properly constituted lineup. I have physical evidence of the crime found in a van belonging to the accused. I have interviewed the accused and am not satisfied with his account of his whereabouts between eight and ten P.M. on the night of the murder."

"Your witness, Mr. Lee," Hunter said, returning to his seat.

Will rose. "Good morning, Sheriff. Did your witness see the crime occur?"

"No, sir."

"Then how do you know the witness saw my client at the scene of the crime?"

The sheriff reddened. "I stand corrected," he drawled. "My witness observed the accused disposing of the body of the victim. I believe the scene of the crime to be in the van belonging to the accused. The van may have been moved after the murder."

"I see. Then your witness did not see my client commit murder?"

"No, sir."

"Did your witness see the face of the person who disposed of the victim's body?"

The sheriff reddened further. "Not exactly, but he is sure of his identification."

"The witness did not see the face of the person, but he is certain it is my client. I see." Will shot a glance of disbelief at the Judge, who remained expressionless. "Now, Sheriff, you say you have physical evidence from Mr. Moody's van. Is that evidence found by the State Crime Lab?"

"It is."

"May I see a copy of the lab's report, please?"

"Uh, I don't have it yet. I've had a telephone report from the lab saying the fibers found on the victim's body came from the van."

"Now, Sheriff, the report didn't say exactly that, did it? Didn't it say that the fibers were the same as some found in the van?"

"Yes, sir."

"So, that means only that the fibers are similar or the same, not that they came from the same source; am I right?"

"I guess so."

"Good. Now, you say you aren't satisfied with the accused's account of his whereabouts at the time of the murder. Is that right?"

"That's right."

"In what respect are you not satisfied?"

"I didn't believe him."

"That's all? No evidence that he was lying—just that you didn't believe him?"

"I've got my witness."

"What you mean, then, is that you prefer to believe your witness—who admits he didn't see my client's face."

"Yes, sir."

"My client had an alibi, didn't he?"

"Yes, sir. He said he was home with his girlfriend."

"That would be Miss Charlene Joiner. Did you question her?"

"Yes, sir."

"And did she corroborate his story?"

"Yes, sir."

"But you didn't believe her, either."

"No, sir."

"Why not? Any evidence to the contrary?"

"Just what I've told you already."

"So you preferred to believe your witness rather than Miss Joiner, is that it?"

"Yes, sir." The sheriff was becoming annoyed now.

"Sheriff, was an autopsy performed on the body of the deceased?"

"Yes, sir."

"Did the autopsy show that the deceased was raped before she was murdered?"

"Yes, sir."

"Then why is my client not charged with rape?"

"You'll have to ask the prosecutor about that. It wasn't my decision."

"Very well; I'll excuse you, Sheriff, and we'll hear directly from Miss Joiner herself. Your Honor, the defense calls Miss Charlene Joiner."

The sheriff and Charlene changed places, and she was sworn. She was composed and seemed almost demure.

"Miss Joiner, where were you on last Thursday night?"

"I got home from work a little after six."

"Were you home all evening?"

"Yes."

"Where was Larry Moody during that time?"

"At home with me."

"Did he leave the house after you came home from work?"

"No."

"Not at all? He didn't go to the grocery store? He didn't go out for a beer?"

"No, he was at home with me until he went to work at eight o'clock the next morning."

"Did you leave the house at all during that time?"

"No."

"Miss Joiner, do you understand that you are under oath, and that, if you lie to this court, you are liable not only for a charge of perjury, but one of being an accessory to murder?"

"Yes, I understand that, but I'm not lying. Larry was home with me from just after six that evening until eight the next morning."

"I have no further questions for this witness, Your Honor."

The Judge looked at Elton Hunter, and Hunter shook his head. "You have any other witnesses, Mr. Lee?" the Judge asked.

"Yes, Your Honor, one more. I call Mr. John Morgan."

Morgan took the stand and was sworn.

"Mr. Morgan, how long have you known Larry Moody?"

"Well, since he was in high school, I guess. He played football, and I was a member of the Quarterback Club. I got to know him then."

"And when did he come to work for you?"

"Right after he got out of high school. Larry was a little light for college ball, and he wanted to go to work."

"How long ago was that?"

"I guess it was nearly seven years ago. He came to work

in our La Grange store. We trained him, and eventually, two years ago, we sent him over here to Greenville. We have a lot of accounts here, and it seemed like a good idea to have a service office here."

"Why did you choose him to come to Greenville?"

"Because he was real good at his work—excellent, you might say—and because he was always absolutely reliable."

"Do you pay him well?"

"He's the best-paid employee we've got."

"Mr. Morgan, you told me you were willing to put up substantial bail for Larry Moody. Why are you willing to do that?"

"Because I believe in Larry. He's a fine young man, and I'd trust him with my life."

"Thank you, Mr. Morgan. No further questions."

Again the Judge looked at Elton Hunter, and he declined to question the witness. "All right, Mr. Hunter," the Judge said. "Sum up for me."

Elton Hunter rose. "Your Honor, you've heard the testimony of the sheriff, an experienced law-enforcement officer, who has explained his case. The prosecution wishes the accused bound over for the grand jury." Hunter sat down.

"Mr. Lee?" the judge said.

Will stood. "Your Honor, you have heard the sheriff say that his witness did not actually see my client's face, and that his physical evidence has not been exclusively connected to Mr. Moody's van. You've heard a reliable witness say that Mr. Moody was at home with her for the entire evening. You've also noted that, even though this was clearly a rape and murder, my client has not been charged with rape, which indicates to me a shaky case for the prosecution. Your Honor, I move that, in view of lack of substantive evidence, the charge against Larry Eugene Moody be dismissed." This was form; Will had no expectation that the charge would be dismissed.

"Denied," the Judge said. "Do you have a request for bail?"

"Yes, Your Honor. I would ask you to consider that the evidence against my client so far presented here is, to put it politely, inconclusive. My client has corroboration of his whereabouts at the time of the crime; he has shown himself to be a stable person with roots in the community; he is gainfully employed and has an excellent employment record, as you have heard. Although employed, he has no savings and has many financial obligations to meet, so it is important to him that he resume work immediately. There is no reason whatever to fear that he might flee the jurisdiction. I request that bail be set in the amount of ten thousand dollars."

The Judge looked at Elton Hunter and raised his eyebrows.

Hunter half stood. "Your Honor, the prosecution opposes bail—"

"Oh, come on!" Will said. "We're willing to offer substantial bond, if necessary, but surely there is no reason to deny bail in this case."

The Judge looked at Will. "Sit, Mr. Lee," he commanded. "You've had your say."

Reluctantly, Will sat down.

"Your Honor," Elton Hunter continued, "Mr. Moody

is charged with a capital crime—the brutal murder of an outstanding citizen—that has shocked this community. He cannot be let loose on the streets."

The Judge hardly paused. "Bail is denied. The accused is bound over for the grand jury, which"—he looked inquiringly at Hunter—"is in session this week?"

"Correct, Your Honor," Hunter replied. "I intend to present the case on Thursday, when copies of the autopsy and lab reports are available."

"Good," the Judge said. "Mr. Lee, if the prosecution's case is so shaky, I'm sure the grand jury will decline to indict, and your client will be free before the week is out." The Judge stood. "This hearing is concluded."

"All rise!"

When the Judge had gone, Will sat down next to his client again. "I'm sorry, Larry, but our chances were never good for bail—not in a case like this."

"But you heard the Judge say that the grand jury might not indict me," Moody said hopefully.

Will shook his head. "I won't be able to plead for you there. A prosecution can get just about anything he wants from a grand jury. I'm afraid you're going to be in jail until your trial. We'll see that you're made as comfortable as possible. Charlene can bring you food, so you won't have to eat the jailhouse stuff."

Moody nodded sadly. "Well, thanks for doing such a good job, anyway. You really gave that sheriff hell."

Will grinned. "Just wait until I get him on the stand at the trial."

While Moody was allowed to kiss Charlene and speak to his boss again, Will glanced around and saw a number of people he had not noticed in the courtroom earlier. An elderly black couple, both light of complexion, stood talking to a very tall, very black man. Will recognized him as Martin Washington, head of a lawyers' group called Attorneys for Racial Equality, or ARE, as it was known. That meant publicity, maybe even demonstrations. Bad news.

Another man, white, whom he did not recognize, was talking with Elton Hunter at the back of the courtroom. As Will watched, the two concluded their discussion, and the man walked toward him.

"Mr. Lee," the man said, extending his hand, "I'm Nick Donner, Southern Bureau of the *New York Times*.

Will shook the man's hand. Oh, Christ, he was thinking, this is all I need.

8

Will leaned over the bed and looked into Benjamin Carr's eyes. They shone brightly back at him. The Senator's face was expressionless, and it occurred to Will that he had never before seen Carr's face without expression. Even the poker face for which he was famous was different from this. His features had relaxed into a visage that was soft and childlike, and his mouth seemed to smile slightly.

The doctor had told Will that Carr might be able to understand him—there was no way of knowing—but that even if he could comprehend, he would be unable to respond by speaking, writing, or signaling. That was the meaning of "aphasic."

Will pulled a chair up to the bed and took Carr's limp hand. "Senator," he said, "it's Will. I know you can't talk, but I hope you can understand me. I just want you to know that you've had a stroke, but now you're stable. The doctor doesn't know much more than that. He doesn't know . . . when you'll regain your speech." He had almost said "whether." Will paused and tried to think what else the Senator might want to know. "Miss Emmy has been here, and so has Jasper, right along. They're both resting now. The Governor came right down as soon as he heard, but he had to go back to Atlanta." He paused again, then decided to tell him about his sister. "The doctor and I had a talk with the Judge, and he signed a temporary order giving me authority to handle your affairs. I didn't think Miss Emmy was up to it. Minnie and Jasper will take care of the household, paying the bills, and so forth. I'll be available to make any other decisions until you're on your feet again." He stopped again. He wanted to say something to encourage the man, to make him want to get better. He wasn't sure it was the right thing to do, but he did it anyway. "Senator, I know you real well, and I know you'll be yourself before long. I'm still planning on running your reelection campaign, so don't you let me down, you hear? I've already told the staff that nothing has changed," he lied.

Carr's face never showed a flicker of change, but to Will's astonishment, there was a movement in his hand, as if he had tried to grip Will's.

"That's the way, Senator," Will said. "I felt that; I know you can move that hand. You just keep at it, all right?" Carr closed his eyes as if he was sleepy. Will squeezed his hand and left him.

In the hallway he encountered Dr. Daniels. "He moved his hand, Doctor," Will said excitedly. "He gripped my hand for just a fleeting moment."

The doctor looked doubtful. "I don't think he's capable of that in his condition. What you felt was probably an involuntary muscle spasm."

"Well, what are his chances of regaining some movement and speech?"

"It's hard to say," the doctor replied. "I've seen some patients bounce right back after a very serious stroke. I've seen others become vegetables after what I thought was a minor one."

"What if he did grip my hand? What if it wasn't an involuntary spasm?"

"That would be a very good sign. If he can make that sort of movement now, so soon after his stroke, then, with therapy, he could recover quite a lot. If he remains stable, I'll send him home in a few days, maybe even for Christmas. After he's comfortable at home, then we can start him on some therapy and see how he reacts."

"Doctor, I'll tell you in confidence that he was planning to run for another term next November. Has he any chance of being well enough for that? He wouldn't have to campaign, as long as he could look into a television camera and speak. As long as he can think and express himself. I think if he couldn't be in the Senate, he'd curl up and die."

The doctor didn't speak for a moment. "Will," he said finally, "I can't encourage or discourage that idea. I just don't know enough. But any patient will respond better if he has something to look forward to. It can't hurt to keep talking to him about it."

"Doctor," Will said, "can I ask a favor of you?"

"Of course."

"When you talk to the press, will you say that he's responded in some way to treatment? I don't mean for you to lie—after all, he did try to grip my hand; he really did. It's just important right now that nobody thinks he's a vegetable."

"Like Mack Dean?" Daniels asked. "I suppose our Governor would like to be in the Senate, wouldn't he? After all, he can't run for a third term."

Will smiled. "Thank you, Doctor," he said.

At home, in his cottage by the lake, Will began to make decisions. It was Monday night, the twenty-first of December, two days since the Senator had had his stroke. He had not been returning phone calls since Saturday. He sat at his desk and opened his briefcase, looking for his address book and diary. On top of those, he found the padded envelope of anonymously sent money. There was a small safe in a cupboard in his bedroom; he opened it and tossed the money inside, spinning the lock. He had the odd feeling that he might want to give it back at some stage, if he ever found out who had sent it to him.

Back at his desk, he switched on his computer and composed a telegram to the Senator's other staff members.

SENATOR CARR HAS HAD A SERIOUS STROKE, BUT HE SEEMS TO BE RESPONDING TO TREATMENT, AND I AM HOPEFUL HE WILL RECOVER. IN THE MEANTIME, I AM SURE HE WOULD LIKE TO HEAR FROM YOU. I WILL SEE YOU BACK IN THE OFFICE ON JANUARY 2ND. PLEASE DON'T DO ANY JOB HUNTING—AT LEAST, NOT UNTIL YOU HAVE TALKED WITH ME. I AM AVAILABLE AT HOME IN DELANO IF YOU NEED ANY FURTHER INFORMATION. WILL LEE.

He typed a few keystrokes, instructing that it be sent to the list of staff names, already on file. They would have his message the following morning.

He telephoned Jasper and instructed him to set up a room at home with a hospital bed for the Senator, and to have a television set there so he could watch Cable News Network and C-Span. "Go ahead and get a tree decorated, too," he said. "Make it like it always is at Christmas."

"Yes, sir, Mr. Will," Jasper said.

"Jasper," Will said, "you're in charge down there. Don't let Miss Emmy push you around, you hear? Just do what's right for the Senator, and let me know if you can't handle her."

"Yes, sir!" Jasper said emphatically.

As soon as he hung up the telephone, it rang again.

"Will, it's Dudley Wendell," the voice said.

"How come I always rate an editor instead of a reporter?" Will asked.

"I hope you don't mind," Wendell replied. "I've had to bring my man at the hospital back to Atlanta, and I wanted something from you for tomorrow's edition."

"I don't mind, Dudley," Will said. "I saw the Senator this afternoon. He's in good spirits and responding to treatment. His doctor says he'll be home for Christmas."

"What about next November?" Wendell asked.

"The last thing the Senator and I talked about before his stroke was the election. He had already decided to run again, and until I hear differently from him, that's the way I'm going to leave it."

"Do you really think he can recover from a major stroke in that time?"

"It wouldn't be the first time a strong man had bounced back," Will said. "Now, if you'll excuse me, Dudley, I've got to get some sleep."

First, though, he looked up Kate Rule's number at her parents' house and dialed it.

"Hello!" she said, sounding both enthusiastic and relieved.

"I'm sorry I couldn't call you sooner," he said. "It's been wild."

"I can imagine. How is the Senator? And how are you?"

"It just about killed me when I saw him helpless in a hospital bed, but I think he's going to make it out of this," Will replied. "It's just a feeling. You know how tough he is."

"Is he going to be able to run again?"

"Who knows? To tell you the truth, it wouldn't surprise me. My plan is to go on just as if he is." Will was uncomfortable with this and changed the subject. "Also, I've gotten myself into defending in a juicy murder case down here." He gave her a blow-by-blow account of Larry Moody and the case against him, surprising himself that he didn't say much about Charlene Joiner.

"You sound beat," she said.

"You're so perceptive," he replied, laughing. "Is it because my lips are out of touch with my brain? Am I mumbling?"

"You are. You get yourself into a bed right now, you hear me?"

"All right. I wish you were in it, though."

"So do I. One piece of news before you crash."

"I'm sorry. I've hardly given you a chance to talk, have I?"

"I got the job. As of January one, I'm the Central Intelligence Agency's new Assistant Deputy Director for Intelligence. The fourth is my first day, actually."

"Oh, that's great, Kate. I know how much you wanted it. You'll be great. Before those guys know what hit them, you'll be DDI. Hell, Director!"

"I appreciate your faith, lover. Now put your body in bed. Good night."

He hung up and set his answering machine to answer on the first ring, then switched off the bell. Will felt a sense of relief that she'd gotten the job. Without it, she'd have been frustrated and unhappy, he knew, but now they'd have another two years, stable ones, in Washington. If the Senator recovered. Will could not allow himself to face the prospect of the Senator's not recovering.

He moved sluggishly toward the bedroom, struggling out of his clothes. He had been going nonstop since Saturday, dealing with the Senator's affairs, defending Larry Moody, and flying all over hell and back. He was through for at least eight hours.

9

Manny Pearl was the kind of man who, if he had been bald, would have worn a bad toupee. He was short, plump, and expensively but carelessly dressed in a gray sharkskin suit that was not a perfect fit. Still, he exuded a certain confidence and charm that stood him in good stead with his girls.

Manny looked up at the girl above him and winked at her.

Her name was Lauren, or so she said. She winked back, and followed the wink with a huge, sweeping bump, aimed right at him, then turned, stroking his hair with her fingertips. Her G-string was festooned with greenbacks, and all along the runway, men were beckoning her with more.

Manny tapped his watch and made a key-turning motion, then a sign that meant half an hour. She winked again, then turned her attention to a middle-aged businessman waving a twenty.

Manny moved his plump shape slowly toward the door of the club, watching the customers and the waiters. It was

Christmas Eve, and the place was a lot less than half-full. Still, he couldn't complain about business. Smooth as silk, it was. He'd cleared better than half a million bucks out of this place in the past year, and it was only one of three. The bookstore, though, that was another thing altogether. He'd go lock it up and be back with Lauren in no time. He stopped by his office and picked up an envelope with the checks in it.

In the parking lot, he inhaled the scent of the Mercedes leather interior once more, then started the car and moved off toward the bookstore, only a few blocks away. The car was new, less than a hundred miles on it, and he still felt the euphoria of ownership every time he got into it. He had paid cash for it; he paid cash for everything these days.

It was a damn shame about the bookstore, he reflected as he drove through the Atlanta streets, shiny with rain. It wasn't working. The rent was too high, it took too many people to run, and, worst of all, the place had been getting picketed lately. It was that goddamned TV preacher, Calhoun, sending his wild-eyed troops of housewives and children around with their signs, followed by the TV cameras. Then, when the local stations had tired of filming this ritual, Calhoun had sent his own cameras out and was showing the footage on one of his television programs.

What the hell? Manny thought, pulling into a parking spot outside the store. Why would guys want to buy pictures and videotapes of girls when they could come to any one of his three spots and see the real thing? He fished the envelope out of his pocket and looked at the three checks again. He was giving every man a month's pay in addition to what he had coming. That was generous, wasn't it? None of them had worked for him a year yet. A lot of employers would have just booted them out and shut down, even if it was Christmas Eve.

He swung out of the Mercedes and started for the door, glancing at his watch. Five minutes to four A.M., which was closing time. He'd make this short and sweet, get back to the club, give Lauren a quick hump, and be home in bed next to his wife by five. His daughter and her husband, the bum, would be over for Christmas dinner tomorrow.

Manny opened the door and stepped into the store. He didn't notice the van that had pulled into the parking lot and was sitting, its engine idling, as he looked around the store for customers. None, and no surprise. There was a man at the cash register, another dozing against a wall, and as Manny greeted them, the manager stepped out of his tiny cubicle at the rear.

"Hi, Frank," Manny said, pulling the envelope out of his pocket and waving it. "Merry Christmas, huh?"

Frank started to speak, but stopped, and his expression suddenly changed from greeting to something else, something Manny couldn't figure.

"What's the matter?" Manny asked. Then he felt a cold draft on the back of his neck and realized that Frank was looking past him, toward the door. So was the man at the cash register, and the one against the wall was suddenly awake. Manny turned around.

Two men stood inside the door, and two others quickly joined them. They were wearing camouflage fatigues and black berets, and three of them were holding some sort of small automatic weapons. The fourth, a tall, thin, deeply tanned man with barn-door ears and a hooked nose, held an automatic pistol.

This was not the first time Manny had faced men with guns, what with the business he was in, and he did not panic. "All right, fellas," he said, holding his hands out in front of him in a placating gesture, "no problem. No problem at all. We'll give you what we've got—whatever you want—and there won't be any fuss, all right?" He turned half around. "Frank, get all the cash together, whatever you've got, and do it right now."

"No."

Manny turned back toward the four men. "What?"

The tall man spoke again. "We don't want your filthy money."

"I'm sorry?" Manny said, bewildered. "You want pictures, tapes? Take whatever you want. Whatever."

"You three," the tall man said to Manny's employees. "Over here; on the floor."

Manny didn't like this at all. A stickup? Sure, take your loss like a man, don't get anybody hurt. But what was with these guys? What was it with the uniforms? He held out his car keys. "Listen," he said, "there's a brand-new Mercedes 560 SEL out in the parking lot—sixty grand's worth. Take it and have a Merry Christmas, okay? Let's not get crazy here."

"Lie down on the floor," the tall man said harshly. One of his companions grabbed Frank, the manager, and threw him onto the floor at Manny's feet. "Face that way," the tall man said, "all in a row."

Manny was suddenly very frightened. This was very weird. He looked out the window at the deserted street. A patrol car, he thought. We gotta have a patrol car, right now.

"You're Pearl," the tall man said. "We didn't expect to get this lucky."

"What lucky?" Manny said, his voice breaking. These guys wanted *him*. Was this some mob thing? He'd never had any of that kind of trouble, always made it a point to get along with those guys. His three employees were lined up on the floor at his feet now.

The tall man nodded to one of his companions and pointed at Frank, the manager. The uniformed man, who was young and fresh-faced, stepped forward, quickly aimed his weapon, and fired a single shot into the back of Frank's head. The manager emitted a sort of sigh.

"Jesus God!" Manny said. "Please don't do this! These people have never done anything to you! Neither have I!"

"Shut up," the tall man said. He nodded to another of his companions, who stepped forward and shot the cashier, then to the third companion, who shot the remaining employee.

Manny stood, staring at the three bodies. He looked helplessly out the window again. Would nobody come to help him?

"Pearl!" the tall man barked.

Manny turned and looked at the man, suddenly angry. "You sons of bitches, all of you!" he shouted.

The tall man raised his pistol and fired point-blank into Manny's face.

Manny flew backward, knocking over a bookstand, and ended up facedown on the floor. Amazingly, he was still conscious. He heard the tall man speak again.

"Good work, men," the man said.

"Pearl's still breathing," another voice said. "You better put another one in him."

"Yeah," the tall man said.

Manny clenched his fists. His right hand was full of blood. The shock and the noise came at the same time.

10

At midmorning on Christmas Day, Will set the airplane down on fifteen hundred feet of pasture at Flat Rock Farm. He taxied as close to the house as he could, then walked the last hundred yards, bearing his Christmas gift. Jasper met him at the back door, all smiles.

"I sure am glad to have him home, Mr. Will," the black man said, "and I sure am glad to see you down here on Christmas. Minnie wants to know—can you stay for Christmas dinner?"

Will shucked off his coat and handed it to the man. "I'm afraid not, Jasper," he said. "My folks are expecting me back. I haven't had a meal with them since I got home from Washington."

"Come on upstairs," Jasper said. "We got him all fixed up in his own room. We put a bed in there that sits up, and wait till you see what the Governor sent down here."

Will followed Jasper up the stairs and down the hallway to the big corner room. The Senator was sitting, supported by the new bed, facing the biggest television set Will had ever seen.

"Twenty-seven-inch screen. Ain't that something!" Jasper crowed. He leaned closer to Will. "There's a therapist lady coming every day, starting tomorrow. I sure hope she helps him. I hate seeing him like this."

Will went to the bed and pulled up a chair. He took Ben Carr's hand. "Merry Christmas, Senator," he said. The hand moved a bit. A muscle spasm? Will set his gift on the bed beside the Senator and removed the wrapping. "It's a speaker telephone," he said to the old man. He unplugged the instrument beside the bed and plugged in the new phone. "When you get a call, Jasper can just push the button, here, and you can listen without having to fool with the handset."

The same childlike expression greeted Will, the same bright eyes. Did they understand what they saw? They had to. Will wouldn't have it any other way. He sat beside the bed for half an hour bringing the Senator up to date on everything he could think of. He told him about the preliminary hearing for Larry Moody, and about Katharine Rule's promotion. The Senator knew her from CIA budget hearings before his Intelligence Committee.

Finally, Will said his good-byes. "The folks are expecting me home for Christmas dinner. I'll call you often and get down here as much as I can." He left the old man still pointed at the massive television set and went back to the airplane.

As the late-afternoon sunshine streamed through the library windows, Will sat with his mother and father and sipped coffee. They were all sated from a fine Christmas feast, and they had about run out of things to talk about, Will thought. He was wrong.

"Are you going to run?" Billy Lee said out of the blue.

Will sat up. "Run for what?" he asked, puzzled. "If you're talking about Jim Barnett's seat, well, I guess so. Nothing's changed."

"Everything has changed," Billy said. "Can't you see that, boy? I'm talking about running for Ben Carr's seat."

Will looked at his father, dumbfounded. "You can't be serious. With him lying down there on that farm, paralyzed? Besides, he could recover and run himself."

"Come on, son," Billy said, "it's time to face it. Ben Carr is never going to run for anything again. He's out of it, and the sooner you get a grip on that, the better."

"I've talked with his doctor at length about this," Will insisted. "He's seen more than one person the Senator's age snap right back from something like this."

"Will, even if his recovery surpassed his doctor's wildest dreams, he's through; can't you see that? The vultures are already circling, boy, just waiting for the earliest decent moment to pounce."

"Well, I'm not one of 'em," Will said emphatically. "That seat is the last thing he's got to cling to, and I love him too much to try to take it away from him."

"It has already been taken away from him," Billy said, standing and beginning to pace around the room. "And if he has a mind left, he knows it. Ben Carr is as much a realist as any man on earth, and you ought to know that by now. If he can still think, he's lying down there right now trying to figure out how to get you elected to replace him. I believe that, and you should, too."

"Daddy, my heart wouldn't be in it. I could never go around this state asking people to vote for me while the Senator is still alive and in office."

"Mack Dean could," Billy said bluntly. "Our beloved Governor will not only run for the seat, but if Ben dies, he'll appoint himself to the remainder of his term. He told you so himself."

"He didn't say he'd run for the seat."

"Of course he will," Bill said adamantly, "and so will half a dozen others, though none of them has the wherewithal and the organization to do it, except Mack Dean."

"Well, you can include me in that group, Daddy," Will said. "I don't have a political pot to piss in, let alone any real money or any way to raise it. Sure, with the Senator's help, I might have a chance at Barnett's seat, but not without his help."

Billy Lee looked at his wife for a moment, then went to a bookshelf, removed a handful of books, and worked the combination on the small safe behind them. He took out a bundle of blue-bound documents, closed the safe, replaced the books, and tossed the bundle into Will's lap. "There's the wherewithal," Billy said. "It won't buy you the election, but it will get you started."

"What's this?" Will asked, wary of the documents.

"It's the farm," Patricia Lee said.

"What?"

"We've been putting parcels of land in your name for years. It's all yours, really. We've kept the house and eight acres. The rest belongs to you, including the herd." Will's mother had been building a herd of Black Angus cattle for more than forty years, and she now had some of the finest breeding stock in the world.

"Mother, Daddy, you can't do this," Will said.

"It's done," Billy replied. "Of course, we hope you'll hold on to the land. A lot of it has been in the family since the 1820s, but the herd—that's readily salable."

"I couldn't sell the herd. Mother has worked too hard to build it up."

"Why do you think I did it?" Patricia asked. "Oh, I had a good time with it, but it was always for you, so you'd be free to do whatever you wanted to. I'm seventy years old, Will; your father is seventy-eight. We've no business raising cattle. I know you don't want the herd; your interests are elsewhere. I've sold off all but the best stock over the last couple of years. Why not sell them now, when they'll serve your purpose? That's what I want. That's what your father wants."

Will sat and looked at his parents. He tried to speak and failed.

"I've never seen you at a loss for words"—his mother laughed—"and this is it, I guess. Well, Will, are you going to run?"

"I can't even let myself think about it right now," Will said. "I'm so grateful to both of you for doing this. I'm overwhelmed, I really am. But what you're suggesting just seems unthinkable."

"You keep thinking about it," Billy said, "and you'll be surprised how much more thinkable it'll get." He flopped into his chair and reached for the television remote control. "We'll talk about it some more," he said. "Right now, it's time for the news." He switched on the set. The six-o'clock news was a nightly ritual in the family.

"Good evening," a young woman said. "In the early hours of Christmas morning, three men were murdered in an Atlanta adult bookstore." A shot of the interior of the store filled the screen. "The execution-style slayings took the lives of the store's manager, Frank Smith, and two of the store's employees. The store's owner, Manfred Pearl, who also owns three Atlanta nude dancing clubs, miraculously survived and is in critical condition in Piedmont Hospital, with two gunshot wounds to the head." The camera moved through the store and stopped at the counter next to the cash register. A crudely lettered sign in marking pencil was scrawled across the countertops: DEATH TO QUEERS AND JEWS, it read. The picture went back to the newscaster. "Police say that robbery was not a motive, since the store's cash register was undisturbed. A message left by the murderers made reference to homosexuals and Jews. Mr. Pearl is Jewish."

The picture switched to a group of women and children parading outside the store with signs. "A women's group from the Gospel of Freedom Church of Atlanta has been picketing the store in recent weeks. The church has a large congregation and a big following on television for its pastor, Dr. Don Beverly Calhoun"—the picture switched to a shot of a sleek, gray-haired man preaching from a pulpit— "who has also founded Freedom University, on the church grounds. Dr. Calhoun is with us in our studios."

The woman turned to her right, and the camera pulled back to reveal the minister, gorgeously tailored and groomed, sitting next to her. "Dr. Calhoun, do you think that the recent targeting of this store by your ministry might have, in some way, led to these killings?"

Dr. Calhoun placed his hands on the desk before him and folded them together. "Sheila, this sort of tragic thing could never have been done by anyone even remotely associated with our ministry. And I hope, in the midst of all this, none of us will lose sight of the tragedy which this so-called bookstore and others like it have brought to our community and our nation. This Mr. Manny Pearl, who, of course, we wish a speedy recovery, is a kingpin of the thriving Atlanta pornography industry, reaching to the very heart of our Christian—"

"But Dr. Calhoun," the woman interrupted, "Mr. Pearl's activities have all been within the law, have they not? Do you have any evidence to the contrary?"

"Sheila, Mr. Pearl's activities have never, at any time, been within God's law, and that is the law we hold supreme."

"Thank you, Dr. Calhoun."

Will turned to his father. "He's a pretty slick article, isn't he?"

"Oh, yes," Billy replied. "And he and Mack Dean are as thick as thieves, which is not an inappropriate simile, now that I think of it. Mack attends the Gospel of Freedom Church about once a month, and the television camera always finds him in the congregation. Calhoun raised a huge chunk of the money for Mack's two campaigns."

"You think Calhoun's crooked in some way?"

"Probably not, unless you consider separating little old ladies from their Social Security checks crooked. I sure do."

"He raises a lot of money outside Georgia, too," Patricia interjected. "He has a national audience on television.

He's pulled in enough money from around the country to invent that so-called university of his, cranking out little automatons for Jesus." In her scorn, Patricia's Irish accent came to the forefront. "God help us if they call what he's feeding them an education."

"When Governor Mack Dean announces for Ben Carr's seat," Billy said, "you can be sure Dr. Don, as he likes to be called, will be at his side—or leading him by the nose, depending on your point of view."

"You really think Mack will run for the Senator's seat?" Will asked, incredulously.

"Son, sometimes I think you're still a babe in the woods. Mack, I promise you, views Ben Carr's illness as a God-given opportunity to propel himself farther in politics than he ever believed possible. He's been a lackluster governor, and next November, he'll become a lackluster senator." Billy paused. "Unless somebody of substance runs against him."

Will found that notion nearly as depressing as he, himself, running for the Senator's seat. He couldn't do it, he knew that, and some part of him still doubted that Mack Dean could.

II

In the four years they had been seeing each other, they had never been to a restaurant together. Her position at the Central Intelligence Agency and his—first, as counsel to the Senate Select Committee on Intelligence and, later, as chief of staff to the chairman of that committee—made for a conflict of interest that, if known, might seriously undermine her career at the Agency. They had kept their secret well, always dining at his house, since he enjoyed cooking, and sleeping together in his bed or hers. It had been an odd love affair, but a successful one. Now, for the first time, they gazed at each other across a restaurant table, though not in Washington. On New Year's Eve, they sipped champagne at the Café des Artistes in New York, while the nudes by Howard Chandler Christy looked down upon them from the walls.

Will raised his glass. "To a new day at the Agency," he said, smiling.

She tapped his glass with hers and drank. "That may be something of an overstatement, you know. I'm not sure anything is going to change."

"It will with you in the job. You've already changed some things at that place, and from a lot weaker position than you're now going to be in."

"Let's hope," she said.

The waiter brought their first course, a selection of pâtés and a rillette from the charcuterie table.

"Now to the important stuff," Kate said. "What are you going to do with yourself now?"

He was surprised. "Well, I've still got a job, you know."

She took a deep breath. "Will, I don't think you're being realistic. From what you've told me about the Senator's condition, this is certainly his last term, and, moreover, he could have another stroke and die at any moment. It seems to me the very best you can expect is to stay on for the rest of his term, and then do something else."

Will sighed. "You're probably right," he said.

"Probably? You know I'm absolutely right. Do you really believe that the Senator might rise up from his bed, get reelected, and continue as if nothing has happened?"

Will put down his fork. "You know," he said sheepishly, "that's exactly what I have been telling myself. It's not very smart, is it?"

"Look, this isn't the end of the world. You can still do just what you'd planned to do. You may not have the Senator's help, but, on the other hand, he might recover enough to do something for you. In any case, you've got four years to build a candidacy for yourself. Your father will help; he's still got a lot of political clout in Georgia, hasn't he?"

"Probably not as much as he'd like to think. It's been more than twenty years since he was governor, and there are still a lot of Democrats who haven't forgiven him for pulling out of politics rather than support Lester Maddox when he was elected governor. He couldn't abide supporting a racist clown, but there were a lot of people who thought he should abide anything for the party's sake." Will paused. "You have to remember, too, that in four years' time he'll be eighty-two, and he's already had a heart attack. What he wants me to do is declare now; run for the Senator's seat."

Kate's eyebrows went up. She started to speak, but reconsidered, took another bite of her food. "You think," she said finally, "he's rushing you into running so he can be around to see it?"

"Oh, maybe that's part of it; that's a natural enough reaction. He also thinks the Governor, Mack Dean, will run, and he's always thought Mack was a spineless do-nothing. But he really believes it's the right thing for me to do. I'm having an awful hard time with it."

She placed her hand on his. "You don't want to run for the Senator's seat?"

"Not while he's alive. And, of course, if he dies, Mack Dean will appoint himself to serve out the term, and it would be extremely difficult to beat him as an incumbent. Hell, it would be difficult under the best of circumstances. He's just coming off two terms as governor, and he would have most of the party behind him."

"You'd be starting from scratch if you ran against him," she said. "You don't really have a political base, do you? Just a well-known name."

"That's about it. I think what I'll do is see that the office is run as well as possible for the rest of the Senator's term, then repair to Delano, practice law, and start to work on Jim Barnett's seat, four years down the road."

"Sounds like the prudent thing to do," Kate said. "If you run against Dean and lose, wouldn't that make things more difficult in four years?"

"Oh, sure. First of all, Mack would be mad at me for opposing him. He'd throw his support to somebody else in the primary. Then, of course, I'd be a loser in the electorate's eyes."

"Sounds like you've got this pretty well worked out. Practice for four years, build a base, then run against the Republican."

Will nodded. "And with Dean's support, if I support him this time. It's not something I relish, supporting him."

"Well," she said, smiling and raising her glass, "let's drink to four years well spent—as long as you spend a lot of that time in Washington, near me."

Will raised his glass. "I'll drink to that," he said. "And a wedding two years hence. Is that a deal?"

"You're on." She smiled. "I think you're smart not to run now, unprepared. It's better for us, too. It will take the pressure off me where the Agency's concerned. And I expect that, after a couple of years, I'll have the job out of my system."

"Just as long as you don't have *me* out of your system."

"Fat chance," she laughed. "Remember now, we've got a deal."

They drank deeply of the wine, never taking their eyes from each other.

12

Will sat on a desk in the large, common workroom of Senator Benjamin Carr's office, addressing the Senator's staff gathered there. They gazed back at him with interest and uncertainty, a young, talented, and enthusiastic group, three-quarters of whom Will had himself recruited over the past years. They were always coming and going, these Capitol Hill staffers—young lawyers out for Washington experience they could later exploit with D.C. law firms and as lobbyists; a journalist or two who had decided to work for someone who made news; a couple of bright young women who were answering phones and stuffing envelopes while using the office as a base for Capitol husband-hunting; a few dilettantes with rich daddies and high ideals; and a hard core of professional staffers, people who found it satisfying to be involved in the business of making law and running the country. It was this last group, more than the others, that Will was addressing.

"Now," he began as if in midsentence, "I can't make

any of you any promises about when or even if the Senator will be back. But, at the very least until the end of the year, we have an office to run, and for some of that time, it's going to have to be run without me. I got myself involved, with the Senator's permission, representing an indigent defendant in a murder trial at home, and the judge won't release me—believe me, I tried. So I'm depending on every one of you to stick here and make it work. I know full well that you're going to be getting calls from other staffs, and I hope you'll put them off until we know what's what around here—no matter how attractive the offers are. If you're tempted, talk to me first. I think you owe the Senator that, at least."

Jack Buchanan, the Senator's chief legislative aide and one of the professional staff group, came and leaned close. "Will, Jasper is on the phone from the Senator's house. Do you want to talk to him now?"

"Tell him I'll call him back, unless it's an emergency. Be sure you find out about that," Will whispered back. Buchanan went back to the phone, and Will continued. "Naturally, the legislative side of things is going to be sharply curtailed, under the circumstances, so I've asked Jack Buchanan to fill in for me when I'm out of the office. What won't stop, what we really have to keep going, is constituent services, and Jack and I will be pulling some of you off your regular assignments to help with that. I want every phone call or letter from a constituent to be handled as if the Senator were taking a personal interest in it. Letters to federal agencies and any other letter in support of a constituent will go out over my signature, for the Senator. I don't think anybody is going to buy it if we send out letters signed by the signature machine." He swept the room once more, making eye contact and holding it with an occasional staffer. "One final thing: if the Senator should die before his term expires, the Governor will appoint someone to succeed him, and I hope every one of you will stay and serve that person just as you would have served the Senator. He or she will need the help of all of us until the new senator can put his or her own staff together. That's it. Any questions?"

There were none.

"Good. Any problems, see me, or, if I'm not here, Jack."

People ambled back to their desks, and Will returned to his own office. He picked up the phone and began dialing Flat Rock Farm. Before he could be connected, Jack Buchanan thrust his lanky figure through Will's door, looking worried.

"Will, come look at this, quick!"

Will hung up the telephone and followed Jack back into the common workroom. The staff were fixed on the television set high up on one wall. They were looking at Emma Carr, the Senator's sister, who was speaking into a microphone.

"Ladies and gentlemen," she announced in her broad south Georgia accent, "I would like to announce that Senator Carr has decided to run for another term. He made his wishes known to me last night."

"It's CNN, Will," Jack whispered. "They just said they were going live to the Senator's house for an announcement."

"How is the Senator feeling, Miss Emmy?" a reporter asked.

"He's doing just fine, feeling a whole lot better. He's having a therapist over every day, and she's working with him a lot."

Will stared unbelievingly at the set.

"Has the Senator recovered his speech, Miss Emmy?" the reporter asked.

"He's communicating his wishes," Miss Emmy replied. "Now, that's all I have to say to the press today," she concluded, waving coquettishly at the camera. She turned and went back into the house, and as she did, the camera caught a brief glimpse of Jasper, looking anguished.

"Jesus Christ," Will muttered, striding back into his office. "What the hell is going on down there?" He picked up the phone and redialed Flat Rock Farm. Jasper answered on the first ring.

"Jasper, I just saw Miss Emmy on TV. What's happening?"

"Lord, I'm glad to hear from you, Mr. Will," Jasper panted. "Miss Emmy, she done gone nuts. I couldn't do nothing with her."

"What about the Senator? Is he talking? Has he said anything?"

"He ain't said a word," Jasper said, "just like he's been since the stroke. He wrote something, though."

"*Wrote* something? He can *write*?"

"He managed a little bit," Jasper said. "That's what got Miss Emmy so crazy."

"What did he write?" Will demanded.

"Mr. Will, you better come down here," Jasper said. "I'm gon' need your help to get Miss Emmy back under control."

"What did the Senator write?" Will asked again.

"I think you better come down here and look at it before I say something," Jasper replied. "You might want to talk some to the Senator when you see it."

Will realized that Jasper had dug in his heels and was not going to say any more. He had seen the man do this before. "All right, Jasper, I'll get down there as quick as I can. I've got a few more things to do here; it'll probably be noon before I can take off. Look for me about three-thirty or four. Is the weather good?"

"Yes, sir. Clear as a bell. You can set down out back."

Will hung up and looked at Jack Buchanan, who was standing in the door. "He says the Senator has written something."

"I thought he was paralyzed," Jack said.

"So did I, but a therapist has been working with him since Christmas. He must be making a lot of progress."

Jack looked over his shoulder at the television set. "Uh-oh," he said, "here comes Mack Dean."

Will went back into the common room in time to see the harried-looking Governor of Georgia hurrying down the Georgia Capitol steps, followed by a couple of television reporters.

"Yes, I just heard," the Governor said. "Wonderful news."

"He doesn't look like he thinks it's so wonderful." Jack chuckled.

"I'm delighted to hear that the Senator seems to be on the road to recovery," Dean said, "although that's quite a surprise, given the reports I've been getting from his doctors. Gentlemen, you'll have to excuse me. I'm late for a meeting."

The camera followed him to his car and watched as he was driven away, then panned to a young reporter. "That was Governor Mack Dean, expressing his pleasure at the news of Senator Carr's improvement. There had been rumors that the Governor was about to announce for the Senator's seat, so the news might not have been all good, from the Governor's point of view."

Jack laughed aloud. "No, I guess it isn't all good news for Mack," he chortled. "You going down there, Will?"

"Damn right. I'm going to have to do something about Miss Emmy. It looks like Jasper can't handle her."

The afternoon shadows were long when Will taxied the airplane toward the house at Flat Rock Farm. Jasper was out of the house to meet him even before he could shut down the engine. Jasper reached the airplane as Will was getting out, and they walked briskly toward the house together.

"Now, tell me exactly what happened," Will said.

"Well, it was late yesterday afternoon. That therapy lady was over here working with the Senator. She had him gripping a pencil with that one hand, trying to write on a pad, but he couldn't do it. Then the lady left, and me and the Senator was watching TV. The Governor was on, being interviewed by this fellow, and he was hinting around like he might want to run for the Senator's seat."

They reached the house and went in through the back door. Before Jasper could continue, Miss Emmy suddenly appeared from the kitchen.

"Goddamn vultures," she spat at Will. "That'll show you all! He's going to run!"

Minnie came out of the kitchen and led her away, looking over her shoulder at Will, shaking her head.

"She's been just like that since yesterday, Mr. Will," Jasper said. "I swear, I didn't know she'd done called up that TV station, not till I see her out on the front porch, talking to them. Wasn't nothing I could do."

They started up the stairs toward the Senator's room.

"Go on, Jasper," Will said, "tell me about yesterday."

"Oh, well, me and the Senator was watching the Governor on TV, and I think the Senator must've got mad, 'cause that pencil was still in his hand, and he started moving it around on the paper. You could tell he was really struggling with it."

"And he wrote something?"

"Yessir, he did," Jasper said, pulling a folded piece of paper from his coat pocket and holding it back when Will tried to take it. "He wrote something, and Miss Emmy took it all wrong, I think. I think he wrote it to you." Finally, having said his piece, Jasper surrendered the paper to Will.

Will unfolded it and looked at what the Senator had written. At first, it wasn't clear; it was nothing like the Senator's handwriting. But after a moment, Will realized what the scrawl said. He stopped outside the Senator's door. There were two words on the paper, written in uneven, poorly drawn capital letters. Together, they made a message that rocked Will when he read it.

The words were: WILL RUN.

Will stared at the message, reading it over and over, to be sure he was not mistaken. He leaned against the door and took a few deep breaths; then he turned and walked into the Senator's room.

The Senator was awake, sitting up, supported by the elevated hospital bed. Will pulled up a chair and took the old man's hand. His face was still soft and featureless, but his eyes burned brightly. "Hello, Senator," Will said. "I hear you're feeling better."

The hand squeezed Will's softly. It was no mere muscle spasm.

"Senator," Will said, "I want to ask you something. Try and squeeze my hand once for yes and twice for no. Can you do that?"

The hand squeezed once.

"Good." Will grinned. He held up the piece of paper. "Did you manage to write this yesterday?"

The hand squeezed once.

"That's wonderful!" Will said. "You're going to recover! You'll be back with us in Washington before you know it."

The hand squeezed twice, emphatically.

"Senator," Will said, "in this note, did you mean you wanted to run again?"

Two squeezes. No mistaking.

Will took a deep breath. He didn't want to ask the next question. Finally, he asked, "Did you mean you want *me* to run?"

Will was astonished at the firmness of the grip. One squeeze. Just one. Hard. The Senator stared at Will and held tightly onto his hand.

13

Leah Pearl sat and knitted and, occasionally, glanced at her husband. She had been knitting for most of the day, rising only to have a bite to eat and go to the bathroom. She had been sitting there every day since Manny Pearl was shot.

Leah smiled, remembering what Manny liked to say about her knitting. "It gives her something to think about while she talks." Manny had always been funny, since the day she first met him, nearly forty years before, when she had been selling tickets at the Fox Theater, and Manny had been an usher. They had been married before a month had passed, and Leah had never regretted a moment of it. Oh, a lot of people would have thought Manny unreliable, what with all the businesses he'd been in—novelties, costume rentals, ladies' sexy underwear, marital aids, and now the nightclub business. What people never seemed to understand was that Manny had made money at them all; he had only changed businesses when he got bored. Manny was steady, in his way. He'd been a good father—strict, the best schools for the boys; he'd been a good husband, an honorable man—religious, even, although he only went to synagogue on the holidays. Still, he'd given and given to the congregation and to Israel. A good man. She'd never minded about the girls. Men had to have them, she believed, and as long as she didn't know the details, she didn't mind. She knew he didn't have to work as late as he said he did, but she didn't mind. Manny enjoyed, and it was all right with her.

She glanced at Manny and saw that his arm was dangling from the bed. Alarmed, she went and checked his pulse. Still there, still steady. It had been steady since the third day, when they had taken him off the respirator. Tenderly, she passed a hand over the bandages that swathed most of his head above the nose. Satisfied, she tucked his arm under the covers and went back to her chair and her knitting. A moment later, for the first time since Christmas Eve, her husband moved in his bed.

"Putz!" Manny said suddenly.

Leah dropped her knitting and ran to the bedside. Manny was staring at the ceiling. "Gonif!" he yelled. "Schmuck!"

"Now, dear," she said, breathing hard and reaching for the call button, "just lie quietly, and the doctor will be here in a minute." She hoped he'd mind his language when the doctor came.

A nurse, blond and pretty, put her head inside the door. "What is it, Mrs. Pearl?"

"He's awake!" Leah stammered. "Get the doctor!"

The nurse walked over to the bed, took Manny's bandaged face in her hands, and checked his pupils. "Can you hear me, Mr. Pearl?" she said loudly.

"Of course I can hear you, sugar," Manny said, smiling. "You should be in show business, you know. You want a job?"

"Manny!" Leah said. "Watch your mouth!"

The nurse left the room, and Manny turned to her. "Hello, sweetheart." He looked around him and frowned. "They killed those three boys, didn't they? I saw them do it."

"Yes, Manny," Leah said. "But they didn't kill you."

"Damned right, they didn't. The putz! He didn't have to do it! They could have had everything! I even offered them the car!" He looked at her. "Did they take the car?"

"No, Manny. It's home in the garage. Not a scratch on it."

"Thank God for small favors," Manny said.

A young doctor appeared and began examining Manny. He held up his hand. "How many fingers, Mr. Pearl?"

"Two," Manny replied. "It was that fucking preacher that was behind it," he said.

"Manny, watch your language!" Leah commanded.

"Follow my finger," the doctor said, moving his hand back and forth in front of Manny's face.

"I'm sorry, Leah," Manny said. "I apologize for my language, Doctor."

"That's okay, Mr. Pearl. I'm glad to hear you talking."

Manny looked at him narrowly. "How old are you?" he demanded.

"Why do you want to know that?" the doctor asked.

"How long you been a doctor?"

The doctor laughed. "Long enough to know that you're an amazing medical phenomenon. You want somebody with a little gray at the temples; is that it?"

"I don't trust young," Manny said. "Get me old."

"Not a gray hair around, I'm afraid. I'll have to do until the real thing comes along. Now, I want you just to lie quietly. I'm going to order some more X-rays and I want a neurologist to see you. I warn you, though, he's pretty young, too."

"Never mind X-rays," Manny said.

"Mr. Pearl, you've been shot twice, and you've had a lot of surgery."

"I have? Am I all right?"

"That's what I want to find out—just how all right you are."

"Okay, do your worst," Manny said. "But first, I want a cop."

"A cop?"

"Lots of cops. I got a lot to say. I'm not seeing this neurologist guy until I've seen a cop. Tell them to put the siren on. I got a lot to tell them."

The detective sergeant looked up from his notebook. "Is there anything else, Mr. Pearl?"

"The tall one with the barn-door ears and the nose, he shouldn't be too hard to find. Nobody else could look like that."

"We'll get his description on the wire right away."

"I think he's military," Manny said. "I was in the army. I think he was, too. Or maybe the Marines."

"What about him makes you say that?" the detective asked.

"Everything about him. The way he stood, the way he gave orders. Retired, maybe. You know how they join young, get out after twenty years or something? Like that."

"Well, we can check with the Pentagon, but do you have any idea how many retired military people there are in Georgia?"

"Not an officer, though. A noncom," Manny said. "A master sergeant, I'll give you odds. You know what pricks sergeants are."

"Manny!" Leah blurted.

"Sorry, Sergeant," Manny said sheepishly. "I meant army, not cops."

"That's okay, Mr. Pearl," the sergeant said. "I was in the army, too. I know about sergeants."

"Do you know about TV preachers?" Manny asked.

"Now, listen, Mr. Pearl," the detective said seriously. "I wouldn't go around saying that, if I were you. Granted, Calhoun had some pickets from his church at your store, but that doesn't connect him with what happened. A lot of people in this town think Calhoun is some kind of saint. My mother is among them, although I think she's nuts. She's been sending part of her Social Security check to that guy. It burns me up."

A doctor who was leaning against the wall of the room spoke up. "If that's about it, Sergeant, I'd like to see if Mr. Pearl can wiggle his fingers and toes."

"I'll tell you something, Doctor," the sergeant said, "I wouldn't want to arm-wrestle Mr. Pearl for money right now." He turned to his partner. "Let's get out of here and let Mr. Pearl wear out this doctor."

"Okay, Doc," Manny said, "you're next. Let's get on with it."

14

It was after midnight when Will got back to George-town, and he was exhausted. He started for his own house, but ended up at Kate's. He let himself into the house, tapping the burglar-alarm code into a keypad and ringing the doorbell three times to alert her. There was a 9 mm automatic pistol in her beside-table drawer, and he didn't want any accidents.

"What's up?" she asked sleepily, moving over to let him under the covers.

"A lot," he said, climbing in beside her. He told her about the Senator's new note-writing skills.

She listened in silence, now fully awake, and when he had finished, she still didn't say anything.

"You see where I am," he said finally.

"Yes, I suppose I do," she replied. "You're going to run, aren't you? In spite of our deal."

"Yes," Will said. "I don't have any other choice. It's the mirror image of the way things were last week. Then, I couldn't run, because I thought I would hurt him. Now, I have to run, and for exactly the same reason."

"I know," she said.

"You know, a couple of weeks ago, everything was in such good shape. We both had what we wanted—me, the Senator's support against Barnett; you, the new job at the Agency."

"And we both had a plan to marry," she said.

"Yes. And now everything has changed, been moved up, and we both have commitments to others."

"Yes. Commitments we both have to keep," she said quietly.

"You can't do this with me, can you?" he asked.

"You know I can't. I'm already up to my neck. Two people took early retirement when they didn't get the job. I could never live with myself if I walked out now."

"And I could never live with myself if I didn't run now."

She snuggled close and put her head on his shoulder. "I wish I could go down there with you and do my part."

He put an arm around her and turned to face her. "So do I. But I understand why you can't. Really, I do."

"We can keep on the way we are, can't we?" she whispered.

"Sure we can," he whispered back, but he wasn't sure. "I won't be able to get up here much between now and election day," he said.

"I won't be able to come down there," she said. "Or even meet you anywhere. I'm at a new level in the Agency; I have access to a lot more information than I did before. They'll put me through a new security-clearance investigation, and I'll have to turn in an accurate log every time I travel—no exceptions. You can see that it's more important than ever that we keep our relationship quiet; the slightest thing in the papers might make my position at the Agency untenable. You can see that, can't you?"

"Yes, I can." He hugged her. "You're just going to have to remain the best-kept secret in town."

They lay in each other's arms until they fell asleep. Neither of them made any move to make love.

15

Will sat in his small office, filling the pages of a legal pad. It was just after eight, and he had been at it for an hour. He heard footsteps in the common room, and Jack Buchanan put his head into the office.

"Come on in, Jack," Will said. "I'm glad you're in early; I need to talk with you." Jack arranged his long frame in the only other chair in Will's office. Will looked at him. He had brought Jack Buchanan onto the staff, stolen him from the office of a Massachusetts congressman, where he had been languishing as an assistant. Will had met him while doing committee work and had been impressed with his easy manner and bright mind. Will had been best man at Jack's wedding four years before and was godfather to the elder of his two daughters. Jack had been resented by some of the Georgians at first, a Yankee on a mostly Southern staff, but he had won them over quickly. It was Jack whom Will had planned to recommend for his own job when he eventually left the Senator's staff.

"Jack," Will said, "I wanted to talk to you before I talked with anybody else." He paused. He had made this decision, but he was still uncomfortable with it. Things were happening too fast. He explained to Buchanan what had occurred at the Senator's house. "I'm going to run for his seat, Jack. I had planned to run against Barnett next time, but now it can't wait. I'm satisfied it's what the Senator wants, too."

Jack was grinning. "That's terrific news, Will. I'm glad for you. I'll miss you around here, though."

"Thanks, Jack, but—"

"I'll hold the office together, though. You can count on it."

"Jack, I don't want you to hold the office together. I want Ed to do that." Ed Tanner was the Senator's press secretary.

Jack's face fell. "I see. Well, whatever you want . . ."

Will laughed. "I'm sorry. I'm not making myself clear. I want you to sign on with me, help me run my campaign."

Jack smiled broadly. "I'd really like that, Will." He frowned. "But I'm not sure I can handle it."

"I've got some money. I can pay you what you're making here, right through the campaign. If we make it, then I want you to run my office."

Jack stood up and grabbed Will's hand. He seemed to be having a hard time speaking.

"It's going to mean a lot of time away from Millie and the kids, you know."

"She'll go along; you know she will. She's nuts about you."

"I'm glad to hear it. Listen, I'm going to ask Kitty Conroy to join us, too. The two of you are all I can afford at the moment."

"I'll call Millie now, and see what she has to say," Jack said.

"Thanks, and as soon as Kitty comes in, ask her to see me, will you?"

"Sure." Jack turned to go.

"One more thing, Jack. What do you think of Hank Taylor?"

"I don't have much direct knowledge of him," Jack replied. He grinned. "We've never had much need of a political consultant around here."

"I knew him slightly when he was a deputy press secretary to Jimmy Carter."

"He's done mostly New York and California campaigns, hasn't he?"

"Yeah, but television is a New York and California business. Anyway, he's a Southerner. He won't have forgotten what it's like."

"If you say so." Jack turned to go. "I'll send Kitty to you when she comes in."

Kitty Conroy jumped at the chance. "I'll do a good job for you, Will," she enthused. Kitty was in her late twenties, redhaired, smart, and pretty. She was from Savannah's large Irish community, where her father was a city councilman.

"You always have. That's why I'm asking you. I know you've chafed a bit at working as a deputy, when you were perfectly well qualified to be press secretary yourself. Well, now you're my press secretary, as of next Monday. Type out a resignation for the files, and ask Jack to do the same, will you? Spend the rest of the week cleaning up around here and doing what you can to see that it runs smoothly when you're gone."

"Sure, Will."

"And plan to come down to Delano this weekend. Bring what you'll need for a long stay."

Will arrived at the Watergate and took the elevator to Hank Taylor's floor. He was asked to wait by the pretty receptionist. Will sat down and took in the cool decor, the expensive furniture, the art. From the other side of the wall behind him, he heard a stirring march strike up. "Heald, Heald, he's our man, if he can't do it, nobody can!" a male chorus sang. Will winced; it was awful. That would be Michael Heald, who was running for Congress in New York City's Silk Stocking District, Will remembered. He had begun to think that maybe he should look elsewhere for a campaign consultant when a door opened and another pretty girl asked Will to follow her. They went down a long corridor toward the corner office, and Will caught glimpses of people designing ads and editing film. The Heald music was farther away now, and Will tried to put it out of his mind.

Hank Taylor came from behind a large glass table to greet him. Short, wiry, athletic-looking, black-rimmed glasses, silk shirt, red suspenders. "Will, how are you, boy?" He had not lost his accent.

"Good, Hank."

"How's the Senator?"

"Doing better. He's having therapy every day now, and improving."

Taylor waved him to a chair. "Not fast enough for November, though, huh, boy?"

Will shook his head. "I'm afraid he's out of it, Hank.
That's between you and me for the moment, though."

"And you're going to go for his seat?" Taylor asked,
leaning back in his chair and grinning.

"That's the way the Senator wants it," Will said uncomfortably. "I hadn't planned to run until Barnett comes
up."

"Sure, sure." Taylor grinned.

Will flushed. "Let's be clear about this, Hank. I
wouldn't be running if the Senator hadn't asked me to."

"Sorry, Will," Taylor said, holding up a placating hand.
"You're going to need a lot of help, then."

"That's why I'm here," Will said. "You're the only guy
I know in this business, you're a Southerner, and your
reputation is good."

Taylor stood up and started to pace. "Okay, boy, let me
tell you what you'll get for your money around here. We'll
do your television, radio, and design all printed materials.
We think it's important to have an overall look that runs
right through everything."

"Sounds good," Will replied.

"I give my personal attention to every single thing that
comes out of this office, boy. This firm's biggest asset is my
feel for things, and as a client, you'll get the full benefit of
that."

"Glad to hear it."

"My guys will get your positions right on all the
issues."

"Well, Hank, I've got a lot of ideas of my own," Will

said. "I've been writing Senator Carr's position papers for years."

"Sure, sure, boy, but we want to home in on one or two out-front issues, you know? For instance, education. We've been getting a lot of playback on the idea of a bill offering parents government vouchers that they can spend at any private school. Hot response, sexy stuff."

"I'm a Democrat, Hank. I believe in public education."

"Sure, sure, boy, I'm just throwing around ideas off the top of my head. We'll be in sync with your convictions, don't worry." Taylor walked back behind his desk and sat down. "Now, let's get down to brass tacks," he said. "You got any money?"

"I've got enough to get us set up. Of course, fund-raising is going to be very important to us."

"Yeah, I know. We don't handle that end, though. We're primarily a media outfit."

"I understand that. Now, what's this going to cost me?"

"Our fee is seventy-five grand, thirty-seven five now and the rest the day after you win the primary. That covers all our creative fees. We'll bill you for production costs and add our standard 17.85 percent commission. Our media service will place all the advertising, and we split the 15 percent commission from the stations with them. Got it?"

"Seems clear," Will said, swallowing.

"Good. When can you let me have your check?"

"Well, we haven't even got a bank account yet. Will next week be all right?"

"Sure, sure. Can I expect your check on Monday, then?"

"All right, I'll have it in the mail by Friday."

"Use Federal Express," Taylor said, rising from his chair. "More reliable." He took Will's arm and steered him toward the door. "I want to send one of my guys down to see you next week, soak up some atmosphere, get your slant on the campaign, okay?"

"Sure."

"I'll send Tommy Black down there. He's one of my best. You'll like him." Taylor walked Will to the door and down the hall to the reception room. There he stopped and took Will's hand. "Will, boy, I don't want you to worry about a thing. You've got the best outfit in the business on your side. You're going to be the next senator from Georgia."

Will shook Taylor's hand and left. As he walked toward the elevators, he could still hear the music hammering away through the walls. "Heald, Heald, he's our man! If Heald can't do it, nobody can!" He shuddered.

Driving back toward the Capitol, though, Will felt somehow better prepared, more in the race. Now he had some professionals on his side. Now, too, he was seventy-five thousand dollars in debt.

16

Detective Sergeant Charles Pittman sat at his desk at downtown Atlanta police headquarters on Decatur Street. His partner, Mickey Keane, sat facing him across the desk.

"This is everything we've got?" Pittman asked.

"This is it, Chuck," Keane replied, ticking information off a list. "We got some slugs and shell casings—Mac Tens and a Beretta handgun; we got some red mud from the shoes of these guys . . ."

"Red mud. Swell. The whole state of Georgia is made out of red mud."

"Yeah," Keane said. "We got a tire track that's used on a dozen General Motors vans and pickups, and some Chryslers, too. That's it."

"We got Manny Pearl," Pittman said. "He's worth a lot. He'll make ol' Sarge, if he gets a chance." "Sarge" was their name for the leader of the assassins. "And we got this," he said, opening a drawer and tossing a thick stack of computer printouts onto the desk. "An answer to my Pentagon inquiry. Just information, no pictures. There's five hundred and eighteen of them, and the guy I talked to balked at printing five hundred and eighteen photographs. The reason there's so many is, we've got half a dozen major army bases in the state, thank old Senator Ben Carr for that, and a lot of guys who serve in the state like it and retire here. Thank God we're not Florida; we'd have ten thousand to go through."

"What were your parameters for the search?" Keane asked.

"Army, retired less than ten years, buck sergeant or better, Georgia resident."

Keane picked up the stack of sheets, tore off half, and tossed the remainder to Pittman. "How you want to do this?"

"Pearl says he's tall and skinny. Pity they don't keep track of ear size in the army. Let's look for what—six feet and under a hundred and sixty?"

"Pearl's short. Five-ten might look tall to him."

"Okay, five-ten."

"What if our man weighed two-twenty when he retired, then lost fifty pounds?"

Pittman laughed. "Nobody loses weight in middle age. I'll bet our man has been skinny all his life."

Both men began going through the sheets, painstakingly reading height and weight on the forms and setting aside the shorter, heavier men. At lunchtime, they ordered a pizza and continued working while they ate. By the end of their shift, they had finished.

Pittman counted the forms. "Eighty-one more-or-less tall, skinny retired sergeants," he said. "Why don't we separate out the Atlanta addresses? I doubt if these guys drove up from south Georgia just to blow away a dirty bookstore."

They went through the papers again. "An even dozen," Pittman counted. "Now we can ask the Pentagon for pictures." He typed out a telex, left it with the operator, and called it a day.

It was just after lunch the following day when the photographs came back. Pittman and Keane shuffled through them.

"Funny how most tall, skinny guys seem to have big ears, ain't it?" Keane said.

"Let's go see Manny Pearl," Pittman said.

Manny was sitting up in bed when Pittman and Keane entered the room.

"How you feeling, Mr. Pearl?" Pittman asked.

"The kid neurologist says my left side is impaired," Manny says. "They're talking therapy now."

"You'll be jogging again in no time," Pittman said.

"Hah!" Pearl snorted. "I should get over getting shot in the head so I can wear myself down to nothing, running around?"

Pittman pulled a chair up to the bed and took the photographs from an envelope. "Mr. Pearl, we've got some pictures to show you. Your army idea sounded good to us, so we've got twelve pictures here that the Pentagon sent us. Every one of these guys is tall, skinny, retired from the army as a sergeant, and lives in the Atlanta area. I want you to look at each one carefully and tell me if any one of them is the man who shot you. Take your time."

Manny took his time. With his half-glasses perched on his prominent nose, he gazed solemnly at each photograph, running his eyes over the face and ears. When he had finished, he handed the photographs back to Pittman. "Nope," he said emphatically, "he's not among them."

"Why don't you look at them again, Mr. Pearl," Keane said. "Let's be absolutely certain about this."

"All right," Manny said. He repeated his performance, taking even more time. "Sorry, you haven't found him yet, gentlemen." He handed back the photographs.

Pittman stood wearily. "Okay, Mr. Pearl. Thanks for your time. We'll keep looking."

"Sergeant," Manny said, "when you find him, I'll know. Believe me."

"I believe you, Mr. Pearl," Pittman said.

"What next?" Keane said, when they were in the hallway.

"We'll talk the Pentagon out of shots of the other sixty-nine in the tall/skinny group. If that doesn't work, we'll start on the Marines." Pittman sighed. "What the hell, it's all we've got to go on."

17

Will stood before Judge Boggs. His arguments for bail were pretty much as they had been in Larry Moody's preliminary hearing: no previous record, roots in the community, gainfully employed, necessary to the conduct of his employer's business. John Morgan sat in the front of the courtroom, ready to make bail. Charlene Joiner sat next to him.

Elton Hunter then had his say. "Your Honor, the defendant has been indicted for a capital crime, that of first-degree murder. The circumstances justifying bail on such a charge would have to be extraordinary, and they are not extraordinary. To release the defendant on bail at this time would constitute a danger to every woman in the county. The prosecution requests that application for bail be denied."

The Judge shuffled papers for a moment, scribbled something, then looked up. "Bail is denied. The defendant is bound over to the sheriff until trial. Is there any objection to setting a trial date at this time?"

Will stood. "Your Honor, the defense requests a meeting in chambers."

The Judge looked at him blankly. "Why? I'm prepared to set a date now."

"If Your Honor please, I would be grateful for a meeting in chambers."

The Judge looked at Elton Hunter, who shrugged. Boggs sighed. "All right. We'll meet in chambers in ten minutes. I got a call of nature to answer."

Will took Larry to the rail to speak with Charlene and John Morgan. "Folks, I'm afraid this is as expected. There was never much chance of bail, not on this charge."

"Larry," John Morgan said, "I'm going to service Greenville out of the La Grange office until you're out. I know you didn't do this, and I'm not going to replace you. I'm going to keep you on salary, too."

"Thanks, Mr. Morgan," Larry said. "That's awful nice of you."

Morgan shook Larry's and Will's hands and left. Charlene lingered at the rail. "I'll bring the bills to the jail, and you can sign checks," she said to Larry, stroking his arm.

"Naw, that would be a lot of trouble," Larry said. "Just get one of those cards from the bank, and I'll sign it so you can sign on my account."

Charlene nodded.

"Larry," Will said, "I've got to meet with the Judge now. I'll come over to the jail when I'm finished."

"Why didn't you want the Judge to set a trial date a minute ago?" Charlene asked.

"I've got something I need to talk to him about first,"

Will replied, avoiding her steady gaze. "We'll only be a few minutes."

A deputy walked over. "I'll have to return him to his cell now, Mr. Lee." Larry left with him, and Will made to leave, too.

"Wait a minute," Charlene said, placing her hand on his arm. "What's going on?"

"Hang around," Will said. "I'll see you here in a few minutes. We'll go see Larry together." He left her and went to the Judge's chambers, where Elton Hunter was waiting for him.

"What's up, Will?" Elton asked.

"Let's wait for the Judge; it'll save me repeating it."

The Judge strode in and settled himself behind the huge desk. "All right, Will. What can I do for you?"

Will took a deep breath. "Judge, a lot has happened since the preliminary hearing. The Senator has improved enough to make it known that he doesn't intend to run for reelection." He paused. He had the same feeling about this that he had had about the bail hearing. "He has suggested that I run in his place." He stopped and waited.

The Judge looked at him, interested. "Yes, go on."

"Judge, it must be clear to you that I cannot conduct the defense in a capital case and run for the Senate at the same time. If the man were to be convicted, he would have every right to ask for the verdict to be set aside on grounds of a less than competent defense."

"Well, you might be right, Will," the Judge said amiably. "I'm real sorry about your ambitions for the Senate."

"What?" Will said, momentarily baffled by the response.

"If you can't conduct a proper defense and run for the

Senate at the same time, well, I guess you'll have to run for the Senate another time."

In spite of his expectations, Will was stunned. "Now listen here, Judge," he began.

"No!" said the Judge, pounding on the desk and rising to his feet. "I told you when you signed on for this that you were in it for the duration, and now you've come to me twice and tried to beg off!"

"And with damned good reason!" Will shouted back, standing up to face the old man.

Elton Hunter leapt to his feet, his hands out before him. "Gentlemen, gentlemen, there's no need for this. Let's talk about this sensibly."

"You shut up!" the Judge roared at him, then turned back to Will and shouted, "You're in this to the finish, do you understand me?"

"Hell no, I don't understand you!" Will shouted back. "I'm giving you notice right now, before you set a trial date—I'm out of it!"

"In that case, goddammit, you can run for the Senate from a jail cell!" The Judge turned toward the door. "Bailiff!" he shouted. "Get in here this minute!" He turned back to Will. "I'll hold you in contempt and postpone the trial until such time as you decide to continue!"

"Shut up!"

Both Will and the Judge turned and stared at Elton Hunter, who was beet-red. "Get out of here!" Elton shouted at the bailiff, who had just run into the room. The astonished bailiff stood and stared at the three men. Elton banged his palm flat on the desk, making a noise like a bass drum. "Now both of you sit down and get hold of yourselves" he demanded. "I said, get out of here!" he shouted at the bailiff. The bailiff turned and fled, closing the door behind him. "Now," Elton said, more quietly, "let's all sit down and discuss this calmly."

Will and the Judge, both surprised at the ordinarily mild Elton's outburst, sat down. "Judge, this is completely unreasonable," Will said.

"It may be unreasonable, but that's the way it is, and you're going to have to live with it," the Judge said, clearly trying to maintain control of himself. "I've arranged this trial so that both the prosecution and the defense are conducted by the best lawyers available. If either one of you should drop out and I replaced you with anybody else, then we'd have a lopsided trial, and I intend to see that both the defendant and the people get a fair trial. Now," he said, opening his desk calendar, "Will, if you want some more time to prepare, I'll give it to you. How about the sixteenth of February?"

"The sixteenth is fine with me, Judge," Elton said.

"Mr. Lee?" the Judge asked, an edge in his voice.

Will gritted his teeth and nodded. "All right. I apologize for my outburst."

"Good," the Judge said. "Now this meeting is adjourned. I will see you both on February sixteenth at ten o'clock sharp.

Will found Charlene waiting for him in the courtroom. "Come on," he said, "let's go see Larry." Five minutes later, he was seated in the interview room with the two of them.

"I may as well tell you," Will began, "I've just tried to get out of representing you again."

"Why?" asked Larry, looking hurt.

"It's nothing against you or your case, Larry. It's just that my boss, Senator Carr, is ill and is not going to run for reelection, and I'm going to run for his seat. I really don't see how I can represent you properly and run for the Senate at the same time."

"What did the Judge say about this?" Charlene asked.

"He refused to let me resign from the case. That's why I wanted to talk with you two. Larry, I know we've been over this before, but I think you should tell the Judge you want another lawyer."

"But why? I don't understand." Larry looked like a little boy who had been told he couldn't go to Disneyland.

"I've just explained it to you, Larry." He turned to Charlene. "Help me here, will you? Surely you can see that this is not good for Larry's case. If he asks the Judge for a new lawyer, then the Judge will have to give him one."

Charlene looked at him evenly for a moment, then shook her head. "This is between you and Larry," she said.

"I want you, Mr. Lee," Larry said earnestly. "I don't care about you running for anything." He folded his arms. "I won't have anybody else," he said stubbornly.

Will rested his elbows on the metal table and massaged his temples. This was insane. This case was a tar baby, and he was Br'er Fox. Neither Larry nor Charlene said anything. "Larry, do you know what the maximum penalty for first-degree murder is in this state?" he asked wearily. There was no reply. "It's death," Will said. "It's the electric chair in this state. That's what you get if I lose this for you. You're gambling with your life. Do you understand that?"

Larry Moody nodded his head. "I'll take my chances with you."

18

On Saturday morning, as he waited for Jack Buchanan and Kitty Conroy to arrive from Washington, Will sat at the computer in the lake cottage and tried to write a campaign plan. It wasn't coming very quickly, because he had never done it before. Running a campaign for the re-election of Benjamin Carr, which he had done, was an entirely different thing from running a campaign for the election of a little-known Senate assistant, and as he labored, it became increasingly clear to Will how difficult his position was. He was contemplating withdrawing from a race he had not yet entered when he heard a car pulling into the gravel parking area a few yards from the cottage. Will looked at his watch. It was too early for Jack and Kitty, who were driving down from the Atlanta airport. He got up and went out onto the front porch.

Two men and a woman were getting out of a station wagon. Led by the shorter of the men, they walked up the gravel path to the cottage. The second man and the woman were carrying camera equipment. The short man, who seemed to be in his early twenties, reached the porch and stuck out his hand. "Hi, I'm Tom Black, from Hank Taylor's office," he said.

Will shook his hand. "Hello, I wasn't expecting you until next week."

"I wanted to get an early start," Black said. "This is Jim and Betty—they're freelancers out of Atlanta. I want to get some footage of you and how you live down here."

"Well, sure. I guess it's a good time for you to come. My first two staffers will be here in an hour or so, so you can sit in on our very first campaign meeting."

"Good," Black said. "I'd like that." He looked around him at the cottage and the lake. "This is nice," he said. "It'll look good on film. Can I see the inside of the house?"

"Oh, sure, come in," Will said. "There's coffee or tea, if you'd like." He led the people into the cottage.

Jim and Betty immediately started shooting pictures, the man with a video camera, the woman with a 35 mm flash camera. Black wandered into the kitchen and out again.

"I'm sorry it's a bit messy," Will said.

"No matter," Black said, strolling into the bedroom. "You mind if I take a look at your clothes?" Without waiting for an answer, he began pulling suits out of the closet and rummaging in the shirt drawers. "Uh-huh," he was muttering to himself. He came out of the bedroom and flopped down in an easy chair.

"I was just working on a campaign plan," Will said, indicating the computer.

"We'll talk about that later," Black said, surreptitiously nodding at the two camera people. "Have a seat at the computer; let's get some shots of you working. Roll up your shirtsleeves, will you?"

Will did as he was asked, while the photographers circled him.

"Jim, Betty, get some shots of the house from across the lake, will you?" Black asked. When they had gone, the young man went back to the easy chair.

Will looked him over. He had sandy hair and a smooth face and was dressed in a bush jacket and desert boots, like something out of a Banana Republic catalog. He couldn't be more than twenty-five, Will thought. This was one of Hank Taylor's best people?

Black seemed to read Will's mind. "Just so we'll get off on the right foot," he said, "I'm thirty-one; I know I don't look it. I got my start in national politics with Jimmy Carter's campaign in '76 as an advance man. I was nineteen. In the '80 campaign I was in charge of all the advance people in the eastern half of the country. In between I was a press assistant in the White House. After Carter lost, I followed Hank into the political consultancy business, and since then I've done eleven campaigns and won eight."

"Okay," Will laughed, "so I underestimated you right off."

"It's an easy mistake to make." Black smiled. "In fact, it's one of my chief weapons. I get quite a lot done by managing not to look like an important person. Who's coming to this meeting today?"

"Jack Buchanan, who was chief legislative aide in Carr's office, and Kitty Conroy, who was deputy press secretary."

"I know about them both," Black said. "Anybody else?"

"My mother and father, and my Aunt Eloise. They've all had a lot of experience in political campaigns, and they want to help."

"Good," Black said. "It's good to have a lot of family around, especially since you aren't married. You got a fiancée, maybe, or even just a girl?"

Will hesitated for a moment. "No, neither," he said. "Nobody special. My job has taken up most of my time."

"Uh-huh," Black said noncommittally. "How come you buy all your clothes in London?"

"My mother's Irish, she and my father met during World War Two, and we still have her father's house over there, so I've spent a lot of time on that side of the water. I've been going to my father's tailor and shirtmaker since I was in law school."

"Uh-huh," Black responded. "Well, your old man has great taste in tailors, but that stuff won't do for this campaign."

"Why not?"

"Too slick. You're back in Georgia now, not in Washington. Side vents and bold shirts aren't going to work. There's a guy named Ham Stockton in Atlanta who has a men's store."

"I know Ham."

"It's just right. Not as square as Brooks Brothers, but nice, quiet stuff. I want you to go up there and get two each of suits in navy blue, dark blue pinstripes, and gray pinstripes, and two navy blazers, plain buttons. Get yourself a couple dozen white button-down shirts, no short sleeves. In hot weather, I like rolled-up sleeves. Get some regimental-stripe ties, lots of red. No bow ties—we'll leave that to Paul Simon. Get yourself a couple pair Weejuns—penny loafers—and two pairs of black wingtips."

"Wingtips?"

"I'm not kidding. They're coming back, anyway. You're going to be spending a lot of time on your feet, and you need heavy shoes with thick soles. I don't want you crippled in the middle of the campaign. Get a tan, single-breasted raincoat with a zip-out lining. It's the only overcoat you'll need, and it'll keep you from looking like a banker. The Rolex watch you're wearing is fine. A Swiss watch is all-American. You wear glasses?"

"No."

"You object to wearing them for appearance's sake?"

"Yes."

"Okay. But if you find yourself going blind, check with me, and I'll pick the frames. Very important. You need a haircut. Is your barber here or in Washington?"

"In Washington."

"Call a guy in Atlanta named Ray Brewer, make an appointment, tell him I sent you. He'll know what I want. After that, get it cut every ten days, without fail. You're going to be on television a lot. If you can't get to Atlanta, tell your people to get Ray to you."

"Listen, do I really look so wrong the way I am?"

"Yes. Trust me, I'm giving you good advice, and you're paying a lot for it."

Will sighed. "All right. How much are you going to be around during the campaign?"

"A lot, but not all the time. I'm running a guy named Heald in New York for Congress and another guy in North Carolina."

"I see."

"I hope so. If you had me down here full time, it would cost you three times as much as you're paying. What I'll do is I'll look over your operation from the media point of view, and I'll make suggestions. I expect my suggestions to be taken seriously. You're not likely to have anybody on this campaign who's as smart as I am when it comes to running a campaign, and I say that advisedly."

"I'm sure you do," Will said, and meant it.

"Is that your Wagoneer outside?"

"Yes."

"Get rid of it. Get a Ford or a Chevy. They've both got assembly plants in Atlanta. American Motors, who makes the Wagoneer, is in God-knows-where. The guys who build them don't vote in Georgia. You don't want any of your people driving foreign cars, especially expensive ones, but not even Hondas or Toyotas."

"Okay, that makes sense."

"You sure you're not about to get married?"

"No hope, I'm afraid."

"Maybe we can rent you somebody," Black deadpanned. "A nice blonde who looks like Tipper Gore and works weekends with the homeless."

Will laughed.

"You got a dog?"

"Yeah, a golden Labrador retriever."

"That'll have to do, I guess." He got up from his chair. "Come on, let's get some shots of you out by the lake. We'd better take some with the dog, too."

19

After introductions, they all gathered around the dining room table in the main house, Bill and Patricia at each end of the table, Will in the middle, and the others scattered about. It was too small and intimate a group for opening remarks, so Will got right down to it.

"What I want to do today is to get everybody assigned to particular areas, and then get everybody's ideas on everything. Aunt Eloise, how's your shorthand?"

"Still pretty good, I guess," his elderly aunt replied.

"I'd appreciate it if you'd take notes about what we decide and type it up later."

"Glad to."

"I'm going to act as my own campaign manager, at least for the time being. We're going to be shorthanded, at first, anyway, and I don't want to saddle anybody with overall management." He turned to Jack Buchanan. "Jack, the first thing I want you to do is to find us some space in Atlanta for a campaign headquarters."

Billy Lee raised a hand. "I can probably help with that. I'll make a few calls."

"Good," Will said. "Kitty, you're in charge of press relations, of course, and I want you to handle the scheduling of my appearances. There'll no doubt be a lot of other stuff for you to work on, too. I don't want anybody to get too attached to a title, just yet." He turned to Billy. "Dad has agreed to take on fund-raising, for the moment. There's nothing more important than that right now."

The meeting droned on through the morning, through a light lunch, and on into the afternoon. The sun was low in the sky when Will took a deep breath and said, "That's it, unless anybody has anything to add."

Patricia stood up. "I've rooms prepared for Jack, Kitty, and Tom. Why don't you all go and have a nap and freshen up, and we'll meet at seven for drinks and dinner."

As they stood and stretched, Henry came into the room to announce a telephone call for Will. He took it in the hall.

"Will? This is Rob Cutts at the *Atlanta Constitution*. We've just learned that Governor Dean is announcing for Senator Carr's seat. We're running the story front page tomorrow. Do you have any comment?"

"Hang on a minute, Rob," Will said. He caught Tom Black's eye and waved him into the hall. "Mack Dean is announcing tomorrow. The *Constitution* wants a comment."

Black shook his head. "Nothing now. Just say you're not surprised."

"I'm not surprised to hear it, but I don't have any comment at this time," Will said into the phone.

"Okay. Miss Emma Carr has given the Governor her blessing. Anything to say about that?"

Will winced. He didn't defer to Black this time. "Only that nothing Miss Emmy says is a reflection of the Senator's views. Can we go off the record here, Rob?"

"All right, we're off."

"If you're recording our conversation, please switch it off."

"Okay, the recorder's off."

"You met Miss Emmy at the hospital, didn't you?"

"I saw her going in and out of the Senator's room and ordering people around."

"Well, then, you'll understand when I tell you that Miss Emmy is not herself. She's under the constant care of a nurse; her affairs and those of the Senator have been placed in my hands by the court. She's not responsible for anything she might say."

"I understand, Will," Cutts said. "Anything else to say?"

"Not at this time."

"Are you considering running yourself?"

"I've nothing to say at this time about that."

The reporter thanked him and hung up.

"Don't worry about Dean," Black said. "He's gonna do what he's gonna do, right now, and there's nothing you can do about it. Let him blow his hot air for the time being."

"I don't mind Mack spouting off, but Senator Carr's sister is going to drive me nuts."

"The famous Miss Emmy? You did a good job of undercutting her just now. Keep it up, but don't attack her. By the way, when were you thinking of announcing?"

"Early next week, I thought."

Black shook his head. "Too soon. Let's wait until we've got the act together a little bit. Let's have some announcements to make about fund-raising and an Atlanta office and some staff appointments. Let's look ready when we announce."

"Okay," Will said. "I guess it can't hurt."

Black took his arm. "Come on, I'll walk you down to the cottage." The two men left the house and strolled toward the lake.

"Your dad," Black said, "how do you think he'll do on this fund-raising thing?"

"He's still got a lot of friends from the old days. A lot of them have a lot of money."

Black nodded. "That's good, but remember, none of them can give more than a thousand bucks each for themselves, their wives, and children."

"I know."

"It won't take long for your dad to run through his list. After that, we're going to have to go about it in a more systematic way. I want you to start by making a list of everybody you know who thinks well of you, and I mean *everybody*. Go right back to your college days. As soon as you announce, I want you to get on the phone and call every one of them; ask for money; ask for contributions in kind; ask them to volunteer and to lend their children to volunteer. Get them to hold fund-raisers and invite their friends. You went to the University of Georgia; that means you went to school with somebody from just about every town in this state. We're going to want a local chairman in every county, and it would be good if those people came from your list of friends."

"I'm not sure how many of the people I know I would feel comfortable about asking for money," Will said, shaking his head.

"Listen," Black said, "we're not talking personal loans here. You're not asking them to bail you out on a drunk-driving charge. It's their civic duty to support political candidates, and you've got to very quickly acquire enough chutzpah to ask them. All they can say is no. Believe me, a lot of them will be flattered to be asked. Tell them you need a thousand bucks from each of them. If they don't have that, ask for eight hundred, five hundred, a hundred. Don't turn up your nose at ten bucks. Keep a list, and later, you'll go back and ask them for more, for their wives and children and parents and friends to give. The enthusiastic ones, appoint them as official fund-raisers on the spot, and mail them a copy of the rules."

"Okay," Will sighed.

"Another thing: I didn't want to break in too much during the meeting, but when you get space for your Atlanta headquarters set up, get Buchanan to get a whole bunch of telephones. We're going to need a hundred lines before we're done. If the space is expensive, we can put the phones somewhere cheaper, in a warehouse or something. Atlanta has the largest toll-free dialing area in the United States, and you want to take advantage of that. A volunteer talking on the telephone is the cheapest campaign tool you've got."

"Good idea."

"Another thing. On the day you announce, you need to appoint a couple of well-known blacks to your staff. You got any contacts in the Atlanta black community?"

"Yes, I've done a lot of favors there since I've been in the Senator's office. I know half a dozen ministers and a couple of city councilmen. I was thinking of approaching Marty Banks."

"The Billy Dee Williams of Atlanta politics? Good. He'll charm the socks off the ladies.

"Oh, by the way, did you hear the *Constitution* has a new editor for their Sunday magazine, a lady from the *Washington Post* named Ann Heath?"

"Yeah, I read something about it in the paper. She's doing over the magazine, isn't she?"

"Right. Her first redesigned issue will be out in about a month. You're going to be on the cover."

Will's eyebrows went up. "Yeah?"

"Yeah, she'll be down here tomorrow with a photographer. I told her you'd give her lunch."

"You're not wasting any time, are you?"

"Nope. Let's go talk about what you're going to say to her. And what you're going to wear. You got a beer at the cottage?"

20

Chuck Pittman reflected that, since he had been a policeman, most of his cases had been roughly divided into two categories: fairly easy and almost impossible. If you did your work properly, if you followed police methodology, most of them were fairly easy. It was the almost impossible ones that intrigued him, though, the ones that took some imagination and, often, some luck. His luck in the Dirty Bookstore Case, as he thought of it, was the survival of Manny Pearl.

That was it, though; there hadn't been any other luck, and, so far, his imagination had failed him. He was reduced to relying on the imagination of the victim. Often, when he was stuck on a case, he would devote his time to another, and while he worked on that, an idea, an inspiration would come to him about the first case. This time, however, he and Keane had been pulled off everything else to work on the Dirty Bookstore Case.

He sat on the sun porch and watched the rain beat against the glass. He had been divorced two years before, and his wife had remarried almost immediately. Another cop. It wasn't his weekend with his two little girls, and he was lonely. Next weekend, he'd take them out to Stone Mountain, if the weather was good. He thought he might go out for a drink, a singles bar he knew, but it was too early; it wasn't even dark yet.

He went into the living room and switched on the six-o'clock news. Central America, he was tired of that. There was a bill in the Georgia legislature to prevent alcoholic beverages from being sold in clubs that featured nude dancing. He laughed. Manny Pearl would love that! Now Pittman began paying attention. Three people had been murdered at a pornographic movie house in Charlotte, North Carolina. He picked up the phone and dialed his boss's home number.

"Captain, this is Pittman. There's been some killings in Charlotte, sounds like our Dirty Bookstore Case. I'd like to go up there."

"Come on, Chuck, you're just bored. What are you go-ing to do, go up there and solve it for them? You haven't gotten anywhere on your own case yet. Besides, I haven't got the budget for junkets. Use the telephone, for Christ's sake. They'll give you what they've got." He hung up.

Pittman started calling. Ten minutes later, he had the right unit in the Charlotte Police Department. The detec-tive in charge of the case had gone home. Pittman asked that he be contacted and asked to call him in Atlanta.

Nearly an hour passed before the call came in. The Charlotte detective's name was Miller.

"I just saw your case on TV," Pittman said. "It sounds like one I've got here. Can you give me some details?"

"You show me yours, I'll show you mine," Miller said.

"Okay. Four men in camouflage fatigues hit a dirty bookstore, executed the manager and two employees, shot the owner twice in the head, but he lived. They were carrying three Mac Tens and a Beretta nine-millimeter automatic. We got some tire tracks—Goodyears that are used on GM and Chrysler vans and pickups. The store owner has described the leader as forty-five to fifty, six feet or better, thin, big ears, big nose. He couldn't give us much on the others, just that they were young. Now, let's see yours."

"I got some nine-millimeter slugs and a lot of double-aught buckshot. That's it. No descriptions, no nothing. No robbery, either. It was an execution."

"Any notes? We had something about death to queers."

"No."

"I'd appreciate it if you'd fax me the ballistics reports on the nine-millimeter metal. I'd like to compare."

"Sure. You got anything you can give me?"

"I'm working on a make of the leader by the bookstore owner. We're waiting for pictures from the army. When I get something, I'll send it to you." Pittman thanked the man and hung up. He had hoped for more, some little thing that would help.

It was dark now. Pittman got into a coat and looked for his car keys. He'd get a bite to eat; then he'd have a few drinks. Tonight, he wanted to talk with somebody about something besides murder.

21

Ann Heath, the new editor of the *Atlanta Constitution*'s Sunday magazine, turned out to be quite pretty. She was in her mid-thirties, tall, fashionably dressed, and wore her dark hair long and loose around her shoulders. She made Will immediately nervous, because he was attracted to her. "She can be charmed," Tom Black had said of her, by way of advice. She could be more than charmed, Will thought, and in a different time and place, he might have wanted it. All he knew about her was that on the *Washington Post* she had covered fashion and had written features. She had not been a political reporter.

Will greeted her and her male photographer on the front porch of the cottage and asked them into the kitchen, where he was preparing lunch. The weather had turned chilly after the rain the night before, and he had built a fire in the stone fireplace in the living room. He settled her on a stool at the little bar that closed off the kitchen from the living room and asked her if they'd like some refreshment.

"I'd love a glass of wine," she said.

Will had not expected booze to be a part of the interview, but he dug a bottle of California Chardonnay out of the fridge. "How about you?" he asked the photographer.

"Just pretend he's not here," she said. "He'll take his pictures and go." As if on cue, the man began snapping away.

"Why don't we go into the living room for this?" Will said, untying his apron. He hadn't expected to be photographed in the kitchen.

She guided him around the room, seated him first in an armchair, then at the computer, then leaning against the mantel. They got a few shots on the front porch and some by the lake; then Ann Heath dismissed the photographer, and he got into a car and drove away.

"You came in separate cars?" Will asked, disquieted about being alone with her.

"He was taking some shots at Roosevelt's Little White House in Warm Springs, so we met here," she replied, re-settling herself on the barstool. She raised her glass. "To politics?"

"I'll drink to that," he said.

"You don't mind?" she asked, switching on a small tape recorder and setting it on the bar between them. "It's just for accuracy."

"Fine," Will said. He was unaccustomed to being interviewed and had assumed she'd be taking notes in shorthand. He had also assumed she'd be short and plump.

"Tom didn't give me a bio," she said. "Why don't you just tell me a little about yourself—family, school, all that?"

Will explained that he'd been born and raised here on the farm, how his parents had met, and the Irish connection; he told her about college and law school, about practicing law in a small town, about how he'd been hired by Senator Carr eight years before. "That brings us up to date," he said.

"Most men your age entering politics have a wife and kids and a dog to parade for a reporter," she said. "Why have you never married?"

Will laughed. He had been asked that question before. "Just lucky, I guess. I can dig up a dog, if that'll help."

She smiled only slightly. "I expect you must have some special girlfriend."

"No one in particular," he lied. He was going to have to get used to pretending Kate didn't exist.

Her eyebrows went up. "No wife, and not even a girl in the picture? You must be one of the most eligible bachelors in the state, maybe the country."

"I doubt it," he laughed. "But I'm hardly the first bachelor to run for the Senate. John Kennedy was still single when he was elected to his first term."

"And something of a womanizer, too, from all accounts," she said. "Funny, there's no word around Washington on you. I checked."

"Oh, I went to a lot of cocktail and dinner parties when I was first in Washington," he said. "I was often invited as an odd man, but I soon discovered that nobody in Washington is interested in people who don't have power, and since I was a Senate aide instead of a senator, people seemed to sort of look through me. I wearied of that, I suppose, and anyway, working for Benjamin Carr has always been more than a full-time job."

"Odd man, huh?" she muttered. "Is that why you're

running for the Senate? So you'll have some power of your own, and people won't look through you at dinner parties?"

"Hardly," Will replied.

"Just why are you running, then?" she demanded.

"I was brought up to believe that I had an obligation to serve others," he said, aware that he was sounding pompous. "I mean, everybody in my family, even those who weren't in public life, always worked hard at some sort of community work. After I had been in Senator Carr's office for a couple of years and had learned how the Congress worked, I began to think I might one day want to run for office."

"But why do you think you can do it?"

"I've seen it done from up close; I know what's involved better than most people who have never actually been elected to the Senate. You have to understand that even a very good senator is pretty dependent on his staff, and at one time or another during the past eight years, I've done just about everything a staffer can do for a senator."

"Are you implying that a senator is run by his staff?"

"Certainly not, at least not in the case of a man like Ben Carr."

"There are some senators who are run by their staffs, though?"

"None that I know of." He wasn't about to let himself be quoted on something like that. He picked up the salad bowl and his wineglass and headed for the small dining table, followed by Ann Heath and her tape recorder. They sat down and continued their interview.

"Why do you think you would make a better senator than Mack Dean?" she asked.

"Well," he said, feeling his way, "I don't think it's a reflection on his performance as governor to say that what a governor does has very little to do with what a senator does."

"But Dean has been both a representative and a senator in state government."

"No argument there. I just feel that, with the experience I've had under Benjamin Carr over the past eight years, I'm better prepared to serve Georgia in the Senate than anybody else in the state."

"Even though you've never held elective office?"

"I've been as close to being a senator as you can get without actually being elected. I don't claim that would qualify me for governor but it certainly qualifies me for the Senate."

"Do you think you can be as good a senator as Ben Carr?"

Will laughed. "I'm not sure *anybody* can be as good a senator as Ben Carr. You're talking about a man whom a great many knowledgeable people have called the greatest senator in this century. I have, however, had the benefit of serving under him, and it has been a great education."

"Is Senator Carr going to endorse you?"

"I have no way of knowing if the Senator will be well enough to endorse anyone, but before he became ill, he gave me to believe, in no uncertain terms, that if I ever decided to run for the Senate, I would have his whole-hearted support."

"That's easy to say, now that he can't speak for himself, isn't it?"

Will fought the urge to raise his voice. "It would be

impossible for me to say if it weren't so. I still have to look the Senator in the eye every time I visit him."

"You mean we'll just have to take your word for it?"

"I hope the Senator will recover enough to say so himself."

"Isn't it unusual for a man of your age to live at home with his parents?"

Will felt himself redden. "Most of the time, I live in Washington. When I'm in Georgia, I have my own home not far from my parents'. You're sitting in it."

She seemed to miss the rebuke. "Tom says you built this place yourself. Is that true?"

"I designed it and built it with the help of two men who worked on the farm. I guess I can take credit for a third of the work."

"That's becomingly modest," she said, holding out her glass for a refill.

"It's the truth of the matter," Will replied, filling her glass. "I worked on the framing and the roofing, but not the electrical or the plumbing. If I had, the place would have burned down or floated away long ago. I did most of the interior finishing myself. Of the skill required to build the place, carpentry is the one at which I am least deficient."

She took a large swallow of the wine. "How are the working people of Georgia supposed to relate to a man who owns a yacht, a Porsche, and an airplane?" she asked archly.

Will managed a laugh. "I'll try to explain about all three," he said. "I spent two years in Ireland when I was in my early twenties, and I helped a couple of friends build the boat. The woman was killed in an electrical accident after the boat was finished, and the man was lost overboard in a single-handed race across the Atlantic. A merchant ship recovered the boat, and I was astonished to learn that my friend had left it to me in his will. That was more than fifteen years ago. I've kept the boat all these years, although the maintenance has been a strain, because I associate it so strongly with those friends and that time of my life. Before I would sell it, I would take it out to sea and scuttle it.

"The Porsche is eight years old; I bought it cheap four years ago from a senator who shall remain nameless, who had to get rid of it in a hurry because cars were built in his state, and he was up for reelection.

"The airplane is ten years old. I bought it six years ago to make it easier for me to get home to Georgia when my father was more dependent on me to help out in our law practice. It has had the incidental effect of making me knowledgeable about the air-traffic system in this country, something I'm going to take a great interest in if I'm elected to the Senate."

"Are you a rich man?"

"A poor man might think so; a rich one wouldn't."

"Are you going to use your own money to run for the Senate?"

"If I depended on my own funds, I wouldn't get past next month. I'm going to need every campaign contribution I can get."

She continued with her questions, but less pugnaciously, asking about his positions on defense, social programs, and agriculture. She accepted brief answers, not seeming terribly interested. They finished lunch and the bottle of wine, of which Will had drunk very little. She didn't seem affected, though. Will wondered if she drank a bottle of wine for lunch every day. He was clearing up the dishes when she switched off the tape recorder.

"Enough of business," she said. "Can I use your john?"

"Sure," he replied, pointing. "It's through the bedroom, there."

She was gone for quite a long time; then, as he was closing the dishwasher, she called from the bedroom. "Who did this picture?"

"Which one?" he asked.

"Come here, and I'll show you," she called back.

Will walked into the bedroom to find her looking at an abstract painting that hung at the foot of his bed. "Oh, that's by an Atlanta artist, Sidney Guberman. He's a friend."

She stepped closer to him, as if to see the picture from a different angle. "Really. Do you have many artist friends?"

"A few, I guess." He was suddenly aware that she had used perfume while she had been in the bathroom.

"It's a nude, isn't it?" she asked.

He laughed. "Maybe. It can be hard to tell in an abstract."

"I think this is a breast, right here," she said, pointing. She turned to face him and stepped back, placing her hands on her hips. "Tell me," she said, "do you like large breasts or small breasts?"

Will sucked in a breath. "Are we off the record here?" he asked, regretting it immediately.

"Oh, we're all through with business," she said. "I'm inquiring into your personal tastes now."

"Well," he said, "I don't think it would be politic of me to take a position on that subject, even off the record." He tried to make it sound funny, but it came out wary. He was starting to sweat when he heard footsteps on the front porch.

"Hello?" Tom Black called out.

Will, relieved, turned and walked into the living room, followed by Ann Heath. "Hi, we're just finishing. Ann was asking about a picture in there."

Tom hardly missed a beat. "I see," he said. "Listen, I need a ride to Atlanta. You got room for me in your car, Ann?"

"Sure," she said. She turned to Will. "Well," she said, holding out her hand, "I hope we can continue our discussion on art another time."

"Ah, well, ah, sure," Will stammered, as she clung to his hand. "Thanks for coming down here. I appreciate it."

She gathered up her handbag and recorder and walked out.

"Be right with you, Ann," Black called. He turned to Will. "What the hell was going on in there?" he demanded.

"She asked about a picture," Will said, wondering why he felt guilty. "She'd had a lot of wine. I'm glad you showed up when you did," he admitted.

"Listen," Black said, "a Gary Hart I don't need."

"A Gary Hart you haven't got," Will said with feeling.

"Good. I'll call you from Washington in a couple of days to get a progress report. I'll read your position papers; then I'll get together with Hank. We'll do some preliminary work on a TV campaign, maybe even do some storyboards."

"Fine," Will said, "but don't go beyond that until we've talked about the idea, okay? I don't want to spend any unnecessary production money."

Black held out his hand. "Take care."

Will grinned. "*You* take care. You're the one who's going to be in the car with her."

Black rolled his eyes and headed for the door.

22

On Monday morning, Will went to the law office in Delano, read his mail, and made his daily call to the Senator. Then he moved to face what he had been dreading. He got into his car and drove to Greenville.

As he entered the jail, the sheriff saw him coming. "I guess I know what you want." He grinned, waving some papers. "I was just going to put them in the mail to you."

Sure he was, Will thought. He accepted the papers and put them in his briefcase. "I'd like the van, too, Sheriff," Will said. "You've raked it over pretty good by now, I expect."

"Well," said the sheriff, scratching his chin, "I don't know about that."

"I can walk over to the courthouse and get an order from the Judge, if you like."

"Now, Will, no need to go to extremes," the sheriff chided. He reached into a desk drawer and pulled out a set of keys with a large tag attached. "Here you go. He's not going to be driving for a while, anyway. Maybe not ever." He grinned.

"Don't be such a pessimist, Dan," Will laughed. "I'll have that boy free as a bird in another month."

"Yeah, sure you will," the sheriff laughed back.

Will left the jail and walked around back to the parking lot. The chocolate brown van was parked in a corner, dusty and neglected-looking. Will unlocked the rear door, and sunlight flooded into the back of the van. The carpet was missing, and everything was covered with black finger-printing dust. The cushions had been removed from all the seats and were piled in the back bay. He closed the rear doors, went around to the driver's door, unlocked it, and got in. He switched on the ignition and cranked the engine; the battery was weak, but the engine caught. He let the engine run while he looked through the papers the sheriff had given him.

On top was a receipt for the carpet. There was a lab report attached. The carpet had harbored a bloodstain, type A positive, that matched the victim's blood type; fibers had been found matching a sweater worn by the victim. The sweater was described in some detail; it was from Rich's department store in Atlanta, a size medium, of black lamb's wool. Carpet fibers matching those from the van had been found on the victim's clothes.

Will laid the lab reports on top of his briefcase, got out of the van, and made a note of the vehicle identification number on the plate attached to the windshield post; then he got back into the van and drove it toward the Luthers-ville highway. He pulled into the MagiMart parking lot and went inside.

Charlene Joiner was helping a customer, and he looked idly around the place while she finished. When the customer had gone, she came from behind the counter and offered her hand, cool and soft, as always.

"Hi," he said, "I managed to get Larry's van released. If you can take five minutes off, you can drop me at my car, and then you'll have wheels."

"Oh, good," she said. "It's been a bitch without a car." She looked over her shoulder. "Mavis, will you cover for me for ten minutes?"

"Sure," the woman called back. "We're not busy, anyway."

"Have you got a men's room here?" Will asked.

"Right through there," she said, pointing at a door.

"I'll meet you in the van in two minutes," he said. When he emerged, Charlene was in the driver's seat. He got into the passenger seat, and she drove off toward the jail.

"I got the lab reports, too," Will said.

"How do they look for Larry?" she asked.

Will had trouble not watching her breasts as she turned the van's wheel. "Too soon to say. There was some blood on the carpet and some fiber evidence, too. I'll do what I can to rebut the findings. What's your blood type?"

"I don't know," she replied.

"I want you to go to a doctor or a clinic as soon as possible, today, if you can, and get it typed. Get something in writing."

"All right," she said. She glanced sideways at him. "Are you really going to run for the Senate?"

"Yes, I am, but keep it under your hat, will you? I won't be announcing for another couple of weeks."

"You'll have to run against old Mack Dean, then?"

"That's right."

"Think you can beat him?"

"I'm sure going to try."

She pulled the van up in front of the jail, and Will put the papers into his briefcase and closed it. "I think you can beat him," she said, smiling. "I'll vote for you, anyway."

"Thanks for your confidence."

"Don't mention it," she laughed.

It was a pleasant sound, her laugh. "See you soon, then," he said, and got out of the van. She drove away, and he got into his own car. He had one more stop to make in Greenville.

He drove out to the La Grange highway and found a sign directing him to the spot. Half a mile down a dirt road, he saw smoke rising ahead. A moment later, he stopped the car and surveyed the scene. There were half a dozen fires burning here and there. A hundred yards away, a bulldozer was pushing landfill over garbage. Will retrieved the papers from his briefcase and got out of the car. Flipping to the last page, a hand-drawn map, he walked along, referring to the paper and trying to get his bearings. After a couple of minutes, he stopped. A dozen yards away, he saw a strip of yellow tape on the ground. Printed on it were the words CRIME SCENE. DO NOT CROSS. He walked over, referred to the map, and saw the spot where Sarah Cole's body had been abandoned.

Will stood and looked around him, turning slowly through 360 degrees. Plastic bags, garbage, and more garbage. Then he stopped turning. Thirty yards away, in the trees at the edge of the Greenville City Dump, was a shack. Will started toward it, pacing off the distance. At the door, he stopped and had a good look. The shack had been put together from bits of everything—plywood, chipboard, scrap lumber, and tar paper. The front of the place was nearly covered in old hubcaps, shiny, dull, and bent. Will recognized one from a '68 Oldsmobile, like one he used to own. There was a length of pipe protruding from the roof of the shack, and a wisp of smoke curled up from it.

"Good mornin'," a voice said from behind him.

Will turned to find a black man of indeterminate age, dressed in tattered overalls, approaching him from the trees. "Good morning," he said. "You live here?"

"I sho' do," the man said, smiling to reveal a number of missing teeth. "Make my living out here," he said. "Do right well out of other folks' leavins."

"My name is Will Lee," Will said. "What's your name?"

"I'm Roosevelt Watkins," the man said. "Pleased to meet you." He stuck out a hand.

Will shook it and reflected that he had known half a dozen black men called Roosevelt. It had been a popular name among blacks during the thirties. "Mr. Watkins," Will said, "I wanted—"

"Oh, you can call me Roosevelt," the man interrupted, grinning. "Everybody calls me Roosevelt. I met Mr. Franklin D. hisself one time, back during the war, and he called me Roosevelt."

"Well, Roosevelt," Will said, "I wanted to ask you something."

"Yassuh," Watkins said, "you go right ahead. I'll tell you the answer if I know it."

"Tell me, then," Will said, "have you had any conversations with the sheriff lately?"

"Why, I sho' has," Roosevelt said, grinning and slapping his thigh. "I been a right popular fella with the sheriff right lately."

"Ah." Will grinned. "I think you're the fellow I'm looking for." He stood in front of the shack and had a long talk with Roosevelt Watkins.

23

Chuck Pittman was driving to work when the radio call came.

"Your partner says a package from the Pentagon arrived," the dispatcher said.

"Roger," Pittman replied. "Tell my partner to meet me at Piedmont Hospital." He made an illegal U-turn, nearly sideswiping a limousine in the process. Ten minutes later, he was at the hospital; Keane's car was parked in the emergency entrance. Pittman flipped down the sun visor, which displayed the car's ID, and went inside. Keane was waiting at the front desk.

"Pearl has checked out," he said, handing Pittman a thick brown envelope. "Here's the package; the nurse is getting me his address now. Apparently, his chart wasn't back in the files yet."

Pittman drew Keane to a bench and sat down, opening the package and handing his partner half the photographs. "You got a picture in your mind of Sarge?"

"Sure."

"You pick him out; I'll do the same." Both men moved quickly through the sixty-nine photographs. When they had finished, Keane had picked one photograph, and Pittman had two. They spread them on the bench between them.

"Christ," Keane said, "they could be brothers."

"Shit. I don't like this. I was hoping for a clean ID."

Keane signed. "All we can do is try."

A nurse called to Keane from the desk. "Here's Mr. Pearl's address."

"It's in Brookhaven," Pittman said. "Follow me; I know the street."

Pittman drove faster than he should have, straight out Peachtree Road. A mile past Lenox Square, he turned left and quickly found the street. He was surprised by the house; it didn't look like the sort of place where the owner of strip joints would live. He and Keane walked to the front door of the red brick Queen Anne house and rang the bell. Leah Pearl answered the door.

"Oh, hello, Sergeant," she said. "Won't you come in?"

"Thank you, ma'am," Pittman replied, stepping into the house, which was quiet and smelled of something good cooking. "I was glad to hear Mr. Pearl was home. May we see him for a minute?"

"Of course," the woman replied. "Follow me." She led them to a glassed-in porch that ran the width of the back of the house. Manny Pearl was struggling along the floor with an aluminum walker, dragging his left foot. It was the first time Pittman and Keane had seen him without his head swathed in bandages. Now there was just one large one on his face, under his right eye, and one on the back of his head.

"Hey, Sergeant, Officer Keane, how you doing?" Manny said, beaming at them. "Check out my chariot here."

"You're doing great, Mr. Pearl," Pittman said. "Can we sit down for a minute? We've got some pictures to show you."

Pearl waved them to a metal porch glider covered in flowered plastic cloth. The two detectives sat on either end, with Manny Pearl in between.

"Now just take your time," Pittman said, "and even if you think you recognize the guy, I want you to look at all the pictures before you decide for sure."

Manny went carefully through the pictures, one at a time, dropping them in a stack onto the glass coffee table in front of him. Pittman and Keane watched him anxiously. Suddenly, Manny stopped. He looked hard at the photograph, then put it down beside the stack before continuing. Twice more, he did this, until the three men Pittman and Keane had picked were in a stack by themselves. The two policemen looked at each other, and Keane rolled his eyes.

Manny spread the photographs out before him and looked from one to another. He held up a finger, and in a diving motion, zoomed it down to the picture on the right. "This one," he said, emphatically. "No doubt about it."

"You're sure, Mr. Pearl?" Pittman asked. "Those three guys look enough alike to be brothers."

"So maybe they're brothers," Manny said. "What do I care? This is the putz who shot me. He was the leader. I wouldn't forget the face."

Pittman turned over the photograph and read aloud.

"Senior Master Sergeant Perkerson, Harold C. (retired), 400 Airport Road, East Point, Georgia." He looked at Keane. "That's South Atlanta. How come he wasn't in the Atlanta area batch that we showed Mr. Pearl?"

Keane shrugged. "We screwed up there, I guess."

"Mr. Pearl, thank you," Pittman said. "Can I use your phone?"

"Sure, right beside you, on the table," Manny said.

Pittman called his captain on his direct line. "Captain," he said, "Manny Pearl has made an identification of his assailant from photographs we got from the Pentagon. The man is a retired army senior master sergeant named Harold C. Perkerson, of Airport Road in East Point."

"Good going, Chuck," the captain replied. "What do you want to do?"

"I want to take him *now*," Pittman said.

"What do you need?"

"I want a warrant, a SWAT team, ready for anything— this guy is a pro and has access to automatic weapons—and an East Point Police Department liaison."

"Where?"

"There's a gas station at the old airport exit from I-85 South. We'll rally there in"—he looked at his watch— "twenty minutes; make it ten A.M."

"You got it," the captain said. "Anything else?"

"I don't mind press, if you don't," Pittman said.

"Why not? The crime got a lot of play, why not the arrest?"

"And, Captain, I'd like the Pentagon to fax us this man's service record. We're going to need it eventually anyway, but I'd like to have it when I question him."

"I'll make the call myself, as soon as I've got this together."

"Thank you, sir." Pittman hung up the phone. "Let's get going," he said to Keane.

Manny Pearl grabbed Pittman's sleeve. "Listen," he said, "you be careful. This guy's a hard one."

Pittman used the siren all the way, and so did Keane, right behind him. There was an East Point police lieutenant named Brown waiting for him at the gas station.

"What we got here, Sergeant?" Brown asked.

"You remember the killings at the dirty bookstore Christmas Eve?"

"Oh, yeah. Those guys?"

"One of them, anyway, the guy in charge."

"I'll stay outta your way, unless you need my help," the lieutenant said.

"I think we've got it covered," Pittman replied. "Thanks for coming out, though."

The SWAT team van pulled into the station, followed by a brightly painted van with a microwave dish on top. Pittman shook hands with the SWAT commander, a captain named Meadows, then went to the TV van. A young man in a tweed jacket got out and approached him.

"Sergeant Pittman? Jerry Cross, Channel Six News."

"Hi, Jerry," Pittman said. "Now listen, this is a dangerous one." He explained whom they were arresting. "Now, first, I have to case the location; then I'll come back for you. You stay behind the SWAT van at all times, got that?"

"Sure," the reporter said.

Pittman, Keane, and Captain Meadows got into Pittman's car to reconnoiter. They drove down Airport Road, but they couldn't find number 400.

"Wait a minute," Keane said, "I think it's in that little shopping center there. Maybe we've got his address at work."

Pittman drove into the center and circled the parking lot slowly. "There you go," said Meadows, pointing at a small shop. "Number 400."

A sign outside proclaimed that printing and passport photographs were available inside.

"Let's have a look around back," Meadows said.

Pittman drove back into Airport Road, then turned into an alley behind the shopping center. He drove slowly along the alley, checking numbers.

"There," Keane said, pointing.

There was nothing but a back door and a small loading platform.

"I'll place my van behind the Dumpster, there," Meadows said. "I'd suggest you and Keane and the East Point guy go in the front door like customers. I'll bring my men in through the back."

"Sounds good," Pittman said. "That'll give us a chance to get any customers out."

They drove back to the gas station, where Meadows briefed his men, and Pittman explained things to Lieutenant Brown.

"You sure I won't be in your way?" Brown said.

Chickenshit, thought Pittman. "Tell you what, you back us up from outside, okay?"

"Okay," Brown said, looking relieved.

Pittman walked over to Captain Meadows. "Listen,

maybe I should go in and ask for the guy. We got a lot of civilians around that store. I'd hate to see a lot of live ammo flying around there."

"Take it from me," Meadows said. "Go in heavy; don't take any chances with this guy. My people aren't going to start shooting indiscriminately, and if they do shoot, they'll hit what they aim at."

Ten minutes later, they were all in place. Pittman parked his car a row away from the storefront, then picked up a handheld radio and punched in a frequency. "Team leader?" he said.

"Read you loud and clear," Meadows said. "I need one minute to get my men in position. Stand by."

"Roger," Pittman said. He took out his service revolver and checked it. Keane and Brown did the same. Meadows came back on the radio.

"We're in position."

"Roger," Pittman said. "Don't call me. I don't want the radio going off in that shop while we're waiting for the customers to leave. I'll call it with one word—'go'—okay?"

"Roger," Meadows said, "you'll call it with the word 'go.'"

"Keane and I are going in," Pittman said.

The three men got out of the car. While Brown waited, using the car for cover, Pittman and Keane walked toward the front of the shop.

"I see one woman inside," Pittman said.

"Right," Keane replied. "Let's be sure, though."

The two detectives walked into the shop. A tall, thin man behind the counter was waiting on an elderly woman.

"Be with you in a minute," the man said to Pittman.

Pittman nodded and looked around. There was a sign identifying the shop as a pickup point for Federal Express and United Parcel Service, and a wall of mailboxes on the other side of the room.

"Thank you so much," the woman said to the tall, thin man.

"Thank you, ma'am," he replied. "Come back to see us."

The woman walked slowly past the policemen and out the door.

Pittman and Keane approached the counter. There was a blank wall behind the counterman, so they could not see into the next room.

"Hi," said Keane to the tall, thin man, "I wonder if you could help me."

Pittman turned away from the counter, took the hand-held radio from his belt, and spoke into it. "Go!" he said.

Immediately, there was a loud pounding from behind the wall—the back door was being knocked down. Pittman and Keane simultaneously produced badges and guns.

"Police! Freeze!" Pittman shouted, holding the pistol and the badge out in front of him.

The tall, thin man backed away from the counter, his hands out in front of him. "Hey, now . . ." he was saying.

Pittman vaulted over the counter, spun the man around, and threw him against the wall. Then, signaling to Keane to cuff the man, he edged toward the end of the wall and executed a quick peep behind it, exposing himself to view as briefly as possible. The back room was full of SWAT policemen. Two store employees were braced against the walls, being searched. Pittman turned to Keane, who had the counterman handcuffed. "It's okay," he said. "Everybody's nailed down."

Pittman, followed by Keane and the counterman, walked into the back room.

"See your man?" Meadows asked.

Pittman looked at the two back-room employees, then at the counterman. "This guy looks a little like him, but younger," he said. "All right," he said, raising his voice, "where is Harold Perkerson?"

"Huh?" the counterman said. "What the hell is going on here? What do you mean, busting into my place of business?"

Pittman looked at the man and held up the photograph. "We're looking for this man. His name is Harold C. Perkerson. This is his address."

"Yeah?" said the counterman scornfully. "That name sounds familiar. Come here, I'll show you." His hands still cuffed behind his back, he walked over to where Pittman stood and nodded down a hallway. "He lives right down there in one of those mailboxes," the man said.

"Oh, shit," Keane said mournfully.

"What's your name?" Pittman said to the counterman.

"Robert Wickman," the man said. "I own this place. Now, will you take these goddamned handcuffs off me? Then I'll see if I can help you."

Pittman nodded to Keane, who began unlocking the cuffs. Then he looked up and found himself staring into a television camera.

24

Chuck Pittman and Mickey Keane stood before their captain's desk and sweated.

"A *mail drop*?" the captain demanded, incredulous. "A fucking private postal box? That's all it was?"

"Yessir," Pittman said. "We had no way of knowing until we got there."

"And Channel Six News got the whole thing?"

"Yessir, I'm afraid so."

"Are they going to run it?"

"Ah, I was hoping you'd speak to their news director, sir. If they run it and this guy Perkerson sees it, or somebody who knows him sees it, then he'll go to ground."

"Jesus Christ," the captain said in disgust. He picked up the telephone. "I hate asking favors of press people," he said, dialing a number.

Pittman and Keane stood and sweated some more while the captain pleaded his case with the TV newsman, alternately cajoling and demanding. Finally, he hung up the phone.

"I'm going to owe that guy now," he said to the two detectives, "and it's your fucking fault. I'm going to remember that."

"He won't run the tape, then?" Pittman asked, hardly daring to believe it.

"Oh, you're not that lucky, Pittman," the captain said. "He won't run it on the noon news, but he's running it at six. You've got till then to find Perkerson."

"We got a phone number from the guy we raided," Pittman said. "It's outside the city; I'm having it run down now."

"You be sure you've got local support before you go crashing in someplace," the captain said. "And for Christ's sake, don't take any TV people with you. Now get out of here."

Pittman and Keane returned to their desks. Pittman sat down and called his telephone-company contact again, making notes. He hung up and turned to Keane. "We got lucky. It's a rural address, east of La Grange, in Meriwether County. Who's the sheriff down there?"

"Dunno," Keane said. He reached into a desk drawer and pulled out the Georgia Law Enforcement Directory. "Dan Cox, it says here." He read out the phone number.

Pittman called the number and asked for the sheriff.

"Dan Cox," a deep voice said.

"Sheriff, this is Detective Sergeant Chuck Pittman of the Atlanta Police Department."

"Morning, Sergeant, what can I do for you?" the sheriff drawled.

"I have to make an arrest in your county today, and I'd like your support."

"What do you need?"

"As many men as you can spare."

"Who's your man?"

"One Harold C. Perkerson. Know him?"

"Know him to see," the sheriff said. "What do you want him for?"

"Three counts of murder one."

There was a brief silence, then Pittman heard the sheriff say to somebody in his office, "Says he wants that fellow Harold Perkerson on three counts of murder one." Then the sheriff spoke into the phone again. "You sure about this?"

"I've got an eyewitness, made him from his army photograph."

"Well, I'll be damned," Cox said. "I wouldn't have thought he was the type. War hero, they say."

"Yeah, I had a look at his military record. That's why I want everybody you can spare. This guy's an expert with just about every weapon you can think of."

"I think I can get three or four deputies together, if I call some in who're off duty."

"Thanks, that'll be good. Please don't tell 'em who we're arresting. I've already screwed up once today, and I want it nice and neat this time."

"I understand. When you coming down here?"

"How about we meet at the Moreland exit off I-85 South at three P.M.?"

"Okay, my men and I will be there. We'll want shotguns, I reckon."

"That's right, and one more thing: I'd like an ambulance."

"I'll call the county hospital and get one out there."

Pittman thanked the man, then called the Georgia Bureau of Investigation and the Georgia State Patrol. Within an hour, he had a twenty-man posse together, with automatic weapons, tear gas, and flak jackets. He hung up the phone and looked at Keane. "Well," he said, "if we don't get him this afternoon, we're fucked. As soon as this morning's episode hits the tube, he'll run."

At two o'clock, Pittman gathered his force in the parking lot of a fast-food restaurant on a highway outside Luthersville. He shook hands with Sheriff Dan Cox and introduced the GBI and State Patrol commanders.

"I know the place where he lives," Sheriff Cox said. "He bought it from a fellow I know about three or four years ago. My boy and his boy used to play high school basketball together."

"What's the layout?" Pittman asked.

Cox got a notebook from his car and began drawing. "The house is about a quarter of a mile off the road, behind a stand of pines," he said. "There's a barn and a couple of animal pens right behind it; there's woods on three sides, here, and one side of the house faces a pasture."

"We can go in from the woods on three sides, then," Pittman said.

"Yep," Cox replied. "I reckon we should park on the road and circle the house on foot."

"Right," Pittman said. "Let's saddle up." He gave them a radio frequency; then the group got into their cars and drove the two miles to where Perkerson's mailbox stood beside the road.

As they got out of their car, Keane said to Pittman,

"Chuck, how come this guy had a private mailbox in East Point when he's got his name on his mailbox right here?" He looked into the mailbox and found it empty.

"I don't know," Pittman said. "He gave the army the East Point box for an address, but he's living down here, fifty miles away. It doesn't make much sense."

"It bothers me," Keane said.

"Well," said Pittman, "let's just hope he's at home today." He assigned the GBI to the woods in front of the house, the State Patrol the side stand of trees; then he, Keane, and the sheriff and his men trudged around toward the rear of the house, making a wide circle so as not to be seen.

Half an hour later, Pittman was making his way slowly through the pines toward the house, swearing under his breath at himself, because he had not brought any rough clothes. He was wearing his best suit, and the trousers were now full of cockleburs. He could see the back of the barn now, and he began moving stealthily from tree to tree.

He stopped and lifted the radio to his lips. "This is Pittman; I'm in position about twenty yards behind the barn. Everybody ready?"

He got acknowledgments from the GBI and State Patrol contingents.

"We'll move to the barn and check out the house from closer in," Pittman said into the radio. "Hold your positions for now." He turned to Keane and the sheriff. "I'll go first, and if the area between the barn and the house is clear, I'll wave you in."

Keane and the sheriff nodded.

Pittman worked his way to the edge of the trees and

took one last look around. Nothing moved. Staying low, he ran to the back of the barn, then worked his way around to the side, near the front. He could see the back of the house now, and a gray Chevrolet van was parked next to it. To his left was a small corral with a few bales of hay stacked beside it under a tarp. He turned and waved Keane and the sheriff's men forward. In a moment, they were all flattened against the side of the barn.

"Look at that," Keane said, indicating the corral.

Pittman had not noticed it the first time; the bales of hay had been in the way. There were two horses in the corral, and they were lying on their sides, unmoving.

"They're dead," Keane said. "I don't like this, Chuck."

"It's weird," Pittman said. "Why would he kill the horses?"

The sheriff interrupted. "Let's make a move here," he said.

Pittman fastened his flak jacket and spoke into the radio. "I don't want to rush the place; I'm gonna move to the back of the house and see what I can see. If I yell 'go,' then move in fast, okay?"

The GBI and State Patrol commanders confirmed his instructions.

"Okay," Pittman said, and sprinted the remaining twenty yards to the house and ducked under a window. Quickly, he popped his head up above the sill, and brought it back again. He had seen no one. Slowly, this time, he raised his head above the sill and looked into a kitchen. The room was empty; there were a coffee cup and a folded newspaper on the kitchen table. He pressed the transmit button on the radio again.

"There's nobody in the kitchen." He had the odd feeling that the place was empty, and he made a decision. "I'm going in the back door alone," he said into the radio.

"Chuck, don't do that," Keane's voice said over the radio. "I got a bad feeling about this."

"You're too Irish, Mickey," Pittman said. Keane was always going on about his hunches. He moved to the back door of the house. The door stood open; only a screen door separated him from the kitchen. He hoped it wouldn't squeak. It turned out to be amazingly quiet.

Pittman slipped out of his shoes and moved into the kitchen, holding the riot shotgun before him at port arms. He put his hand on the stove. Cold. The refrigerator came on, startling him. He took a few deep breaths and moved toward the door on the other side of the kitchen. Suddenly, a sound came to him, one he disliked. It was the theme music for a television game show. He hated them, hated the noise they made. The TV must be in the living room, he thought. He'd catch Perkerson sitting in front of it.

He stepped through the door and into a hallway, and the music got louder, leading him toward the living room. There were no lights on in the hall, but he could see dimly by the ambient light from the kitchen and living room doors. Pittman started down the hall. Then there was a familiar smell, one that took him a moment to identify, because it didn't belong in a house. In front of him in the hallway was a low row of objects. Curious, he moved forward. As he did, something thin and sharp came into contact with his ankle. Too late, he knew what the objects were: jerry cans; and what the smell was: gasoline.

*   *   *

Mickey Keane leaned against the barn and clenched his teeth. He didn't like the dead horses, and he didn't like Pittman going into that house by himself. He would have used the bullhorn and tear gas, himself. What the hell was taking Chuck so long? He peeped around the corner of the barn, and as he did, the side of the house facing him buckled outward, and a millionth of a second later the shock wave and the noise hit him. He flinched and pulled back; then, when the shock had passed, he looked around the corner of the barn at the house again. As he did, the van exploded, a giant orange fireball enveloped everything, and debris was flying everywhere.

Keane drew back and pressed his body against the barn again, hoping it would hold, gritting his teeth at the pain caused by the fragments of debris that had struck his face, cursing himself for letting his partner go into the house. When the explosion subsided, he didn't look at where the house had been; he didn't need to. He sank to the ground and began to cry.

BOOK TWO

I

Will Lee stood on the steps of the Georgia capitol and waited for a television cue. The gold-plated dome of the building behind him rose and disappeared into the fog, and a light rain began to fall on the little crowd gathered there. He was dressed in his new H. Stockton blue suit, white button-down shirt, red necktie, and wingtips, and at the curb his new Chevrolet station wagon waited. Beside Will stood his father and mother, Jack Buchanan, Kitty Conroy, and, well to one side, Tom Black, the political consultant.

As the rain started, Patricia Lee raised an umbrella and held it over Will's head.

"Mrs. Lee," Tom Black called softly from the sidelines. When he had her attention, he shook his head, and Patricia closed the umbrella.

"Coming up on six o'clock," a man called from one of the television equipment trucks parked at the nearest curb. "Five, four, three, two, one . . ." He brought his hand down.

Will looked out over the heads of the three television

cameramen and spoke. "Today, I am announcing my candidacy to represent Georgia in the United States Senate. I
run because I believe I am better qualified to do the job
than any other person in Georgia—except one, who is not
well enough to run." He stopped speaking and continued
to look at a point over the cameramen's heads until he was
sure all three cameras had stopped turning. Back at the
stations, the anchors were beginning their newscasts with
his candidacy as their lead stories. Will didn't know how
Tom Black had managed to get him at the top of all three
newscasts, but he had done it. Now, as Tom had arranged,
Will turned to the first camera and waited for his cue. He
would give three interviews in tandem, and each would go
out live on one of the three main stations.

A reporter stood and pressed a hand to his ear, waiting
for a cue. Having received it, he turned to Will. "Mr. Lee,
you've said you're better qualified than anybody in the
state but one man; that would be Senator Benjamin Carr?"

"That's correct," Will said. "I wouldn't be running if
the Senator were able himself to run again."

"But you do believe you're better qualified than Governor Mack Dean?"

"I do," Will said emphatically, "for a lot of reasons, but
for two principal ones: first, I have a real program to un-
dertake in the Senate, an agenda of specific proposals that
will help establish national priorities in defense, foreign
policy, education, and social progress, among others; and
second, I have behind me eight years of service and training at the side of the greatest senator our country has produced in this century, and if he were able, I believe Senator
Carr would be here today to back me."

"When are we going to hear about this program of yours, Mr. Lee?"

"As soon as you'll give me more than two minutes of air time." Will laughed. "I'll be taking this message to every corner of our state over the coming months, and I believe the people of Georgia are going to like what they hear."

The reporter turned to his camera. "You heard it. Will Lee has kicked off his campaign by stating flatly that he is better qualified than Governor Dean to serve in the United States Senate. We'll be getting the Governor's reaction a little later in the program, but right now, back to the newsroom."

Tom Black stepped up, thanked the reporter, and began setting up the next interview, with the capitol dome in the background. Will repeated his performance with the other two stations, then spent five minutes with three print reporters from around the state. When he had finished, Tom herded him toward the station wagon.

"All right," Tom said, as they slid into the backseat. "Off to a good start. Now, on Sunday, we've got feeds set up for live, thirty-minute interviews with stations in Augusta, Savannah, Macon, Columbus, and Waycross. That'll cover just about every TV household in the state."

Will mopped the rain from his face. "Well, I guess if I can get through what you've got planned for the next week, I can get through anything."

"Don't worry," Tom said, "it's going to get worse, if you're lucky."

They drove to Will's new Atlanta campaign office on Spring Street. Inside the storefront building were a dozen desks, with volunteers looking busy. Upstairs was a large room with more desks, and offices for Will, Jack, and Kitty. Will sat down at his desk and Jack shoved a large stack of three-by-five cards in front of him.

"Okay," Jack said, "these are for each of the people on the personal acquaintance list you made. Each card has everything we know about the person—job, family, kids. Go to it."

Will stared at the top card. Willis Perkins, fraternity brother at the University of Georgia, twenty years before. "Here goes," he said, dialing a number, while Tom Black listened on an extension. A small child answered, and Will finally persuaded him to call his father to the phone.

"Hello?"

It was a deep, rich voice, one that Will remembered immediately. "Willis, this is Will Lee. How you doing?"

There was a brief silence before Perkins spoke. "Will Lee from school?"

"That's right."

"Jesus Christ."

Will glanced at the card before him. "How's the pulpwood business these days? You went into the family business, didn't you?"

"That's right, and it ain't bad."

"Listen, Willis, did you watch the six-o'clock news tonight?"

"Nope. I was taking a nap. You woke me up."

"I'm sorry about that, but if you had been watching, you'd have seen me standing up there on the capitol steps, announcing for the Senate."

"The state senate?"

"The United States Senate."

"Well, I'll be damned."

Will took a deep breath and forced himself to go on. "Listen, Willis, I need your help."

"Aha!" Perkins laughed. "Now I get it. You're looking for a campaign contribution, right?"

"You always were a quick one, Willis."

"You a Republican or a Democrat?"

"I'm a Democrat, Willis."

"Then you're out of luck, boy. I'm a born-again Republican. Jimmy Carter turned me into one."

"He damn near turned *me* into one," Will said, pressing on. Why the hell did I say that? he wondered. It isn't true.

Across the desk, Tom Black drew his finger across his throat. "Forget it," he mouthed silently.

"Willis, I don't want you to go against these newfound Republican principles of yours, but I want you to pay attention to what gets said in the campaign, and if you start agreeing with me, I want you to call me, all right? We'll always be ready to welcome you back to the fold."

"Don't count on it," Perkins said.

"Thanks, Willis. Good to talk to you." Will hung up and mopped his brow. "That guy never had a brain in his head," he said. "I don't know what made me put him on the list."

"It's time well spent," Tom said. "Hell, you might hear from him. At least he'll tell everybody he knows that you called him. He'll be proud of that."

Kitty Conroy came into the room. "This was left for you earlier," she said. "It's marked 'personal.'" She placed a large brown envelope on the desk.

Will opened the envelope and looked at the papers inside. "Good," he said. "This is the stuff my investigator has been rounding up for Larry Moody's trial." He went quickly through the papers and grinned. "Good stuff; I can use it."

"How long do you reckon this trial is going to last?" Jack Buchanan asked.

"Three days, maybe five," Will said. "We start jury selection Monday morning—that shouldn't take more than a day. The prosecution will take a day to present; then I'll take a day. There won't be that many witnesses. Just to be on the safe side, don't schedule anything for me in the daytime until the weekend."

"The good news about the trial is that you're going to get TV coverage every day."

"Why is that so good?" Will asked. "If Moody's found innocent, it will offend most of the black people in the state; if he's found guilty, it'll offend a lot of whites—and I'll look like an incompetent, too."

"Don't worry about that," Tom said. "Kitty's getting the word out to the press that you had no choice about defending the guy. The main thing is, every night on the six-o'clock news, you'll be walking out of that courthouse and talking to a bunch of cameras. Remember what P.T. Barnum said—'as long as they spell your name right.'"

"I buy that," Kitty said.

"I'd worry about it if it were later in the campaign," Tom said. "But early on, it'll just get people used to looking at your face."

"I hope you're right," Will said, picking up another card from the stack before him. "Harry Maples," he read aloud. "Banker? Harry?"

"That's what the University of Georgia Directory says," Jack replied.

"To tell you the truth," Will said, "I never thought Harry would even get a job after college." He dialed the number.

"Hello."

"Harry Maples?"

"That's right."

"This is Will Lee. I—"

"Will, how are you, boy? I just saw you on television. What can I do to help?"

Will covered the receiver and looked at Tom Black. "Maybe this isn't going to be so bad after all," he said.

When Will hung up the phone, he had Maples's pledge of a thousand-dollar contribution and a promise to raise more from his friends.

Kitty went to a large TV set in a corner and turned up the volume. "The Governor is going to be interviewed in a minute," she said.

Will put down his index cards and turned his attention to the set. After a moment, the anchorman switched to the capitol, and Mack Dean stood on the steps, in exactly the same spot where Will had stood.

"Governor, Will Lee says he's better qualified than you to represent Georgia in the Senate. What do you have to say about that?"

A slow smile spread across Dean's face. "Why, I've known Will since he was a little boy," he said, "and he's always been a real polite little fellow." A tiny frown crept into Dean's expression. "Course, young Will's never run for public office before, and you have to wonder if maybe he isn't biting off a little bit more than he can chew, running for the United States Senate first time out. I think Will ought to get some experience at a lower level, maybe his local school board, or something like that. Then, when he's learned something about what folks want from their government, maybe he could take on a race for his county board of commissioners, or maybe even the state legislature."

"Governor, Mr. Lee has worked for Senator Ben Carr for eight years, and he says he has the Senator's support."

Mack Dean looked sad. "Well, now, I'm sorry to hear that young Will has already started comparing himself to Senator Carr, and as far as having his support, well, from what I hear—and I'm very well informed about the Senator's condition—Ben Carr is just not able to communicate his desires. I guess Will thinks it's easy to claim Senator Carr's support, when he knows the Senator can't speak up for himself. Still, I'm looking forward to introducing young Will Lee to Georgia politics. He's got a lot to learn, and I'm going to do what I can to teach him."

"You son of a bitch," Will said to the television screen.

"You'd better get used to it," Tom Black said. "He's just getting started."

2

"Well, Harry," the Archon said, "you'd better come in." Harold Perkerson shook his raincoat before stepping into the foyer. "A filthy night," the Archon said, taking Perkerson's raincoat and hanging it in a closet.

Perkerson followed the man across the marble floor and into a small library. A fire crackled in the hearth as the Archon went to a bookcase and opened a door to reveal a mirrored liquor cabinet. He poured them both a stiff bourbon on the rocks.

"Have a seat, man," the Archon said, indicating a leather club chair before the fire.

Perkerson sat stiffly and watched the Archon take his place in an identical chair opposite. He was as calm and hospitable as if he were receiving the President instead of a soaking-wet fugitive. Perkerson's awe of the man went up yet another notch. "I . . . I'm sorry I had to call you," he said.

"Nonsense," the Archon replied, shaking his massive head. "It was the proper thing to do. I'm sorry it took me these days to get things organized."

Perkerson took a deep swig of the bourbon. It was better than anything he had ever tasted. He wondered what brand it was. "I know I've destroyed my effectiveness," Perkerson said, his voice trembling.

"What? Do you really believe that? Let me put your mind at rest, Harold. Up until now, you've been an effective training specialist and team leader, but now you're much more." The Archon leaned forward and rested his elbows on his knees. "Now you're a hero to all the young men in our organization—and other sympathetic organizations, too. All those in the know are aware of what you've done. You're a paragon, man."

Perkerson could hardly believe what he was being told. He had telephoned the Archon as soon as he had become a fugitive, and had been told to wait, to call back later. He had come to the man's house ready to receive a bullet in the head or to put it there himself, if asked, and now he was being called a hero.

"That was a fine piece of work at the farm, too," the Archon said earnestly. "A proper scorched-earth retreat."

"I killed a policeman," Perkerson said. "I know that's bad."

"Don't worry about it. They're in a frenzy, of course, but they're baffled. They know who you are now, but we can fix that. They don't know *why,* and that's driving them nuts. I've got a source in the department, so I know. And the sheriff down there is an amiable fool, so that's nothing to worry about. You always kept to yourself, so there's no trail of friends and acquaintances to follow." He winked. "None that would say a word."

"But my picture has been in every newspaper in the state," Perkerson said.

"Well," said the Archon, rising and walking toward the liquor cabinet, "that's true, but we're going to fix it."

"Fix it?" How the hell could even the Archon fix a thing like that?

The Archon fiddled with something at the side of the liquor cabinet, then took hold of a shelf and pulled. The mirrored back panel of the cabinet swung outward to reveal a large, old-fashioned safe, nestled in yet another concealed cupboard. He worked the combination, took hold of the handle, and pulled it open. The contents were hidden from Perkerson by the door, but the Archon reached into the safe and withdrew a small zippered canvas duffel and dropped it onto the floor beside him. He secured the safe, swung back the liquor shelf, retrieved the duffel, and came back to his chair. "Now, let's see what I've got for you," he said, dropping the duffel at his feet and unzipping it. He removed a smaller bag from the duffel and tossed it to Perkerson. "Ten thousand dollars in twenties and fifties," he said.

Perkerson placed the bag in his lap without opening it.

The Archon held up a small bundle of plastic cards secured with a rubber band, then tossed it to Perkerson. "Visa, MasterCard, and business cards in the name of James Ross; he's a salesman for a company owned by friends of ours. If you get caught, he'll report the cards stolen. There's a Georgia driver's license, too, in the same name, using my file photo of you. You'll want to burn that after a few days."

Perkerson caught the bundle and looked at the license. "My ears show up anywhere, don't they?"

"Your nose, too," the Archon replied. "But we're going to fix all that." He took a notebook from his pocket and wrote down something, then passed it to Perkerson. "He's a very fine surgeon, practices out in Cobb County, one of our most enthusiastic supporters. He's already had a good look at your photograph, and he says he can make a new man of you. You're to go there when you leave here; he'll start working on you tonight." The Archon grinned. "You won't have to worry about the ears anymore." He tossed the empty duffel to Perkerson.

Perkerson caught it and began refilling it with the things he had been given.

"Do you have any weapons?" the Archon asked.

Perkerson nodded. "There's an Uzi in the raincoat, and I've got an H&K automatic in a shoulder holster."

"Were the weapons used in any of your assignments?"

"All of them."

The Archon rose and left the room for a moment. He came back carrying an automatic pistol and a leather briefcase. "Take this," he said, "and give me your weapons. I'll dispose of them."

Perkerson handed over his pistol and accepted the new one. He looked at the briefcase.

"Ah, we've something special here," the Archon said. He opened the case. "It's Czech, a silenced sniper's rifle that breaks down. Look, you can even use the briefcase; the rifle only takes up half the room."

Perkerson took out the pieces and quickly assembled the weapon. It was very light.

"I'll have some new assignments for you before long, when you've sufficiently recovered from your surgery," the Archon said, as if he had been reading Perkerson's mind. "You'll need the rifle then. What are you driving?"

"I ditched my pickup truck yesterday. I took a cab to about a mile from here, then walked."

"Good." The Archon fished in his pocket and handed Perkerson some keys. "There's a Mazda in my garage, registered to the company you now seem to work for. Go straight to the doctor's from here. I'll let him know you're on your way."

Perkerson broke down the rifle and packed it into its case; then he stood up. "Sir, I don't know how to thank you."

The Archon took his hand. "I don't know how to thank *you*," he said. "Go carefully in the rain, and don't run any stop signs. If you can just make it to the doctor's office, you'll be fine."

A few minutes later, as Perkerson crossed the Chatta-hoochee River into Cobb County, he wondered at the thing he belonged to, that owned him. It could do anything, this Elect, under its Archon. It could change his face, his very identity, as easily as the government could for a federal witness. It could protect him, nurture him while he did his work. It could change him from a retired army sergeant to a harbinger of a new order, of a new world to come. He drove joyously into the wet night.

3

Will had been up since six, and at seven, he dialed
Katharine Rule's Washington number.

"Hello," a sleepy voice said.

"It's Will."

"Oh. What time is it?"

"It's seven in the morning. I thought you'd be up."

"I'm not up. Can we talk later?"

Will tried to keep the irritation from his voice. "I've
been trying to reach you for a week. All I get is an answering machine. You haven't returned any of my calls."

There was a brief silence. "I've been very busy," she
said finally.

"I've been pretty busy myself," he said, letting his irritation get the best of him.

"You know I can't go into it on the phone," she said.
"When are you coming up here?"

"I don't know," he replied sullenly.

"Can't you take some time? I think we need to talk."

"Look, I'm running for the United States Senate, remember? And I've got a murder trial starting this morning. There just isn't any time. I had hoped you might understand that."

"And I'm only a few weeks into a new job, remember? I didn't get home until after two this morning, and now, when I had hoped to make up a couple of hours' sleep, I've got you on the phone at the crack of dawn, making noises like a resentful child."

Will took a deep breath. "I'm sorry I woke you. Go back to sleep. Call me, if you get a chance." He hung up without waiting for her to reply.

He spent two minutes pacing up and down, swearing at Kate, calling her names he would have never used to her face. Then he grabbed his coat and a necktie and strode out of the cottage, slamming the door behind him. When he was almost to the car, he heard the telephone in the cottage ring. He paused for a moment, then got into the car and drove away.

By nine o'clock, Will had gone through his notes on questions for jurors and had packed his large briefcase and stuffed his exhibits into a large plastic garbage bag and knotted it at the top. He left the law offices of Lee & Lee and got into the Chevy station wagon. Still angry with Kate, he drove faster than he should have to Greenville and parked in one of the spaces on the courthouse square reserved for lawyers. To his surprise, a television crew had set up on the courthouse lawn, and he was waylaid on his way into the building.

"Mr. Lee, can we have a moment?" the reporter, a young black man, asked.

Will's inclination was to brush him off, but Tom Black wouldn't like his passing up television time. "Sure," he said, "what can I do for you?"

The young man nodded to his cameraman, got a signal back, and turned to the camera. "This is Dave Willis, at the Meriwether County Courthouse with Will Lee, candidate for the U.S. Senate and lawyer for Larry Eugene Moody in his trial for the murder of Sarah Cole." He turned to Will. "Mr. Lee, why are you defending Larry Moody?" There was accusation in the man's tone.

"Well, Dave," Will replied, "I'm sure you'll agree that Mr. Moody has a right to a lawyer. I—"

"Yes, of course, Mr. Lee, but why you? You're a candidate for public office. Do you hope to win some votes by defending a man accused of a brutal rape and murder?"

"Of course not," Will said, restraining himself. "The Judge asked me to defend Mr. Moody before I decided to run for the Senate."

"As a public defender?"

"That was the basis on which I originally agreed to act for the defense," Will said carefully.

"You said 'originally,' Mr. Lee. Does that mean your status has since changed? Are you now being paid to defend Larry Eugene Moody?"

The reporter was quicker than Will had given him credit for. "Someone has since expressed a desire to pay for Mr. Moody's defense," Will said. "I explained that to the Judge, and I am no longer a public defender."

"Who is paying for Moody's defense?" the reporter asked.

"The party wishes to remain anonymous," Will said.

"Now, if you'll excuse me, I have to get into court." He made to leave.

The reporter walked along after him. "What outcome do you anticipate?" he asked.

"I expect an acquittal," Will called over his shoulder. "Good morning." God, was it going to be like this every day? He trudged into the courtroom, which was already full. A line of spectators waited in the hallway.

Larry's boss, John Morgan, and Charlene Joiner sat together in the first row of seats, directly behind the defense table. Will set his briefcase on the defense table and tucked the garbage bag underneath it; then he shook hands with Morgan and Charlene. She was, he noted, demurely dressed in a navy blue cotton dress with a high neck. Will found her even more striking in such clothes. He looked up to see a deputy at a side door removing Larry Moody's handcuffs.

Larry, in a tan cotton suit and necktie, looked quite presentable, too. His hair had been cut, and he was cleanly shaven, at Will's insistence. Will shook his hand, and they sat down to wait for court to convene. Will noticed that Larry's greeting to Charlene was only a curt nod, though he leaned across the railing and shook John Morgan's hand.

They sat for another ten minutes. Will looked at his watch; it was after ten o'clock, and Elton Hunter had still not arrived. Neither had the Judge. As they waited, the murmur of the spectators' voices filling the courtroom, the clerk emerged from the Judge's office and came to the defense table.

"Judge Boggs would like to see you in chambers," he said to Will.

"I'll be right back, Larry," Will said. "Just relax." He rose and walked to the Judge's chambers.

"Come on in, Will," the Judge said from behind his desk. He was on the telephone.

Will took a chair and waited for the Judge to finish.

"So, exactly what is his condition?" the Judge asked, then waited for a reply. "No, I am not a family member, I am Judge of the Superior Court, and that man was due in my courtroom ten minutes ago. Now, is he going to make it?" He waited again. "Thanks very much," he said at last, then hung up with a sigh and turned to Will. "We got problems, boy," he said.

"What's wrong?" Will asked.

"Elton Hunter is what's wrong. They took him to Callaway Hospital in La Grange this morning with stomach pains. Turns out it's a ruptured appendix, complete with peritonitis. Elton's in the recovery room now, and he's not good."

Will couldn't think of anything to say.

"Well, the son of a bitch better not die," the Judge said.

"Is there anybody to stand in for him?" Will asked.

"Not a soul," the Judge said. "I'm going to have to reschedule, and it's not going to make it onto this calendar, I can tell you. I'm right up to here." The Judge held a hand to his chin.

"We're talking another three months, then?" Will said, incredulous.

"That's about right, I reckon."

Will leaned back in his chair and massaged his temples. His day was not going well. "Judge, I ask you once more—"

"No," the Judge said emphatically. "Don't even bring it up again."

"All right," Will said, standing up. "I want bail for my client. There's no reason to keep him locked up. He's got a job, his employer's willing to stand bail, and he's not going anywhere. I request bail in the amount of fifty thousand dollars."

"I'll hear your request in the courtroom," the Judge said, rising.

Will went back to the defense table and sat down.

"What's happening?" Larry Moody asked.

"Hang on a minute," Will said. "You'll see."

"All rise!" the clerk said.

Everyone got to his feet as the Judge entered the courtroom and sat himself down behind the bench.

"Ladies and gentlemen," the Judge said to the room at large, "we've brought you here for naught. The prosecutor has been hospitalized with appendicitis, and I'm moving this case to the next calendar." He looked at Will and nodded.

Will stood. "Your Honor, I request bail for my client."

The courtroom erupted in a loud murmur.

"Bail is set at two hundred and fifty thousand dollars," the Judge said.

"Shit!" Will said under his breath. He turned and looked at John Morgan. To Will's surprise, Morgan nodded solemnly. Will turned back to the Judge. "Your Honor, the defendant will post bail."

"See the clerk," the Judge said. He banged his gavel. "This case is adjourned. Court will recess for one hour to allow the sheriff time to bring the next case." He rose and went into his chambers.

Larry Moody looked stunned. "Does that mean I'm free?" he asked, wide-eyed.

Will looked at Morgan, who patted his coat pocket.

"I brought some deeds, just in case," he said.

Will turned back to Larry. "Then you'll be out before lunch." He looked for Charlene, but she was gone. Surprised, he turned to Larry. "Where'd Charlene go? She ought to be pretty excited about this."

Larry looked away. "Wherever she wants, I guess. I don't much care." Then, seeing Will's alarm, he said, "Don't worry, she'll be here to testify when the time comes. You can count on that."

4

When Will got back to the cottage, the light was blinking on his answering machine. He punched the button and sat down with a pencil and pad.

"Oh, the hell with it," Katharine Rule's voice said. "Go fuck yourself." The telephone was slammed down.

Fine, Will thought. Before he could think further, another voice came from the machine. "Will, this is Hank Taylor in Washington. Boy, have we got some advertising for you! I want you to come up here just as soon as you can and have a look at some TV stuff. Call me right back, will you?"

Will jotted down the number; then he called the Atlanta campaign office and asked for Jack Buchanan. "Moody's trial has been postponed," he said. "Looks like I've got the whole week free. Can you reschedule something for me?"

"Jesus, Will," Jack replied, his voice hoarse, "I don't know what we can come up with on short notice, but next week is full."

"You sound awful, Jack. You sick or something?"

"No, just a late night, I guess. I was . . . ah, working on some stuff."

"Well, get some rest; you're no good to me dead on your feet."

"Okay. Listen, about all you can do this week is continue with the fund-raising, but you've already been through the initial list."

"I got a call from Hank Taylor this morning; says he's got some advertising for me to look at. I think I'll go to Washington today."

"Okay," Jack replied. "When you thinking of coming back?"

"Tomorrow—no, make it the next day. I've got some personal business to take care of."

"Will, would you mind if I come with you? I haven't seen Millie and the kids for weeks, and she's pretty down. I think Kitty can manage here without me."

"Sure." Will looked at his watch. "I'll pick you up at Peachtree De Kalb Airport in, say, two hours' time. We'll be in Washington by late afternoon."

Will hung up and started getting ready to leave. He was going to have it out with Kate once and for all.

Will landed at PDK, refueled, and picked up Jack Buchanan. Jack looked tired and worried, Will thought. "Is something wrong?" he asked.

"Oh, nothing much," Jack said. "Just a little domestic quarrel with Millie. We'll sort it out while I'm home."

"Jack, if you need some time at home, we can work something out."

"Oh, no, it's not as serious as that. We'll fix it."

Will started to press, then backed off; it wasn't really his business. "Let me know if I can help," he said.

Jack dozed off shortly after takeoff and slept the whole way to the airport at College Park, Maryland. On the ground, Will called for his car to be brought, while Jack got a cab to his home in Bethesda. Then Will called Kate at her CIA office, something he had rarely done.

"Office of the Deputy Assistant Director for Intelligence," a man's voice said.

Will nearly hung up, but he wanted badly to speak to her. "May I speak to Katharine Rule?" he said finally.

"Who is calling, please?"

"This is William Henry," he replied, using only his first two names. He had done this before on the rare occasions when he had called her at work.

There was a very long silence; then Kate came on the line, cool and businesslike. "Yes?" she said.

"I've just arrived in town," he said, matching her tone. "May we meet this evening?"

"I'll call you late in the afternoon," she said. "Good-bye." She hung up.

Will wondered whether she was being curt because it was an Agency line. It ate at him all the way to Hank Taylor's office.

He was kept waiting a few minutes in Taylor's reception room, which gave him more time to worry about Kate. It was much quieter than the last time he had been here, he reflected, remembering the music for the New York candidate, Heald, coming through the walls. Shortly, he was shown to a conference room, where Hank Taylor waited for him alone.

"Will, how you doing?" Taylor asked, pumping his hand.

"Fine, Hank," Will replied, still annoyed with Kate and trying not to sound it. He was in no mood for Taylor's backslapping, either.

"Sit down, boy. I've got some great stuff to show you," Taylor said, pulling a chair out for him. "My guy's threading the projector now."

Film? Will thought. He had specifically asked Taylor to show him rough ideas before making actual commercials. "Where's Tom Black?" Will asked.

"He couldn't be here today," Taylor said evasively. "In fact, I'm not sure he's the right man for your campaign. He's spending a lot of time on the Heald thing in New York, you know. I'm going to give you somebody better."

Will started to speak, but the lights went down, and Taylor held up a hand. "Wait till you see this," Taylor said. "Hell, wait till you *hear* it."

Will sat back in his chair and directed his attention to the screen at the end of the room. A countdown appeared on the screen, giving Will time to be annoyed again that Taylor had gone straight to film without discussing the idea with him first. And what the hell was this about Tom Black? He had begun to rely on Tom, and he wasn't going to let go of him without a fight. He tried to clear his mind and concentrate fully on the film, which was now coming up on the screen.

Will was surprised to see himself standing next to the lake by the cottage at home, his sleeves rolled up, the Labrador retriever at his side. A march was playing softly in the background, as an announcer's deep voice came in. "Georgia needs a new kind of senator," the announcer rumbled, "one with his feet in the red clay of the state, and his mind on the stars." The camera pulled back as Will walked along the lakeshore, throwing a stick for the dog to retrieve.

"A man who believes every Georgia parent should choose the school that's right for his child, public or private, with tuition paid by a voucher bought with his own tax dollars."

Will's eyes widened. He had specifically told Taylor that he was opposed to such a plan.

The camera zoomed in across the lake on Will's face, and the film froze. "A man every Georgian can count on," the announcer said, and the music swelled up, joined by a hearty male chorus. "Lee! Lee! He's our man! If he can't do it, nobody can!" The screen went black, and a title appeared: "Paid for by the committee to elect Will Lee." The film ended, and the lights came up.

Will turned to Taylor. "The hell you say." He was right at the boiling point.

"What?" Taylor said, taken aback.

"If you think I'm paying for that piece of crap, you're out of your mind," Will said.

"Now look, Will, it's only a rough idea at this stage, but we think it's great stuff."

"I told you specifically I was against that cockamamy school-voucher idea. I'm a Democrat, for Christ's sake."

"Now, Will—"

"I told you specifically not to go to film with any idea until we had discussed it."

"Will, this is just a rough—"

"And the last time I was in this office, I heard that music with Heald's name on it. What's the matter, did he throw it back at you? I don't blame him—it's lousy. But you thought you could palm it off on me, huh?" Will stood up. "Where's Tom Black? I can't believe he had anything to do with this crap."

Taylor stood up too. "I told you, Will, he's off your campaign."

"So are you," Will said, walking toward the door. He stopped and turned around. "You can send me a bill for Tom's time and expenses on my campaign. Anything else, anything like that piece of film, you can eat. I'll expect a refund of any part of my thirty-seven thousand five hundred bucks that wasn't spent on Tom Black. And if I don't have it by a week from today, I'll sue you and send a copy of the writ to the *Washington Post*."

Taylor stood, red and sweating, next to the conference table. He seemed to be trying to say something but couldn't get the words out.

Will slammed the door behind him and walked out of the office.

5

Mickey Keane sat in the steel armchair in his captain's office and waited for the captain, whose back was turned to him, to hang up the telephone. Finally, the captain closed his conversation and turned to face him.

"Jesus Christ, Mickey!" he said.

Keane's hand went to his face. The swelling had mostly gone down, but there were still many jagged, red welts where the glass fragments had been removed. He was lucky to have his eyes. "Yeah, I know, Cap."

"Can anything be done about that?"

"Aw, they're talking about some plastic surgery, but I haven't got the time for that right now."

"You take all the time you need," the captain said. "Besides, the way you look right now, you're bad for morale around here." It was only half a joke.

Keane tried to chuckle. "It's not what I've got on my mind just at the moment."

"Yeah, I know," the captain said sympathetically. "Let me bring you up to date."

"I read all the reports you sent to the hospital. Thanks for that."

"Well, there isn't much more, I guess. That place was an arsenal, or had been. We found a kind of pit, a room, under the barn, set up as a firing range. We dug a lot of metal out of the dirt behind the targets, every sort of caliber, a lot of Mac Ten and Uzi stuff, shotgun pellets, nine-millimeter handgun stuff. The police range wouldn't have that kind of variety."

"So it's some sort of group, then. It's the only thing that makes any sense. There has to be more to it than the four who hit Manny Pearl's store."

"Who knows?" the captain replied. "I guess you want to be on the hunt for this guy Perkerson, huh?"

"Yes, sir."

The captain leaned back in his chair and locked his fingers behind his head. "I read your report, Mick, but I want to hear from you why Pittman went into that house alone. More important, I want to know why you let him do it."

"I tried to talk him out of it, Captain, but I didn't have much time, and he wasn't listening. When I saw that the horses had been shot, I felt we had a bad one, but Chuck wasn't listening. He was my senior; I couldn't order him not to go in."

"I see," the captain said. "Well, he always was a little on the headstrong side. Brave, too. Pittman always had guts."

"It was the brave thing to do that day," Keane said, looking at the floor. "If we'd rushed the place, a lot more of us would have died." Keane looked up at the captain. "I guess it'd look a lot better on my record if I was dead with my partner."

The captain reddened. "I don't want to hear any of that shit from you, Keane. I'm not blaming you. Nobody is."

Keane looked through the glass partition into the squad room. Nobody in there looked at him in quite the same way anymore. He'd lost his partner, and they wondered why. "I don't want another partner right off, if that's all right, Captain."

The captain nodded. "Okay, I can understand that. We'll let it cool off awhile."

"I'd like to run the search on Perkerson, though."

"It's a little late for that," the captain replied. "We've already run down every contact of the man's we could establish. It's a cold trail now."

"He'll surface," Keane said. "He's on some kind of goddamned crusade—first the dirty bookstore, then the X-rated movie house in Charlotte. Nobody has that sort of firing range setup to train for dove hunting. It's some sort of paramilitary thing, something political. It's like some of those far-right-wing groups out west we've heard about, that Posse whatever."

"We've never had that sort of thing around here," the captain said.

"The Klan is that sort of thing," Keane answered, "just not as well organized or trained. This isn't a bunch of good ol' boys with rifle racks in their pickups and a couple six-packs on a Saturday night before some hell-raising."

The captain looked at him but said nothing.

"You see it some other way?" Keane asked.

The captain shrugged. "You want me to go tell the chief we got a little army working the city and the state? You want him to tell the mayor that? You want the mayor to tell the Governor?"

"My partner's dead," Keane said. "He died in a booby trap that would look good on the Viet Cong. He died chasing a guy who led three other guys in some sort of uniform in the murders of three people—lucky it wasn't four. It wasn't a stickup; it wasn't a grudge; it wasn't Manny Pearl's wife trying to collect on the insurance. What do you make it, Captain?"

"Let's let the newspapers put the labels on it," the captain replied. "We'll just run it down in our own plodding way."

"Let me go after the guy," Keane said.

"I told you, we've run down every lead. I've had fifteen men on it."

"He's going to do it again, you watch. Before long, we'll have another killing, something sexy again. It'll be Perkerson or his people. When that happens, I want it."

"Okay," the captain said, "you'll get it when it happens."

"I'll know when it's him," Keane said. "You'll let me call it?"

"You'll call it," the captain said. "You hear something sounds right, it's yours. Meantime, I want you to take another week of sick leave, go to Florida or something. I don't want to see that particular face around here. Get some sun on it."

Keane nodded. "Yessir." He got up and left. Walking through the squad room, he looked straight ahead. One detective stopped him.

"Tough break, Mick," the man said.

"Yeah," Keane replied, and continued out of the room. He'd go to Florida and get some sun, get rested. Perkerson wouldn't move yet; he was too hot. But he'd move, and when he did, Keane would be on the job. Mickey Keane wanted Perkerson. He wanted to stick a service revolver in his ear and pull the trigger until it was empty.

6

Will Lee let himself into his Georgetown house, dis-armed the burglar alarm, and turned up the ther-mostat on the furnace. There was a distant rumble, and warm air began to flow into the stale house.

The telephone rang.

Will ran to get it, but the answering machine picked up on the first ring. He snatched the phone from its cradle. "Hang on a minute," he said. He waited patiently until his own recorded voice spoke the answering message and the beep went. "Hello," he said.

"Can we meet at Pied de Couchon at seven?" Katharine Rule's voice said.

At a restaurant? Not at her place or his? They hadn't seen each other for weeks. "If that's what you want," he said.

"Seven, then," she said, and hung up.

Will slammed down the phone, furious. He was furious at Hank Taylor for his shabby performance, furious at Tom Black for not having the guts to be at the meeting, and, above all, furious with Kate. He stood and took deep breaths, willing himself to be calm. He looked at his watch. Five-thirty. What could he do until seven? He went into his study, grabbed a legal pad, and started to make lists, lists of things to do in the campaign. Turn all this angry adrenaline to good use.

He made a list for Kitty Conroy, then a list for Jack Buchanan. He looked at his watch again: six-fifteen. He had to do something about another political consultant, or maybe an ad agency would be better. He had to do something about Jack, too. He had asked him onto the campaign without giving him full charge of anything. He would make Jack campaign manager, officially. Jack was smart, imaginative, and hardworking; he deserved it. At the beginning, he'd had some notion of being his own campaign manager, but that was stupid. He'd be in charge, anyway, and it was wrong of him to withhold the title from Jack.

Will looked up Tom Black's home phone number and called it. He got an answering machine. "Tom, this is Will Lee. I had a meeting with Hank Taylor this afternoon, and I fired him. But I want to talk to you. I'll be at the Georgetown house at least through tomorrow night, then back in Delano. Please call me as soon as you possibly can." He wanted some answers from Tom Black.

Six-thirty. Will went upstairs to his bedroom, ran an electric razor over his face, and changed shirts. He got into a tweed jacket and grabbed his trench coat. Six-forty-five. He was downstairs, about to arm the alarm system, when the doorbell rang.

Jack Buchanan stood on the doorstep, looking as if he had been hit by a truck.

"Jack, what's the matter?" Will asked. "Come on in." He hung their coats on the hall rack, then led Jack into the living room and got him into a chair.

"I'm sorry to barge in on you like this, Will," Buchanan said.

"That's okay, Jack. You look as if you could use a drink."

"Thanks, yes, I guess I could."

Will went to the liquor cabinet and poured a bourbon on the rocks, then handed it to Jack and took a chair opposite him, glancing at his watch. Six-fifty, and it was a ten-minute walk to the restaurant. "What's the matter, Jack?"

Buchanan took half the drink at a gulp and shook his head as it went down. "It's Millie and me," he said. "It's over."

"Oh, come on, Jack," Will said, "not you and Millie. You've had an argument or something, but you could never leave Millie."

"It's she who's left me," Jack said. "Thrown me out. Said not to come back, ever."

"Jack, you know she can't mean that. You two have the best marriage I know."

"We did, once," Jack said. "We never will again, though." He began to cry.

Will was embarrassed. He and Jack had been co-workers for a long time, but apart from a couple of dinners at Jack and Millie's house, he hadn't known them as a couple all that well, even though he was godfather to their daughter. Glancing at his watch again, he went and sat on the arm of Jack's chair. Six-fifty-five. He was going to be late. Awkwardly, he put a hand on Jack's shoulder. "Take it easy, Jack. This isn't going to look nearly as bad tomorrow. Why don't you let me put you up here tonight? I've got to go out, but you can make yourself at home."

Jack took a deep breath and wiped his face with his sleeve, seeming to get hold of himself. "All right, Will, thanks. I guess I haven't got anyplace else to go."

Will stood up. "Come on upstairs. I'll show you where things are." He led the way up the stairs, stopping in the upper hallway at a utility closet filled with tools and other household stuff. "I'd better get you an electric blanket. The radiator hasn't been on in that room." He led Jack to a guest room at the end of the hall and switched on the light. "Sheets are clean, I think, and the bath's through there. There's a razor and some other stuff in the medicine cabinet." He spread the electric blanket on the bed and plugged it in.

"This is fine, Will. I'll try not to be in the way."

"Don't worry about it, Jack; why don't you lie down for a while, and when you're feeling better, there's food in the freezer. You know how to use a microwave?"

"Sure." Jack nodded. "I can manage." He sat down on the edge of the bed. "Will," he said, "I want to tell you about all of this. It's been going on for a long time now."

Will looked at his watch. Seven o'clock. Dammit, she'd be there by now; she was never late. "Listen, Jack, you don't feel like talking right now, and I've got to be somewhere. I won't be in until late, but we can talk in the morning. Things will look better in the morning, anyway, I promise you."

"Will . . ."

"No arguments," Will said, pushing him back onto the bed and covering him with the blanket. "You can tell me everything in the morning. You know I'll do whatever I can to help."

Jack nodded and turned onto his side, away from Will. "Good night, Will," he said. "I'll see you in the morning."

"Good night, Jack. I'll see you at breakfast." He switched off the light and ran quickly down the stairs, grabbing his coat from the hall rack. No point in arming the alarm system.

He half walked, half ran down the street toward the restaurant. He had meant to be exactly on time; he didn't want to give her any ammunition. When he arrived, she wasn't there. It was early, and the restaurant was half empty.

"How many, sir?" a waiter asked.

"Two," Will replied. "I haven't booked, I'm afraid."

"Quite all right this time of evening," the waiter said. He showed Will to a table and left him with two menus and some bread.

Will looked at his watch; seven-fifteen. She was never late. He started to get angry with her for being late. He broke a roll and buttered it. Suddenly, he was hungry. He ate half the roll, then the other half. He ordered a bottle of red wine, one she liked. At seven-thirty-five, he looked up, and she was standing there.

"Sorry I'm late," she said, shucking off her coat and handing it to the waiter.

"That's all right," he said, as evenly as he could manage. "I was late myself. Jack and Millie Buchanan have had a fight, and he turned up at the house as I was leaving. I gave him a drink and put him to bed." He poured her a glass of wine, but she didn't pick it up.

"He's the one in your office? I mean, Senator Carr's office?" She had never met any of his coworkers, but she had heard their names often enough.

"Yes, he left to come onto the campaign. He's going to be campaign manager; if I win, he'll probably be my chief staffer."

"Nice to have a staff waiting for you," she said. "How's the Senator?"

"Improving, but slowly. I get down there once a week."

"And the campaign? How's that going?"

"Hardly begun. I'd blocked off this week for the Moody trial, but the prosecutor was hospitalized. It's postponed for at least three months, which is a pain in the ass."

She nodded. "Must be tough, having to try that case in the middle of a campaign."

"I'll let you know," he said.

The waiter came over. "May I tell you about this evening's specials?" he asked.

"I won't be having dinner," Kate said to the man. She turned to Will. "I've got to be somewhere at eight."

"Give me a few minutes," Will said to the waiter. The man left, and he turned to Kate. "Looks like a few minutes is all I get from you, too," he said.

"Will, we've got to talk."

"And fast, apparently."

"I'm sorry, but I didn't expect you, and I made other plans. You can't just call from the airport and expect me to drop everything."

That was exactly what he had expected. "I suppose not," he said.

"Listen to me," she said wearily. "I'm under a lot of pressure at the moment."

"Tell me about it."

"We've got a new director, and the usual shake-up is going on. I told you, I have to sit still for a whole new security check because of the promotion; and quite apart from that, I'm under a lot of scrutiny in general. I'm the first woman to get this high in the directorate, and it's unsettled some of the old-timers."

"I didn't know there were any old-timers at the Agency anymore."

"Comparative old-timers. Simon's gone, but some of his friends haven't." Simon Rule was Kate's ex-husband, who had been forced to resign in a scandal some time back. "They're hoping I'll screw up, do you see? There's always been this problem of you and me seeing each other, what with you working for the chairman of the Senate Intelligence Committee, and right now it's worse than ever. I don't know how deep this security-clearance investigation is going; they could be tapping my phones, they could be surveilling me. I just don't know how to read it."

"If you think you might be under surveillance, then why the hell did you choose to meet me in a public place?"

"I didn't want to come to your place, and anyway, Jack Buchanan is there, isn't he?"

"Afraid I'd jump you?"

"Will, stop it."

"And they're watching your place, of course."

"I don't know. Maybe. Anyway, I've got company coming tonight." She looked at her watch. "He's . . ." She stopped.

A wave of jealousy flashed through Will. "Oh, I see, somebody the Agency approves of."

"He *is* Agency."

"Oh, that's all right, then. I'd forgotten; the Agency likes its employees to cohabitate, marry. Much cozier that way, fewer security problems."

"We're not cohabitating," she said wearily. "If you had just given me some notice, I could have arranged something, but now I've bought all these groceries, and—"

"*You're* cooking?" He had never known her to boil water. He had always done the cooking when they were together.

She flushed. "I've taken it up, sort of. It's not as bad as I'd thought."

"I'm amazed you can find the time, what with all your new responsibilities," he said. "You haven't even been able to find the time to return phone calls lately."

"I don't have to explain myself to you," she said angrily.

"You certainly don't." He waved the waiter over. "I'll have the shell steak, medium; baked potato, loaded; a Caesar salad to start. The lady is not dining; not with me, anyway." The man scribbled the order and went away. Will turned back to Kate, glancing at his watch. "I don't want to keep you."

"Will, *please* try to understand what I'm going through," she said. "I'm not sleeping with him; he's just a friend, a good friend, and I need as many of those as I can get these days."

Will stared at her for a moment, thinking how beautiful

she was—the auburn hair, the creamy skin, the full mouth. He wanted her desperately. "You don't seem to need me anymore," he said.

Kate looked down at the tablecloth, then up at him again. She started to speak, then stopped; she got up, took her coat from the nearby rack and, without another word, walked out of the restaurant.

Will drained his wineglass, refilled it, then sat staring into the wine. The waiter put his salad in front of him, but he ignored it. What was he supposed to do, resign from the Senate race? Change his name? Somehow become acceptable as an escort to a senior official of the Central Intelligence Agency? Soon, the waiter moved his untouched salad to one side and put his steak on the table.

Will made an effort to eat it, but his throat was so tight, he could barely swallow the meat without washing it down with the wine. Halfway through the meal, he asked for the check. While he was waiting for it, he finished the bottle of wine; then he paid the bill and left the restaurant.

He went out of his way to pass her house on the way home. He stopped for a moment and stared at the curtained front windows. From behind them came a dim, perhaps flickering, light; candles, he supposed. Angrily, despondently, he turned and trudged on toward his own house.

Five minutes later, he put the key into the lock and turned it. He opened the door, stepped across the threshold, then stopped and stared, wide-eyed, agape.

Jack Buchanan, a thick orange electrical extension cord noosed about his neck, was hanging in the entrance hall, his feet only inches from the floor, the other end of the cord tied to the upper stair railing.

7

The detective was bored but not unkind. Will tried to put his own problems aside and answer the man's questions as dispassionately as he could.

"How did he know where to find the extension cord?"

"I got a blanket for him from the upstairs closet. The cord was in there; he must have noticed it."

The detective nodded. "Have you notified any of his people?"

"I tried to call his wife as soon as the paramedics took over the CPR, but she hung up on me."

"Why would she do that?"

"I can only think she must have thought I was calling her on Jack's behalf, to try to mediate. He said she was very angry with him. I tried to call her back a couple of times before you arrived, but I got a busy signal. I think she left the phone off the hook."

"Did you have any indication that he was depressed enough to take his own life?"

Will shook his head. "No." He paused. "I knew he was

upset, of course, but . . . he wanted to talk about what had happened to him, but I was late for an appointment, and I sort of rushed out. Perhaps if I'd stayed and listened . . ."

"This appointment—who was it with?"

"I'd rather not bring the person into it. I don't think it's necessary."

"You let me worry about what's necessary, Mr. Lee," the detective said.

Will shook his head. "The person was entirely removed from these events. You'll just have to take my word for it."

The detective's face darkened. "All right, then, maybe you'll tell me where you were."

"I had dinner at Pied de Couchon, a few blocks from here."

"With this unnamed person?"

"I dined alone."

"Can anybody put you there?"

"The waiter, I suppose. I sat on the right as you enter. The third or fourth table, I think. I paid with a credit card." He dug into his pocket. "Here's the receipt."

The detective glanced at it and nodded. "In the time you knew him, would you say that Jack Buchanan was prone to depression?"

Will shrugged. "I don't think so. Jack was a worrier, though; he worried about things."

"What sort of things?"

"Oh, just about everything. It was one of the things that made him good at his job. He worried about it."

"Is there anything else you can think of to tell me?"

Will thought for a moment. "He seemed very tired on the flight up here; he slept a lot. I thought he had lost weight. Maybe he had been worrying more than usual. I don't know. I guess you'll have to talk with Millie, his wife."

"I'll do that," the detective replied, closing his notebook. "I'll send a patrol car out there."

"I'd rather you didn't do that," Will replied. "I'll drive out there myself when you're all through here."

The detective turned to watch the medical examiner's people carrying Jack Buchanan's body out of the house. "I think we're about done," he said.

In the patrol car, the detective was quiet, but his young partner wanted to talk.

"So, what do you make of Lee's story?" he asked.

The detective sighed. "I think it happened the way he said."

The younger man was incredulous. "You gotta be kidding, Sarge. There's more to it. I think they're gay."

"What?"

"They're queer—Lee and Buchanan. The wife found out about it, threw him out of the house. Won't talk to Lee."

"You got an overactive imagination gland," the detective said. "I been listening to people's stories for a long time. I can tell when they're lying, covering up something. This guy Lee is covering up something, but not much. He was calm, he wasn't nervous, his eyes weren't moving all around, he was breathing slow. He wasn't scared, either. He was sad, not scared. He was telling the truth."

"I don't buy it," the partner said. "There's more to it."

The detective, who was driving, pulled over to the curb.

"Why're you stopping?" the partner asked.

The detective nodded. "The restaurant," he said. "Third or fourth table on the right. You go question the waiter."

"Okay," the partner said, getting out of the car.

The detective sat and waited the five minutes it took for the waiter to be questioned, then looked at his partner as he got back into the car.

"Well . . ." the partner began.

"Let me tell you," the detective said. "He got here when he said he did; he met a woman; they argued; she left and he had dinner alone, left when he said he did. Am I right?"

"How'd you know about the woman?" the partner asked.

"Because he wouldn't say who he was with. Listen, kid, don't you go mouthing off to any of your reporter buddies about this. Lee works for Ben Carr, and he's got a good reputation on the Hill; I heard about him. Buchanan worked for Carr, too, and only good people work for Carr. I don't want the papers and the TV people making more out of this than it is."

"So why wouldn't he give us the woman's name?"

"In addition to being young, you're dumb," the detective said. "It's not too tough to add up. The woman is married."

Will switched off the Porsche's engine and sat in front of the house in Bethesda. He hadn't been nervous about talking to the police, but he was afraid of talking to Millie Buchanan. Finally he took a deep breath, got out of the car, and walked to the front door. A light came on down-stairs; she had been in bed.

The door opened, and she was there, tying a robe around her. "Now, Will," she said. "I know why you're here, and I don't want to talk to you right now. This is none of your business."

Will looked at her—small, pert, a little disheveled from the bed. He had picked out birthday presents for her chil-dren; he had eaten her cooking, and she had eaten his. Her life was about to change forever. "Oh, Jesus, Millie," he said.

8

The funeral was a quiet nightmare. The little church in Bethesda was full, half by staffers from Benjamin Carr's office, half by friends, Will reckoned. Jack Buchanan had been a popular man. His coffin stood before the altar as his widow stared straight ahead of her, not weeping, not blinking.

After the service, when Will approached Millie Buchanan and bent to kiss her on the cheek, she shrank from him. Her mother and father, who were standing next to her, looked away.

Kitty Conroy, who had flown up from Atlanta for the service, approached Will while he was still surprised by Millie's reaction. Her eyes were red. "What happened, Will?" she asked, trying not to cry. Other Carr staffers crowded around to hear his answer.

Will gave them a blow-by-blow of the events of two nights before, and they wandered away, except Kitty.

"Will, I've got to put out some sort of statement to the press in Atlanta." She cocked her head. "Are you sure you've told me absolutely everything? I wouldn't want this to blow up on us later."

Will looked at her, puzzled. "That's everything, Kitty," he said. "What did you think I might be holding back?"

"It's not that," she said uncomfortably. "It's just that this sort of thing can take on a life of its own, if it's not handled absolutely frankly."

"You mean you think this might be some sort of Chappaquiddick?"

"I certainly wouldn't want to see that happen," Kitty said.

Will put his arm around her and walked her toward her car. "Kitty, love, you now know everything about this that I do. I've told you exactly what happened." Everything but Millie Buchanan's behavior that night. "Now I'd appreciate it if you would put together a press conference in Atlanta for tomorrow. I'll make a statement, say how shocked and sad we all are and how much we valued Jack."

Kitty shook her head. "I don't think a press conference is the right thing to do; it's too much, in the circumstances. I'd rather just do a release saying what happened. Then you can be available around the office on an informal basis if anybody has any further questions, as they surely will."

"Maybe you're right," Will said, opening her car door. "Go ahead and do it that way. If you'd like a ride back to Atlanta, come by the house in about an hour and you can ride out to the airport with me."

"Okay." Kitty looked at the ground. "I feel like a shit for bringing this up, but have you thought about who you want to replace Jack on the campaign?"

Will shook his head. "I don't have a clue at this point."

A voice behind Will interrupted their conversation. "Mind if I make a suggestion?"

Will turned to find Tom Black standing behind him. Instantly, the scene in Hank Taylor's office popped into his mind. He didn't reply.

"I left Taylor last week," Black said. "You didn't really think I'd have anything to do with that crap he presented, do you?"

"Didn't you?" Will asked, wary.

"If you have to be told, I didn't," Black said. "We had a discussion about it, to put it mildly. He said he was going to show the stuff to you whether I liked it or not; I told him to go fuck himself, and then I took a hike. That's it."

Will managed a grin. "I should have known better than to think you'd have anything to do with that stuff. I apologize."

"No apology necessary. Now, about my suggestion: I think you should sign me on to replace Jack Buchanan."

Will looked carefully at the younger man. "I don't think you could afford the salary cut," he said.

"I'm not worried about the money," Black said. "Pay me whatever you were paying Buchanan. And I'll be right up front with you, Will; I'm not looking for a ticket to a Senate staff job. What I want to do is get you elected, take as much of the credit as I possibly can, then start my own political consultancy."

Will laughed. "That's candid, I guess. So, if I get elected, who's going to run my office?"

"I'll find you somebody who's cut out for administration and fighting legislative battles. Me, I'm cut out for late nights and high drama on the campaign trail."

Will turned to Kitty. "Well, I guess that answers your question."

"It's okay by me." Kitty grinned.

Will turned back to Tom Black. "You better pack your bags and meet me at College Park Airport in a couple of hours."

Tom snapped off a salute and walked away.

"Will?" Kitty said.

"Yeah?"

"What was that business with Millie Buchanan a few minutes ago?"

Will looked back to where Millie and her parents were still receiving mourners. "I don't know," he said. "I guess she's just upset."

"I hope that's all it is," Kitty said.

On the flight back to Atlanta, everyone wore headsets, and they talked on the intercom.

"How much money you got in the bank?" Tom Black asked.

"I'm embarrassed to tell you I don't know," Will replied. "That was Jack's department."

Kitty ripped a sheet of paper off a yellow legal pad and handed it to Tom. "How's that for the press release?" she asked.

Tom read it over quickly. "Good," he said. "I think you're right about not holding a press conference," Tom said. "We don't want him staring into a white light and expressing his grief on the tube. The statement does it best."

"I want reporters to be able to talk to him informally," she replied.

"Okay, if you think so."

Will piped up, "Anybody care what I think around here?"

"Not much, pal," Tom said. "You're just the candidate. Kitty and I will do the thinking; you just smile a lot."

"I think I like it that way," Will laughed.

Kitty got the press release hand-delivered in time for the eleven-o'clock news and the morning papers. Will had three or four phone calls from reporters, mostly to express sympathy. They watched the eleven-o'clock news on all three local channels. Jack Buchanan's suicide was treated respectfully.

Will stood up and stretched. "I'm turning in," he said, heading for the small bedroom set up in the back of the Atlanta headquarters. "What about it, Kitty? You happy with the way it went?"

"Couldn't have been better," she said.

"I agree," said Tom.

"Good," Will said. "Tom, there's a cot upstairs somewhere. We'll find you a place to stay tomorrow."

At the Georgetown police station, a young detective walked up to his older partner's desk and dropped a sheet of paper on it. "I told you so," he crowed.

The older detective looked at the document. "Oh, shit," he said.

9

They forded the river about two miles from the main highway. The jeep went in up to the doorsills and Harold Perkerson thought for a moment they were going to get wet. The woman drove surely and quickly up what was now little more than a track. Nothing but an off-road vehicle would have made it, he thought. Another mile along, they came to a gate. She took a remote-control box from the glove compartment and pointed it; the gate creaked noisily out of their way and closed again when they were through. Another half a mile passed before the cabin came into view up a steep rise.

It was perfect, Perkerson thought. Good field of fire.

"Okay, sport," the woman said, "you're here." She grabbed one of his bags and led the way to the front porch, unfastening the two padlocks that secured the door. "You want to be careful right here," she said, easing the door open a couple of inches and reaching in to unfasten something. She swung the door open and showed him the hook and wire, then the sawed-off, double-barreled shotgun at the other end of the wire, pointed at the door. "The Archon doesn't like smart-asses." She grinned. She flipped a switch by the door and lights came on in the cabin.

"Where's the power come from?" Perkerson asked. "I didn't see any wires."

"There's a water-driven generator in the creek, a couple hundred yards back up in the woods; it tops up a bank of batteries in the cellar. There's two years' worth of food down there, too." She handed him a clump of keys. "Weapons and ammunition, the works. Be sure and keep a list of every single thing you eat," she said. "I'll replace it when you're gone."

"It's a survivalist's dream," Perkerson said admiringly.

"Damn right," the woman said. "Now, you sit down over there; I want to change your bandages." She went back to the jeep and returned with a medical bag, then scrubbed her hands at the kitchen sink.

Perkerson thought he looked a little like Claude Rains in *The Invisible Man*. The bandage across his nose joined with the turban enclosing his ears, and the dark glasses made him look as if there were nothing behind them. "Are you a doctor, or something?" he asked, as she laid out bandages and scissors.

"Something, I guess; I'm a nurse/anesthetist. I passed the gas during your surgery, but you were still pretty groggy when we left the doctor's. Don't worry, the doctor has already checked on the results of the surgery. All we're concerned about now is secondary infection." She snipped at the bandages, then unwound the gauze from his head. "Oh, boy," she laughed, "you've got a couple of great shiners there. You look like a raccoon!"

"Thanks," Perkerson said dryly.

"Don't worry, sport," she said, "you're looking real good. A lot of the swelling has gone and . . . uh-oh, here's the start of some infection." She swabbed the area with something and took a bottle from her bag. "I want you to start on antibiotics today. Take two, then one after every meal. Use up the whole bottle, okay?"

"Okay," Perkerson said. "Can I look at myself?"

"Oh, you don't want to do that yet," she said. "A few days and the shiners and the swelling will be gone, and then—boy, you're going to look great. The nose has a nice shape. Now, let's get some fresh bandages on."

She began winding gauze around his head, and as she did, her breasts brushed his face. She was a big girl, Perkerson thought, five-eight or -nine and not skinny. He felt himself stirring.

"There you go," she said. "Now let's get some tape across that nose. Don't want the cartilage moving around before it heals." She held his head in her hands and had a good look at him. "Those are the handsomest bandages I ever saw," she said. "And you're not so bad yourself."

"Neither are you," he said, putting his hands on her hips and pulling her toward him.

"Hey, tiger," she purred. "Plenty of time for that later. We don't want to mess up the doctor's good work, do we?" She put her hands on his shoulders and rubbed.

"How long do I have to wait?" he said. He was breathing rapidly.

"Tell you what," she said, pushing him back onto the bed. "I don't guess it can do any harm if you just lie there and enjoy yourself for a little bit." She knelt between his legs and swiftly unbuckled his belt and undid the zipper.

Perkerson drew in air as she took him into her mouth. "Oh, God," he moaned.

"It's been a long time, hasn't it, tiger?" she asked, pausing from her work, then returning to it.

"Too long, too long," Perkerson said, then gave all of himself to her.

When he woke, the lights were off, and it was dark outside. There was the noise of one stone striking another, and Perkerson was on his feet immediately. He unzipped his bag and came up with the automatic pistol the Archon had given him, then crept to the door, which was open. The moon was up, and he saw, standing ten yards away, chewing on a sapling, a large buck deer. His hunter's instinct made him want to kill it, but the sight was too beautiful. He stood silently and watched for a few moments, then the wind changed, and the buck caught his scent. The big deer raised his head, sniffed, and listened for a moment, then moved off down the mountainside toward the trees.

Perkerson went back into the cabin and sought the bed in the darkness. The painkillers the doctor had given him had worn off; he sat on the bed and rummaged in his bag for more. Then he lay back on the bed and tried to turn off the wariness he had felt for the past days of being hunted. He was safe here; he had food, shelter, weapons, and—most important—a woman. When he had healed a little more, he was going to screw the socks off her. He let the pistol slip from his fingers and fall to the rug beside the bed; then he closed his eyes and drifted with the morphia.

Pretty soon, he would be himself—no—better than himself, because he wouldn't match the pictures in the papers anymore. He'd go among them again, hunt them down, the queers and pornographers and liberals. He sighed and dreamed of The Day.

10

Will slept late on Sunday morning, allowing himself to wake only when he heard the thump of the Sunday newspaper on the front porch of the cottage. He got out of bed slowly, stretching and yawning, and it was a moment before the dread came to him—the memory of Jack's death. He took a few deep breaths and tried to banish the thought, to enjoy, instead, the comfort of a Sunday morning at home on the farm.

He went to the kitchen and spooned the strong Italian coffee he loved into the maker and switched it on. While the coffee brewed, he scrambled eggs and toasted English muffins; then he put everything on a tray, took it to the bedroom, and settled down to breakfast and the newspaper. There was nothing more in the news section of Jack Buchanan's death, but there was a moderately long obituary, detailing Jack's education and service on congressional staffs. He read it carefully, learning nothing new about his friend, then went through the travel and arts sections before picking up the Sunday magazine. To his surprise, his photograph was on the cover, walking along the lake with the dog. He had forgotten the interview he had given the magazine's new editor, Ann Heath. He found the article inside and began to read.

This November, if the Georgia electorate decides to take a new course and choose a man not from the traditional core of the Democratic party, like Governor Mack Dean, then its other choice will be a young man very unlike those usually found on Southern slates of candidates.

Not bad, Will thought.

Born to wealth and position, political heir to a father who was a controversial governor, and now attempting to inherit the power of a great senator who gave him his most recent job, Will Lee is conventionally handsome, conventionally charming, conventional in just about everything, it seems, except his personal life.

Now, what the hell does she mean by that? Will asked himself. The phone rang, and he picked it up. "Hello?"

"Will, it's Tom Black. Have you read it?"

"I've just started to," Will replied. "What do you think she means by the second paragraph?"

"Forget the second paragraph; turn to page fifteen, about halfway down."

Will fumbled with the newspaper while cradling the phone between shoulder and head. "Where?"

"Dead center on the page. It begins, 'His social life . . .'"

Will found it.

His social life, if he has one, is another matter entirely. For, to the best memory of anyone who knows him that this reporter has been able to contact, Will Lee has not been seen in any social situation with a woman in years. Since there is no clear, substantiated evidence of proclivities to the contrary, it seems that Georgia is considering electing a man who might be the first United States Senator who has never lost his virginity to anyone of any sexual orientation.

"Jesus H. Christ," Will said.

"I shouldn't have barged in on the two of you," Tom said. "I should have let you fuck her."

"Christ, maybe I should have," Will said. "I'm stunned. I can't believe that anybody would write something like this, or that anybody would publish it."

"Welcome to politics," Tom said.

"Tom, I want you to hand-deliver a letter demanding a retraction, and if we don't get it within twenty-four hours, we'll sue for libel."

"Easy there, Will, easy. I know you're upset, but we have to consider some things before we go off half-cocked."

"What things? I want her scalp. I want to raise such a stink that the paper will pack her off back to Washington."

"First of all," Tom said, "I want to ask you a blunt question. Are you now or have you ever been a homosexual?"

Will paused and took a deep breath. "I don't have to answer that question to you or anybody else."

Tom paused, too. "Of course you don't, but nevertheless, I wish you'd given me a blunt answer."

"All right, I am not now nor have I ever been a homosexual. Is that good enough for you?"

"It would have been ten seconds ago," Tom said.

"What does that mean, Tom?" Will demanded, starting to get angry.

"It means that the proper answer to that question or any other like it is a prompt and visceral *no*!" He paused again. "And you hesitated."

"It's not a question that deserves an answer, Tom. I answered you because you're running my campaign, and you have a right to know. I won't ever answer it again—to you, the press, or anybody else. Is that clear?"

"All right, Will. For what it's worth, I believe you; I want you to know that. You're right, of course. It isn't a civilized question, but getting elected to the Senate is not always a civilized process."

"I think I'm beginning to understand that," Will said, cooling a little.

"Of course, she hasn't exactly called you queer," Tom said, and his voice contained ill-concealed amusement. "She's left the door open to an alternative; you may simply be a neuter. That way, we don't even get the gay vote."

Will burst out laughing, in spite of himself.

"All right, let me handle this," Tom said. "I'll ask for a meeting with the editor of the paper, in confidence, tomorrow morning, and I'll demand that he discipline his new Sunday magazine editor. I doubt if the man has even read the piece, and he'll probably be pretty annoyed when he does."

"Don't you think we should make some sort of public statement on this?" Will asked.

"That's the last thing we should do at the moment," Tom said. "This may blow right over, who knows? If it doesn't, I'll handle that, too. You don't mind if *I* tell people you're not queer, do you?"

"Feel free."

"Listen, I don't suppose you've got some old girlfriend who'd like to go out on the campaign trail with you for a few days and hold your hand in public now and then?"

"Nope."

Tom was quiet for a moment. "*I've* got an old girlfriend who'd do it. You might even like her."

"Tom, get stuffed."

"All right, it was a bad idea. Now put down that magazine and read 'The Week in Review' or something. We'll talk again tomorrow."

Will hung up and tried to do as Tom suggested, but his anger kept boiling up. The bitch; she'd practically offered herself to him on a platter. A woman scorned, he guessed, but then, he hadn't even had time to scorn her before Tom had interrupted their conversation. Still, as he remembered, he may have been walking backward at the time.

He cleaned up the dishes and got dressed. He didn't feel like reading the papers anymore; he felt like a walk. He was about to leave the cottage when the telephone rang again. Probably Tom with another idea on how to handle the situation. He picked up the telephone. "Hello?"

"Will Lee?"

"Speaking."

"This is Bill Mott with the Associated Press. I assume you've heard about Jack Buchanan; I just wanted a comment."

"Of course I've heard about it," Will said, annoyed. "I found him. Didn't you know that? You'd better start reading your own dispatches."

"I guess you haven't heard," Mott said. "There's a story in this morning's *Washington Times* that Jack Buchanan had been arrested in 1982 in a Georgetown gay bar when he propositioned a vice cop. Do you have any comment?"

"I don't believe it!" Will blurted. He turned away from the phone and took several deep breaths.

"The paper published a copy of the arrest report, with photograph attached. Did Jack Buchanan have a security clearance?"

"Of course," Will said absently, trying to absorb this news. "All the senior staff people had clearances because of Senator Carr's chairmanship of the Senate Intelligence Committee."

"Do you have any idea why this didn't turn up during the FBI investigation of his background for the clearance?"

"No, I don't. As I say, it's news to me, and I'm sure that neither Senator Carr nor anyone else in the office knew about it."

"Well, I guess the FBI is getting sloppy."

"I still find this impossible to believe," Will said. "What was the disposition of the case? Did the story say?"

"He pleaded guilty, and as a first offender, he got off

with a thirty-day sentence, suspended. He was lucky somebody didn't spot him in the courtroom, I guess."

"I still can't believe it," Will said.

"Mr. Lee, did you ever have any indication at all that Jack Buchanan might have been a homosexual?"

"None whatever. He was happily . . . he was married and had two children."

"Do you think his homosexuality might have led to the domestic difficulties he told you about when he turned up at your house the night he died?"

"I have no idea about that," Will said. "He never told me the nature of his problems with his wife. Until that night, I thought they were very happily married. Now, if you'll excuse me, I was just on the way out of the house."

He put the phone down, and it rang immediately.

"It's Tom. I've got more bad news."

"I've heard. The AP just called."

"What did you tell them?"

Will related his conversation with the wire-service reporter.

"I hope you sounded flabbergasted."

"I think I must have; I certainly was."

"Kitty Conroy knew," Tom said.

"*What?*"

"Now, don't blame Kitty, Will. Jack told her about it when he was arrested but swore her to secrecy. She was only keeping her promise to him."

"Christ, what a day!"

"Will?"

"Yeah?"

"It's time to get uncivilized again. Why haven't you been seen socially with a woman in years?"

Will nearly didn't answer. "Because I've been seeing only one woman during that time, and we don't go out together in public."

"Oh, shit," Tom said, "a married woman." He brightened. "Still, that's better than no woman at all. How big a flap will it cause if her name comes out?"

"Her name isn't going to come out."

"Now look, Will, you're in serious trouble here."

"And she's not married. It's just that . . . for reasons I can't go into, we can't . . . we couldn't be identified with each other."

"Why not?"

"I told you, I can't go into that."

Tom Black drew in a deep breath, obviously trying to keep his temper. "All right, I think you'd better come to Atlanta today. We've got to agree on a way to deal with this."

"All right. I'll leave right after lunch. I want to have lunch with my folks."

"I'll see you later in the afternoon at headquarters, then." Tom hung up.

Will sat slumped for a moment; then he did what he knew he had to do sooner or later. He got his address book and looked up Jack Buchanan's home number.

Millie Buchanan answered the phone.

"Millie, it's Will. The AP just called me about the story."

"You bastard," she said.

"I don't know what I've done to deserve that," Will said. "I didn't know about Jack's arrest. I didn't have the slightest idea that he . . . had some sort of problem."

"Well, I knew about it, and I don't see how you couldn't have known it," Millie said hotly.

"He never gave the slightest indication," Will said. "How do you think I could have known?"

"Look, Will, I know you want to get elected, but you don't have to pull this with me. I know too much."

"Millie, what on earth are you talking about? You can't think that Jack and I were . . . involved, can you?"

"Can't I?"

Will was speechless.

"Don't worry, I'm not going to say anything to the press," she said.

"Say anything? What would you say? That's complete nonsense, and you know it."

"I *don't* know it," Millie said. "All I know is that less than a year after we were married, Jack told me."

"Told you what? There was nothing to tell!"

"That he was in love with you."

"What?" he yelled at her, but she had already hung up.

11

Mickey Keane had been a burglar during his teens, in a small way. He had broken into a dozen houses—neighbors, people in the surrounding homes. He had never stolen anything of real value, just some small souvenir of each place—a Zippo lighter, a cheap manicure kit, a girl's panties, once—to prove to himself that he'd been there, that he'd done it. It had always been a thrill, and he had never been caught. The need to do it had passed.

Now the need had come again. He crouched at the back door of the shop and worked quickly with the picklocks he always carried. A snitch of his, an old con, had taught him how. Only the fancy stuff could stump him. The lock, a cheap Yale, yielded after less than a minute. He opened the door gingerly, in case there was an alarm he hadn't found. There was no noise; he let himself in, left the door ajar.

His masked flashlight played over the small offset press, the copying machine, and the other paraphernalia. He knew what he wanted; he had seen it when they had pulled the raid. Thumbtacked to a small bulletin board was a typed list of the names of the boxholders. He took it to the copying machine and quickly made copies of all four pages, then tacked it to the bulletin board again, careful to use the same holes in the paper. He stuffed the copies into a pocket and walked into the small office off the printing room. He started with the desk drawers; only one was locked, and he picked that in no time.

The most interesting thing was a photograph of a girl in a bikini. Short, plump, but fairly sexy, Mickey thought. There was a picture on the desk of a woman and two small children. The guy had a girlfriend; that was why the drawer was locked. There was nothing else in it. He turned to the filing cabinets, which weren't locked. Invoices, copies of dunning letters, nothing of interest. He tried another drawer. There must be applications for the boxes somewhere, at least a record of the boxholders' actual addresses. But there wasn't. He closed the filing cabinet and turned toward the door. He had just entered the printing room again when the flashlight hit him.

"Freeze! Police!"

Mickey shot his hands into the air. "Okay, okay, it's all right, I'm on the job!"

"Shut your mouth; up against the wall!" The voice was very young. "Turn that light on, Bob." The light went on, but by this time, Mickey was leaning on the wall, his legs spread; hands were patting him down.

"He's carrying," said another voice. "We got a live one, Hal."

"Yeah, yeah," Mickey said, still careful not to move. "Just check the wallet, left-hand hip pocket."

A hand removed the wallet. "Jesus, he's Atlanta PD," the younger voice said.

"I'm going to turn around, real slow," Mickey said. "For Jesus' sake, don't shoot me, okay?" Without waiting for a reply, he pushed away from the wall, and, holding his hands protectively in front of him, he turned around to face his apprehenders. "There was a silent alarm, right?"

"Right," the younger of the two uniformed East Point policemen said. The older one wasn't older by much.

"You're Hal, right? And you're Bob?"

Bob, the older one, looked at him. "So, what are you doing in here, Keane?" he asked, looking at Mickey's ID.

"You remember the cop got killed a little while back? Down in Meriwether County? Booby-trapped house?"

"Yeah, I heard about it."

"Well, I'm his partner."

"So?"

"So, there's a connection with this place."

"What kind of connection?"

"The guy who owned the house had a box here."

The younger cop, Hal, interrupted. "I don't much care what it's connected to. You're breaking and entering, pal, and if you're a cop, well, that makes it all the worse. You're under arrest. You have the right to remain silent—"

"Jesus Christ, man," Mickey said. "You're not arresting another cop, are you? Don't you know anything? How long you been on the job?"

"What's that got to do with anything?" Hal said, reddening.

Bob spoke up. "Listen, Hal, let's be sure we're doing the right thing here. The guy's a cop, after all."

"Bullshit," Hal said. "I don't buy that shit at all. He's in here where he shouldn't be, and that's it as far as I'm concerned. We let him go, we're accessories to a B&E, right?"

Keane felt the situation slipping away from him. He turned to the older cop. "Listen, Bob, you've been on the force awhile, right? You know that no cop would ever bust another cop. Now talk some sense to this kid." As he said it, Keane knew, too late, that he should never have called the younger cop a kid.

Hal's face was set hard now. "That's it, up against the wall," he said, spinning Keane around and shoving him into the position. He snapped handcuffs onto Keane's wrists. "You have the right to remain silent; you have the right to—"

"Shove it up your ass, kid," Keane said. "I know the drill."

Keane stood uncomfortably before his captain's desk.

"I'm sorry I couldn't get you out sooner," the captain said. "The cop was within his rights. Even his commander tried to get him to change his mind, but he stuck to his position."

"Thanks, Captain," Keane said, unable to keep the sarcasm from his voice. "I enjoy a night in the tank every now and then."

The captain regarded him somberly. "Your tit's in the wringer, Keane, don't you know that? What the hell do you mean going off on your own like that, breaking and entering? We've got a homicide squad here that investigates murders; we're investigating this one."

"Well, you're getting nowhere fast, aren't you?" Keane

snapped back. "If you'd put me on it, where I belong, maybe I could come up with something."

"You don't get it, do you, Keane? I'm not putting you back on homicide. I'm not even transferring you to traffic. You're finished around here, don't you understand?"

Keane jerked involuntarily. "Finished? You mean you're kicking me off?"

"Keane, you've never been anything around here but a pain in the ass. First, there was the drinking—"

"Listen, Captain, I've got a better record of busts than ninety percent of the guys in the department—"

"You were doing okay with Chuck; he was keeping you straight, but now—you're just hell-bent on flushing yourself down the toilet."

"You're recommending me for involuntary discharge, then? I thought this department took care of its own."

"We do, Keane, we do. But when you go out into another jurisdiction and commit a felony, what the hell can we do? East Point won't play ball, or at least this young cop won't, so what the hell can I do?" He sat back in his chair. "No, I won't make that recommendation, but it doesn't make any difference. In a few weeks, you'll come to trial on this charge, and you'll fall. You'll get a suspended sentence, sure, but you'll be a convicted felon, and that boots you right off the force automatically. You won't even get a hearing."

Keane could not bring himself to speak, could not believe what was happening to him.

"Listen, Mickey, here's the only way out for you. You retire from the force and go quietly. The kid's commander tells me he won't press it if you take out papers."

"Papers, what papers? I'm two years and two months short of a pension. I won't have nothing, and I won't be a cop anymore, either," Keane said.

"You'll be a retired cop instead of a fired one, and you won't be in jail, either. Anyway, you stopped being a cop when you picked that lock," the captain said. He reached into his desk drawer, pulled out a folder, placed it on his desk, opened it, and spun it around. He pulled a pen from his pocket and placed it on the stack of papers. "There's three places to sign," he said. "I marked them."

Keane stared at the man. What were they doing to him? He had seen commanders get cops out of worse scrapes than this. The captain wanted to be rid of him; that was it. He picked up the pen, signed the documents, then placed his gun and his badge on the captain's desk.

"You need any money, Mickey?" the captain asked.

"Not from you, I don't," Keane spat. He turned on his heel and walked out of the captain's office, out of the precinct.

12

"You might have told me, Kitty," Will said. He sat on the edge of his desk in the Atlanta campaign headquarters and dangled his feet.

Kitty looked miserable. "I promised Jack I wouldn't," she said.

"It wouldn't have changed anything, would it?" Tom Black asked. "I mean, when Jack showed up at your house, you wouldn't have kicked him out, would you?"

"No," Will sighed, "I wouldn't have done that. I'm sorry, Kitty, this isn't your fault in any way. I'm just feeling sorry for myself." He turned to Tom. "All right, what's next? A statement to the press?"

"What sort of statement?" Tom asked.

"That I'm out of the race."

Tom laughed aloud. "You really are feeling sorry for yourself, aren't you?"

"You mean you think I still have a chance?"

"I didn't say that. But what's the alternative? You drop

out, and you're queer, right? And what the hell are you
going to do with yourself? Practice law in Delano?"

"I could get another Senate staff job," Will said.

"Get serious," Tom shot back. He tossed a copy of the
Washington Times at Will. "It says there that there are 'reports' of a ring of homosexuals operating among Senate
staffers. You drop out of the race, and you're the chairman
of their board. Who'd hire you? People on the Hill would
fall all over themselves getting away from you."

"I see your point," Will said.

"Anyway, I like a challenge. It was too easy before; you
were a shoo-in. Now there's work for me to do."

Will laughed. "Okay, where do we start?"

"We've been working on your schedule," Tom said,
handing him some papers. "You start at the Atlanta Rotary
Club at lunch today; then you hit the shopping malls in
the afternoon. I want you on Atlanta TV tonight charming
housewives right out of their socks. I think given our press
over the weekend, we'll make all three channels. Tomorrow, we head for south Georgia. We've got three fund-
raisers, in Thomasville, Waycross, and Savannah, later on
in the week, and half a dozen speaking engagements in
small towns."

"I sound pretty busy," Will mused.

"You are, as of this moment," Tom said. "Let's get
started. I've written you a stump speech." He handed over
more papers. "There are three main points: a strong defense, education, and family values."

"Not Mom and apple pie?" Will asked.

"Oh, we'll get around to that," Tom said. "And listen
to me. This is important: Every time you meet a woman

from now on in this campaign—I don't care if she's eight or eighty, beautiful or ugly—I want you to gaze into her eyes and squeeze her hand. I want five seconds of seduction for every one of them, okay?"

"I'll do my best," Will said.

"Do you like women, Will?"

"Sure I do."

"Then it won't be such a chore, will it?"

They hit the road at sunup the next morning. By noon, Will had given the stump speech three times, and he knew the words by heart. He marveled at the advance work that Tom's people had done. In every town they hit, there was a stand of some sort, with a public address system, a Dixieland band, and a small crowd, getting bigger. In every town, there was a white leader and a black leader to shake hands and be photographed with.

Will paid particular attention to the women, and they responded. By late afternoon, what had begun as a tactic was second nature to him. He kissed cheeks, hugged, and grinned into a hundred Instamatics.

That night, in a motel somewhere south of Macon, Will sat on the bed and massaged his feet. "You were right about the wingtips," he said to Tom. "This is no territory for Gucci loafers."

Tom laughed. "I'm nearly always right. Better start getting used to it."

Will lay back on the bed and sighed. "My face hurts from smiling. What time is it?"

"Just after ten. Sorry about the food at the Kiwanis meeting, but we couldn't pass it up."

"Don't worry, I didn't eat much of it," Will murmured. He was drifting off.

"All right, up and at 'em," Tom cried, pulling him upright. "We've got to get a steak inside you. You can't campaign and diet at the same time."

"Have mercy," Will moaned. "I want to sleep."

"We've got to get you on a schedule," Tom said. "You go to sleep too early, you'll wake up too early. And you've got to eat. Come on."

Will trudged into the motel restaurant behind Tom and Kitty. As they slid into a booth, a blowsy-looking woman at the bar raised her glass to him. Will waved and started to sit down.

"Will . . ." Tom said reprovingly.

Will groaned, got up, and went over to the bar. "Hello, how are you?" he asked, smiling broadly. "I'm Will Lee. I sure need your support in the Democratic primary."

On Saturday night, in Savannah, Will stood in a private dining room at a local country club and asked for questions from people he hoped would give him money. They came to the point quickly.

"We've been reading some funny stuff about you in the papers," a man said. "What's going on, Will?"

"Mr. Partain," Will said, glancing fleetingly at the man's name tag, "I'm a great believer in a free press. But I don't have to believe everything I read in the papers. Neither do you."

There was laughter, and Will thought he was over that hurdle, but then a man at one side of the room stood up.

"Mr. Lee, let's get this right out in the open," he said, and his accent was sharp. "Are you a homosexual?"

Will looked at the man for a moment; he didn't bother with the name tag. "Where were you born?" he asked. This was dirty, but it was a dirty question.

"Ohio," the man said, a little too boldly. "I've been down here for two years."

"Then," Will said, "you've been down here long enough to know that, in Georgia, a man doesn't ask another man that kind of question"—he paused—"unless he *really* wants to know."

There was a mixture of laughter and applause; a Yankee had got himself nailed by a home boy.

At a table near the rear of the room, a woman leaned over to her female friend. "You know something?" she whispered loudly. "There ain't *nothing* queer about that boy."

Tom Black, who was standing nearby, allowed himself a large grin.

13

Mickey Keane looked up at the girl's crotch. Funny, he thought, it was the only part of her that had any clothes on it, and it was the only part he wanted to see. He tucked a five-dollar bill into her G-string and hoped for the best. She squatted in front of him and made the money in the G-string move around, but her crotch remained covered. Then, having given him something less than his five bucks' worth, she moved on down the bar. Keane waved at the barman. "Gimme another Johnny Walker Black," he shouted over the din of the music and the screaming customers.

"Why don't you let me buy that one for you?" a familiar voice behind him asked.

Keane turned around to find Manny Pearl leaning on an aluminum crutch. "Hey, Mr. Pearl, how are you?" he yelled. He liked Manny Pearl, and he was glad to see him.

"Call me Manny," Pearl said, "and come on back to my office." He waved the bartender over and took the bottle of Scotch from him. "Follow me," he said to Keane.

In his office, Manny waved Keane to a huge sofa, then stumped around his desk and settled into a large chair. "I read it in the papers," he said. "I was sorry to hear about it."

"Thanks," Keane said, pouring himself a shot from the bottle.

"What the hell is going on down there, anyway?" Manny demanded. "Letting good officers like you leave the force."

"I don't know what's going on down there," Keane replied, downing the whiskey, "but I'd sure like to know. Nothing has gone right since we identified the Perkerson guy. People just seemed to draw away from Chuck and me, you know?"

Manny looked solemn. "Pittman was a fine detective," he said. "I felt like I lost a son when he was killed."

"I shouldn't a let him go in that house by himself," Keane murmured, pouring another shot.

"So, you should have died with him? Is that what you're telling me?" Manny shook his head. "That's dumb. It wasn't your fault. Tell me, did this burglary thing have something to do with Pittman?"

Keane told him about the raid on the shop and his reasons for breaking in.

Manny nodded. "I figured. Listen, don't take that drink, okay? I want to talk to you, and I want you to understand me."

Keane paused with the glass at his lips, then put it on the desk. "Okay," he said, "I'm all ears."

"What are doing for a living?" Manny asked.

"Drinking," Keane replied.

"I thought so. I want you to do me a favor."

"Sure."

"I want you to stand up, take that shot of whiskey, and pour it back in the bottle."

Keane stood up, steadied himself against the desk, and poured the Scotch into the bottle, not spilling a drop.

"That's the first thing," Manny said. "The next thing is, I don't want you to take it out again."

"Huh?"

"Listen, Michael—can I call you that?"

"Call me Mickey."

"Mickey, I been in this business long enough to know when a fellow doesn't have no business drinking whiskey."

"Yeah?"

"Yeah. Have you got enough guts to give it up?"

"For what?"

"For me. I want you to come to work for me. But I want you sober."

Keane shook his head. "Thanks, Mr. Pearl, I appreciate the thought, but I'd make a lousy bouncer."

"I don't want you for bouncing."

"I'd make a lousy bartender, too."

"Not that, either."

"What, then?"

"I want you to go find this fellow Perkerson. For me." Keane sat up straight.

"It looks like, to me, the police department isn't too interested."

"It looks that way to me, too," Keane said.

"I will pay you one thousand dollars a week to find him."

"And kill him?"

"No, that would make me no better than him. You, too. I want you to arrest him and put him in jail. Please don't misunderstand me: I don't want you to put yourself in danger. I got reason to know how dangerous a man he is, and if you have to kill him to protect yourself, I would understand. Just like you were still a policeman. Nobody expects you to die."

"And just why do you think I can find Perkerson when the whole department can't?"

"Because you've got motivation, my boy. It's important, motivation—in business, in everything. You *want* Perkerson. So do I."

"You understand, I don't have access to the homicide bureau anymore, to computers and all that."

Manny smiled. "You'll get what you need. I'm not worried. That's what you were doing in that printing shop." He held up a finger. "Just don't get arrested anymore. And when you catch Perkerson, I'll give you fifty thousand dollars more."

"That's very generous, Mr. Pearl, especially when you know I want him bad anyway."

"Manny. And it's not so generous. You've got to live, like everybody else. Another thing: I'm going to offer a hundred-thousand-dollar reward. I'll run an ad in the paper. That should get you a few clues, yes?"

"That should," Keane agreed. "It might also make it easier to get a little help from inside the department. If somebody in there helps me nail Perkerson, you'll take my word? He'll get the reward?"

"I'll slice it any way you say," Manny said. "Now, you didn't answer my question—about the whiskey."

"I'm off it as of right now," Keane said.

"Good. Tell me, you have a few debts, you're behind on a few payments, maybe?"

"You're a good judge of character, Mr. Pearl."

Manny shrugged. "Manny. Don't call me Mr. Pearl no more. Even my girls call me Manny."

"Manny."

Manny went to his safe, opened it, and took out a steel box. "Here's five thousand," he said, peeling bills off a stack. "I'll take it out of your fifty when you're done. Will that get you off the hook?"

Keane nodded. "It will."

"Good. I don't want your mind distracted by unimportant things." He reached into a desk drawer, took out a box, and handed it to Keane.

Keane opened the box. In it was an expensive-looking 9 mm automatic pistol.

"Keep it," Manny said. "I've got two, since Mr. Perkerson."

"Thanks," Keane said. "I had to turn mine in."

"I figured," Manny said. "Wear it in good health."

14

When Will got back to the Atlanta office, it was humming. His Aunt Eloise was prowling among a corps of young volunteers, watching their telephone manners. There was a stack of credit-card chits in front of each of them, and a growing stack had been filled out.

"The money looks fair for this stage, considering our unwanted publicity," Tom Black said. "Your dad's on the phone now, and he's doing okay."

"Come on, Tom, what's the bad news?"

"You're getting to know me, aren't you?" Tom said, shaking his head. "The bad news is, the telephone company demanded a fifty-thousand-dollar deposit for the phone bank."

"What?"

"The good news is, I got them down to thirty."

"That's good news if we had the money," Will said.

"We had it. When I wrote the check, it left eight dollars and forty cents in the account." He held up a hand. "We've taken in some more since then; your aunt Eloise is doing a great job."

"She's been doing it a long time," Will said. "All my father's campaigns. Where is he?"

"Upstairs in your office."

"Come on, let's see how he's doing."

"He's working on something special," Tom said.

They went up the stairs and into Will's large but ill-furnished office. Billy Lee was on the phone, and he waved them in and put a cautionary finger to his lips.

"Tell you what, Marvin," he was saying, "how about we each pick one, and they each pick another one? Fair enough? All right. Yes, Sunday afternoon. The station's standing by for confirmation. You get Mack's okay. No, I'll hang on. I know damn well he's standing right there." He covered the phone. "I think we've got him," he said to Tom.

Will was puzzled. "Got who? Mack Dean? Got him for what?"

"Just hang on a minute," Billy said. "Yeah, Marvin, all right, you're on. Three o'clock Sunday at the PBS station. Who are you choosing? If that's who you want, that's who you get. I don't know; I haven't talked to Will yet. I'll let you know. Bye." Billy turned to Will. "Your first debate with Mack is Sunday at three."

"How'd you get him to do it?" Will asked, astonished.

"Oh, I've still got a card or two up my sleeve. He's agreed to two meetings; I tried to get him to agree to three, but he won't. If he thinks he does well enough in this one, he might agree to another."

"Well, I'll be damned," Will said. "I never thought I'd get a shot at him face to face."

"Hang on," Tom said, "don't get too excited. You haven't won the debate yet. Don't underestimate Mack

Dean. I've seen some tapes of his debates last time around, and I want you to see them, too."

"Mack's picked Shirley Scott, the anchorlady at Channel Six, for his panel member. We get to pick somebody; then they each pick one."

"I hear Mack's screwing her," Tom said.

"You're kidding," Will said. "He's got twenty-five years on her."

"I told you not to underestimate him, didn't I?"

"Who do you want, Will?" Billy asked.

"I don't care. Pick somebody fair who'll pick somebody else fair. Anybody but the lady at the Sunday magazine."

"I hear she doesn't like Atlanta, is thinking about going back to Washington," Tom said.

"Did she get canned?"

"Nobody will admit it, but I know somebody who knows the guy who's subletting her apartment in D.C., and he's been told to get out."

"I hope it's true. Good riddance."

"Yeah," Tom laughed, "but she'll just be waiting for you when you get to Washington."

"A nice thought; thanks."

On the Saturday before the debate, Will got his hair cut and his suit pressed; then he went to headquarters and was grilled by Tom Black, Kitty Conroy, and his father for nearly six hours, until none of them could think of anything else to ask.

"I give up," his father said finally. "I can't stump you."

"You're in good shape, Will," Tom said. "Mack will have to get awfully lucky to take you."

"One thing, Tom," Will said, "I have a tendency to sweat when it's the slightest bit warm. See if you can get the studio refrigerated, will you?"

"I'll do the best I can, but when the microphones go on, the air-conditioning will go off, so here's what you do: keep a fresh handkerchief in the palm of your hand, and when Mack's talking, give your face a quick pat—don't wipe; that'll screw up the makeup—and don't try to figure out which camera is on; it'll just confuse you. Chances are, if Mack's talking, the camera will be on him."

"Okay. Any other advice?"

"Yeah. Don't look into the camera when you're answering questions; look at the questioner—answer him. I know there's a school of thought that you ought to face the viewer when answering, but I don't buy it; it's artificial. Also, when you sit down, sit on your coattails, so that when you lean forward with your hands on the desk, your suit won't ride up."

"I saw that movie, too."

"Good. Be sure and pee right before you go on. And try not to be too serious. You have a tendency to do that when the questions are serious. You've got a sense of humor; use it. Don't call Mack Governor, unless he calls you Mr. Lee. If he calls you Will, call him Mack; it'll keep you on a more equal footing. I don't want you referring to papers or index cards; you're good on your feet, and I don't want what you say to sound written. For an opening statement, use some stuff from the stump speech—you've already taken that far beyond what I wrote. It sounds like you now. That's all I've got. Anybody else?" He looked around, but nobody had anything. "Okay, get a good night's sleep; I don't want you hoarse tomorrow."

That night, when the campaign headquarters had finally emptied of volunteer workers, Will settled down in his makeshift bedroom and tried to sleep. Instead, he found himself thinking about Kate, something he had not had much time for recently. He wanted to be angry with her, but all he could feel was desire. They had not slept together since before Christmas, and he missed her beside him in bed. He supposed she'd seen the stories in the Washington papers about Jack's suicide, and the subsequent revelations about his homosexuality, but she had not called. He wondered how she could simply stop seeing him after four years, with no explanation and no apparent regrets. It didn't make any sense to him, and it didn't make him want her any less, either.

He slept, finally, and his dreams were erotic.

15

Will woke with hardly a thought of the debate. He got through the morning papers, made a couple of fund-raising phone calls, and listened with Tom to a proposal from Moss Mallet, head of a local polling operation. They agreed to a statewide poll, their first, immediately following the debate.

On the way to the television station in the car, Will listened to a dozen ideas from Kitty and Tom and agreed with most of them. At the station, they walked into the studio and Will immediately began mopping his brow. "You've got to get it cooler in here," he said to Tom.

"Damn it, they promised me," Tom said, disappearing into a glass-fronted booth, where Will could see him gesturing emphatically to a young woman. Shortly, the air-conditioning came on.

"How you doing, Will?" a booming voice behind him said.

"Hello, Mack," Will replied, remembering to keep on an equal footing. "You're looking well." He wasn't at all,

Will thought. He was puffy around the eyes and pinker than usual.

"You look pretty good yourself," the Governor replied. "You enjoying the campaign trail?"

"Oh, there's nothing I like better," Will came back. Jesus, he wanted to get away from Dean. He found this artificial bonhomie a strain. He was rescued when a makeup lady came and led the Governor away.

Tom came back into the studio. "That better?"

"Yeah. I hope there's time for it to get really cold before we go on." He mopped his face again; then a young man came and led him into a makeup room. Pancake was applied to his face, the first time Will had ever had the experience. He didn't like it; he was starting to feel uncomfortable.

When he walked back into the studio, the four reporters who would be questioning the candidates were in place, as was the moderator, a woman from the League of Women Voters. Mack Dean took his place at a small desk opposite Will's. As Will sat down, he got a look at Dean's image on a monitor and was surprised at how good he looked. His pinkness was now a tan, contrasting with the Governor's wavy gray hair and gold tie. It was not until he had seated himself opposite Dean that Will began to be nervous.

He listened absently as the moderator went over the rules; then the stage manager called one minute, and everyone seemed to become absorbed in their notes. Will, who had none, tried to think about his opening remarks but couldn't concentrate. The air-conditioning went off, the lights went up, and he began to feel the heat.

"Good afternoon," the moderator said suddenly, "and

welcome to the first in what we hope will be a series of debates between the two Democratic candidates from Georgia for the United States Senate: Governor Mack Dean on your left, and Mr. William Henry Lee the Fourth on your right."

Will tried not to wince at the recitation of his full name. He hadn't heard it spoken out loud since he had graduated from law school.

"We will begin with a brief opening statement from each candidate," the moderator said, "and then they will be questioned in turn by our guest panel." She introduced the panel, two print reporters from the *Atlanta Journal-Constitution* and the *Gwinnett Daily News* and two television reporters from local stations. Will took note of Shirley Scott, the tall blond anchorwoman with the dramatic hairdo, who Tom Black had said was sleeping with Mack Dean. She looked up from her notes and smiled professionally at the camera.

"We will begin with Mr. Lee," the moderator said.

The words came like a clap of thunder to Will. He had won the toss; hadn't he chosen to go second? Rattled, he swallowed and faced the camera. "Good afternoon," he began. The stage manager was waving frantically at him, pointing to another camera. Will found the red light, shifted his position, and stared at the lens.

"Good afternoon," he repeated, "my name is Will Lee, and I'm running for the United States Senate." Why the hell had he said that? Everybody watching knew it. "For the past eight years, I've had the privilege of working at the side of the greatest United States Senator Georgia has produced, the last four of those years as his chief of staff. I know Senator Carr is watching today, and we all bid him hello and a speedy recovery from his recent illness." He hadn't meant to say that; it had just popped into his mind that the Senator would be watching. "Under Senator Carr, I've had what amounts to a postgraduate education in how the United States Senate works, and now I want to put that knowledge to work for the people of the state of Georgia." A trickle of sweat ran down his forehead, then traveled down the side of his nose and to the corner of his mouth. He tried to ignore it. "I've just come from a week of campaigning around the state, and I'm encouraged by the interest the people of Georgia are showing in this race. They tell me they want a strong defense for our nation, and I do, too; they tell me they're interested in family issues, and I am, too; they tell me they want their government run sensibly and economically, and I do, too." Where was he going with this? He tried to remember the stump speech and failed. "Naturally, this program will be brief, and if you're not satisfied with any answer of mine here today, if you want to know more, just write to me, and I'll see that you have a prompt reply. Thank you." Jesus Christ, had that been a good idea? He didn't know. It had only just occurred to him.

"Thank you, Mr. Lee. And now we'll hear from Governor Dean."

Will saw the face of a relaxed and confident Dean pop onto a monitor screen, and he took the opportunity to run a handkerchief over his face, forgetting for a moment that he was supposed to pat, not wipe. Quickly, he dabbed at his face, hoping he hadn't done something horrible to the makeup.

"Hello," Mack Dean said warmly to the camera. "I'd like to begin today by welcoming Will to the race. I've known this boy most of his life, I guess. When he was in high school, we gave him his first tour around the Georgia House of Representatives, his daddy and I; when he was in college, he worked as an assistant reporter on a committee I chaired in the Georgia State Senate; and when he was doing his postgraduate work with my very old friend, Ben Carr, I was serving as your governor. It's good to see Georgia's young people taking an interest in politics, and I'm sure that one of these days, Will is going to make a fine elected official."

The goddamned fucking son of a bitch, Will thought, squirming under a heavy load of patronization. He mopped at his face, again forgetting the makeup.

"Through twenty-five years of public service I have always tried to put the people first," Mack Dean continued smoothly, "and you have always responded by electing me to public office. I hope and trust that, when you have considered the issues in this campaign, and my service to Georgia, you will see fit to elect me once again, this time to our most august deliberative body, the United States Senate. And when you do, you may be sure you will always have a friend in the Senate."

Will struggled hard to get hold of himself and mostly succeeded. A procession of questions came from the panel to the candidates, and Will tried hard to give detailed and specific answers, while Mack Dean generalized, reassured, and postured skillfully. For the better part of the hour, without a break, they went on, while Will struggled to gain the upper hand on at least one question. Finally, there was three-quarters of a minute showing on the clock.

"We have time for just one question from Shirley Scott, of Channel Six News, for Mr. Lee," the moderator said.

"Mr. Lee," Scott said earnestly, concern showing in her face, "as you know, there have been reports of your involvement in a ring of homosexuals on Capitol Hill, and I wonder—"

Will did not let her finish; he wanted to rise from the chair and strangle the life from her. "I know nothing of the sort, Miss Scott," he said, his voice trembling with anger, "and neither do you. Name your sources."

Scott managed to look as though she had been struck. "Why, I—"

"There has been no such report anywhere, to my knowledge," Will said, "and the moment that any member of the media, including you, makes such an allegation, I promise you I will sue before sundown—"

"I'm afraid our time is up," the moderator interrupted, alarm in her voice. "Thank you for joining us, and good day." Music filled the studio.

Will stood up and started toward the long table where Shirley Scott sat; then he was yanked to a halt by the microphone clipped to his lapel. He jerked it off and continued toward the Scott woman. When he was halfway to her, the stage manager shouted at him.

"For God's sake, we've still got picture!"

Will stopped, and a split second later, the studio lights went dark. He was blind for a moment; then Tom Black was hustling him out a side door.

16

"Oh, Christ," Will said, scrubbing the makeup from his face with a handkerchief as Kitty Conroy drove rapidly toward the campaign headquarters. "What have I done?"

"Just relax," Tom Black said. "It's probably not as bad as you think. You got mad, that's all."

"I think your response was appropriate," Kitty said. "If I'd had a gun, I'd have killed her on the spot."

"But I screwed up everything! I forgot my opening remarks; I was sweating and constantly wiping my face; and the whole time Mack was just sitting there like the Cheshire Cat, spouting platitudes that probably went down great with the audience."

"Well, maybe you got a little specific here and there," Tom said, "but that's okay."

"You sounded like you knew what you were talking about, anyway," Kitty chimed in.

"Look, I appreciate your trying to cheer me up, both of you, but it was a disaster."

"We'll look at the tape when we get to the office," Tom said. "Moss Mallet will be calling us later with the results of his telephone poll, too; that'll give us a better idea of what the effect was in the electorate."

Will sat staring out the window, saying nothing. Kitty and Tom exchanged a worried glance. Kitty stopped the car in front of campaign headquarters, and they all got out.

Will dug into a pocket for his car keys. "I'm not going inside," he said. "I'll call you later." He strode toward the parking lot, leaving Tom and Kitty staring after him. Will got the station wagon started and pulled out of the car park faster than he had meant to. He made himself slow down, fighting his panic. Gradually, he calmed himself, and his mind seemed to reject all thought of anything to do with the debate or the campaign. He was surprised, a few minutes later, when he passed through the entrance of Peachtree De Kalb Airport, since he had not consciously driven there. He continued to the parking lot near his airplane, parked, got out, and began walking methodically around the Cessna, performing his usual pre-flight inspection. Shortly, he was taxiing toward the runway.

Once out of the airport area, he switched off the airplane's radios and shucked off his headset. The drone of the engine filled his head, obliterating everything else. He flew southeast toward Stone Mountain, and when he had reached the huge lump of granite, he turned due south, taking care to keep his altitude at three thousand feet, in order to stay under the Terminal Control Area for the giant Hartsfield Airport. When he was past the TCA, he climbed to nine thousand feet, leaned on the engine, and turned in the Macon VOR beacon. He knew by then that he was not going to Delano, but farther south. He switched on the autopilot and let the airplane fly itself. Then he did something he had never before done at the controls of an airplane: he loosened his safety belt, cranked the seat back a couple of notches, and laid his head against the headrest. In a moment, he was asleep. The airplane droned on into the late afternoon.

"November One Two Three Tango, Macon approach control, do you read?"

Will sat up and looked around him. The airplane was flying steadily south. He checked the instrument panel and found all gauges normal, but the radios were still off. He glanced at the distance-measuring-equipment readout: ten miles from the Macon VOR, the point where he should be calling Macon approach. But Macon approach had called him, hadn't it? He was sure he had heard it. He switched on the radios and dialed in the frequency. "Macon approach, November One Two Three Tango."

"November One Two Three Tango," a woman's voice came back. "Macon approach."

"I'm entering the Macon radar area, ten miles north, course one eight zero, a Cessna 182 RG, VFR."

"Would you like radar advisories?" she asked.

"Affirmative," he replied.

She assigned him a transponder code, and he dialed in the number.

"Two Three Tango, radar contact," she said. "What is your destination?"

"Private field," he said, "near Thomasville."

"Roger. Maintain your heading, resume your own navigation at the Macon VOR."

"Thank you, Macon." He knew where he was going now, but he didn't know what good it would do.

The sun was low in the sky when he found the house and set the airplane down in the pasture behind it. Jasper was out of the house, all smiles, by the time Will had shut down the engine.

"Mr. Will, how you doing?" he asked, shaking Will's hand.

"I'm all right, Jasper. And you and Minnie?"

"We're just fine. You were awful good on the TV this afternoon. Me and the Senator watched you."

"You're too kind, Jasper," Will said, meaning it. "How's the Senator?"

" 'Bout the same, I reckon; maybe a little bit better. You come on upstairs to see him. He's awake."

Will climbed the stairs and found the Senator propped up in bed, watching CNN. He went and sat by the bed and took the old man's hand. "I'm glad to see you, Senator," he said.

Jasper backed out of the room and closed the door behind him.

The Senator's eyes locked on Will's face. His hand made a tiny squeezing motion.

Will looked down at the long face, empty of expression, still childlike in repose. "I had a bad day today," he said. "I wanted to talk to you about it."

17

Harold Perkerson peered into the mirror as he shaved, wondering how he looked behind the bandages. Today was the day he was to find out, and he was excited. He had not been shaving his upper lip, because the bandages interfered. As he finished, he heard the jeep pull up outside the house, and he checked, as he always did, to be sure it was Suzy, the nurse.

She came into the cabin with her bag and gave him a playful poke in the ribs. "This is it, huh? Let's see what you look like." She sat him in a chair, took some scissors from her bag, and began snipping through the gauze. "Oh, yeah," she said. "I like the mustache, too. Suits you."

"Let me see," he said, starting to rise.

"Just a minute now, don't get into a rush." She doused a cotton ball in alcohol and began dabbing at his face. "Let me get all the adhesive off." She finished. "There."

Perkerson stood up and walked to the bathroom mirror. He was stunned by the man who stared back at him. The ears were snug against his head—that would have changed his appearance a lot, but the nose, the nose changed everything. Somehow, it all went together. He was reminded of a teacher he had had in high school, a man who always wore tweed jackets with leather patches on the elbows. The new Harold Perkerson looked . . . professorial; that was the only word that described him. The mustache helped, too. He had never had hair on his face before. His mother, if she had been alive, would not have recognized him.

Suzy walked over with a hand mirror. "Want to check the profile?"

Perkerson held up the mirror and turned sideways. The big hook of a nose had gone; there was a little bump, though; it looked like a real nose, like a nose he had been born with. The nostrils had been made smaller, too. It worked.

"There's just a tiny bit of bruising," she said. "Come sit down, and I'll fix it." He sat, and she took a compact from her purse and applied a dab of powder here and there. "Perfect," she said.

He pulled her down and kissed her. He felt elated. He pulled at her shirt and unsnapped her bra. He buried his face in her large breasts.

"Come," she said, "come with me." She pulled him toward the bed, shucking off clothes.

"Are you awake?" she said later.

"Just barely," he said. "I never felt so good."

"Me neither."

He turned and looked at her. "What now? When do I get out of here?"

"Today," she said. "Now." She rolled over, got up, went to her purse, and retrieved two envelopes.

He watched as she crossed the room toward him. She wasn't exactly beautiful, but she had a great body, he thought.

She handed him the first envelope. "Here's your new address and phone number. It's a furnished condo in Marietta, right outside Atlanta. Lots of singles; you'll fit right in. Down in your car, there's a sample case with stationery in it. You're still James Ross, a printing salesman for the company on your credit cards. It's a tight cover."

"Good," he said. "What's in the other envelope?"

"Let's save that for later," she said. "I want you one more time before you're gone."

When they had made love again, she helped him get his things together and get them into the jeep, then drove him down the mountain. The Mazda was parked at the bottom, and she showed him the sample case in the trunk.

"Well, that's it," she said. "I guess you're on your way. Go out there and do good."

"Thanks," he said. "I will. Now how about the other envelope?"

She smiled and handed it to him. It was sealed.

He tore it open and read the single typed page.

"Good?" she asked.

"I like it," he said. "I like it a lot."

"Tell me," she said.

"You know better than that."

She blushed.

"You'll read about it in the papers."

"When?"

"As soon as I can set it up. You'll know it when you see it."

She wrote down her telephone number. "Memorize it and call me if you need me. Say you're Hank, and I'll know."

"Does the Archon know about that part?"

"No," she said. "That's personal between me and you."

He kissed her again, got into the car, and turned toward Atlanta, memorizing her number. When he had it, he threw the paper out the window. Then, a little farther along, he stopped and read his assignment again, memorizing the name and address. When he had that, he put the car's cigarette lighter to the paper and dropped it out the window, then drove on.

He thought about the assignment. He liked it; he really did.

18

Will was awakened by sunshine streaming through the windows. Disoriented, he looked around the room. It was old-fashioned, with floral-print wallpaper, a brass bed, and wicker furniture. It took him a moment to locate himself in a guest room at Flat Rock Farm, Senator Carr's home.

A few minutes later, he appeared in the kitchen, drawn by the scent of frying bacon. Minnie, clad in an apron, was scrambling eggs.

"Morning, Mr. Will," she said. "There's a piece 'bout you on the editorial page of the *Constitution*." Will poured himself a cup of coffee and sat down to the newspaper. It was the lead editorial, and it damned Shirley Scott for her question to him during the debate of the day before and quoted Governor Mack Dean disassociating himself with her question. It called "baseless" any suggestion that Will might be anything other than a heterosexual bachelor and concluded:

This newspaper has not yet determined which candidate it will support in the Democratic Primary, but it has concluded that Will Lee is, by background and experience, a credible candidate for the United States Senate and that false accusations from the other camp are likely to cause a backlash in Lee's favor. Governor Mack Dean and his supporters would do well to give some thought to that notion.

Will took a deep breath and let it out. The editorial should have made him feel better than he did.

Jasper walked in. "Pretty good, huh?" he said.

"Pretty good, Jasper."

"A Mr. Tom Black been on the phone looking for you this morning, but I told him you was asleep."

"I'll call him in a few minutes," Will said, "but right now, I want some of that bacon and some scrambled eggs."

Will ate in silence, wondering what Tom would have to tell him. He had already decided that he was in the race to stay, but still, he wondered what Tom's attitude would be. He drank the last of his coffee and called campaign headquarters.

"You okay?" Tom asked.

"Sure."

"We were worried about you."

"I just wanted some time alone, and I wanted to see the Senator."

"How's he doing?"

"Maybe a little better, Jasper says."

"Good. The news I've got should make him feel a little better still."

"What's the news?"

"Well, we've got our first statewide poll from Moss Mallet, and you're eleven points behind."

Will's heart sank. This confirmed his worst fears. "That's the good news?"

"The good news is that it was taken before the debate. There's better news."

"I can use it."

"Moss's hurry-up poll taken of people who saw the debate puts you three points behind; that's within the margin of error."

Will couldn't believe it. "You reckon this race is tied?"

"Nope, and neither does Moss, because not all that many of the electorate saw the debate. But I reckon that right now you're closer than eleven points, and the after-debate poll indicates to me that the more often you're seen head to head with Mack, the better you'll do."

"I can't believe the comparison yesterday was a good one."

"It looked different on the tube than it felt in the studio. Kitty was in the control room the whole time, and she's an old friend of the director, who seemed sympathetic. When you were mopping sweat, he was shooting the panel of questioners or Mack. He managed to catch Mack looking uncomfortable a couple of times, too."

"What about at the end?"

"He cut to the panel when you stormed across the studio, so the TV audience missed that."

"I'm glad to hear it."

"The result is, you looked pretty good. But next time we can't trust to luck or a friendly director; we'll have to prepare a little better."

"Right, but if we did this well this time, we can do a lot better next time. We've one more debate to go."

"I don't know if we have."

"What do you mean? They've agreed to two debates."

"Mack's campaign manager has already called this morning. I haven't returned his call yet."

"You think they'll renege?"

"I think they've got a pollster, just like we have, and when they see the results, Mack may decide to cut his losses. He'll notice an eight-point drop in his popularity after one debate, and he won't want to give you another shot at him.'"

"Shit."

"Exactly. What we've got to do is redouble our efforts on fund-raising so that we'll have enough to get you on TV all over this state. Kitty's already working on more TV interviews for you. At least they're free."

"I like free, but how are we going to raise more money?"

"You ever heard of a businessman named Lurton Pitts?"

"The fried-chicken king?"

"One and the same. He's been on the phone this morning to your dad. He saw the debate and was impressed; he wants you to meet with him and a group of his friends."

"When?"

"Today. Lunch at the Capital City Club."

"I'd better go straight there from here, then. Can you have somebody meet me at the airport with a clean shirt and a pressed suit? All that stuff is in my office."

"Sure. Let me warn you about Pitts, though. He may, after he talks with you, offer to raise some money for you. He and his group have raised a hell of a lot for some others."

"What's he going to want?" Will asked.

"I don't know, but it won't be small."

"How do you think I ought to handle him?"

"That's up to you, Will. I can't tell you to promise him the earth, or to tell him to go to hell. You're going to be alone in a room with these guys, and nobody's going to know what you say except you and them. You'll be on your own."

"Well," Will said, "it won't hurt to listen, I guess."

"Be careful, boy," Tom said. "It could get rough."

Will hung up. He was back in the race. Now he had to stay there.

19

Will was met by his father in the foyer of the Capital City Club in downtown Atlanta.

"Here's the way it goes," Billy said, as they rose in the elevator. "I take you up and introduce you; then I leave. They want you alone. Don't give them any more than you have to. In fact, you may decide you don't want to give them anything at all. I won't blame you if you don't." The elevator doors opened, and they walked down a hallway to a set of double doors. "Here we go," Billy said, opening the door.

A group of a dozen men were standing before a drink-laden table. They turned as the Lees entered.

One of them, a short, middle-aged, stocky man with thick fair hair and a freckled face, detached himself from the group and stuck out his hand. "Hello, Will, I'm Lurton Pitts."

The leader of this merry little band, Will thought. "How do you do, Mr. Pitts."

"Call me Lurton, boy; everyone does." He began making introductions.

Will had met two of the other men, a banker and an architect/developer; he had heard of another half dozen; only three or four were unknown to him. A black man in a white coat stepped up.

"Would you like something to drink, Will?" Lurton Pitts asked.

"I'd like some iced tea, please."

"Nothing stronger?"

"I think I'd better keep my wits about me today."

Pitts laughed. "Billy, how about you?"

"Thanks, Lurton," Billy replied, "but I have to be going." He waved to the others and left.

There was a brief period of desultory chat, then Pitts herded them toward a large round table, seating Will next to him. Lunch was served and eaten with a minimum of talk, followed by coffee. Will was surprised at how relaxed he felt. They would get to it now, he thought.

"Well, Will," Lurton Pitts said, "we—all of us—were just wondering if you'd like to be our man in Washington."

Will paused for effect, something he had seen his father do many times; it gave weight to his answer. "I'd be very pleased to be your next senator," he said.

Pitts paused, too, to let Will know that his answer was unsatisfactory. "We're all looking for more than just a senator, Will. We want somebody in the upper house who's looking after our interests."

Will looked around the table. "This looks like a pretty diverse group to me. Do you all have exactly the same interests?"

The banker spoke up. "We have a great many interests in common."

"We're businesspeople," a manufacturer said. "How do you feel about business?"

"I think we wouldn't have much of a country without a successful business community."

"You think the business of America is business, then?"

"I don't agree about much of anything with Calvin Coolidge. This country is never again going to have the sort of economy we had in the twenties, and everybody had better get used to it."

"You believe in a free-market economy?" someone asked.

"Gentlemen, we all know there's no such thing; there hasn't been, really, in this century. I believe in a well-regulated capitalism."

"Regulations!" the manufacturer snorted. "Ronald Reagan got rid of those for us."

"No," Will replied, "his administration just ignored a lot of them. That's going to be expensive, especially in terms of the environment, and your businesses are going to have to help pay for that laxity."

"You're sounding like a socialist," somebody said.

"Nonsense," Will said. "There isn't a socialist in the entire Congress. If Ted Kennedy were British, he'd be in the Conservative Party. I'm not an ideologue of any sort; I'm a realist, I think. I don't think we've had enough realism in government during the Reagan years."

"God knows that's true," said the developer.

Will was relieved to hear somebody agree with him on something.

"Your boss, Ben Carr, supported Reagan a lot of the time."

"Senator Carr supported him when he thought he was right, and, occasionally, when he thought he wasn't. He's a politician; he knows how to live in the real world."

"Do you hold with Senator Carr's views on defense?"

"I think I'm a little more conservative than the Senator on that subject."

"More conservative than Ben Carr?"

"By 'conservative,' I mean I'm a little more tightfisted than the Senator."

"Oh, you mean more liberal, then."

"No. I think the words 'liberal' and 'conservative' have lost most of their political meaning. Nowadays, they're accusations more than anything else. If you insist on applying those labels, then I'm a moderate, generally speaking. But I'm a conservative when it comes to the budget, and that includes the defense budget."

"You'd vote to cut the defense budget?" Pitts asked.

"I think we ought to get more of our money's worth. I think we can have just as effective a national defense on less money. Too much of it is being stolen from us."

A man across the table leaned forward. "I'm a defense contractor," he said, "in a small way. Do you think I'm stealing from my country?"

Will smiled. "You don't look like a thief to me, sir." He leaned forward and looked the man in the eye. "But if you are, then I think you ought to be in jail, and the money ought to be either put to better use in another program or put back in the taxpayer's pocket."

There was an uncomfortable silence; then the man said, "Fair enough."

"Will," Pitts said, "we're in a position to raise a lot of

money for you, if we believe it's to our advantage. If we do, just what sort of cooperation can we expect from you?"

Will leaned back. "Mr. Pitts, the people who support my candidacy are always going to have my ear. When I'm in office, I'll return your phone calls; I'll listen to your problems; and if I think you're right, I'll support your positions. You may not always be happy with the way I vote, but you will have had an opportunity to express your opinion before I cast that vote."

"You'll listen to us personally?" somebody asked.

"Whenever I can. But, as soon as I'm elected, I'm going to find somebody like me and put him to work doing for me what I've been doing for Senator Carr these past years. He'll be the kind of man you'll like talking to when I can't talk to you myself."

A man who had not spoken before, one of the ones Will did not know, leaned forward. "Young fellow, I think you'd better understand right now what we're talking about, what we want from you; if you expect to get our money, then we're going to have to know that you're ours when we need you."

"Mr. Williams," Will said, dredging up the man's name, "it sounds to me like you want to buy yourself a politician. Well, if that's what you want, buy Mack Dean; he's for sale."

It got very quiet in the room.

Will broke the silence. "But Mack Dean is not going to be your next senator. Come September, Mack's going to be back in the farm-implement business, whence he came. Come September, I'm going to be the Democratic nominee. And come November, I'm going to be the senator-elect."

Lurton Pitts pulled a sheet of paper from his pocket. "I've got some poll results that say if the election were held tomorrow, Mack would beat you, say you're eleven points behind."

"Fortunately," Will said, "the election is not going to be held tomorrow, and I suspect you've also got some post-debate figures on that sheet of paper that tell a different story. No, Mack Dean is on his way out. He's been a do-nothing governor who got elected only because a couple of other people shot themselves in the foot. And suppose he did get elected to the Senate? He'd be the invisible man. I think it's in your best interests—in the state's best interests—to have a man up there who understands how the Senate works, who, in time, can gain some real influence that he can exercise for the benefit of his constituents."

"What about the Republican candidate?" Williams asked. "How do you know you can beat him?"

"I hear," Pitts said, "that the Republican state convention is going to have to choose between Jim Winslow and the Reverend Don Beverly Calhoun, and I hear the choice is likely to be Jim Winslow."

"Mr. Pitts," Will said, "I don't think Jim Winslow could beat Mack Dean."

That got a good laugh from the whole table at a moment when Will thought a laugh was needed.

"I think you're right," Pitts chuckled. "Oddly enough, I think old Calhoun would be a hell of a lot harder to beat than Winslow, but he embarrasses a lot of Republicans."

"I think you might be right on both counts," Will said.

"You going to vote to raise taxes?" Williams asked, cutting across the laughter. "Democrats love to raise taxes."

"That's a myth, I think," Will replied. "I don't know any politician who likes to raise taxes, and I'm no exception. I'll vote to raise taxes only when we can't raise the revenues we need any other way, and if it comes to that, then I'll vote to raise taxes. But I think we can do a lot of trimming and realigning in the budget to help get this god-awful deficit down and to fund the right programs."

"You talking about social programs?"

"We need some social programs," Will said. "Private enterprise, as important as it is, just can't handle all our problems in a fair way. There are always going to be people who need help, and our government is always going to have to help them. Maybe not to the extent it did in the sixties and seventies, but we can't let people starve to death in this country. It's in the interests of all of us to help the poor become self-supporting, to learn something about the work ethic, and to get them on the tax rolls."

" 'The poor ye will always have with you,' " somebody quoted.

"Maybe so, but I'm not willing to let them starve to prove the point. I think this country has the capacity to do something for all its people. I know it's been a long time since anybody in this room missed a meal, but I expect there are some of you who can remember how it felt."

Lurton Pitts looked at his watch. "Will, I promised to have everybody out of here by two o'clock, and it's ten past." He stood up and stuck out his hand. "Thank you for meeting with us, and if you'll excuse us, we have some business to discuss before we adjourn."

Will got up. "Thank you for your time, gentlemen," he said. He turned and left the room.

Outside, as he waited for his car to be brought, he tried to remember the atmosphere in the room, judge it, but he could not. Some of the men had been silent; one or two had been hostile; nobody had really seemed sympathetic, only polite. There were men in that room, maybe most of them, who would be more comfortable with Mack Dean or Jim Winslow, maybe even some who would be more comfortable with the Reverend Don Beverly Calhoun.

Will reported back to his father and to Tom. By the end of the day, they had heard nothing from Lurton Pitts and his group. By the end of the week, they had still heard nothing. Mack Dean's campaign manager held a press conference, canceling the remainder of the debates; he said that his candidate would be too busy traveling the state. There was a rumor, though, that the Governor had suddenly found some new money for television commercials.

20

Harold Perkerson drove slowly down the alley, looking up at the backs of the buildings on both sides. There were few windows; that was good. His car was an anonymous-looking Ford, stolen half an hour before from a parking lot at a MARTA station a couple of stops up the line.

He came to a garage door with the correct number; he stopped, retrieved a small remote-control device from his briefcase, and pointed it at the door; it slid creakily upward. He pulled forward, reversed the car into the garage, and signaled the door to close itself. He got out of the car, taking the briefcase with him. He found himself in a loading bay, wide enough, perhaps, for three trucks to occupy. Following a roughly sketched map, he climbed onto the loading platform, walked through an unlocked door, and came to a large freight elevator. He pressed the button for the third floor and, after a moment's wait, emerged into a wide hallway. He followed that until it turned into a large carpeted room, dimly lit by what sunlight was able to get past the draperies drawn across the wide windows at the front of the building. The room was empty, except for half a dozen telephones resting on the carpet; until recently, this had been a furniture showroom for a manufacturer who was now out of business.

Perkerson walked to the right-hand end of the wide draperies and, with the back of his hand, lifted the curtain away from the wall. The sunlight hurt his eyes for a moment, but as he became used to the brightness, he could look down at the street to where the crowd was. The first thing he saw was a large sign, carried by a fat woman, which read MURDERERS OF CHILDREN, GOD IS WATCHING.

The fat woman was sitting on the pavement outside a low building set back from the street; she was surrounded by, perhaps, thirty other people, most of them carrying placards with messages similar to her own. A sign in front of the building read MILTON PRE-NATAL CLINIC. The word "Clinic" had been crossed out with spray paint and the words "Horror Chamber" substituted.

A dozen uniformed policemen stood about, keeping close watch on the group. Perkerson noted that the walk leading from the curb to the clinic door had been kept free of demonstrators. He looked at his watch: a quarter to nine.

Perkerson shucked off his raincoat, removed a small folding stool from one of the inside pockets, and set it up at the corner of the curtain. Then he opened the briefcase and began assembling the rifle, fixing the large telescopic sight to it, and, finally, screwing a long suppressor into the barrel. He laid the rifle on the carpet, took a lightweight photographer's tripod from the other raincoat pocket, and set it up, adjusting the height carefully. He checked his watch again. Not long, now.

Perkerson reached behind the curtain and pushed open a small window, hinged at the top, propping it open wide. The sound of singing reached him from the demonstrators. It was a hymn he had sung many times as a boy in church. He pulled the curtain away from the wall and draped it over his knee, holding it away from the window. He shoved a full clip into the rifle, screwed the tripod fitting into the stock, and checked the distance. About four hundred feet, he reckoned. He saw a column of steam coming from a manhole and noted that it rose straight into the air. No wind; excellent. He worked the action of the rifle.

He adjusted for distance, then sighted through the scope. A policeman's black face leapt at him, magnified by a factor of ten. Perkerson panned from the curb to the front door. With the rifle set back from the window and not protruding, he could still pan through three-quarters of the distance. But it should not be a moving shot; Milton and the woman were supposed to stop. He panned again anyway, for practice, just in case. Five minutes to nine. A red van pulled up in front of the clinic and stopped.

They were early! Good! He'd be more relaxed, not having to wait. A man he immediately recognized as Milton got out, then turned and helped a woman in a white nurse's uniform from the van. They hurried toward the clinic door as the voices of the demonstrators rose in a cacophony of shouted slogans.

Perkerson leaned into the rifle and made a conscious effort to relax. He had not had time to position himself perfectly; he'd have to shoot quickly.

As Milton was about to reach for the door, a demonstrator flung himself onto the walkway in front of the doctor, stopping his progress. Milton turned to one of the policemen and raised his hands with a shrug. What are you going to do about this? he seemed to be asking.

The turn was perfect for Perkerson. He moved the crosshairs to the center of the doctor's chest, took a breath, let half of it out, and squeezed. The doctor flew backward as the bullet struck home. At the end of his vision, Perkerson could see a policeman diving for the woman. The rifleman panned left two feet and squeezed off a second shot. The nurse's head seemed to explode.

The noise coming from the demonstrators changed character immediately. The chanting turned to screaming as people ran or flung themselves onto the ground.

Perkerson did not wait to see what happened next. He left the window open and moved his knee, letting the curtain fall against the wall. Quickly, but calmly, he disassembled the rifle, packed it into the briefcase, folded the tripod and the stool, put them into the raincoat's inner pockets, draped the coat over his arm, and stood up. He looked around him to be sure he had left nothing behind, then walked with long strides toward the elevator. When he walked out onto the loading platform downstairs, his pulse and breathing were up, but not much.

Perkerson tossed the briefcase and raincoat onto the front seat, got into the car, and punched the remote control. The door slipped upward, and he nosed into the alley, pointing the controller at the door behind him. He turned left and stopped. The alley before him was filled with an enormous garbage truck. Two men were emptying cans into an automatic feeder.

Perkerson made a conscious effort not to make quick, panicky motions. He turned and looked up the alley behind him. A large, brown UPS truck sat there, twenty-five yards behind him, empty. He turned and faced forward again, sitting very still. His pulse and breathing were suddenly up sharply. What were his options?

He could abandon the car and walk. Not a good idea; the police would be all over the place in a minute or so; a good two minutes had already passed since the shoot. The whoop of police cars could already be heard in the distance. He could back into the garage again and leave the building by the front entrance—an even worse idea; he'd be walking straight toward the police. Or he could sit here and wait for the garbage truck to move.

As he considered his options, he glanced into the rearview mirror and saw the UPS deliveryman climbing back into his truck. Momentarily, the truck moved toward his car and came to a halt a few feet behind him. He could see the driver drumming his fingers on the wheel.

There was nothing to do but wait. He couldn't even shout at the rubbish collectors; he didn't want to attract attention to himself. He reached into an inside pocket, retrieved his sunglasses, and put them on. He crossed his arms and rested a hand over his mouth. The garbage men weren't paying any attention to him, but if they did, he wanted them to see as little as possible. Now they would see a hand and some dark glasses. He glanced into the rearview mirror again; the UPS man was climbing down from the truck. Perkerson's blood was pounding in his ears now. Sweat broke from his brow and poured down his face. He checked the side mirror; the UPS man was walking down the alley toward the garbage truck. He would pass a foot from Perkerson's window.

Perkerson mopped his brow with a gloved hand, and then a miracle happened: the garbage truck moved forward. Perkerson let his car creep forward behind it. He could see the UPS man in his side mirror, walking back toward his truck. The police whoopers were no more than a block away now.

The garbage truck stopped again. But this time, it moved to the left and the alley was wider here. One of the rubbish collectors waved him on. Rubbing at his face with one hand to keep it covered, Perkerson pulled slowly around the huge truck, managing the gap between the truck and the wall by inches. He was free.

At the corner of the next street, Perkerson jammed on his brakes as two police cars crossed his path from right to left. Slowly, deliberately, he turned right and began to accelerate. A traffic light loomed ahead at the next corner. It turned red. Perkerson stopped and checked the rearview mirror in time to see two police cars careen around a corner to their left. He looked up and saw two more heading toward him. The light changed as they sped past. He accelerated moderately and, as soon as he could, turned left, looking for the expressway. Five minutes later, he was driving north.

Perkerson turned up the air-conditioning full blast and loosened his collar. The cold air stopped the sweat. Breathing deep breaths, he drove north at fifty-five miles an hour.

He got off at Piedmont Road and drove to the Lindbergh MARTA station. The parking space from which he had stolen the car was still vacant. He pulled into it, got out with the briefcase and raincoat, checking the car for anything left behind, then walked away from it. When the commuter returned in the late afternoon, he would never know the car had been taken.

Perkerson stripped off the driving gloves he had worn since stealing the car and walked briskly to another part of the car park, checking to see that he wasn't noticed. He found his own car, tossed the briefcase and raincoat into the trunk, and drove away, heading north to Marietta and his comfortable new apartment. He switched on the radio.

"We have a preliminary report of a disturbance, no, it's a shooting, at an abortion clinic in midtown. Our mobile unit is on its way there now, and we expect to have a report directly from the scene in a very short time, so please stay tuned."

Perkerson drove languidly, letting the sweat dry on his body. The satisfaction came with a rush. He was back in business.

21

Mickey Keane got there almost as soon as the police; he had heard it on his car police radio, which was illegal, except for a retired cop. The paved area in front of the clinic was chaotic when he arrived. There were four black-and-whites parked every which way, lights flashing; women were crying, men trembling; the bodies lay where they had fallen, while a patrolman took Polaroids, waiting for the medical examiner and a photographer to arrive.

Keane flashed his badge, which, as a retiree, he had been allowed to keep, at a uniformed youngster and stepped under the yellow tape that separated the crime scene from the sidewalk. He glanced at the bodies, at the way they had fallen, then looked up the street. There were low trees planted along the property line; he reckoned the shots had come from an elevation. Quickly, he scanned the opposite side of the street. People were gathered at office windows, looking down; in some cases they were hanging out the windows, pointing. Except for one building. The storefront at street level had its windows soaped, and on the third floor, a single window was open.

If he had still been on the job, he would have had to follow procedure, start questioning witnesses; but now, he could follow his hunches. As he started to move, an unmarked police car screeched to a halt at the curb, and the first detectives got out of it. Keane ran over and grabbed the first man's sleeve. "Come with me, Frank, and right now; let your partner work the scene!"

The detective waved his partner to the crime scene and trotted after Keane. "What you got, Mickey?" he panted. The man was pushing fifty and overweight.

"Just come on, Frank. We might have a shot at this guy. Probably not, but maybe." Keane crossed the street, dodging traffic, and ran to the storefront. There was a doorway to one side, and Keane already had the picklock in his hand.

"Shit, Mickey, what the hell are you doing?" the detective asked.

"Just shut up, Frank, if you want this guy. You can blame everything on me." He got the door opened, pulled his gun, and ran straight ahead up the two flights of stairs. At the top, he stopped and listened, putting a finger to his lips. From there, they worked automatically, covering each other as they searched the floor.

"Nothing," the detective said disgustedly. "Wild-goose chase. Thanks a lot, Keane."

"He was here," Keane said, holstering his pistol. He walked down the hallway and paused at the entrance to the empty showroom. He ran his fingers along the wainscoting. "Dust," he said, holding up his fingers. "Thick dust."

"So, dust," the detective said.

Keane squatted and looked along the carpet from a low angle toward the windows. "Look at that," he said, pointing. Indistinct tracks led to and from the windows, traced in the dust on the gray carpet. Keane and the detective crossed the room, avoiding the footprints. "Your shooter was right there at the corner of the window. He left the little ventilating window in the plate glass open. Two to one you find powder on it."

"Okay, I'll buy it," the detective said.

"He didn't leave by the front," Keane said, punching the elevator button.

"Watch that. Prints."

"This guy didn't leave any prints," Keane said. "He didn't leave nothing, not a shell casing, not a cigarette butt. Nothing. You won't even get a shoe size from those tracks in the dust." They rode the elevator down a floor and Keane walked to the loading platform. "He came and went this way," he said, pointing at the tire tracks in the dust on the garage floor. "Your best shot is a witness in the alley."

The detective began speaking into a handheld radio. He gave the address, asked for a crime-scene team with a tire ID kit. "We'll have some kind of idea on the car in half an hour, if the tires have never been changed," he said to Keane.

"Jesus, Frank, you wait half an hour, then forget it. Somebody didn't see him in the alley, you're fucked anyway. This guy's a pro. You know who he is, don't you?"

The detective looked puzzled. "Huh?"

"It's the guy who greased Chuck. Don't you see that?"

"What's his name, Perkins?"

"Perkerson. Harold Perkerson."

"It's been weeks, Mickey. I'm not gonna get fixated on that guy. I heard you were."

"It's him, Frank; I can feel it in my bones," Keane said. "Old Harold's back. Come on." He stepped down from the loading platform, taking care to avoid the area where the car had been parked, found the switch for the garage doors, and opened them. He stepped into the alley, followed by the detective, and looked both ways. "Now looka there." Keane grinned. At the end of the alley was a garbage truck, but there were no garbage collectors. "I'll bet our witnesses are at the scene of the crime," he laughed.

They went back through the building, meeting the crime-scene team on the way, then stepped out into the street. There, behind the yellow tape, were three uniformed garbage collectors. Keane pointed. "There's your witnesses, if you're lucky." He let the detective handle them, then went back to the crime scene and had one more look around. The bodies were being loaded into a meat wagon, and somebody from the clinic was hosing down the pavement. It was all over here. He went back to find the detective and his witnesses.

"You were right, Mickey," the detective said, as Keane approached. "We got witnesses, but no description. Nobody got a good look at the guy." He grinned. "We got half a license number, though."

"Good luck with it, Frank," Keane said, waving goodbye and heading for his car.

"Don't you want to stick around while we run the tag?"

"Nope, you can have all the glory." Keane got into his

car, started it, and punched a number into his new car phone. He picked it up and listened.

"Pearl," a voice said.

"He's back, Manny," Keane said, unable to keep the grin from his voice.

"Is it the thing at the abortion clinic? It's on TV already."

"Yeah, it's him; I can feel him; He's gone, though. They've got part of a license number, but if they ever find the car, Perkerson won't be in it. He's long gone."

"Damn it!" Manny Pearl shouted.

Keane took a breath. "But not too far gone. He's around. Now I'm going to find the son of a bitch."

22

Will arrived at the cottage at dusk, exhausted. He had made fifteen campaign stops during the past three days, flying himself from town to town. It was Saturday night, his parents were in Atlanta, the servants at the main house were off, and he looked forward to a Sunday of rest and solitude. For days he had been unable to think about anything but the place he was visiting and the question he was being asked. He needed a few hours to think about nothing at all, and he was determined to get them.

There was mail on the desk, most of it ignorable. Two pieces weren't. The first was from the court, and he ripped it open.

Dear Will,

Elton has recovered and is back in form, but in the meantime, my calendar is extremely overcrowded, and I don't see how I'm going to be able to do justice to a murder trial during this session. I'm inclined to think it's going to get held over until next session, unless I get a

postponement on another big case, probably until late
November. I guess you won't mind that, but let me know
if you do.

It was signed by Judge Boggs.

Will felt a wave of relief. He had not had time to think about the case for weeks, but it had always been there, under the surface, waiting for him. Now he could separate the trial from the election, and forget about the deleterious effect the two might have on each other. He found his address book. The phone was answered immediately.

"Hello?" The voice high and young, as always.

"Larry, it's Will Lee. How you doing?"

"Mr. Lee, I'm glad to hear from you. Any news about my trial?"

Will told him about the Judge's letter. "I really think it's the best thing, Larry."

"Yessir, I guess maybe it is."

"I think the longer we're able to put off a trial, the cooler things will be for you. It's always good to let some time pass in a murder case."

"I get your point," Larry Moody said.

"Of course, you have a right to a speedy trial, and if you can't stand it, I can always go back to the Judge. His letter sounds as if he's holding out the possibility of an earlier trial, if we demand it."

"No, I think you're right; we ought to wait. I can handle that. Things aren't so bad for me. I'm doing my work, just like before."

"I'm glad to hear it. How's Charlene?"

"To tell the truth, I don't really know. We split."

Will felt a stab of alarm. "Where is she? Has she left town?"

"Oh, no, she's moved in with a girlfriend; they got a trailer down near Warm Springs."

"There's no problem about her testifying?"

"Oh, no—no problem at all. She'll stand up for me. Charlene's okay, she'll do the right thing."

Will was relieved. Charlene was Larry Moody's only alibi. "I'm glad to hear it. You take care of yourself, then. If there's anything I can do for you, call my Atlanta headquarters and leave a message. They'll know where to reach me."

"I sure will, Mr. Lee, and thanks."

Will hung up. He should have asked for Charlene's new address and phone number, he realized. He called information and got a listing in Warm Springs, then dialed the number.

A familiar voice answered, honeyed and Southern. "Hello, this is Charlene. Ruby and I are out right now, but you can leave a message at the tone, and we'll get right back to you."

Will waited for the tone and left his number. Then he turned to the other piece of mail. It was addressed in her clear, straightforward hand, one he would have recognized anywhere. He ripped open the envelope. There was only a single page.

Will,

I've been unhappy about the way we left things when I saw you last. I don't want to lose your friendship. I know you're probably overwhelmed with the campaign right now, so I'll wait and call you after November. Things

*should be quieter for me at the office then, too, and per-
haps we can have lunch and catch up. In the meantime,
I wish you the best of luck in the race. I know you'll do it
well, the way you do everything. You'll make a fine senator from Georgia.*

Kate

He read the note again. It stank of detachment. Not so
much as a "Dear" in the salutation; its mention of friendship, not love; its suggestion of lunch, not dinner; the gra-
tuitous, sugary compliment at the close. He took a sheet
of notepaper from its pigeonhole and wrote:

My Dear Kate,

    *Thank you for your kind note. Of course, your friend-
ship will always be important to me. Thank you, too, for
your good wishes, and I look forward to hearing from you
after early November.*

Warm regards,
Will

Always best to be a little warmer than necessary in these
situations. He addressed an envelope and sealed the letter,
then wadded her note and tossed it in the wastebasket. He
stamped the letter and left it in the mailbox on the front
porch for collection on Monday. Then he heated a can of
chili and washed it down with half a bottle of California red.
He fell asleep almost immediately after hitting the bed, but
not before he was gripped by a long, wrenching moment of
pain, regret, anger, and sexual longing. Tomorrow, first
thing in the morning, he was going to stop missing her.

23

The dream slipped away, and Will was left with only the erection it had caused. He allowed himself to wake slowly, willing his body to return to normal. What had he dreamed? It had been so vivid, and yet, instantly, it was gone.

He lay on his back and watched the shadow of a tree play on the ceiling. Almost no movement; it would be a typical July day in Georgia, still and hot.

He struggled from the bed, still groggy, and made coffee, wolfing down a bowl of cereal while he waited for the pot to do its work. Two cups later, he was able to handle the newspapers, deliberately skipping the political coverage. The funnies seemed the most important part today; he lingered over *Doonesbury* and *Bloom County*. The phone rang once, then he got up, turned off the bell, and adjusted the answering machine to pick up on the first ring. So much for that. They could do without him for this single day, probably the last he would have to himself before the primary.

He puttered around the house through the morning, rearranging some books on their shelves, throwing out a lot of debris that had begun to fill various corners of the house, hanging a couple of pictures that had been leaning against a cupboard for months. By noon, he was hot and a little tired. Clad only in a light cotton bathrobe, he walked out onto the front porch of the cottage. It was like stepping into a sauna; heat radiated from everything. He opened the robe and flapped it to cool his body, but that only admitted more heat. He looked at the placid little lake; it would be warm from the surface to about a foot down; below that, it would be cool. Impulsively, he shucked off the robe and ran, naked, toward the water; he sprinted down the small dock and, with a whoop, flung himself as far out as he could reach. He had been right about the temperature at the surface; it was blood-warm. He had been wrong about the water below that, too; it was not cool, it was icy. The spring that fed the lake had kept it that way. Holding his breath for as long as he could, he swam underwater, letting the cold depths sweep along his heated body. He broke the surface half a minute later and let out another whoop. He hadn't had this much fun since he was a teenager. How long since he had swum in the lake? During college? Law school?

He swam along the warm surface for a minute or two, heading back toward the dock, then turned and dived under the surface again. He counted the seconds as he swam and got to fifty before he shot upward again, gasping for air. As he broke the surface, an odd thing happened. Behind him, near the dock, there was a loud splash. He turned, but there was nobody there. The water, however, was disturbed. Then, suddenly, before he could even take a breath, something grabbed his ankle and yanked him underwater.

Shocked and panicky, he fought to the surface again, sucking in air. Something, somebody was in the water with him, but he could see no one. What the hell was going on? He looked all around him, but there was nothing, not a bubble. Then, just as suddenly as before, somebody was crawling up his back. This time, though, he had a chance to grab some air. He turned and grabbed at a form that twisted away from him; then they both broke the surface, face to face.

"Well, hi there," she said, brushing strands of long blond hair from her face.

It took him a moment. "Charlene!" he laughed, astonished. "Where the hell did you come from?"

"Well, I got your message, and I was coming down to Delano anyway, so I thought I'd drop by. I got here about the time you took your running dive, and you couldn't seem to hear me calling you, so I thought I'd just join you." She reached out, grabbed him by the hair and dunked him with both hands.

His face slid down her body, past her breasts, down a flat stomach, and over pubic hair before she vaulted over him and tried to swim away. He grabbed an ankle and pulled her down with him. They surfaced together, his hand on her bare waist, hers on his shoulders. He looked at her, gleaming wet, the outline of her breasts just beneath the water. Here they were, he thought, naked; the farm was deserted; just the two of them, alone; she and Larry Moody had broken up—Larry himself had said so. What the hell?

"Why, Mr. Lee," she laughed. "You look as though you just made a decision."

"I did," he replied.

"Hey, Will," she said. She put her arms around his neck, pulled him close, and kissed him. Her mouth was soft and warm; her body, the full length of her, pressed against him. Her legs were clamped together around his penis, which had been erect since he had realized who was in the water with him. They sank for a moment, locked together; then she broke from him and swam back to the surface. "Is there a bed in that little house over there?" she asked.

"There is," he sputtered.

"I'll race you to it," she said. She turned and made for the dock.

He swam after her, but she was already out of the water, running for the cottage, by the time he made the dock. He pulled himself out and ran after her. She went through the front door and ran straight at the bed, diving toward it. He was right behind her.

She grabbed at him, pulling him on top of her. "I want you right now," she panted, "right this minute."

He tried to answer, but her mouth was clamped to his. They rolled about in the bed; his hands were on her breasts, then her buttocks; she found him and took him inside her. "Oh, God!" she sang out. "I want you, I want you!"

"You've got me!" he yelled back, and proved it to her.

In moments, they had both come, noisily, grandly, with abandon. They lay, locked together, wet from the lake and each other.

"My goodness," she panted, "you do know how to seduce a girl."

"Me? Seduce you?" He roared with laughter.

"And make her happy, too," she said.

"Happy?" he asked. "Is that what this is? I thought it was better than happy."

"It's going to be, Will." She brushed his hair from his face. "That one was fast, and I wanted it that way. But this one is going to be slow."

"I don't know if I can handle it right this minute," Will said, beginning to get his breath.

She rolled him onto his back and ran her tongue around his nipple. "Oh, you can," she said, taking his testicles in her hand. "You just wait and see."

Will stroked her breasts, pinched a nipple softly. "You may be right," he said.

And she was. The next time took the better part of an hour.

As it got dark, they lay in bed, on fresh sheets, having showered together, and ate ice cream.

"We sort of have this problem," he said.

"What?" she asked. "I'm on the pill, and I haven't got any diseases. I just got a checkup."

"It's Larry."

"Oh, him. We split a while back; I forget exactly when."

"Well, that helps, but the thing is, you're an important witness, a critical witness, in a capital trial in which I'm defending."

"So?"

"Well, it could be construed—by unkind persons such

as the prosecuting attorney, the judge, or a jury—that I am attempting to influence your testimony."

"Is that what you've been doing? I thought you were fucking me. When I wasn't fucking you, I mean."

"Yes, well, that apart, it is probably not the smartest thing in the world for you and me to be having a relationship of this sort, if you get my drift."

"Why? Didn't you like it?"

"Oh, boy, did I like it! Still, strictly speaking, this is not proper."

"I'm glad," she said. "I hate proper. Nothing proper about me."

"It's one of your charms."

"Yeah?"

"Only one of your charms."

"Charms like what?" she asked.

"Like this."

"Oooo. I like that."

"So do I. I like it a lot."

"Can I ask you a personal question?" she asked.

"I don't see why not. This is a pretty personal situation."

"Have you ever had a blow job from somebody who was just eating ice cream?"

"I can't say that I have ever been that lucky," he replied weakly.

She put down her ice cream dish. "Well, old sport," she said, "your luck has just changed."

At dawn, she went outside and found the clothes she had been wearing when she arrived. The shorts and cut-off

T-shirt in her hand, she came back and sat on the edge of the bed. "Will, you incredible stud you," she said, "I gotta be at work at eight. Morning shift."

"Am I an incredible stud?" he asked sleepily.

"Are you ever," she said, pulling the sheet from his body. "Just look at that. I do believe you're waking up. You just lie still now." She straddled him and took him inside her.

"You're wonderfully wet inside," he said, sitting up and kissing her.

"All your fault, bud."

He buried his face in her full breasts. "These are wonderful."

"Glad you like them."

"You're wonderful all over."

"You're not so bad yourself," she said, beginning to breathe rapidly. "I'm coming."

"Me, too," he panted.

They held on to each other for a long moment before she gently pushed him back onto the bed. She brought him a damp towel and wiped his belly and his penis.

"What a way to start the day," he said.

"You go back to sleep, bud."

"Charlene, before you go—"

"Listen, Will, this was just grand; I was horny, you were horny, but I know you're going to be pretty busy for a while. Don't feel like you've got to call me up. I know you and me are from different places, and I'm not the kind of girl you take to the country-club dance."

"I think you're terrific."

"I'm glad, but you don't owe me a thing," she said.

"*However,* if you ever start feeling this way again, then I'd like it if you and I could just fuck ourselves silly. Can we leave it like that? That's the way I'd like to leave it."

"Sure. If that's what you want."

"That's it. And you just relax about this trial thing. I know how to keep my mouth shut. I'll be there to testify, and you didn't change my testimony." She stood up and slipped into her two small pieces of clothing. "You go back to sleep for a little bit," she said, kissing him.

"Good-bye, Charlene," he said, in a long sigh.

"Good-bye, Will. Until you want me again."

She left, and Will sank into a rosy haze of sleep.

24

Will arrived at the Atlanta headquarters on Monday morning light of step and of heart. He marveled at the transformation he felt in himself. Could an act of sex—well, several acts of sex—release some rejuvenative hormone into the bloodstream? Or was he simply feeling some primitive elation over a conquest? Not that the conquest had been his. Charlene puzzled him. Here was this perfectly beautiful girl, though country of manners and speech, who had it in her to seek out and seduce a man whom she barely knew, then describe their relationship dispassionately and without rancor, in a way that Will could never have brought himself to do, and say she was available for more whenever he wanted her. Why? Was she simply sexually overheated? Larry Moody had said as much; maybe it was an answer. Still, maybe she had been striking out at Larry. If so, he felt both fortunate to have been chosen as the means, and frightened at the thought that anyone but the two of them might ever learn about it.

Tom Black looked at him, puzzled. "You must have had an awfully good day off," he said.

"An awfully good day off." Will grinned. If Tom only knew.

"Well, I'm happy to see you in such good spirits. I wish I felt as happy."

"What's the problem?"

"Money's drying up, that's what. Every day, our telephone bank is becoming less productive; we've had fundraisers at the homes of everyone who would help; we've been back to the well two or three times with some of our contributors, and I suspect they're getting sick of us. What we need is a shot in the arm, something favorable that will impress enough people to refresh our sources. The debate helped, and a second debate might have helped more. Mack Dean was smart enough to know that; I think it was one of the reasons he canceled."

"Have you talked to my father about this?" Will asked.

Tom nodded. "He's beaten the bushes two or three times with his own network, too. What we need is Ben Carr out there stumping for us and putting the arm on people."

"That we're not going to get," Will said. "He's made progress, I think; he can communicate in a minimal sort of way, but not enough even to give a press interview."

"There's another thing," Tom said. "Emma Carr has been making appearances at teas and fund-raisers for Mack, saying her brother loves Mack and never trusted you."

"There's not a hell of a lot we can do about Miss Emmy," Will replied, "except maybe have her committed, and I'm not about to do that."

"It's a pity we can't," Tom mused. "I'd put out a contract on the old biddy, if I thought I could get away with it."

Will laughed. "Don't say that, even in jest. Suppose Mack had this place bugged."

Kitty Conroy came in bearing a bulky Federal Express envelope. "This just came, addressed to you, Will."

"Open it. Do we get many Federal Express deliveries around here?"

"I can't even remember one," Tom said.

Kitty pulled the string on the package, looked into it, then turned it upside down and shook the contents out onto Will's desk. Several bundles of multicolored paper, secured with rubber bands, lay there.

"What the hell?" Tom said, picking up one of the bundles.

Kitty was fishing a single sheet of paper out of the envelope. "It's a letter from Lurton Pitts," she said, handing it to Will.

Will looked at the letter.

"Jesus, Will," Tom said. "These are checks."

Will's mouth fell open. " 'Dear Will,' " he read from the letter. " 'Our bunch was very impressed with you. We made a few phone calls to some of our acquaintances and rounded up the enclosed. Hope you will find it useful. Regards, Lurton.' " Will looked at the bundles. "How many do you think there are?" he asked.

Tom and Kitty were stripping off the rubber bands and riffling through the checks.

"There's nothing here for less than five hundred dollars!" Tom said. "Most of them are for a thousand!"

The three of them began sorting the checks into stacks by amount; then they counted each stack.

"I don't believe it," Kitty said, looking at the pad before her. "I make it four hundred and ten thousand dollars!"

"This can't be legal," Will said. "We've got to get this money back to Pitts before somebody finds out about it."

"The hell you say," Tom crowed. "There's not a check in here for more than a thousand dollars—that's the individual legal limit. Each of these checks is from a different person. This is entirely legal and proper."

Will stared at the pile of checks. "This is impossible. This can't be happening. There's some sort of catch."

A campaign worker stepped into Will's office. "Will, your father is on the phone."

Will punched a button and picked up the phone. "Good morning, Dad, how was your weekend?"

"Never mind that," Billy Lee replied. "How's your morning going? If what I hear is true, it ought to be going great."

"You know about the package from Pitts?"

"He just called me. He wanted to reassure me that every penny was raised in accordance with the campaign laws. He asks only that you don't reveal that he or any of his group was behind it."

"We have to give a list of contributors to the campaign commission," Will said.

"That's all right. Lurton and his friends will be down for only a thousand each."

"I'm still trying to think of something wrong with it," Will said, shaking his head.

"Boy, stop worrying about it, and start spending it!" Billy said good-bye and hung up.

Will looked up at Tom. "It's legal, proper, and okay, too. But only the three of us know who assembled all this. Pitts has demanded that we keep it to ourselves, and I don't want it to go beyond this room, got that?"

"Got it," Tom and Kitty responded simultaneously.

"Will," Tom said.

"Yes?"

"We've got our TV campaign."

Will was fumbling in a desk drawer; he came up with some campaign stationery. "I think I'd better write Lurton Pitts a personal thank-you note. Get somebody started on the computer—I want an individual letter to each of these people over my signature."

"Will," Kitty said, "your mama brought you up right."

"One more thing," Will said, beginning to write. "Somebody get these checks into the bank immediately. It makes me nervous having all this money on the premises."

Kitty began raking bundles of checks back into the big envelope.

25

Will sat nervously with Tom Black, Kitty Conroy, and his parents in a small screening room that smelled of stale cigarette smoke; he stared at a large, blank television monitor and waited for something to appear on it.

Will had just spent two days in a tiny studio down the corridor, staring into the lens of a camera and speaking to it as if it were a person. It had been a disconcerting experience; Tom had not allowed him to see himself on a monitor during all that time; he had been constantly patted on the face by an elderly woman with a sponge and a jar of makeup; and at no time had he been given anything to read from. Tom had forced him to talk about himself in a way he would never normally have done, until he spoke of his own accomplishments as if they were those of someone else. At the end of the time, he had been weary, hoarse, and disoriented. Now he was to see the result of his effort.

The monitor flickered, and suddenly Will's face appeared on the screen. It was alarmingly large and close, but Will was immediately aware of how beautifully it was lit.

The voice of a professional announcer spoke. "Will Lee is running for the United States Senate, to represent Georgia. Here's what he has to say about it."

Will, looking directly into the camera, began to speak; his voice was relaxed, natural, and richer than it ordinarily sounded to its owner. "For eight years now, I've been working for Senator Ben Carr in the United States Senate. I've done just about everything in his office. I've been his press secretary, his chief legislative assistant, and counsel to the committee he chairs, the Senate Intelligence Committee." He permitted himself a small smile. "I've gone for a few cups of coffee in my time there, too." Then he became more serious. "I've had the opportunity to learn, first-hand, from the man I believe to be Georgia's—perhaps America's—greatest senator in this century. And now, since Senator Carr can't himself run again, I'm running to replace him—to the extent that anybody can replace Benjamin Carr. I want your vote, so that I can put my experience to work for you in the Senate. I think that experience qualifies me to do a better job than anybody else who's running. I hope you think so, too."

A title came up: "Paid for by the Committee to Elect Will Lee." The monitor went blank.

Will found that he had been holding his breath; he released it.

"That was fine," Patricia Lee said.

"Careful, everybody," Will laughed, "that woman is a mother."

"She's right, you know," Kitty Conroy said.

"I think it's perfect," Billy Lee chimed in. "You've done a magnificent job, Tom."

"Thanks," Tom said. "We've got seven more one-minute spots." He signaled for the technician to start the tape again.

Will watched himself as the spots ran. It was an eerie experience; he felt both a participant and a detached viewer. By the time the spots had all run, he felt comfortable watching them, even liked them a little. "I feel too close to this to make any sort of rational judgment," he said to no one in particular.

"Let me tell you what I wanted to accomplish," Tom said, "and you tell me if I got it right. Mack Dean's stuff is all flag-waving and patriotic music; I wanted a sharp contrast to that. I wanted to keep the message simple, friendly, and believable; I think Will is a believable man, and I wanted that to come out. I framed the shot so closely because I wanted intimacy, too. One of the criticisms that has been made of Will is that he's too cool, too hard to figure out, that his charm is superficial. I worked him until that went away, until I felt we were right down to the core of the man. In the beginning, he was stiff, was trying to project earnestness; in the end, he was relaxed, maybe even a little tired, and I like him that way."

"It's an outstanding job, Tom," Billy said. "I think you accomplished exactly what you wanted to."

"Thank you, Billy."

"Hey, don't I get any credit for any of this?" Will asked with mock hurt.

"Maybe a little," Kitty said.

"I'm also doing a thirty-second version of each of these spots," Tom said. "That'll give us a bank we can use right through the general election."

"Thank God for that," Will said. "I wouldn't want to go through this again."

Somebody came into the room and called Billy to the phone. When he returned, his face was neutral.

"I've got some news," he said.

Everyone looked expectantly at him. "A source of mine says that a few minutes ago the State Republican Committee picked Jim Winslow as the Republican candidate."

"Whew!" Tom said, slumping in his seat.

"You were afraid the Reverend Don Beverly Calhoun would get it?" Billy asked.

"I was," Tom said.

"But why?" Billy asked. "The man's a buffoon."

"So's Ronald Reagan," Tom said, "from my point of view, anyway. But he's good on TV. So's Calhoun. What's more, Calhoun's about as well-known in this state as Ronald Reagan. He's got his own television studios, and he can reach any home in the state two or three times a week; he's got a massive mailing list, too, all computer-catalogued by county and city and all sorts of other things. If Dr. Don wants to send a letter to all the people in metropolitan counties between the ages of forty and sixty who have given him more than one hundred dollars in the past years and who are terrified of gays, he just punches it in, and the computer cranks out a list: I wish we had a database half as good."

"Well," Billy said, "he's out of the picture now, unless he campaigns for Winslow."

"I don't think he will," Tom said. "Winslow is too liberal for him; Winslow thinks abortion should be available in cases of rape and incest."

"When do these spots start running, Tom?" Billy asked. "We've only got ten days until the primary."

"Tonight," Tom said. "Three of them. Big blast, statewide. By primary day, we'll have spent three hundred thousand of our money."

"Aren't you loading too much of your money into the primary?" Billy asked. "What will you have left for the general election?"

"If we don't win the primary, we won't be in the general election," Tom replied. "We're getting poll results frequently now, and I'm prepared to commit our whole budget to the primary, if the figures we get warrant it."

"Sounds risky to me," Billy said.

"Billy," Tom said, "I'd hate to wake up the morning after the primary with three hundred thousand dollars in the bank, having lost the vote by half a point."

"I see what you mean," Billy said.

"Besides," Will chimed in, "if we win the primary, the state party will chip in some bucks, and our fund-raising should pick up, too."

"I hope you're right," Billy said.

Tom stood up. "Well, we'd better all get a good night's sleep. Tomorrow, we're in the home stretch."

26

Ernest Jenkins was accustomed to meeting people in hotel rooms, so, in that respect, there was nothing about this occasion to unnerve him. Still, he was unnerved. He had never expected to find himself in a meeting alone with this man. He could not have been more nervous if he had been meeting the President of the United States. He was shown to a seat and offered a drink, which he declined with thanks; it might stand him in better stead to be abstemious, and anyway, he wanted a clear head. He wanted to remember every detail of this occasion.

The man seated himself across the fireplace from Jenkins, crossed his legs, and dusted something off his neat blue suit. He was impressive even in his smallest motion. "Now, Ernest," the Archon began. "May I call you that?"

"Oh, yes, sir," Jenkins replied. "I'd be honored."

"I'm told you have some interesting information for me."

Jenkins fingered the envelope in his lap. "Yes, sir, I believe it is. May I tell you the whole story?"

"Of course, Ernest," the Archon said smoothly. "Just take your time, and tell me everything."

"Well, I'm in the business of private investigations, and the other day I was contacted by . . . well, can we just say I was contacted by this certain party?"

"By all means, Ernest. I wouldn't want you to betray a confidence."

"Thank you, sir. Well, as I was saying, I was contacted by this certain party and asked to do a surveillance job, a kind of confidential job, you understand."

"Of course, Ernest. A surveillance would have to be confidential, wouldn't it?" There was just a flicker of impatience in the Archon's voice.

Ernest plunged ahead, not wanting to inconvenience the great man. "Well, sir, I was told to follow this certain young lady, that she might be meeting a gentleman, and I was asked to record and photograph the, uh, occasion."

"I see. And did you do this?"

"Yes, sir, I did. I followed this young lady to a certain house in the country, and I found that I was able to set up an excellent surveillance, in spite of the impromptu situation, as it were. I've got some very good camera equipment and a parabolic microphone—that's a highly localized microphone with—"

"I believe I'm familiar with the instrument. Please go on."

"Well, I was able to get an excellent angle through a window and take some very excellent shots, and I got a very nice sound track, so to speak, to go with them."

"I see. And why did you think this would be of interest to me?"

"Well, sir, when I got back to my darkroom and processed my film and started printing, I realized that the gentleman in question was someone rather, ah, politically prominent."

"Ah . . ." the Archon said. "Perhaps you'll let me take a look?"

"Yes, sir, that's why I'm here. I just wanted to get your assurance that this won't go any further. I mean, I haven't even shown the pictures to my client yet."

The Archon gazed at him, saying nothing.

"Of course, I know you'd never mention it to anybody else, sir," Jenkins said, handing over the envelope. "I mean, where you got the photographs."

The Archon ignored him and removed half a dozen eight-by-tens from the envelope and began looking through them. His black eyebrows went up.

"You recognize this gentleman, then?" Jenkins asked.

"Oh, yes, I believe I do." The Archon permitted himself a small smile. "And there was sound, as well, you said?"

Jenkins produced a small cassette recorder from his briefcase and handed it across. "Just push the start button, there; it's all cued up for you."

The Archon pressed the button.

"There," a husky woman's voice said. "Do you like my finger right there?"

"Oh, yes," a man's voice replied. "That's a very nice place."

"And what would you like me to do with my finger?" the woman asked coyly.

The Archon switched off the machine.

Jenkins thought he looked a little embarrassed.

"I believe I get the picture," the Archon said. "Well, Ernest, you were right. This is very interesting material indeed. May I keep these photographs?"

"Oh, yes, sir," Jenkins replied. "Those are extras. You can keep the tape machine, too."

"Thank you. I would like to give some thought as to how this material might best serve our interests. You say you haven't given anything to your client yet?"

"Not yet, sir. I was going to this evening."

"Well, go ahead, then. I'm sure your client has paid very handsomely for this work, and he—or she—is entitled to the results."

"Yes, sir."

The Archon stood, signaling that the meeting was at a close. He took Jenkins's hand in both of his. "Thank you so much, Ernest," he said warmly. "You have done the right thing, and I won't forget it."

"It's been a privilege, sir," Jenkins replied. He walked on air all the way to his car.

When Jenkins had left, the Archon went through the photographs again. The man certainly did good work; he would remember that. The pictures were nicely shot and expertly printed—all the details were there, including the ecstatic faces of both the participants.

The Archon picked up a telephone and dialed a number.

"Hello?" a man's voice said.

"Hello," the Archon replied. "You know who this is?"

"Yes, sure. You heard about Jim Winslow getting the Republican nomination?"

"Yes, within minutes."

"Not what we'd hoped."

"It's unacceptable," the Archon replied, "but don't despair just yet. I've told you we're going to have an effect on elections in this state, and believe me, we're just getting started. To that end, I want to place something of importance in the hands of just the right journalist. This is not the sort of story that might appeal to the nobler members of the profession, if you get my drift."

"Newspaper or TV?"

"Wherever it will get the most play. You're a better judge of that than I; I just don't want it traceable to us."

"Mmmm. I think I might have an idea; fellow on the *Columbus Beacon*, name of Huel Hardaway."

"Does he have credibility with his colleagues?"

"I think so. He's thought to be a little over the hill, drinks a fair bit, but he drinks with other press people. I've heard that he makes more money than he's been worth, lately, and his position at his paper is not very secure. He might jump at something big, even if it was on the questionable side."

"He sounds ideal. How soon can you get some material to him?"

"Tomorrow, if you're in a hurry."

"Not too big a hurry. We've got a few days before the primary. I'd like this to break late; say, the Sunday papers before the Tuesday primary. I don't want the story to have time to cool before the vote."

"You've got something on one of the candidates?"

"When you see the material, you'll know who. Another thing, I don't want this to seem to come from his opponent. We don't want a backfire."

"I think I can manage that all right, but I'm a little confused. What do we care who wins the primary?"

"We want our man to have the opponent who's easiest to beat, don't we?"

"But Jim Winslow isn't exactly our man."

"You let me worry about that."

"Now listen, I know Winslow, and he will never be reliable for us."

"I'm aware of that," the Archon said with some irritation.

"No offense, I just . . . well, I'll let you handle it."

"You do that. I'll leave the material in your mailbox before midnight. You just get it to your man, Hardaway, tomorrow, but stress that he holds it until Sunday."

"Yes, sir."

The Archon hung up, then sat quietly for a moment. The upset he had felt at the selection by the Republicans of Winslow was ebbing away. He saw his way clearly now. This little private detective, Jenkins, had given him the means to control the primary. Now all he had to worry about was the general election. He picked up the telephone again.

"Hello?"

"You know who this is?"

"Yessir."

"Come to my house at three A.M."

"Yes, sir."

The line went dead.

Harold Perkerson hung up the telephone. He went back to the sofa and once again entwined himself with Suzy, the nurse. "A meeting with the Man," he said, glancing at his watch. "We've got plenty of time, though."

She kissed him lightly and put her hand in his lap. "Must be a big one, if he's meeting with you personally."

"Yeah. It's only the second time I've been to his house."

"Where does he live?"

Perkerson sat up, drew back, and hit her hard across the mouth with the back of his hand. "Don't ever ask me a question like that again," he said evenly.

A tear spilled from the corner of her eye. "I'm sorry," she whimpered. "I know better than that."

Perkerson brushed away the tear. She liked being hit, he thought. He'd do that again sometimes, if she got out of line. He cupped his hand behind her neck. "Come here, baby," he said.

She came to him. "I'm sorry," she said again.

"Show me how sorry," he replied.

27

Kitty Conroy was leaving her room at the Best Western Motel in Americus, Georgia, near Plains, when
Rick Barnes, a columnist for the Atlanta papers, fell in
step with her. Barnes had traveled with the campaign off
and on.

"A word, Kitty?"

She stopped. "I haven't got much time, Rick. We're
due at Jimmy Carter's house in half an hour."

"Is Carter going to endorse Will? And, if so, does Will
really want the endorsement?"

"The answer to your first question is, I don't know; to
the second, yes, if he can get it. You might remember that
Mack Dean wants his endorsement, too. Is that what you
wanted to talk about?"

Barnes shook his head. "No. But we have to agree that
this conversation never took place."

"All right."

"I mean, really—it never took place, okay?"

"Okay. It stops here."

Barnes took a deep breath. "First of all, my people are planning to endorse Will on Sunday."

Kitty brightened. "That's good news, Rick. Thanks for telling me."

"Don't thank me yet," Barnes said. "There's more."

"More?"

"Kitty, I'm sorry to have to be the one to tell you this, and I stress, it may just be talk, but . . ."

"What kind of talk?"

Barnes looked embarrassed. "What the hell, I'd better just get it out. You know Huel Hardaway, with the *Columbus Beacon*?"

"Fat, in his fifties, boozer?"

"That's the one. Hardaway's never meant a hell of a lot statewide, but he used to be well thought of in the Columbus area. He's gone downhill a bit the past few years. There were rumors he was going to get the chop."

"I don't follow, Rick. What's this got to do with us?"

"Well, apparently, he's not going to get the chop now; he says he's come up with a real front-pager for the *Beacon*."

"And?"

"Somebody I know had a drink with Hardaway last night in Columbus. Well, a few drinks. It must have taken that to get it out of him."

"Get what out of him?"

"He says he's got pictures of, well, maybe Will in bed with somebody."

Kitty froze. "With who?"

"He wouldn't say."

"When were these pictures taken?"

"Maybe as recently as last weekend."

"Rick, Will Lee is a heterosexual bachelor; he's entitled to a sex life."

"Yeah, sure. Normally, this wouldn't be a story."

"Then why is it a story, now?"

"It's got something to do with who he was in bed with."

"Who?" Oh, God, Kitty prayed. Don't let it be a man.

"Hardaway was being cagey, but my source got the very strong impression that the identity of the person was more important than the fact of the, uh, meeting."

"Rick . . ."

"It was a woman; I got that much."

Kitty tried not to sigh with relief. "No other information?"

Barnes shook his head. "None."

"No respectable newspaper would run such pictures."

"No, but the *Beacon* would run a story saying that such pictures exist. So would we, if we could verify it. In the middle of a campaign for the Senate, it's news any way you slice it."

"I see."

"And there's something else."

"What?"

"A respectable newspaper might not run the pictures, but that's not the only place they could run."

Kitty's heart sank. "Hardaway says he's got a bidding war going between two of the supermarket tabloids. That means very splashy and, of course, national coverage. After a week or two of follow-ups, your man would be as famous as Elvis. And just as dead."

"Does your paper know about this?"

"Yes," Barnes said. "They won't go with it until they can verify all the details, and Hardaway is the only one who has those, so that probably means we'll have to wait for the Sunday *Beacon*. In the meantime, they're holding up on the endorsement of Will until they can check out the story."

"Thanks, Rick. I know you went out on a limb, telling me."

Barnes shrugged. "I think it stinks."

"I owe you one." She turned to go.

"Kitty?"

"Yes?"

Barnes grinned. "Maybe you can still get *Amy* Carter's endorsement."

"Well?" Tom Black said.

"Well, what?" Will answered.

"Oh, come on, Will," Kitty said, "we've got to talk about this."

"My sex life is my own business."

"On Sunday morning, it's going to be everybody's business," Kitty said.

"Let me ask you something," Will said to them both. "Assume the worst. What can we do about it? Can we stop the story?"

Kitty shook her head. "No, not unless we can safely deny it. And they've got pictures."

"Then why worry? Let's continue as planned. If they run pictures of me in bed with somebody, I'll deal with it then."

"What I don't understand," Kitty chipped in, "is who this woman could be that makes her so dangerous."

Will shrugged.

Tom spoke up. "Somebody's wife."

"Oh, shit," Kitty moaned.

The telephone rang, and Tom picked it up.

"Yes?"

"Oh, yes, how are you? Oh, I'm sorry to hear it. Yes, we'll wait for your call. Thank you." He hung up. "That was Rosalynn Carter. The President has asked Jimmy to come to Washington for some sort of meeting. He has to leave immediately. He'll call us when he gets back." Tom collapsed into his chair.

"Well," Kitty said, "word is getting around."

When they had gone, Will stretched out on the bed and closed his eyes. What next? What else could possibly happen to him? He didn't understand. Who could possibly have known they would end up in bed together? He hadn't even known himself. He thought for a minute. There was only one person who could have known, who could have planned the event, including the pictures.

Charlene.

28

It was ironic, Will thought, that his entire Saturday was scheduled for Columbus, a city where polling had suggested that he could gain ground with personal appearances; also a city where his political fate could be sealed on the following day.

It surprised him that he was not depressed. He went about his campaigning like a man enjoying his last day on earth, starting with a country ham-and-grits breakfast with a hundred people in a supporter's backyard; he continued to a shopping mall for a speech and a round of the shops, shaking hands, with a local TV news crew tagging along; that afternoon, he visited a Little League championship game, just in time for a few words to the crowd during the seventh-inning stretch, then another shopping mall on the black side of town. In the early evening, he spoke on defense policy at the American Legion state convention, then, later, wound up with the taping of an interview by the anchorman of a local television station, to be shown the following afternoon.

The interview ran to form, with no questions of an unusual nature, until the last. With a minute remaining, the interviewer asked, "Mr. Lee, there are rumors that one of our local newspapers, the *Columbus Beacon,* is running a front-page story tomorrow morning that might change the course of the campaign. Can you tell us anything about that?"

Will affected mild surprise. "I'm afraid I'm no better informed than you are. I guess we'll both have to go out and buy a paper."

The man thanked him and closed the program.

Will got into a car with Tom Black and Kitty Conroy outside the station.

"That's it," Tom said. "We'd better all get some sleep. Big day tomorrow." There did not seem to be any irony in his voice.

"I'm not bushed yet," Will said. "Let's go on back to Atlanta. I'd just as soon wake up there."

"We've already got rooms booked here. Are you sure you aren't too tired to fly?"

"I'm fine," Will said. "I must be getting used to this."

Tom turned the car around and pointed it toward the airport.

Although there were still two more days of campaigning to go, Will felt, somehow, that the campaign had ended that night. And well it might have, depending on what the *Columbus Beacon* had to say the following morning. He had shut out all thought of what might happen. He supposed he should have been planning as best he could for the eventuality, but he felt removed from the dangers of tomorrow. He still had the feeling, no doubt irrational, that, in spite of all that had occurred so far, nothing so terrible could possibly happen to him.

At the airport, Tom dropped them at Will's airplane, then went to return the rental car. Will got a weather forecast and filed a flight plan, then performed his pre-flight inspection of the aircraft.

As he and Kitty climbed into the airplane, Kitty looked around. "Where's Tom? He's taking an awfully long time getting rid of the car."

Will looked toward the little terminal building and saw Tom standing under a streetlight in front of the building, looking expectantly up the street.

"What's he doing?" Kitty wondered.

As she asked the question, it was answered. From up the street came a large truck, which came to a halt in front of the terminal. Painted on the side of the vehicle in large letters were the words COLUMBUS BEACON DAILY AND SUNDAY. The driver got out, hefted a bundle of papers from the back of the truck, and began filling the coin-operated dispensing machines in front of the terminal building. Tom was digging into his pocket for change. Shortly, he was walking toward the airplane, a paper under his arm.

Will's bowels shrank as a condemned man's might at the first sight of his firing squad. Here it came; it could no longer be avoided. There was nothing but trouble ahead—first, public humiliation and the loss of the election, followed by disbarment and disgrace. He would move to Ireland. The family still had his grandfather's property there. He could farm the place and spend his evenings reading. Nobody there would know or care what he had done to himself in America.

Tom got into the airplane. "How about some light?" he said.

Will reached up and switched on the cabin light.

Tom spread the front page for them all to see. A large black headline read GOVERNOR IN LOVE NEST WITH ANCHORLADY.

"What?" Kitty said weakly.

Will closed his eyes and rested his head on the back of the seat. "Read it to us, Tom," he said.

Tom read:

Exclusive to the *Beacon*, by Huel Hardaway. Earlier this week, this reporter came into possession of photographs taken by a private detective employed by Mrs. Louise Dean, wife of Governor Mack Dean, of her husband in intimate circumstances with Ms. Shirley Scott, anchor of Atlanta's Channel Six News. After verifying the authenticity of the photographs and tracking down the detective, this reporter was able, with the permission of Mrs. Dean, to get his story. Ernest Jenkins, a licensed private investigator of Atlanta, established a surveillance last weekend of Shirley Scott, thirty-seven, a well-known Atlanta television journalist. On Sunday evening, he followed her to a farm in Gwinnett County, north of Atlanta, a property owned by the Governor of the state, Mack Dean, sixty-one. There, he observed the Governor greeting Ms. Scott affectionately at the door of a guest cottage.

The photographs clearly show Governor Dean and Ms. Scott on a bed, nude, performing a variety of acts of sexual intercourse, including, but not limited to, coitus.

Mrs. Louise Dean, the Governor's second wife, has been married to him for the past nine years. The Governor was divorced from his first wife eleven years ago amid unconfirmed rumors of an affair with the current Mrs. Dean. Mrs. Dean, reached by telephone at the Governor's Mansion in Atlanta, said, "I have suspected my husband and this woman of carrying on an affair for some time now, and Mr. Jenkins's photographs and tape recording have confirmed my suspicions. I will be filing for divorce on grounds of adultery Monday morning at ten o'clock at the Fulton County Courthouse." Mrs. Dean added that she will hold a news conference at that time.

Governor Dean, reached at press time and asked to comment on the evidence and his wife's statement, would only say, "I have nothing to say at this time. I am sure that the true facts will become known as time progresses. I would just like to assure the people of Georgia that I have never done anything, publicly or privately, which would bring disrepute upon the office I hold or upon this great state."

Ms. Scott, reached at her North Atlanta condominium, and advised of the evidence by this reporter, would only say, "You son of a bitch."

Tom put down the newspaper and looked at Kitty. They both burst into laughter.

"That's telling him, Shirley!" Kitty crowed. "I'm amazed he printed her response."

"It was too good a line to pass up," Tom howled. "Jesus, Will, why didn't you tell us they had nothing on you?"

Will raised his head weakly from the back of the seat. "Would you have believed me?"

"Probably not," Tom laughed. "God, I never had such an awful day as today."

"Me neither," Kitty said. "Not as bad a day as Mack Dean, though."

"Poor old Mack," Will sighed.

"Don't waste your sympathy," Tom said. "He got exactly what he deserved."

Will shook his head. "I don't think anybody deserves that. God, his wife must really hate him."

"A woman scorned," Kitty said. "Let that be a lesson to the both of you."

"Well, I think we can stop worrying about the primary," Tom said. "As close as we've been in the polls, the wronged-woman vote alone would put us over the top."

Will started the engine and looked at his checklist. "There are still two days to go before the primary," he said over the intercom. "I would have thought that if we have learned anything at all in this campaign, it is that *anything can happen.*"

All the way to Atlanta, the silence was broken only by Will's occasional words to air-traffic control.

29

Harold Perkerson sat in the dark and waited. The stars had disappeared, but the sun had not yet risen. The warm, moist air promised a hot and muggy day, normal for a September Tuesday in Georgia.

He fingered a thick, elongated canvas tube that rested on his knees. Hand-stitched and filled with sand, it weighed perhaps two pounds.

As the light came up, he stood and stretched his body, paying particular attention to his legs. He was not a regular runner, and although he had jogged a mile or so for the past few mornings, he did not want to run the risk of a pulled muscle. He slapped the canvas tube into the palm of his other hand; there was a dull thud, nothing more. It was a quiet instrument. He felt in a pocket of his sweat jacket for another implement, took it out, examined its contents, replaced it. He felt in the other pocket for the rubber tubing.

Perkerson walked through the woods toward the road, careful not to be seen. Finally, he stationed himself behind a large oak, ten yards from where the road curved sharply, and waited. Seven or eight minutes passed. Perkerson glanced at his watch: just past six; he hoped his man would be on time. As if to make a point, the jogger appeared a hundred yards down the road. Perkerson looked just long enough to form an impression. Tallish, slim, not unlike himself; thinning gray hair, glasses, tanned skin: the picture of a healthy, fit man in his fifties. Perkerson moved behind the tree, put on his dark glasses, pulled up the hood of the sweat jacket, and waited for the sound of running shoes passing on the tarmac. It came soon enough.

Perkerson counted to five, then left the shelter of the tree and made for the road. It was slower and noisier going through the last yards of woods than he imagined it would be. He hit the road running fast, afraid he would be unable to catch his man soon enough.

He came around the curve and entered a long tunnel of trees, dark and cool, with a blaze of low-angled sunlight at the far end. The man was twenty yards ahead of him, jogging along with practiced ease. Perkerson had to overtake him before the tree tunnel ended. He increased his pace, and the gap closed. The man glanced over his shoulder and gave a little wave.

The sunlight at the end of the tree tunnel loomed ahead, and Perkerson started to sprint. As he began to draw even with his target, the man half turned his head.

"Morning," he called out. "You're really pouring it on, aren't you?"

"I sure am," Perkerson replied, then swung the cosh. Not too much force, he told himself as his arm came around; let the thing do its own work. The canvas tube met the back of the man's neck, at the base of the skull.

Immediately, he became a rag doll, a limp length of flesh, falling forward, colliding harshly with the black road surface. He was unconscious before he hit the ground; he had not even had the moment it would have taken to throw his hands out to break his fall.

There would be no bruising at the back of the neck, and unconsciousness would last only a short time. Perkerson, breathing hard and working fast, knelt beside the still figure, took a length of rubber surgical tubing from a pocket, wound it around the man's left leg above the knee, and tied it off. He pulled up the leg of the running suit, slapped the bare skin smartly at the back of the knee, and watched the vein come up. He took a disposable syringe from his other pocket, removed the protective cap from the needle, held it up, tapped the thing so any bubbles would rise to the tip of the solution of potassium, squirted a little into the air away from the leg, then slipped the needle into the vein. He released the tied tubing and slowly emptied the syringe into the man's bloodstream. He removed the syringe and wiped away a drop of blood with his finger and a little spit; he returned the tubing to his pocket, pulling down the trouser leg, replaced the cap on the needle, put that into his pocket, and waited. It should take only seconds. The man moaned, started to come around.

Perkerson was nervous; he didn't want to hit him again, didn't want to touch him. He needn't have worried; suddenly the man emitted a loud grunt and convulsed, reflexively drawing a hand to his chest. Then, with a sigh, he relaxed and seemed to melt into the tarmac. It was over, as quickly as that.

There was a noise from somewhere. Perkerson looked

over his shoulder, but before he could move, a car swung around the curve and came toward him through the tree tunnel. Perkerson turned back to the dead jogger, turned him over, and put an ear to his chest. The car screeched to a halt next to him.

"What happened?" a man shouted from the car.

"I don't know," Perkerson shouted back, not turning his head. "I saw him grab his chest and fall; he must have had a heart attack. Do you know CPR?"

The car door slammed, and the driver knelt beside the body. He felt for a pulse at the man's neck, then struck him sharply twice in the chest. "Yes," he said, "I do. Take my car, and call an ambulance." He turned the man's face to him and started to give mouth-to-mouth resuscitation.

Perkerson ran around the car, the engine of which was still running, leapt in, and drove away, fast. He emerged from the tree tunnel into bright sunlight, rounded a curve, and came to a convenience store; a phone booth stood outside it. He whipped into the deserted parking lot, found some change, and dialed 911.

"Emergency," a voice said. "Which service do you need?"

"Ambulance." A click.

"Ambulance services."

"A jogger is down, suspected heart attack, Northside Drive, just outside the Perimeter; need an ambulance at once. Got that?"

"Yes, but I need some more information."

Perkerson hung up the phone, looked around him, then loped off into the woods, back toward where he had left his car.

30

Will woke slowly, disoriented at first, unaccustomed to his own bed in the cottage at the Delano farm. The morning was his; the phone was shut off, Tom and Kitty were in Atlanta. It was over. There was nothing more he could do.

He sat up and groaned. He was still tired; his whole body was sore; his right hand was swollen and tender from shaking hundreds of hands, and his arm ached right up to the shoulder. He felt old and arthritic.

Ten minutes under a hot shower restored something like normal movement, and by the time he had opened the morning papers he was nearly awake.

Louise Dean, brunette, a carefully preserved forty-five, smiled bravely at him from the front page of the *Atlanta Constitution*. She stood, the Fulton County Courthouse rising behind her, a forest of microphones rising before her, cheerfully applying the finishing touches to the destruction of her husband's political career. Will had seen it on TV, sandwiched between two of the twenty-five campaign appearances he had made the previous day. She had stood there, telling the entire state of Georgia and most of the rest of the country, of her husband's infidelity over the years, of his weakness for the bottle, and of his personal and political incompetence. For one brief moment of panic, Will had thought she was going to endorse her husband's opponent. He had prayed that she would end her news conference without uttering his name and she had, finally flouncing off into the courthouse, smug with satisfaction over her morning's work.

Bright and early Monday morning, a tabloid newspaper had appeared at every supermarket in the state and country, featuring well-taken photographs of Mack Dean and Shirley Scott in the throes, with little black bars covering strategic places.

On Monday's noon news, the president of Channel 6 had announced, having ascertained from a recalcitrant Shirley Scott that her affair with Mack Dean had extended back in time at least as far as his television debate with Will Lee, that Ms. Scott had involuntarily left the employ of the station, indeed had left town, taking advantage of accumulated vacation time.

Mack Dean himself was holed up in a suite at the Peachtree Plaza Hotel, and the operators were not putting through any calls. Nobody had seen him since Saturday night except the room-service waiters, who were talking freely to television cameras in their spare time. Old Mack, they all agreed, was drunk as a skunk.

And now Dean's opponent sat alone in the cottage by the lake, a half-eaten bowl of cereal congealing before him, leafing listlessly through the papers, the primary victory all but his, and nothing between him and a seat in the United States Senate but a lackluster Republican opponent with a slight stammer and not much money. To Will, on this hot September morning, it did not seem possible.

Later in the morning, he shaved and dressed for what would be his only public appearance that day, until the election had been decided. Glancing frequently at his watch, Will drove into town, pulling up, as previously arranged by Kitty Conroy with nearly every television station in the state, at precisely ten minutes past twelve, in order to make the noon news, live. As he got out of the car, six—he counted them—television cameras and their attached correspondents rushed at him. He had been expecting only one, the pool camera; it seemed a terrible waste of men and equipment, he thought, just to cover the candidate entering the polling place to vote.

"Good morning, ladies and gentlemen," he said, beaming at them. "Or is it afternoon? I slept late." The reporters, to his surprise, looked momentarily taken aback.

"Mr. Lee," said a young woman, thrusting her microphone into his face.

Will was ready for a question about Mack Dean's predicament, on which he did not plan to comment.

"Do you have any comment on the death of your Republican opponent?"

Will thought he had misunderstood. "I beg your pardon?"

"Sir, perhaps you haven't heard that Jim Winslow suffered a heart attack and died while jogging early this morning."

Will stood speechless before the cameras.

"Will," a young man said, elbowing the woman out of the way, "you obviously haven't heard. To bring you up to date, just after six this morning a jogger was discovered, unconscious, on a North Atlanta street by another jogger and a motorist. An ambulance was called, and he was DOA at Grady Hospital. There was no identification on the body. Mr. Winslow's wife went out looking for him at seven o'clock and reported him missing at seven-thirty, but there was some foul-up at the morgue, and his body wasn't identified until just over an hour ago."

"Well, I'm shocked," Will said truthfully. "I didn't know Jim Winslow well, but from all I knew of him he was a fine man. I was looking forward to facing him in the general election, if, of course, I win today. I can only extend my sympathy to his family and friends. Now, if you'll excuse me, I'd better get inside and vote." He made his way through the maze of equipment and up the steps of the Community Building, pausing to shake a hand or two along the way. Inside, he greeted a few locals who were there to vote, voted himself, and left the building. The cameras were on him again immediately.

"Mr. Lee, how do you feel about all the events of the past few days?"

"Well, frankly, I'm a little dazed. Sunday and yesterday were, of course, very crowded days for me—I think we made something like a couple of dozen stops yesterday in the Atlanta area—and that sort of schedule doesn't afford much time for reflection. Of course, I'm very shocked to hear about Mr. Winslow's death. I just hope that folks won't forget that there's a very important election today, and that everybody will get out and vote. Thank you very much." He made his way back to the car and pointed it toward the airport at Warm Springs.

Will arrived at midafternoon at the Omni Hotel in Atlanta, where a suite had been reserved for Election Day. His parents were already there, manning phone lines to headquarters, where Tom Black was in touch with precinct captains all over the state.

"The turnout is low," Tom said on the phone. "We might have expected that, I guess, but I thought it would be better, even with the news about Mack. Scattered exit polling gives us better than sixty-five percent so far, and it could get better when our people start to vote after work. Any way you slice it, Will, it looks like a milk run."

"Yeah," Will replied, "I wish I could enjoy it more. To tell you the truth, I'd rather have had Mack on his feet at the end and taken my chances with the vote."

"The last polling we did, which was on Friday, had you three points ahead, with an error margin of four points, and that was a gain on early in the week. If it's any consolation, I think you would have won anyway."

"Well, thanks for that, Tom."

"Word is, the Republican State Executive Committee is meeting this afternoon, but I expect it'll be later in the week before we know who the candidate is going to be. Winslow's death must have thrown them for a bad loop, but I can't imagine they'd choose that clown Calhoun."

"But he was their second choice last time."

"Yeah, he was their last choice, too. They couldn't be that crazy."

"Okay, I'll talk to you later. I'm going to try to take a nap; I'm still pretty bushed."

Will surprised himself by sleeping until he was awakened by his mother at dinnertime. They ate well from room service, and his mood improved. It began to sink in that he was going to be the Democratic nominee.

At eight-fifteen, Tom called. "I've had all three television stations on the phone. They'd planned full election coverage from nine o'clock, but now, with the returns so one-sided, they're badgering us for an early statement."

"Suits me," Will said, "but I think we ought to hear from Mack first."

"You come on over here now, and I'll get hold of his campaign manager."

Will arrived at campaign headquarters to find a party in full swing. Nobody was even chalking up precinct returns anymore. He made his way through the crowd of campaign workers and supporters to the front of the room. Tom thrust a yellow sheet of paper at him.

"Call this a telegram. Mack himself dictated it to me five minutes ago. He sounded awful."

Will read the concession statement.

"TV wants to go on at eight-fifty, so they can resume the network schedule at nine. I told them okay."

"Good," Will said. He passed the next few minutes accepting congratulations; then, on signal from a television man, he climbed onto a desk. "Thank you for being here," he called out, quieting them. "First of all, I know you all join me in extending to the family of Jim Winslow our sincere sympathy." He paused for a beat. "Now, I want to read something to you." He held up the yellow sheet of paper. "I have a telegram here; it says: 'I want to extend my congratulations to you, your mother and father, and all your campaign workers this evening. You have fought a fine and clean campaign and have won the right to represent all Democrats in the general election. Come November, you will have my full and unstinting support.' It's signed 'Governor Mack Dean.'"

Will paused for a moment of pandemonium from the campaign workers, and as he did, he saw Kitty Conroy come out of her office and take Tom Black aside. Tom turned toward Will and drew a finger across his throat. "Cut," he mimed.

"I want to thank you all here for working so hard during this campaign," Will continued, wondering what was up, "and all the people across the state who have worked hard and contributed their hard-earned dollars to this victory." He looked at Tom, who was giving him the "cut" sign again. "And finally, I just want to say that about this time on that Tuesday in November, I'm going to throw you a much bigger party than this!"

Will hopped down from the desk, embraced his mother and father, and, shaking hands and kissing cheeks, made his way through the television cameras and celebrants toward his office. Tom and Kitty were waiting for him there. Tom closed the door.

"Kitty just got a call from a friend of hers," he said. "The Republican State Executive Committee has already agreed on their nominee for the Senate."

Will was surprised. "They're not even waiting until Jim Winslow's body is cold?"

"Nope," Tom said. "They don't plan to announce it until after the funeral, but their nominee is the Reverend Don Beverly Calhoun."

"Oh, shit," Will said.

"There's more," Kitty said. "They've already scheduled his first campaign appearance. He's conducting Jim Winslow's funeral."

BOOK THREE

I

When Will arrived at St. Philip's Cathedral for the funeral of Jim Winslow, he could see why Tom and Kitty had persuaded him to come. As Will and his father got out of the car, it was immediately apparent that half the politicians in the state were there. Billy introduced him to a dozen people before they had left the parking lot, and in the vestibule of the cathedral, business was being done. Inside, the church contained a dozen members of the Winslow family, four television crews, and what appeared to be a joint session of the Georgia State Senate and House of Representatives. Seated next to the widow and her two daughters was Governor Mack Dean, looking frail.

Billy Lee broke away from a knot of legislators in the vestibule in time to accompany his son to a pew. "The word is," he whispered to Will, "that Dr. Don is not going to conduct the service after all."

"No? What happened?"

"Apparently, the Bishop took the chairman of the Republican party aside and explained to him, in no uncertain

terms, that a self-ordained minister in the so-called Pentecostal Baptist Church, with a dubious doctorate from a
redneck Bible college, is not entitled to conduct a High
Episcopal religious service."

Will tried not to laugh. "No kidding?"

"However," Billy continued, "the party principals, over
the initial objections of the widow, have prevailed upon
the Bishop to allow Calhoun to do the eulogy."

"Too bad."

"If he promises not to come to the graveside."

The service was glorious. There was pomp, pageantry,
and incense; the Atlanta Boy Choir sang their hearts out;
the Bishop contributed his personal reminiscences of Jim
Winslow's character, then introduced the Reverend Don
Beverly Calhoun, representing the Republican party of
Georgia, he added, dryly

Will had never seen Calhoun in person, only on various
talk shows, and he was interested to see that Dr. Don, unlike some public figures, was actually taller than he seemed
on television. He was dressed in a very correct, severely cut
black suit, a black necktie, and a gleaming-white shirt.
Even the cuff links were muted. This was the man, Will
remembered, who had been described by one columnist as
having "the brains of a Pat Robertson, the preaching skills
of a Jimmy Swaggart, the charm of a Jim Bakker, and the
ruthlessness of a Jerry Falwell."

Calhoun gripped the sides of the pulpit and took in his
audience with one lingering sweep of the cathedral. "My
friends," he began, in a deceptively soft voice that rico-
cheted around the stone walls, "the task falls to me today
to tell you not what Jim Winslow meant to his family and

friends—that has already been beautifully done this morning. I have been asked to tell you what he meant to his
party, his state, and his country—and I have been asked to
be brief. That is difficult, when a man's life has meant so
much, but I will try."

Calhoun shifted his weight and subtly intensified his voice.
"Jim Winslow recognized better than most people the trouble our country is in today, after a succession of too many
godless leaders, too many battles fought and lost, too many
innocent children's lives snuffed out in the abortion mills that
disgrace our nation, too many inroads made by the Commu-
nists and the liberals and the so-called secular humanists, too
many children's prayers banned in our schools, while murderers and rapists and drug dealers are set loose upon our society
by weak laws and liberal judges." Calhoun paused.

God, what a sentence! Will thought. He noticed the
Bishop squirming in his seat.

"And," Calhoun continued, "if Jim Winslow had lived,
he would have done something about it in the United
States Senate!"

From somewhere in the back of the cathedral, a few
people began to applaud, but were quickly shushed by
others. The Bishop looked miserable.

Calhoun looked down at the pulpit until order had
been restored, then went on. "And so it is left for those of
us who remain on this earth to pick up that fallen torch
and carry it on to glory! And so it is left for us to take Jim
Winslow's fight to every corner of this state! And so it is
left for us to lead America into the light of a new day—
under God!" Calhoun bowed his head for a moment of
silence, then stepped backward and returned to his seat.

The boys' choir burst into an anthem, and the pallbearers began carrying the coffin down the aisle and out of the church to the waiting hearse, followed by the Winslow family and Governor Mack Dean. From the front of the cathedral, legislators streamed down the aisle until the building was empty. By the time Will and Billy were outside, the hearse and the family had departed for the cemetery and a private graveside service.

"I've never heard anything like that in my life," Billy said.

"Neither has anybody else," Will replied.

A television crew materialized before them, and a reporter pointed a microphone at Billy. "Governor Lee, what did you think of today's service?"

"I thought the Episcopal service was a fine tribute to a good man, but I must say, I thought Mr. Calhoun's eulogy sounded more like a political oration, maybe even a campaign speech. You have to wonder if there's something he isn't telling us just yet."

The reporter turned to Will. "Will Lee, you're the Democratic nominee for the Senate. Do you think Dr. Don is going to be your Republican opponent?"

"That's a matter for the Republican State Executive Committee, and I'm sure they'll wait a decent time before choosing a nominee. After all, today is hardly a day for politics," Will said, not too piously, he hoped.

They excused themselves and walked toward the car.

"This is going to be one hell of a campaign," Billy said. "I'm not sure I envy you the experience."

"I'm not sure I do, either," Will replied.

2

Mickey Keane entered a steakhouse on Peachtree Road and found his lunch date waiting for him. "Hey, Dave," he said, sticking out a hand.

Homicide Detective Dave Haynes shook hands. "How y'doin', Mickey?"

They got a table near the bar. "I'm doin' good," Keane said.

"How you liking the work?" Haynes asked.

"Better than you might think. Pearl's a decent guy. I've worked for a lot worse."

"Why, I hope you aren't referring to our beloved captain," Haynes said.

"Nah," Keane replied. "I never refer to him at all."

"How are you spending your time?"

"Running leads."

"Yeah, I've seen the ads. Bet you're getting a lot of trash."

"Yeah, I guess I am. That was predictable. So what's going on down there?"

Haynes looked around and lowered his voice. "Funny stuff," he said. "Oh, nothing too funny, everything within bounds, just a teeny bit funny now and then."

"So, tell me something funny."

"Jim Winslow had a heart attack jogging," Haynes said. Keane stopped eating his salad. "What's funny about that?" he asked, playing the straight man. "Guys drop dead jogging all the time, guys in perfect health and great shape."

"Yeah, but those guys turn out to have clogged-up veins. Winslow's veins were clean as a whistle."

"So what does the medical examiner say?"

"He says some jargon that means every now and then a guy pops off because of some sort of freak electrical thing with the heart."

"Why would a person think different, then?"

"Nothing big. Just too many little things."

"Like?"

"Like, Winslow goes jogging every morning of his life at dawn, winter and summer. He's well-known for it. Now, if you were going to hit Winslow, when would you do it? I'll tell you; at dawn, when the paper boy has already been, and nobody else is up and about yet."

"Tell me more."

"Okay, there's two guys find him. One is a neighbor, has to make an early plane at Hartsfield. But when this guy comes around the bend, there's another guy there, with his ear to Winslow's chest."

"The jogger. A natural-enough thing to do. I've done it myself."

"Okay, sure, but the jogger is wearing a hood and dark glasses. It's a warm, humid morning. And then the jogger takes off in the neighbor's car, calls an ambulance, and disappears."

"So he doesn't want to get involved. It happens."

"I canvassed the neighborhood myself. The jogger doesn't live there. Nobody around there jogs at dawn but Winslow. Joggers don't go to other people's neighborhoods to jog. They do it around home."

"Did the neighbor give you a description of the other jogger?"

"Not much. He thinks, tall; the guy had a mustache. That's about it; the guy was covered from head to toe in gray sweat clothes. Remember the hood and the dark glasses?"

"What was on the 911 tape?"

"The minimum. Man down, the address, ambulance. He hung up before the operator could get anything else. His accent is Southern, country Southern, but he enunciates clearly, like he's been practicing a long time."

"Like Southerners in the army, career guys, learn to do?"

"Like that."

Keane looked at Haynes with mock solemnity. "Course, you know, this is the wildest kind of supposition."

"Funny, that's what our beloved captain said." Haynes put down his fork. "Oh, hell, I know it's not enough to go on. I know it's a political hot potato, that the department doesn't want stories in the paper like this without some hard facts. But it ought to be enough for something more than a routine autopsy, for a top-notch forensic pathologist to be brought in. I mean, our loveable old ME ain't no hotshot."

"That would prick up the ears of the press," Keane said.

"Yeah, I know, I'm just burned. It's not the first time I've been warned off something because it's too much trouble for everybody. Hell, I know a little about the allocation of resources and all that. But it burns me anyway." Haynes looked at Keane, who didn't appear to be listening, then followed his gaze to the television set over the bar. The noon news was on, and a group of men stood surrounding a lectern, from where the Reverend Don Beverly Calhoun was speaking.

"There he is again," Keane said.

"Oh, yeah, they picked him for the Republican nominee. I heard about it in the car on the way over here."

"Yeah," Keane said, and repeated, "there he is again."

"He's always on TV about something or other," Haynes said.

"That's not what I mean," Keane replied. "It's just that for the past few months, every time I get interested in something, he's around. His people had been picketing Manny Pearl's bookstore right before Perkerson tried to wax Manny; then there were some of his people at the abortion clinic that day, demonstrating, when the doctor and his nurse caught it; and now you're telling me that Jim Winslow just maybe got hit, and here's Dr. Don again, popping up right on cue."

"Why, Mickey." Haynes grinned. "That's the wildest kind of supposition."

"Ain't it?" Keane laughed. "But I'll tell you something, Dave: I sure hate coincidences."

"I know what you mean," Haynes said, wiping his face and tossing his napkin onto his plate. "And now, if you'll excuse me, Mr. Keane, I'm going to get just as far away as I can from you and your far-fetched ideas." He rose, and as he walked past Keane, he clapped him on the shoulder. "Good luck, Mickey," he said. "We won't be talking again."

3

Mickey Keane stood in the back of a crowded ante-room of the Gospel of Freedom Church of Atlanta and exchanged waves and greetings with members of the press he knew from around town. Nobody asked him why he was there, and that was okay with him.

Keane looked up as the group of men entered through a side door and took seats on the platform at the front of the room. They stood in a group for a moment to allow the photographers to get their flash shots done. Keane took note of an impressive-looking man standing next to the Reverend Don Beverly Calhoun. He was tall and lean and of erect bearing, with thick, close-cropped gray hair and dark eyebrows. A handsome man, who had "military" written all over him.

"Who's the guy next to Calhoun?" he asked a reporter from the *Constitution* leaning against the wall next to him.

"That's Colonel J. E. B. Stuart Willingham," the reporter said, "formerly of the U.S. Marines. Old Jeb, as his friends call him, was supposed to be a shoo-in for commandant of the Marine Corps, until he got in a little trouble in Vietnam, something about too many casualties in his unit for the ground gained, suicide missions, that sort of thing. There were some closed congressional hearings on it, and Willingham was reassigned stateside. He retired not long afterward. Since then he's run something called Americans for a Strong Defense, some sort of right-wing lobbying organization. He's—"

"Good morning, ladies and gentlemen."

The booming voice brought instant silence to the room of television and print reporters. Floodlights came on, illuminating the group on the platform.

The commanding figure looked around the room, blessing the group with a small smile. "My name is Willingham," he continued. "I am chairman of the board of deacons of the Holy Hill Pentecostal Baptist Church, and it is with considerable regret that I must announce that, this morning, our board accepted the resignation of the Reverend Doctor Don Beverly Calhoun as pastor of our church, rector of Freedom University, and chief executive officer of Faith Cable Television, Incorporated." He paused for effect, then continued. "Our regret, however, is lessened by the knowledge that, as a candidate for the United States Senate, Dr. Calhoun will be making an even greater contribution to his state and country, and we feel we must share the talents of this fine man with our fellow Americans.

"But our loss is also our gain, for we now have had the pleasure of appointing to succeed his father the Reverend Ralph Beverly Calhoun, who, until now, has been Dr. Calhoun's right-hand man in the church and its related activities." Willingham turned, and a thin blond figure rose and gave a little wave to the crowd. The Reverend Ralph Beverly Calhoun was a younger, skinnier version of his father, with the same capped teeth and the added attraction of an angry red pimple decorating his left cheek.

"And now," Willingham continued, "it is my pleasure to introduce to you the Reverend Doctor Don Beverly Calhoun."

Calhoun, a flatteringly cut blue suit covering his paunch and a bright red necktie lighting his way, approached the podium. "Good morning to you all," he boomed cheerfully. "I would like you all to know that this is my last public appearance as the Reverend Doctor Don Beverly Calhoun. From this day forward, I am just plain Don Calhoun, Republican candidate for the United States Senate from Georgia." He paused, as if anticipating applause that did not come, then rushed ahead. "As of today, I am severing the ties that for so many years have bound me to the Holy Hill Church, Faith University, and Faith Cable Television. I will preach my farewell sermon this Sunday"—he turned and looked at his son, who grinned back at him— "at the kind invitation of the new pastor of our church, the Reverend Ralph Beverly Calhoun. All of this means, of course, that all business and financial relationships with these organizations will end. I will no longer be paid a salary, nor enjoy any other benefits from this connection. Now I am prepared to take questions from the press." He pointed to a young woman who immediately stood in the front row. "Jane?"

"Dr. Don, does this mean—"

"Please, Jane," Calhoun interrupted, "I have never

liked that particular sobriquet, and it is particularly inappropriate from this time forward. Just call me Don."

"Uh, Mr. Calhoun," the young woman continued, "does this mean that you will no longer have the use of the five-million-dollar business jet in which you have been traveling for the past few years?"

"Jane, as you know, that aircraft is owned by an independently run corporation which has, at times, leased its use to Faith Cable Television, Incorporated. Should I require the use of the aircraft during the coming days, my campaign will, of course, come to appropriate terms with the corporation and pay, in full, for the aircraft."

"What will the hourly charge for the airplane be to your campaign, Mr. Calhoun?" the young woman asked.

"Uh, we have not yet worked that out, but you may be sure it will be fair." Calhoun pointed to another reporter.

"Dr.—ah, Mr. Calhoun—last year, the Holy Hill Church built you and your wife a twelve-thousand-square-foot house on the campus of Faith University, the furnishings of which were rumored to cost more than two million dollars. Will you now move out of that house?"

Calhoun beamed at the man. "Of course you know, Ed, that most of the furnishings of the house were gifts from various members of my congregation, and I'm happy to say that the Board of Regents of the university has agreed to give me a ground lease for ninety-nine years on the property, and I will be buying the house from the university."

"Sir," the reporter interrupted, "your declared salaries from all the positions you hold with the church, the university, and the cable television company come to a total of ninety thousand dollars a year, and now you have resigned those positions. How will you pay for a twelve-thousand-square-foot house?"

"Well, I will be making a modest down payment from funds my wife and I have saved over the years, and the university will extend a mortgage to me for the remainder."

"What is the agreed price of the house, and what will the terms of the mortgage be?"

"That has all got to be negotiated, you see, but I am sure that, in a spirit of Christian love and cooperation, we will come to an agreement that will be satisfactory to everybody concerned. Now, I believe I have time for just one more question." Calhoun turned to a young man wearing a name tag declaring him to be a reporter for Faith Cable Television News. "Yes, son?"

"Mr. Calhoun," the young man said, reading mechanically from a sheet of paper, "what will be the aims and objectives of your campaign for the United States Senate?"

There was an audible groan from the other reporters present, and technicians began packing gear.

"Well, now, I'm glad to have a political question," Calhoun chuckled. "My campaign will be a Christian one, down to its roots."

In the back of the room, Mickey Keane recognized this as his cue. As Calhoun continued his spiel, Keane went to a window and looked out. A large bus was parked across the road from the church. He opened the window, leaned out, and gave a thumbs-up signal. Manny Pearl stepped out of the bus and crossed the road toward the church. He was carrying a sign that said SEPARATION OF CHURCH AND

STATE! A.B.D.D.!!! and he was followed by an even dozen striking young women, each dressed in a very small bikini, each carrying a similar sign.

As Calhoun droned on inside the building, a sound man for a local television station happened to glance out the window. "Holy shit!" he yelled. "Take a look at that!"

The room turned, then, as one man rushed to the windows, nearly trampling the young man from Faith Cable Television News. Calhoun stopped talking and gave his attention to the crowd at the windows. "What is going on?" he demanded, bewildered.

"Lemme outta here!!!" a cameraman shouted, pushing his way toward the doors at the rear of the room. He was followed by two dozen members of the media, flattening the rows of folding chairs as they stampeded from the room.

Calhoun stepped down from the platform and strode to the windows, followed by his son and his board of deacons. He took one look out the window and turned to the Reverend Ralph Beverly Calhoun. "Call the police!" he bellowed; then he turned and ran for the doors.

Mickey Keane was standing on the front lawn, laughing his ass off, when Calhoun burst out of the building, followed by his board of deacons and, finally, his son. Calhoun ran across the lawn and brought himself up short on the other side of a drainage ditch from the parading strippers. Half a dozen television cameras swiveled to take in his arrival on the scene.

"What on earth is going on here?" he demanded.

"Just returning the favor, Dr. Don," Manny Pearl yelled back. "You been picketing my place of business, so I thought I'd picket yours, me and my girls from the Alley Cat, here. That's one of my most popular places."

"For God's sake," cried Calhoun, "get something on those women! They're next to naked!"

"Listen, if you want to see everything, just stop in at the Alley Cat tonight," Manny called back, noting that television was recording all of this. "Or the She Cat, or the Jungle Cat. We're open from five P.M. to four A.M., six days a week!"

The whooping of police cars could be heard in the background. A moment later, two of them screeched to a halt in front of the church, and a large sergeant got himself out of one. "Awright, what's going on here?" he asked nobody in particular.

"Officer, I demand that you remove these people from our church property at once!" Calhoun shouted.

"Awright, Manny," the sergeant said. "You've had your fun, now pack up these girls and be on your way."

As if on cue, a young man carrying a briefcase exited the bus and crossed the road. "Excuse me, Sergeant," he said, "my name is Wilcox, and I am an attorney representing Mr. Pearl and these young ladies. I would like to point out that they are not on church property, but on a public right-of-way, and they are not blocking traffic or impeding the progress of anyone."

A young woman stepped up to Manny Pearl and stuck a microphone in his face. "Excuse me, Mr. Pearl," she said, "but on your signs, there, what does A.B.D.D. mean?"

"That's a political slogan." Manny Pearl grinned into the camera. "It means Anybody but Dr. Don!"

The girls behind him burst into cheers. "Anybody but

Dr. Don! Anybody But Dr. Don!" they began to chant in unison.

An unmarked police car skidded to a stop at the edge of the crowd, and a man in a suit got out. The sergeant saluted him. "Good morning, Lieutenant," he said. "I'm afraid we got us a situation here."

"Hey, Harvey!" one of the girls yelled at the lieutenant. "I haven't seen you since last night! How you doin'?"

The lieutenant reddened. "All right, all of you people are under arrest. Indecent exposure!"

The young lawyer stepped forward. "Lieutenant, I'd like to point out that each of these young ladies is wearing a perfectly proper bikini, which is acceptable attire in public anywhere in this country."

"And I ain't exposed!" Manny Pearl yelled. "At least, not yet!"

"Everybody onto that bus!" shouted the lieutenant. "Sergeant, your car leads, the other car follows. Next stop, city jail! We'll discuss the particulars in front of a judge!"

Mickey Keane rolled helplessly on the grass in front of the church, clutching his sides and howling with laughter, as Manny and his girls noisily boarded the bus, and Don Beverly Calhoun led his party back toward the church.

"Reverend Ralph!" Calhoun was shouting. "Call my lawyer!"

4

Will called the meeting to order at ten o'clock on Monday morning. "All right," he said. "I want to hear from everybody this morning. We're in a whole new ball game here, one we never anticipated, and we've got to find some new ways to deal with it." He turned to his father. "Dad, let's start with you. Where do we stand financially?"

Billy Lee cleared his throat and stared at a sheet of paper before him. "We've got a little over a hundred and ten thousand dollars in the bank; if we deduct our unpaid bills, we're liquid to the tune of about seventy thousand dollars."

Will suddenly felt a little sick. "That's all? Are you perfectly serious?"

"I am," said Billy. "And I reckon we're going to need a million dollars to make it through the general election."

"This is my fault, Will," Tom Black said. "If you'll remember, I insisted on putting nearly everything we had into television in the two weeks before the primary. My insistence was based on what the polls told us would be a close race with Mack Dean, followed by a general-election campaign against Jim Winslow. What we had, of course, was a landslide over Mack, after his wife decided to nail him. I tried to cancel as much television time as possible in the last couple of days of the primary race, but most of it was simply uncancelable. We'd paid for it up front, and the stations didn't want to hear about refunds."

"Well, you couldn't foresee that Mack would be removed as a factor, Tom. You made the best decision you could, in the circumstances, and I agreed with you. Anyway, maybe that flood of commercials we ran will do us some good in the general election."

"I wouldn't count on it," Tom said. "We've got six weeks to go before the second Tuesday in November, and folks can forget a lot in that time. Anyway, they'll be bombarded with new stuff from the opposition." Tom shifted in his seat. "The second part of our campaign plan, running against Jim Winslow, didn't happen, either. We're facing a much tougher race now."

"There's some good news on the financial front," Billy said. "Mind you, there's some bad news, too."

"The good news first, please."

"Well, Lurton Pitts and his group have given the Democratic party half a million dollars."

"That is good news," Will said. "Are we going to get all of it?"

"I'm afraid not," Billy said. "That's part of the bad news. The Democratic State Executive Committee has allocated us a hundred thousand dollars."

"*What?*"

"They say they've got some tough congressional races to fund. That's nonsense, of course; there's only one close congressional race in the state that I'm aware of. Frankly, I don't think they're optimistic about your chances. Later on, if we can show them some gains in the polls, we might get some more money out of them."

"I don't understand," Will said. "I was beating their sitting governor before he shot himself in the foot. They don't think I can beat a TV preacher?"

Billy said nothing for a moment, then continued. "There's more bad news. The Lurton Pitts group has also given the Republican party half a million dollars."

"They're working both sides of the street?" Will asked, incredulous.

"It's not the first time a big contributor has done that," Tom Black said.

"I haven't finished," Billy said. "Word is, the Republicans are giving Calhoun the whole half million, since, the reasoning goes, he's starting from scratch, and they don't have a lot of hope in the congressional races anyway."

"Oh, swell," Will said.

Moss Mallet, the pollster, entered the room. "Sorry I'm late, Will."

"Have a seat, Moss; we'll get to you in a minute."

Kitty Conroy spoke up. "I think you'd better get used to the idea of Calhoun having more money than us to spend. Don't forget his mailing lists; he's been known to raise hundreds of thousands of dollars in a day for his TV show; he ought to be able to do it for his campaign, too. By the way, did anybody see his so-called farewell sermon yesterday?"

"I missed it," Will said.

"So did I," Tom echoed.

"It was a thirty-minute campaign speech on free television," Kitty said. "The only time God was mentioned was when Calhoun said he would strike down his—Calhoun's—enemies. I think he meant you."

Will laughed. "I guess I'd better get used to that."

"You'd better get used to something else, too," Kitty said.

"What's that?"

"He went heavy on the homosexual thing. He didn't mention any names, but I think we all know who he was referring to. There was a lot of stuff about the liberals and the homosexuals distorting the purpose of government, and how he was personally going to prevent any other homosexuals from gaining more political power in this state. Judging from his attitude yesterday, I don't think he's going to let up on this."

Will couldn't think of anything to say to that. "All right, Moss, what have you got on last week's polling?"

"Well," Moss Mallet began, spreading some sheets of paper in front of him, "this is Thursday's stuff, after the strippers at the church, and before Calhoun's Sunday-morning sermon."

"Jesus, wasn't that stripper thing wonderful?" Tom said. "I've never laughed so hard."

Will tapped a forefinger on the table. "Just be sure that we don't get connected in any way with this Manny Pearl and his girls. Screen the donation checks carefully. I don't want any money from that quarter; if it gets out, it could kill us."

"I'm glad you enjoyed the stripper incident, Tom," Mallet said, "but a lot of voters didn't, at least not the little bites of it they saw on the news follow-ups. In fact, I think that might have something to do with our position at the moment."

"Just what is our position at the moment?" Will asked.

"Well, as of Friday—this is phone interviews with six hundred likely voters, a good sample—with a four-point statistical margin of error, Calhoun has forty-six percent, and you, Will, have thirty-nine percent."

Will was stunned. "You mean after a primary victory, and with Calhoun just announced, we're *seven points behind*?"

"Maybe as few as three points, depending on the margin of error," Mallet said, trying to put the best face on it. "Something that particularly bothers me, though, is that only fifteen percent are undecided; that's a very small percentage this early in the race. It means that, if the election had been held on Friday, you would have needed more than eighty percent of the undecideds to win, whereas Calhoun would only have needed less than a third of them."

"I don't believe it," Kitty said.

"I'm sorry," Mallet replied, "I've been over everything twice, and my people tell me that the tone of the interviews backs this projection." He shrugged. "I know it's not good news, but you're paying me for the truth."

"Sure, Moss," Will said. "The results are not your fault. At least we have some idea of where we stand."

"Where did we do well and badly?" Tom asked.

Mallet looked at his figures again. "Best inside the Atlanta city limits and in cities of more than a hundred thousand around the state—Savannah, Augusta, Columbus, like that. Worst in smaller cities and towns and in that part of greater Atlanta outside the perimeter—Marietta and Cobb County, Lawrenceville and Gwinnett County. It's a kind of Republican doughnut around Atlanta—generally, the urban suburbs that the writer, Calvin Trillin, likes to call the 'ruburbs.' "

Billy laughed. "The ruburbs; I like that."

"Is there any other good news in all this?" Will asked.

"Well, blacks don't like or trust Calhoun; you're getting more than eighty percent there; that's better than you were doing with blacks against Mack Dean. I think you certainly want to get the best possible voter turnout in black communities. And, of course, you'll get the gay vote. None of them is going to vote for Calhoun after yesterday. I don't have to take a poll to tell you that."

"Yeah," Tom said, "and if we try to hold so much as a single fund-raiser among the gays, Calhoun will fall on us like a ton of bricks from a great height."

Will took a deep breath. "I've got some more bad news, I'm afraid. I was saving this until last, hoping for something better early in the meeting."

"What now?" Kitty moaned.

"You know Judge Boggs, the judge in the Larry Moody murder case?" He took a piece of paper from his briefcase. "This morning, I got a letter from Judge Boggs. He's had a break in his court calendar; he's scheduled the trial for a Monday morning in late October, eight days before the election."

"I don't believe it," Tom sputtered. "The son of a bitch can't get away with that!"

"Oh, yes, he can," Billy said. "And there's not a god-damned thing Will can do about it."

"Refuse to try the case!" Kitty said.

"If Will does that, the Judge will throw him in jail for contempt," Billy said. "He can't campaign in jail." He paused. "What we've got here, I think, is a judge who's a born-again Republican. I think that, ever since Will announced for the race, Boggs has been laying for him, and he just took his best shot."

The group sat in dejected silence for a few moments. Finally, Kitty spoke up. "Oh, I forgot," she said listlessly. "I had some news, too. I got a call this morning from Calhoun's campaign manager. He's challenged us to a television debate."

Will looked up. "Just one?"

"Just one."

Will managed a laugh. "Thank God for small favors."

5

The pickets showed up almost immediately. GOD DE-STROYED SODOM AND GOMORRAH, one placard read. KEEP HOMOSEXUALS OUT OF OUR GOVERNMENT, another said. Will had to walk past them to get into one of a series of "town meetings" he was conducting around the state, meetings where he spoke, then answered questions from the audience. These had been Tom's idea, and they were showing Will to good advantage, answering the questions of ordinary citizens. They were also picking up a lot of local television time. In every audience, Tom had placed one or two supporters, who would ask questions Will particularly wanted to answer in that area. These were secondary, though; Will saw the greatest advantage of the meetings in his responses to difficult, even unfriendly, questions and it was these that got local television news play.

Will had finished his stump speech in the Savannah meeting and was beginning to take questions from the floor. He was relieved to see that the people carrying the placards had not come inside.

A woman in the front row stood up. "Mr. Lee," she said, "I can't help but get the impression that you have not been candid in your responses about the homosexual issue." This was a bad start; it supposed there *was* a homosexual issue. "Perhaps it would be better if you'd just get it all out in the open and tell us how long your affair with Jack Buchanan went on, and if you have had other homosexual affairs."

There was a gasp from the audience that, fortunately, covered the gasp from Will. He glanced at a TV camera and saw the red light was on.

Will knew he had to attack. "Madam," he said sternly, "what you have just said is a lie, and I have come to this hall tonight to answer honest questions, not to respond to lies."

"Answer the question!" a man shouted from the back of the room, and other voices murmured the demand.

Will turned to the woman in the front row, who was still standing. "Perhaps you'll tell us your name," he said.

"My name is Margaret Thurmond. I am a schoolteacher, and I went to college with Millie Buchanan, Jack Buchanan's widow, and I notice that Millie has not exactly come to your defense in all this."

"Millie Buchanan is a shocked and grieved widow, who is trying to raise her children without a husband. I haven't asked for her help. You are repeating vicious gossip which has no basis in fact, and you ought to be ashamed of yourself."

"Answer the question!" the man in the back of the room repeated.

"What question?" Will demanded. "I haven't heard a

question, not from her, not from you. If you want to ask a question, ask it!"

"Are you a queer?" the man shouted.

"No," Will replied, "are you?"

"Hell, no!" the man shouted back.

"Well, I can see that you don't like answering false accusations any better than I do," Will said.

Mercifully, there was laughter from some of the audience, and a few applauded.

"And now that we've settled the question of sexual orientation—mine and yours—maybe we can get down to the serious business of this meeting."

One of Tom's plants was on his feet, and Will called immediately for the man's question. The moment had passed, and he tried to shake it off.

Later, in the car, Kitty said, "I talked with the reporter covering the meeting and asked her to run the whole exchange; she said she'd try. What bothers me is that the words 'homosexual' and 'queer' got used several times. A lot of people who see the report will hear those words and forget about what was said."

"I checked up on the schoolteacher," Tom said. "She did go to college with Millie Buchanan, or, at least, at the same time, but, you notice, she didn't say she'd actually spoken with Millie. What's more important is that she teaches at one of those so-called Christian academies that were set up by right-wingers so their kids wouldn't have to go to school with blacks. This whole thing smells like a setup to me, though I don't guess we can prove it."

"I wish there were some way to deal with this question once and for all; just get it out of the way."

"I'm afraid there's no way to do that, short of you going out and molesting a few women. If we bring it up, then it makes us look defensive. I think it's better to deal with it as it comes, just as you did tonight. That was good, the way you turned it around on the guy, then made them laugh. Maybe we need to work on some other responses, if it's going to keep coming up."

"That's a depressing thought," Will said.

"Tom's right," Kitty said. "There's just no other way to deal with it. Shit, why couldn't you be divorced, like everybody else?"

6

It was desperation, as much as anything else, that gave
Mickey Keane the idea. He had just run dry. Then he
thought about the mustache. If the second jogger had
been Perkerson, then the mustache meant that Perkerson
was trying to change his appearance, which made a lot of
sense for two reasons: first, Perkerson was a distinctive-
looking man, with his barn-door ears and his prominent
nose; second, in spite of this distinctive appearance, there
had not been a single verifiable sighting of Perkerson since
he had gone to ground, and yet, as the shootings at the
abortion clinic indicated, he could be out there and
working.

Keane had never dealt with a single case where a perpe-
trator had had his appearance surgically altered to avoid
capture; that was the stuff of movies, he reckoned. Still, it
could not be discounted as a possibility, and, since he had
no other leads to follow, this seemed his best chance. He
sat down and thought about it.

If the cops had been doing this, they would have can-

vassed every cosmetic surgeon in Greater Atlanta, if necessary, but Keane was one man, and he had to play the odds.
He got out the Yellow Pages. Eliminate all the doctors in
the city of Atlanta proper, for a start; they were the society
guys, who worked out of Piedmont and Northside Hospitals. Eliminate the south side of the city, because that was
mostly black. Perkerson wouldn't go to a black doctor.
Decatur and the northeast suburbs were solid middle-class
sorts of places; check that last. Marietta would be a good
place to start.

Marietta was an affluent suburb to the northwest of the
city. It was white and seemed to be trying to stay that way:
in a referendum, the residents had voted not to join the
city bus system, and they didn't want rapid transit, either,
the theory being that blacks would be attracted to Marietta by the existence of a rapid-transit system. The district
had been represented for years by a congressman who was
on the distant fringes of the right. Gun stores abounded in
the city; submachine guns were manufactured there, and
you could go out to a commercial firing range and rent
them by the hour. It was a post-redneck, lower-end yuppie
sort of a place, it seemed to Keane, and the place to start,
he reckoned.

Since Marietta was, legally, not part of Greater Atlanta,
Keane had not spent much time there, so he needed a
map. There were eighteen cosmetic surgeons listed in the
Yellow Pages; he would hit each one. He spent a day working his way through half his list, and he discovered that all
doctors' offices had something in common: each had a
nurse or receptionist behind a sliding-glass partition. Not
once did he encounter a receptionist sitting at a desk in a

reception room. Further, he found that each doctor's office had in common, apart from the aging magazines, a clipboard with a pencil attached by a piece of string for the patient to list his name, address, and phone number. Surely, he thought, most of the patients had visited the office before. Why did they have to write down an address and phone number repeatedly?

The second morning of his search, he very nearly didn't go out at all. Maybe he had lost his patience since leaving the force, but he found it extremely boring to face the same blank stares and bored reactions in office after office. Finally, though, after the caffeine of a second cup of strong coffee had found its way to the right places, he got into his car and drove to Marietta to visit the second half of his list. The first office he visited was different. The office was a free-standing one near a shopping mall, and it seemed quite large for the office of a single doctor, but there was only one name on the plaque: Leonard Allgood, M.D. Inside, there were only a few general-interest magazines; in addition to *Architectural Digest* and *U.S. News and World Report,* there were several gun magazines. There was even a copy of *Soldier of Fortune,* and there were political magazines that Keane had never heard of. One he noticed, in particular, while he waited for the receptionist to return to her empty cubicle, was something called *On Guard,* subtitled *The Journal of Americans for a Strong Defense,* and its editor and publisher was Colonel J. E. B. Stuart Willingham, USMC (retired). Before he had a chance to read any of it, the receptionist returned.

Keane flashed his badge. "Good morning," he said, producing a brown envelope. "I wonder if you could take a look at this photograph and tell me if the man has been a patient here during the past few weeks or month."

The woman, who was dressed in a nurse's uniform, displayed the momentary uneasiness which Keane had seen in hundreds of ordinary citizens, who, unexpectedly, had a policeman's badge thrust at them. A plastic placard pinned to her uniform said she was Suzy Adams, nurse-anesthetist. She was fortyish, fairly good-looking, with particularly handsome breasts.

"Sure," she said, although her cheerfulness sounded a little forced.

Keane removed the photograph from the envelope and, without taking his eyes from her face, showed it to her. There was a tiny widening of the eyes, an almost imperceptible flaring of the nostrils, and, a moment later, a deep intake of air.

"I've never seen him before," she said earnestly, shaking her head. She rose from her chair. "Let me see if the doctor recognizes him."

Keane had not released his hold on the photograph, and he did not now. "I'd like to meet the doctor," he said pleasantly, "if he has just a moment."

"I'll see," she said, and disappeared through a door.

In the minute she was gone, three women, one wearing bandages, came into the office and signed the log. First patients of the day, he reckoned.

The nurse reappeared and opened a door to meet him. "The doctor has just a minute before he starts seeing patients," she said. "Follow me."

She proceeded down a rather long hall, and along the way, Keane was able to peek into a number of examining rooms. The doctor must really stack them in here, he thought. Then he stopped before an open door. Beyond it was what looked like a small but very well-equipped operating room.

The nurse looked back. "This way," she said with some irritation.

Keane followed her into a large, expensively furnished office. A smallish man, dressed in a white coat, stood and shook Keane's hand. "I'm Dr. Allgood," he said. "I only have a moment; how can I help you?"

Keane didn't flash the badge again. "I won't take up much of your time, Doctor. I'm conducting an investigation, and I wonder if you'd look at this photograph and tell me if you have ever seen this man before—particularly, if he has sought treatment from you."

The doctor ignored the photograph. "May I see your identification, please?"

"Of course," Keane said, producing the little wallet with the badge and ID card.

Allgood did something no one had ever done to Keane before. He reached out and took the wallet from his hand.

Keane was slightly startled and surprised by his own reaction to having the wallet outside his possession, even for a moment.

"I see you're from the Atlanta department," the doctor said. "Which means you have no jurisdiction here."

"I don't need jurisdiction to ask a few questions," Keane replied.

"Oh, I believe the proper procedure would be for you to go to the Marietta Police Department and have a local officer accompany you." The doctor glanced at the ID card again. "In fact, I see that you are retired from the Atlanta police force, which means you have no jurisdiction anywhere at all."

"I'm a licensed private investigator," Keane said, offering his PI's ID.

Allgood looked carefully at the card. "Michael Keane," he said, mostly to himself. "Well, Mr. Keane, I'm happy to cooperate. I just like to know who I'm talking to." He handed everything back to Keane and turned to the photograph. "Well," he said, "this fellow could certainly benefit from cosmetic surgery. Look at those ears! Although this is not a profile, I suspect his nose could be improved, too." He sighed audibly. "But I've never seen him before; certainly, I've never treated him."

"Thank you, Doctor," Keane said, turning to go. "I see you have your own operating room here in your office. Isn't that unusual?"

"It's increasingly usual," Allgood replied, stepping from behind the desk to usher Keane toward the door. "It saves a lot of my time, not having to schedule at a hospital for most procedures. Not to mention the time used by traveling back and forth." He shook Keane's hand again. "I'm sorry I couldn't be of more help. Good day." He turned and walked back into the office. Immediately, he went to his desk and, as Keane looked back, he scribbled something on a pad.

Keane followed the nurse back to the reception room, thanked her, received a chilly smile, and left. As he got into his car, the adrenaline was humming in his veins. "Jackpot!" he said to himself. His every instinct told him so. He wouldn't be visiting any more doctors' offices. In his notebook, he wrote the name of the doctor, Leonard Allgood, and of his nurse, Suzy Adams. It was a perfect setup here, all self-contained. No awkward questions at a hospital, no patient records outside the doctor's office.

And he had learned something else. Perkerson had not only new ears, but a new nose. No more beak; something nice and straight. And a mustache. A description was coming together.

As Keane drove away from the doctor's office, something pricked at his consciousness, and it took him a moment to figure out what it was. Allgood had seen his private investigator's ID, taken a good look at it, and that ID contained his home address. And when Keane had left Allgood's office, the doctor had been writing down something.

Keane drove into the parking lot of the mall beside the doctor's office and parked. He sat in the car, looking at the medical building, thinking, putting it together in his mind. Nearly an hour passed, but Keane was not bored. He stared at the doctor's office, a couple of hundred yards away, and thought. He also took note of who came to the doctor's office through a pair of field glasses. Suddenly, he saw someone he knew.

As Keane watched through the binoculars, a black Jeep Cherokee pulled into the parking lot of the doctor's office, and a man, impressive in his bearing even at that distance, got out. The gray hair, the black eyebrows, the erect posture identified him immediately. Colonel J. E. B. Stuart Willingham was in the office for less than ten minutes before he exited and drove away.

Finally, Keane thought, something was starting to come

together. He had names and faces, some of them well-known. He didn't have anything that could put anybody in jail, and he didn't have Perkerson yet, but at least he finally had something. He pulled out of the parking lot and carefully began to follow the black Cherokee.

In his excitement, Keane forgot that they had something, too. They had his name and address.

7

As the campaign continued, Will descended, physically and mentally, into a soft, fuzzy rut. He was rarely depressed and never exhilarated. He measured the time in terms of his schedule for the day, rarely thinking beyond the night's sleep, which he relished. Each day, he shook dozens, sometimes hundreds, of hands, and listened to many expressions of good wishes and a few expressions of extremely ill wishes. Each day, he saw a group of people, sometimes a large group, carrying signs questioning his patriotism, his devotion to "family values," whatever that meant, and his masculinity. At each town meeting, there were hostile and well-prepared questions, which he met with equally hostile and well-prepared answers.

Finally, midway through October, he arrived at a community hall in Waycross, in the deep southern part of the state, and there were no placards to greet him. Inside, there were serious questions, but none that seemed prepared, and none with the raw hostility that had met him so far.

"They weren't there tonight," he said to Tom.

"I think it's over," Tom said. "Our polling has shown that, in the beginning, the technique had some effect, but we've been getting local TV play wherever we've been, mostly answering those questions. We haven't caught up with it in the polling yet, but my guess is, their polls show it's no longer working."

"I am a little disappointed," Will laughed. "Those questions had become a part of the routine, and I think I had begun to look forward to answering them."

"I can live without them," Tom said. "One thing our polling is showing is that we're gaining in small towns and rural areas. That's where the connection with Senator Carr helps most, I think, and I suspect that those people have found the opposition's picketing unfair. We're gaining less in the ruburbs, but we're coming up overall in our polls.

"I think we're being helped, too, by Calhoun's heavy use of staged five-minute TV question-and-answer sessions and very few public appearances that aren't completely contrived and controlled. What we're doing is much more spontaneous and, I think, real.

"My great worry is that we don't have time to catch Calhoun. I think, the way we're going, we're going to peak about a week after the election."

"We've got to accelerate the process, then," Will said.

"The only way we can do that is with TV money, and we don't have it. Something else that bothers me is that we've still got the trial to look forward to. That's going to bring a halt to daytime campaigning, and we'll have to spend the evenings near enough to the Greenville court-house to keep from exhausting you with late-night travel."

"I appreciate that. I've been refamiliarizing myself with the case, going over the prosecution evidence and Charlene Joiner's deposition, but I'm afraid it remains fragmented in my mind. There's just too much else going on. Can you schedule me to have a completely free day at home the Sunday before the trial opens?"

"Sure we can. It's not going to do the campaign any good if you do badly at the trial."

"I guess not," Will said ruefully. "The trouble is, it's not going to do me all that much good if I do well. I mean, if I do a really great job and get Moody off, who am I going to please? 'Accused Murderer Goes Free' is not a great headline for us."

"Listen, Will, the worst thing you can do for yourself is to start worrying about how the trial is going to affect your chances for the Senate. You just give the case your best effort, and let me worry about what gets said in the press."

"Then there's my debate with Dr. Don. I didn't do all that well against Mack Dean, you know. How am I going to do against a so-called master of the medium?"

"You did better than you thought, remember? Anyway, I've got some ideas about that," Tom said. "I think we'll want to take a different approach in this debate. Let me work on it some more, and we'll talk about it later."

Will laughed. "Later will be soon enough for me."

8

For three days, Mickey Keane followed Willingham. He was there when the man got up in the morning; he put the man to bed at night. He pulled his car into the trees in the wooded area that surrounded Willingham's house and found a good place up a rise, where he could see the black Cherokee come and go. Keane wanted badly to tap the man's phone, but he was afraid he might not be good enough to avoid a security device, and a sticker on the colonel's mailbox said he had one installed.

Willingham's rounds were disappointing. He went, twice, to meetings at the Holy Hill Church, and he did some light shopping here and there, but mostly, he stayed home. Nobody came to see him, and nobody called at the house except Sears Carpet Cleaners and Federal Express. Keane began to think again about trying to tap the phone.

On the third night, Willingham went to bed early. All the lights in the house were out by ten-thirty, and Keane called it a day. He stopped on the way home, as he often did, at Manny Pearl's office for a chat.

"You think Willingham's behind all this?" Manny Pearl asked him.

"Who knows? I certainly can't prove it. I can't prove anything—that Perkerson got his face reshuffled at Dr. Allgood's, that the nurse, Adams, recognized the photograph, that Willingham's arrival at Allgood's office was connected with my visit. But it all kind of comes together, you know? I just hope that eventually Willingham will lead me to Perkerson."

"What about the doctor or the nurse?" Manny asked. "Maybe you should follow one of them."

"I think Perkerson's finished with them. He got his ear job and split, that's what I think. Give me a week on Willingham, and if I don't get anything, I'll try the doctor." Keane talked a little more with Manny, then went home.

As he walked into his apartment, the phone was ringing, the number that had been advertised in the search for Perkerson. It had been a while since it had rung, and, on impulse, Mickey picked it up before the answering machine kicked in.

"Hello."

"Hello," a woman's voice said. Low, husky—familiar, somehow. "Is this Michael Keane?"

"Yes. Who's this?"

"You want Harold Perkerson, I'll give him to you," the woman said. "I want the reward," she added.

"I want him, and if you give him to me, you'll get the reward," Keane replied. "Now, let's start with your name. I'll have to know who to give the reward to, won't I?"

"Call me Jill," the woman said. "If my information's good, that will be our code word, okay?"

"Okay, Jill it is. Now, where's Perkerson?"

"We'll have to meet and talk about this. I'm going to need protection."

"When I find Perkerson, he'll never breathe free air again. You won't have to worry about him."

"You don't think he's alone in all this, do you?" she said.

"Alone in what?" Keane asked.

"There's more than the dirty bookstore, you know."

"Tell me," Keane said. "Show me you know something."

"There's the abortion mill and Winslow," she said.

Hair stood up on the back of Keane's neck. This woman might have guessed about the clinic—that had been all over TV and the papers—but there hadn't been a word said about the possibility of Winslow's death being anything but a heart attack. "Where can we meet?" Keane asked, trying to keep the excitement out of his voice.

"Take 85 North," she said, "get off at the Lenox Road exit, turn left on Lenox. After a couple of miles there's a restaurant called Houston's, right across from the Lenox Square shopping mall. I'm there now. Fifteen minutes?"

"Okay, fifteen minutes. What do you look like?"

"I'll find you. Don't be late, or I'll leave." She hung up.

This didn't sound like a setup, not in such a public place. Keane knew Houston's; it attracted everybody—families, yuppies—and it was always packed. He ran for his car; using the expressway at this time of night, it would take him just the fifteen minutes she had given him.

Eight minutes later, he was on 85 North, doing seventy. There was almost no traffic. He got off at the Buford

Highway exit, onto a spur that had once been the old interstate. The Lenox Road exit branched off to the left from the spur. He had just taken the left fork for the exit and was about to pass under a bridge when he looked in the rearview mirror and noticed the van, moving up fast behind him, a lone driver.

It was odd that the van was speeding up, just at the moment it should have been slowing for the traffic light ahead. The van pulled around him to pass. "You nut," Keane said to himself. "Can't you see the light is red?" The van came even with his car, and he looked toward the driver. All he saw was dark glasses and a mustache before the van smashed into the left side of his car.

Keane screamed at the van and slammed on his brakes, trying to stay in the road. The brakes held for an instant, then the pedal went almost to the floor, practically useless; the power brakes had gone, and the mechanical brakes that were left weren't doing much. Keane hauled hard on the steering wheel, trying to keep to the left, to stay on the road, but the car's progress to the right was inexorable. The van probably weighed a half a ton more than his car. Then Keane saw the bridge abutment coming at him.

"Goddamn you, Perkerson, you son of a bitch!!!" Keane screamed, then the car struck the sheer face of the mountain of concrete, and all the lights went out.

9

Mickey Keane woke to the sound of groaning machinery and tearing metal.

"For Christ's sake, take it easy with that thing, or you'll tear him wide open!" somebody yelled.

That was the moment when Keane knew he was not in hell, or even purgatory; they wouldn't be so worried about him in either place. There was not much pain, but he seemed to be having some trouble taking a deep breath.

"It's going to be like taking a sardine out of a bent can, getting him out of there," a voice said. "We don't know what internal injuries he's got, so we've got to move him an inch at a time, okay? And let me get a collar on him first."

Keane felt something firm go around his neck, then an arm went around his waist.

"Watch it!" somebody yelled.

"I don't know how else to do this," another voice said. "It's hard to tell where he ends and the metal starts."

Keane felt the arm tugging at him, and there was movement. Then there was pain—sharp, penetrating, complete pain. He screamed, and that hurt, too.

"Oh, shit," the voice said. "His foot is jammed in there. Somebody get the man with the torch over here."

"No," Keane said weakly.

"What? Jesus, he's awake," the voice said.

"Oh, shit," somebody replied. "What did he say?"

"No torch," Keane said. He could smell the gasoline.

"He's got a point, Eddie," one of the voices said. "You'll fry us all with the torch. Use the can opener instead."

A sardine, Keane thought, trying to fill his mind with something besides the pain. Then they moved him again, and he passed out.

The lights were very bright when Keane woke again, and the pain was everywhere. People were all around, tugging at him, pulling at things. He could hear clothing tearing.

"Morphine!" somebody said, and Keane felt a needle in his arm.

"Wait a minute," he said, but too late. He wanted to tell them something, but the pleasant warmth came over him and made him forget.

The next time he woke, he knew it was for real. He wasn't going to pass out again. He was alone in a hospital room, and there was sunlight peeping through the drawn Venetian blinds. He moved his left hand to his face to scratch an itch, and pain shot through his chest. He lay still and let it itch until he couldn't stand it anymore; then he moved the hand the rest of the way and let it hurt. The door opened and a nurse came in.

"Oh, you're back with the living, huh?" she said.

"Am I?" Keane said, and that hurt, too. "I can't tell for sure."

"Let's get you a little elevation," she said, cranking a handle at the bottom of the bed. The upper half of Keane's body rose a few inches, and he could see Manny Pearl standing at the end of the bed.

"You're gonna be okay," Manny said. "Not to worry."

"You're not gonna be okay," the nurse said, "you *are* okay. You're the luckiest man in the ward, maybe in the hospital."

Keane could remember the crash now, or at least the part of it right before the car hit the bridge abutment. "What's broken?" he asked.

"Your ankle and your lower leg," she said, rapping on a plaster cast that suddenly seemed to be attached to his leg, up to the knee. "Good thing you were wearing a seat belt, or everything else would be broken."

"What else?" he asked.

"Nothing else," she said. "You've been CAT-scanned from head to toe. Nobody can believe it."

"*I* don't believe it," Keane said. "I hurt enough for everything to be broken."

"You're just sore," she said. "There's a detective outside who's been waiting to talk to you. You feel up to it?"

"Why not?" Keane said. "Can I have something to drink?"

She stuck a glass straw into his mouth and he sucked water, sloshing it around his mouth and letting it trickle over his whole throat. The nurse left the room.

"What happened?" Manny Pearl asked.

"Hang on a minute," Keane said. "Let's see who this cop is."

Shortly, Dave Haynes came into the room. "Morning, Sleeping Beauty," he said. "You had a nice night's sleep while everybody stood around waiting."

"I didn't know you cared, Dave," Keane said.

"I don't, I'm just curious," Haynes replied. "Listen, the traffic boys are going to be in here in a minute. I want to know what happened."

"Me, too," Manny Pearl said.

"Dave, this is my boss, Manny Pearl," Keane said.

The two men shook hands perfunctorily. "So?" Haynes asked.

"It was him," Keane said.

"Shit, I knew you were going to say that," Haynes said. "Now life gets complicated."

"No, it doesn't," Keane replied. "You're out of it. I'm just satisfying your curiosity."

"That's stupid," Haynes said. "If it was really him, give me what you've got, and I'll get on it."

"Nope," Keane said.

"You want him yourself." It wasn't a question.

"Yeah, and I know how to get him."

"Let me help," Haynes said. "The captain doesn't have to know."

"Nah, Dave. You've got less than a year to go, right? Stick around and collect your pension."

"Isn't there something I can do?"

"Yeah, maybe. Has the press got anything on this yet?"

"A TV crew got lots of shots of you in the car when

they were trying to get you out. They don't know who you are."

"What hospital am I in?"

"Northside. It was the nearest trauma center."

"You know anybody here?"

"A couple people."

"Make me dead."

"I don't think they'll do that, Mickey. You know how nervous hospitals are these days."

"Nearly dead?"

"I'll see what I can do. If you really think he's going to try something else, I'll get some people over here."

"Brain-dead should do it," Keane said. "And keep those traffic people away from me."

10

"Why are we meeting him here?" Will asked, looking around him. It was just after three in the afternoon, and the restaurant was nearly empty. At the other end of the room, a woman was mopping the floor.

Tom Black sighed. "Because I have some things to tell you, and I didn't want to do it in front of your dad and Kitty and Moss."

Will did not feel well. He was catching a cold, and he was tired, and now, he was scared. "All right," he said.

"Our latest poll shows Calhoun with forty-eight percent and you with forty-four—with a four-percent error margin. We've picked up, and he's dropped, but—well, it's what I told you a while back: we're going to peak a week after the election. That's pulling out all the stops, using every dime of the money we have or expect to get before election day, and I'm including all our matching funds—everything."

"So, what do we do?" Will knew what was coming.

"I'll put this as bluntly as I can," Tom said. "We spend

four hundred thousand dollars on television the last two weeks in the campaign, or we lose the election."

"If we could just get some sort of break," Will said.

"It's true, we haven't had any breaks since Mack Dean got it caught in his zipper," Tom said. "You'd think we were due for something, but it hasn't happened. Oh, I suppose Dr. Don might be found in the pastor's study with a Boy Scout, but I don't think we can count on it."

Will had avoided thinking about this moment for a long time, but, he admitted to himself, he should have known it was coming. "Does this happen to every candidate?" he asked.

"Just about," Tom said. "Every one in a close race, anyway. Nobody ever has enough money but Republicans." Tom poked at the ice in his tea. "I've got holds on the TV buys. I have to place orders with cashier's checks by the close of business tomorrow, or we lose the buys."

"All right," Will said finally. "I'll find the money."

"There's something else, Will," Tom said.

"What?"

"If we don't get the money, we'll lose; but if we do get the money, we still may not win. I'm not at all sure that we can."

Will's heart sank to his lower abdomen. He knew how to find the money. He always had known; but he had never really thought it would come to this. Now he was being told that, even if he did do this, it might all be for nothing. Was it worth it? Only two people could tell him. "Wait a minute, will you, Tom?" He rose and went to a pay phone, dialed the number, got both of them on the line, and said his piece, listened to their answer. Then he went back to the table. "I'll have the money for you tomorrow," he said.

Will sat and watched the man's face as he looked over the papers. It was a face he had known since he was a boy, a man he had never liked much.

The man put down the papers. "Are you absolutely positive you want to do this?"

"I am," Will said, with as much conviction as he could muster.

"Have you really considered the consequences if you aren't elected?"

"Yes, I have."

"You understand that you don't have the income necessary to effect repayment."

"I certainly understand that."

"And, since this is the case, we would have no recourse but to sell?"

"I understand."

The man reached into his desk drawer and took out a form. He wrote Will's name at the top, the amount of four hundred thousand dollars, and a due date ninety days hence. He made two Xs at the bottom, turned the form around, and handed Will the pen.

"We'll have to do a title search, but I'll expedite that. Assuming the titles are sound, the money will be in your account by lunchtime tomorrow."

Will signed in both places and stood up. "Thank you, sir," he said, extending his hand.

The man stood and gripped Will's hand. "You're a

braver man than I," he said. "Or, perhaps a more foolish one."

"I hope not," Will said. Then he walked out of the office, leaving the deeds to his family's land on the banker's desk—land that the first Lee in Meriwether County had begun buying in 1826; land that his grandfather had lost to the boll weevil, and that his mother and father, through a lifetime of struggle, had won back; land he had thought his children and grandchildren would live on one day.

In the car, on the way back to campaign headquarters, he wept.

II

Mickey Keane sat on the bed and made the huge effort it took to get a sock onto his left foot. As he did so, every muscle in his back, neck, and shoulders cried out for him to stop.

"I wish you'd stay here another couple of days," the doctor said.

"Why?" Keane asked. "I'm not hurt bad. You said so yourself."

"You were badly shaken up," the doctor said. "It takes time for the system to recover from an accident like that. You're only alive because that car folded up exactly the way it was supposed to when it hit an immovable object. It doesn't always happen that way."

"Hurrah for Detroit," Keane said. "Fuck Germany." He had gotten the sock and shoe on and was trying to tie his shoelace.

"All right, go ahead and discharge yourself," the doctor said, disgusted. "I know there's a heel on that cast, but you'll have to use crutches for a few weeks, or you'll screw up your leg. Come back in two weeks, and we'll pull another X-ray." He started to say something else, then stopped. "I just hope I don't see you back in here," he said finally. He turned and stalked out of the room.

Almost immediately, a man in a suit walked in.

Keane ignored him, struggling with the shoelace.

"Let me do that for you," the man said. He walked over and tied the shoelace.

"Thanks," Keane sighed. "Who are you?"

The man produced a small wallet and flipped it open. "I'm Bob Warren, FBI," he said.

Keane bent over and untied the shoelace, then began the struggle to retie it. "You guys investigating traffic accidents these days?"

"We'd like you to stay away from Willingham," the agent said.

Keane got the shoe tied and sat back on the bed. "Who? Never heard of him."

"No? Then how come you camped outside his house for three days?"

Keane looked at him. "I've always liked the woods."

"Look, Willingham may be important in a group we're investigating. We can't have you rattling him."

"Yeah? I love you guys. What if he's important in something *I'm* investigating?"

"I know what you're investigating," the agent said. "I can tell you that Perkerson will get brought in faster if you stay out of it. We've got a man on the inside. We know some of what's going on."

"What would you want with Perkerson?" Keane asked. "Murder isn't a federal crime."

"He's part of something that is a federal crime," the agent said.

"So why haven't you arrested him?" Keane asked innocently. He put a hand on one of his crutches.

"Because he's more useful to us where he is than he would be in jail."

Keane nodded. "I thought so," he said. He pushed off the bed, pivoted on his good foot, and swung a crutch at the FBI man. It caught him full on the side of the head, knocking him down. Keane tried to put his weight on the foot in the cast, cried out in pain, and went down himself.

The agent scrambled to his feet, pulling his gun. "You stay where you are, you crazy bastard!" he yelled, crouching and keeping the gun pointed toward Keane.

Keane struggled into a sitting position and leaned against the wall. "Oh, I just love you guys," he said. "Perkerson drove me into a concrete wall at seventy miles an hour, and you guys were probably taking movies the whole time. How long have you known where he was? Long enough to have stopped those killings at the abortion clinic? Long enough to have stopped my partner from getting barbecued? Who else are you guys willing to get killed, just so you can make a few headlines?"

The agent stood up and holstered his gun. "We have our own ways of working."

"Yeah?" Keane said. "Well, I have my own ways of working, too, and—"

"You want to kill Perkerson, don't you?" the agent asked. His face was turning red. "You want to just put a bullet in his brain and screw up the investigation that's been going on for two years, one that will result in dozens of arrests on conspiracy charges."

Keane grabbed the bed and hauled himself to his good foot. "I don't know about conspiracy," he said. "I catch guys who kill people; you might call it my life's work. I especially catch guys who kill my partner and try to kill me." He shook his head. "No, I'm not going to kill Perkerson, not that I wouldn't love to do it. I'm going to push his face in the dirt, put my knee on his neck, and handcuff his hands behind his back. Then I'm going to see him booked, printed, photographed, and arraigned, then tried for murder; and, eventually, if I live long enough, I'll go down to Reidsville and sit in the gallery and grin while they fry the son of a bitch."

Keane picked up the crutch and hopped over to the other one. He tucked them both under his arms and checked them for length while the agent watched. Finally, he looked up at the agent. "And I'll tell you something else," he said. "None of you federal fairies had better get in my way while I'm doing it."

Keane staggered out of the room on the crutches and aimed for the nurse's desk, muttering under his breath, wobbling all the way.

12

They lay side by side in the dark—wet, spent, still breathing hard.

"I want to know," she said. "I want to know it all."

He laughed. "You're something else," he said. "You never let it go, do you? You looking to get yourself killed?"

She took his penis in her hand and massaged it. "You could never kill me. You need me too much."

"Oh, Christ," he whimpered. "Christ knows, it's true." He began to become hard in her hand.

"I love the power of knowing," she said. "To be near the power. To feel it throb."

By now he was throbbing himself. "I don't know as much as you think I do," he moaned.

She sat up and mounted him, taking all of him inside her. "I want to know what you know," she said, moving slowly in a way she knew drove him crazy. "That's enough for me, just to know what you know."

"No," he said. "Forget it."

She stopped moving.

"Don't stop," he pleaded.

She sat perfectly still.

"Ask me," he said.

"Who is the Archon?" she asked.

"Allgood," he said. "Your boss is the Archon."

"Liar," she said. She started to dismount him.

He caught her and pulled her back. "No," he said.

She began moving again. "Who?"

"Willingham," he said.

She stopped. "You wouldn't lie to me again?"

"I swear it," he said. "I've met with him alone half a dozen times."

She began to move again. "Where do you meet him?"

"Usually at his house," he panted. "That's the center of everything—weapons, money, everything."

"I thought it was Calhoun," she said.

Perkerson laughed aloud, then caught his breath as she moved a certain way, the way he loved. "That clown? He couldn't find his way to the bathroom without Willingham. When Willingham found Calhoun, he was preaching in an old peach-packing shed and living in a house trailer."

"Where does the money come from?" she asked. "There's a lot of money, isn't there?"

"Some from rich guys who are Elect; some from Calhoun's operations. Any actual cash money that comes into Calhoun's ministry gets siphoned straight to Willingham."

She began moving faster. "How do you know all this?"

"He tells me everything. I think he needs somebody to talk to."

"But why you? You were just a team leader; now you're working alone. Why you?" She moved faster still.

"Oh, God," Perkerson groaned. "Soon."

"Why you?" she demanded.

"Because he's known me since Vietnam; because he knows . . ."

"Knows what?"

"I'm coming, I'm coming!"

"Yes, yes!" she cried. "I'm with you!"

They came loudly together, then sank into relaxation. She did not move from on top of him, but wiped the sweat from his forehead and stroked his face.

"Why you?" she asked again, genuinely puzzled.

"Because he knows I'd put a bullet in my own brain, if he asked me to," he panted. "Because he knows I'll never be taken alive."

13

On a Friday evening in the same Atlanta public-television studio where Will had faced Mack Dean, he now faced Don Beverly Calhoun.

The two men stood under the hot lights, at lecterns facing each other, and engaged in debate, prompted by directions from a single moderator, who chose the points that would be discussed by the candidates. For over an hour, Will had offered closely reasoned answers, backed by a real knowledge of each subject, while Calhoun had generalized, pontificated, and invoked Family Values, the American Way, and God's Blessing at every turn.

Will was growing increasingly frustrated at the preacher's tactics; it had been like firing silver bullets into the heart of a monster who simply kept getting up and attacking. Not a single answer of Calhoun's had been without skillful innuendo directed at Will's maturity, masculinity, and religious convictions. At every opportunity, he questioned Will's moral qualifications for representing Georgia in the Senate.

Finally, Will had had enough. He had avoided addressing Calhoun's veiled accusations for fear of lending weight to them, but they were down to the final minutes of the debate, and he felt that he had to take some sort of stand. When his time came to sum up, Will turned to the camera.

"Since this is the last opportunity I will have to speak to such a large number of Georgia voters in this campaign, I would like to address myself to what I feel has become the single most important issue in this campaign, and that is the consistent campaign of innuendo, half-truth, and name-calling that my opponent has indulged in since the day he entered this campaign. He has implied, time after time, that, because I am a bachelor, I must be a homosexual; that, because I am unmarried, I cannot be responsive to the concerns of families; that, because I have refused to discuss my religious beliefs in a political campaign, where they have no place, I must be a faithless atheist—or, even worse, in my opponent's opinion, a secular humanist, whatever that is. Because I am opposed to the continuous spending of horrendous sums of public money on weapons systems that do not work, I am characterized as being against a strong defense; because I believe that a reasonable part of public funds should be used to help unfortunate Americans participate in the American Dream, I am accused of being a free-spending liberal; because I reject a radical right-wing ideology, I am accused of being a socialist or a Communist sympathizer; because I oppose the death penalty, I am accused of being a coddler of criminals; because I support a woman's right to choose whether she should bear a child, I am named an accessory to murder.

"I believe in my heart that you people out there are too smart to fall for these smear tactics; I believe you want responsible government, free of radicalism of any sort; I believe you want to be represented by honorable men who care about the concerns of your daily lives, not demagogues who see public service as an opportunity to distort the political system in favor of their own radical and rigid beliefs. I don't have a church pulpit from which to speak; I have only the means of any political candidate, and I have used them to the best of my ability.

"If I am right about what you out there believe and want, then I can expect to be elected to the United States Senate a week from Tuesday. If I am wrong, then I deserve to be defeated, for I have misjudged the American heart. I ask you to prove me right. Thank you."

Don Beverly Calhoun now came to his final statement. "My friends," he intoned, "my young opponent has summed himself up better than I ever could. He would have you believe that a man's sexual orientation does not matter, even though God himself damns the sodomites; he would have you believe that a God-created fetus is not a human being and does not matter; he would have you believe that a candidate's religious convictions—or lack of same—are not important to the people who elect him. You have heard him say these things himself, here tonight.

"You have also heard him lament his lack of a pulpit from which to tell you of his faith. Well, tonight, I am prepared to offer him that pulpit."

Will stared at Calhoun. What was the man up to?

"I am prepared, tonight, to offer Mr. Lee the pulpit at Holy Hill Pentecostal Baptist Church, a week from this

Sunday. If he is not afraid to let us know what he believes, then let him deliver the sermon on that day and tell us." Calhoun turned from the camera to face Will. "Do you accept my invitation, sir?"

"I accept," Will said, "on one condition—that is, that if I preach at your church, my sermon will be carried on every outlet of your television network, just as your Sunday sermons have been. Do you accept that condition?"

"Why, sir," Calhoun said, "I would not have it any other way."

"Then I am very pleased to accept your invitation," Will said, with as much confidence as he could muster.

The following day, in the back of a car on the way to a campaign appearance, Will sat and looked at Kitty Conroy and Tom Black.

"You let him sandbag you in there last night."

"Tom's right, Will," Kitty said. "You'll be speaking to Dr. Don's audience, both in the church and on television, and with those people, you can't win."

"Then get me a bigger audience," Will said. "Use some of our TV time to advertise the event. Television isn't selective; it goes into every home in the state; all we have to do is get people to turn it on that morning."

"That's very risky," Tom said. "We've improved dramatically in the polls since we got the TV money. I think we might be in a position to edge him out on election day, *if we don't make any mistakes.* We've already got Larry Moody's trial to contend with; that's unpredictable enough. I just think it's wrong to stick your neck out like this, for Calhoun to chop off publicly from his pulpit."

"It's already stuck out," Will said. "I can't back out of this now. Can't you see that? Tell you what, you watch Calhoun's program on Sunday morning; time everything—the hymns, the sermon, the works. That will be useful to me."

"All right," Tom said glumly. "If that's what you want."

"It is," Will said. "And I want a big audience for that appearance. Start working on that today, all right?"

"It's your funeral," Kitty said.

Will sighed. "Well, at least I'll get to conduct the service."

14

The wind blew across the little lake and piled golden leaves on the porch of the cottage on the Delano farm. It was a Sunday of perfect autumn; the crisp days and bright foliage that New Hampshire had known weeks before had finally slipped south to Georgia.

After a morning of sloth and a good lunch, Will sat down to review the Larry Moody case for the last time before the trial. He went slowly through the prosecution's evidence, looking for traps and pitfalls. It seemed straightforward enough. The discovery rules allowed him access to their case, but did not allow them access to his, apart from a list of his witnesses, of which he had only four. He went through the crime-lab report again, mentally rebutting each point. He had his own exhibits: some clothing of Charlene's and a medical certificate.

He would not be able to prove in court that Larry Moody had not murdered Sarah Cole; the case rested on Will's ability to keep the prosecution from proving that he had.

Will opened the cottage door and let the wind blow in an occasional leaf; the cool air would keep him alert. He paced the living room, formulating questions to the witnesses and saying them out loud. He practiced a summation, though he knew its content would change depending on what the trial brought out.

He was standing, hands in pockets, addressing an imaginary jury, when a particularly large puff of wind blew in a pile of leaves, scattering them around the room; he was so absorbed in what he was doing that he did not notice for a moment that someone had entered with the wind.

She stood watching him, silhouetted against the sunlit doorway, until finally he saw her and stopped, his mouth open.

"Hello, Will," she said.

It took Will a moment to recover. "Hello, Kate," he replied slowly.

Neither of them said anything for a moment.

"I'm sorry to interrupt," she said, breaking the silence.

He was at last able to move from the spot. "No, no, you're not interrupting. Come in, let me get you something to drink."

"Thank you. Something soft, if you have it. I have to drive back to Atlanta in a little while."

He went to the refrigerator, got a pitcher of iced tea, and poured them both a glass. He came back to the living room and put them on a little table between two comfortable chairs, then sat opposite her.

"This is quite a surprise," he said carefully.

"I know it must be," she answered. "I spoke this morning to some prospective analyst recruits at Georgia State University; my plane isn't until six, so I had some time. I rented a car and drove down."

"I see," he said. He couldn't think of anything else to say. He felt oddly unsettled.

She waited a moment before she spoke. "I guess I'm going to have to be the one to speak first." She looked away, out the windows toward the lake. "It seems we've been working at cross-purposes for the past few months."

He still said nothing.

She took a deep breath. "I want to try to make you understand what's been happening. If I can. When I got the new job, it rekindled something in me, something I had forgotten I ever had—a kind of passion for the work. The past few years had been so boring at the Agency that I really was ready to leave it and get married; then, when they offered me this job—well, it was like falling in love again. After two years out of the loop, suddenly, I knew *everything* again; they *trusted* me; I could affect events."

She tucked her feet under her in the large chair and smoothed her skirt, a motion that Will found familiar and appealing.

"I immersed myself in it right up to my ears; I was working fifteen, sometimes twenty hours a day—we had a crisis or two that kept things on the boil. I neglected Peter." She had a small son by her first marriage, who was enrolled in his father's old boarding school in New England. "I didn't go up there to see him as often as I should have, and when I finally did get a day or two off, that was where I had to be."

"I can understand that," Will said. He had not liked it

when she had allowed her ex-husband to send the boy there; he liked Peter and felt he was too young to be at that sort of school.

"I believe I mentioned to you that I had to undergo a new security check."

"Yes, you did."

"It was awful. There are still people at the Agency who think a woman shouldn't be in this job. It was as though they were reinventing the security-clearance process just for me. I was terrified that they would discover my connection with you and use that as an excuse to deny me the job. They're scared of Ben Carr at the Agency, you know. I've heard more than one person there express relief that he's gone from the Senate Intelligence Committee."

"That doesn't surprise me," Will said.

"What may surprise you is that they were scared of you, too. Your staff work on the committee was better than they would have liked. You made life difficult for them at budget hearings."

Will laughed. "I always thought you handled my questions well—too well, if anything."

She smiled. "Thank you, sir. Still, they regard you—some of them, anyway—as the enemy. Believe me, if you're elected to the Senate, there will be some disappointed people at the Agency."

"I hope to disappoint them."

"I know I wasn't returning your calls, and I know how maddening that can be. Part of it was the hours I was keeping—I couldn't call you from the office, and I seemed to be at home only in the middle of the night. Still, that's not a good enough excuse. I think the truth is I didn't want to talk to you."

He felt a stab of hurt; this was nearly his worst fear.

"You were a distraction from the job, and I wanted to give the job everything." She stopped and took a deep breath. "No, I promised myself I was going to be absolutely honest."

"Please do. I need that."

"It wasn't just the job," she continued, lowering her eyes. "I was feeling boxed in, and I used your absence to try and put you out of my mind. I felt guilty about not being down here to help you win this race, where I should have been, if I really loved you."

Will's heart was pounding. This was getting worse.

"There was somebody else," she blurted.

"Ahhh," Will sighed. This was his very worst fear.

"It's not what you think—at least, not all of what you think. He was somebody at the office; he was funny and bright and comfortable to be with. He didn't make any demands on me. And you were right, what you said when I saw you in Georgetown. The Agency does encourage people inside to . . . well, see each other, marry. There's a kind of comfort that comes from being with somebody who knows what you're doing, somebody you can talk about it with. It was normal, acceptable; I didn't have to hide it."

Will nodded, but he did not speak.

"I was having him to dinner the night you turned up," she said. "But I want you to know that I never slept with him. I thought about it, I even wanted to, a little bit, but I never did. That's the truth, and I want you to believe me."

Will felt a stab of shame. He had not been so abstemious. He looked away. "I do believe you," he managed to say.

"When there was any moment I wasn't thinking about work, I missed you," she said with feeling. "In spite of myself. Often, even when I should have been thinking of work, I was thinking of you. But I had this terrible conflict, and I had to resolve it."

Will was frightened now. As angry as he had been with Kate, he knew he still wanted her. Now she seemed about to make a choice.

"On Friday, I went to see the boss," she said. "He bought me a drink, and I talked with him for more than an hour. I told him about you, about the last four years. I made no apologies; I told him I knew what I was doing, and that I had never compromised my position at the Agency. He believed me, I think. He said he was spending the weekend at the Director's country place, that he wanted to talk with him about it. I said I would do whatever he wanted; if he wanted my resignation, fine, he could have it, but that it was my intention to go to you at the first opportunity and throw myself at you. I . . ."

Will left his chair and knelt next to hers, took her in his arms, kissed her hair and her face.

She was crying. "I told him I was going to marry you, if you would still have me, and if he and the Director didn't like it, they could both go to hell." She laughed through her tears. "I think I was a little drunk by then."

Will buried his face in her hair and held on to her for dear life.

She looked at her watch. "I really do have to get a six-

o'clock plane," she said. "I just came down here to propose marriage to you, the moment you're through with
this campaign."

"I accept," Will managed to say into her ear.

"I'll be a senator's wife, if you win. I'll stay at the
Agency, too, if they still want me. Or, if you lose, I'll go
anywhere, do anything with you. I'll come down here and
live in this sweet cottage with you and raise cows, if that's
what I have to do to get you. You're more important to
me than anything else."

Will laughed. "I can just see that," he crowed. "Raising
cattle, a country lawyer's wife. That would be hilarious!"

She cuffed him playfully on the side of the head. "I
mean it!"

"You're sure you're not just horny?" he kidded.

"Oh, that, too. Boy, am I horny, but I've got to catch
that plane. I'm traveling with a colleague, and we have a
long report to go over; there's one of those meetings tomorrow morning that may decide the fate of the Western
world."

He laughed again. "It's a long way from deciding the
fate of the Western world to being married to a country
lawyer in Georgia, which is what happens if I lose this race.
I hope you know what you're doing."

They stayed, she in the chair, he on his knees on the
floor beside her, locked together, until he had to walk her
to her car. Finally, he kissed her the way he had dreamed of
doing and sent her on her way. Then he stood looking out
over the lake into a setting autumn sun, and he knew that,
no matter how the election went, everything was going to
be all right for him. Because Katharine Rule loved him.

15

There were more people at the courthouse than Will had expected, and they were better organized. As he was waved into a parking spot by a sheriff's deputy, he saw two groups, one entirely white, the other mostly black, divided by the walkway leading to the front door of the courthouse. The mostly black group carried signs saying JUSTICE FOR SARAH COLE and STOP RACIST MURDER. Will saw that the black attorney Martin Washington, head of a group called ARE, Attorneys for Racial Equality, was back. Will had met Washington a couple of times and thought him an honest, if rigid and excitable, man.

The group of whites standing opposite was smaller, made up of men and women, with a number of children and babies among them. Their signs said WHITE RACE UNDER SIEGE, DON'T RAILROAD LARRY MOODY, and CIVIL RIGHTS FOR WHITES. The two groups were eyeing each other with some hostility.

"Who are those people?" Will asked the deputy, indicating the all-whites.

"Beats me, Counselor," the deputy replied. "Everything's coming out of the woodwork, I guess."

Great, thought Will. This is all I need.

Larry Moody, Charlene Joiner, and Larry's boss, John Morgan, got out of a car across the street, and Will waited for them. They greeted each other, and Charlene's hand lingered in Will's for a moment. It was the first time he had seen her since their assignation of a few months before, and it took some effort on Will's part to keep his response to her muted. He also felt a moment's guilt that he had suspected her when the rumors had begun about photographs of a candidate and his girlfriend.

They ran the gauntlet through the groups of demonstrators and paused on the courthouse steps, where television cameras awaited them. "Smile when you're asked questions," Will said to Larry. "And be brief."

"We've only got a moment," Will said to the television people.

Microphones were stuck in their faces.

"Mr. Lee, is your client going to take the stand?"

"If I think it's necessary, yes, but I stress that I, not Larry, will make that decision."

"Larry," a woman said, "are you glad to be coming to trial at last?"

Larry Moody grinned his most boyish grin. "No, ma'am," he said, "I can't say I'm looking forward to it, but I'm sure looking forward to getting this cloud out from over my head."

"Any chance you're going to cop a plea, Larry?" another reporter asked.

"No, sir, absolutely not," Larry replied, more seriously. "I'm innocent, and I'm expecting to get acquitted."

"We'd better go inside," Will said.

"Mr. Lee," a reporter said, "do you think this trial is going to have any effect on your campaign?"

"Absolutely not," Will said. "This is a case the Judge assigned me before I decided to run for the Senate, and the two have nothing whatever to do with each other." He began herding his group toward the courthouse doors.

"Miss Joiner," a reporter called out, and she turned to look at him. Charlene was dressed in a dark blue wool dress with a full skirt, but a tight waist and bodice; she managed to look, at once, both elegant and extremely alluring. "What are your views on the trial?"

Charlene fixed the man with a dazzling smile. "I think," she said, "that Larry is awfully lucky to have such a brilliant lawyer representing him." And with that, she turned and, with her chin tucked down and her eyes gazing up at him, gave Will an equally dazzling but somehow more intimate version of her smile. Strobe lights flashed from the print photographers' cameras, and the moment was fixed in time.

Will, disconcerted, hustled his party inside.

Jury selection went more quickly than Will could have hoped. He considered that the jurors who would be most sympathetic to Larry Moody would be white males, and the least sympathetic, black females. He ended up with four of each, but he managed to get black women who, if not particularly well educated, seemed intelligent and thoughtful. He could live with that. There were also one black man and three white women on the panel. Will might have been happier with twelve Klansmen, but he was satisfied.

The jury selected, and the preliminaries over, Elton Hunter, thinner since his illness, stood. "Your Honor, the prosecution calls Janeen Walker."

A trim young woman with a voluminous Afro haircut, dressed entirely in black, took the stand and was sworn.

Elton Hunter addressed his witness from behind his table. "Miss Walker, are you employed at the Meriwether Counseling Center?"

"Yes, I am," she replied.

"Were you at work there on December seventeenth of last year?"

"Yes."

"Did the defendant, Larry Eugene Moody, come into the Center on that day?"

"Yes."

"Please describe the circumstances and what occurred."

The young woman shifted in her seat. "Well, I called the Morgan people about our furnace—it was real cold in the building—and they sent Mr. Moody to repair it. When he got there, he said it was a bad thermostat, and it would have to be replaced. Sarah—that's Sarah Cole, my boss—objected to the price, but he said it was the cheapest one he had, and she wrote him a check for it, and he left."

"What was Mr. Moody's attitude toward Sarah Cole?" Hunter asked.

Will rose. "Objection, Your Honor. The witness has demonstrated no qualifications as a mind reader."

"Sustained. Rephrase, Mr. Hunter," the Judge said.

Hunter reddened. "Miss Walker, did you notice anything unusual in Larry Moody's *apparent* attitude toward Sarah Cole?"

"Well, he stared at her the whole time, like he was hungry for her."

"Objection," Will said.

"Sustained." The Judge turned to the woman. "Miss Walker, you may testify only to those things of which you have knowledge."

"Yes, sir," she said.

"Miss Walker," Hunter went on, "did Larry Moody smile at Sarah Cole?"

"Yes, sir."

"What sort of a smile was it?"

"Objection. Is the witness an expert on smiles?"

"I will rephrase, Your Honor. Miss Walker, did Larry Moody smile at Sarah Cole in a manner you felt was proper for a furnace repairman toward his customer?"

"No, sir. I felt it was not proper."

"In what way?"

"It was kind of a leer, sort of a street-corner leer, that you might see when a man is ogling a woman."

"Larry Moody was, in your opinion, ogling Sarah Cole?"

"Yes."

"For how long?"

"During the whole time Sarah was in the room."

"When Larry Moody left the premises, did Sarah Cole comment on this ogling?"

"Well, I said to her, 'Jesus, what a creep . . .'"

There were chuckles in the courtroom.

". . . and she said, 'Don't worry. He didn't bother me.'"

"When did you last see Sarah Cole that day?"

"When she left the Center, about six o'clock. I stayed on to finish up some typing."

"And how did Miss Cole leave? Was she driving?"

"She usually did, but that day her car was in the shop, so she walked. It was only about a mile to her house."

"And did you ever see Sarah Cole again?"

"No," the young woman said, her voice trembling. "She was murdered before she could get home."

Hunter turned to Will. "Your witness," he said.

Will walked from behind the table and stood a few feet in front of the witness, his hands folded in front of him. He gave her a moment to compose herself; then he smiled in a friendly way. "Good morning, Miss Walker," he said.

The young woman said nothing, but watched him warily.

"Miss Walker, had you known Sarah Cole for long?"

"Yes, for about two years. That was how long I worked at the Center."

"Was Sarah Cole an attractive woman?"

"Oh, yes, very attractive."

"Attractive to men?"

"Yes, she was."

"Were you ever with Miss Cole in the company of men?"

"Yes, lots of times, at the Center and after work, at parties, and so on."

"Did the men at the parties and at work seem to find Miss Cole attractive?"

"Yes. Like I said, she was extremely attractive."

"Were any of the men on these occasions white?"

"Sometimes."

"Did they find Miss Cole attractive?"

"Yes, I suppose so."

"So, to sum up, Sarah Cole was an extremely attractive woman, one that any ordinary, normal man might find attractive?"

"Yes, she was."

"Then was it in any way unusual that Larry Moody, here, a healthy, normal fellow, would find Sarah Cole attractive?"

"No," the young woman said quietly, knowing she was trapped.

"Did Larry Moody, in your presence, make any sort of advances toward Miss Cole?"

"No."

"Did he say anything to her at all that did not concern the repair of the furnace and the replacement of the thermostat?"

"I suppose not."

"Please don't suppose, Miss Walker; you were there."

"No, he didn't."

"So the conversation was a perfectly normal one concerning the repair of the furnace, with no untoward remarks on the part of Larry Moody?"

"Yes."

"Tell me, Miss Walker, do you regard yourself as infallible with regard to judging the attitudes of men toward women?"

"No, I don't."

"Then is it possible that another person present, a reasonable person, might have put a different light on whatever . . . glances might have passed between Larry Moody and Sarah Cole?"

"Well *I* didn't . . ."

"Please, Miss Walker, we're talking about another possible view. Might another reasonable person have viewed this meeting differently?"

"Maybe."

"And after Larry Moody left the Center, having done his proper job, and when you remarked to Sarah Cole about him, she said, and I quote, 'Don't worry. He didn't bother me.'"

The young woman was sullen. "Yes, but—"

"So Sarah Cole, by her own account, wasn't bothered by Larry Moody. But you were bothered?"

"Yes, I was."

"Miss Walker, do you approve of white men being attracted to black women?"

She seemed to have difficulty speaking. "I guess it's all right," she said finally.

"Miss Walker, have you ever had a white boyfriend?"

Elton Hunter was on his feet. "Objection."

"This is proper exploration of the witness's attitudes," Will said.

"Overruled," the Judge said. "Witness will answer."

"No," she said.

"Have you ever been asked out by a white man?"

"Yes."

"Did you ever accept such an invitation from a white man?"

"No."

Will was careful to keep his voice conversational, not to seem to badger the girl. "Miss Walker, would it be fair to say that you are uncomfortable with the idea of a white man asking out a black woman?"

"Yes, I suppose so," she admitted quietly, looking down at her hands.

"Then wouldn't it be fair to say that you are uncomfortable with the idea of a white man being attracted to a black woman?"

"I suppose so," she said again.

"And isn't it just possible that your interpretation of the meeting of Larry Moody and Sarah Cole might have been affected by your strongly held attitude?"

"I don't think so," she said firmly.

Will looked at her in silence for a moment. "Thank you, Miss Walker," he said sympathetically, "that will be all."

Will returned to the defense table and sat down.

Larry Moody leaned over and whispered, "You won that one."

"If we're lucky, it might be a tie," Will said under his breath.

"We'll take one hour for lunch," the Judge said.

16

"The prosecution calls Roosevelt Watkins," Elton Hunter said.

Roosevelt Watkins took the stand and was sworn. He was dressed in a neat gray suit that looked new. He looked amiably at Elton Hunter, then turned and smiled at Will, who smiled back.

"Mr. Watkins," Hunter began.

"Just call me Roosevelt," the black man said. "Everybody calls me that. Fact, I met Franklin D. hisself, one time, and he called me Roosevelt."

"Fine, Roosevelt," Hunter said. "Where do you live?"

"I got me a place out off the La Grange highway; real comfortable place," Roosevelt said, smiling broadly at Hunter.

"Does your place have a view of the city landfill site?"

"Yessir, a real good view."

"And on December seventeenth of last year, were you looking out your window at the landfill?"

"You mean, when I saw the truck?"

"That's right, Roosevelt."

"Yessir, I saw it."

"Tell us what happened that day, please."

"Well, I reckon it was 'bout quarter to seven in the evening, and I was frying up some fatback to have with my cornbread—my daughter, she fix me the cornbread. And I looked up from the stove, and I seen this light brown truck—a van, like—pull up out in the dump, and this fellar get out, and he go around to the back, and he take a big bundle out of the truck, the van, and he kind of drag it over a pile of stuff and he leave it there, and then he gets back in the van and he drive off."

"You say it was a big bundle that he removed from the van, Roosevelt?"

"Yessir, pretty big."

"Was it as big as a woman?"

"Yessir, if she wasn't too big of a woman."

"Do you see the man who drove the van in this courtroom?"

"Yessir, he sitting right over there next to Mr. Lee, there." Roosevelt pointed at Larry Moody.

"Your witness," Hunter said to Will.

"Good morning, Roosevelt," Will said.

"Good morning, Mr. Lee," he replied.

"That's a very handsome suit you're wearing," Will said.

"Why, thank you, sir." Roosevelt grinned. "Mr. Hunter over here give it to me."

The courtroom laughed, and Elton Hunter looked uncomfortable.

"Roosevelt, you say you saw a truck?"

"Yessir. Some calls it a van."

"Did you tell the sheriff you saw a truck?"

"Yessir, he come out there the next morning when they find that girl, and he ask me. I told him I saw a truck."

"And did the sheriff say it was a van?"

"Yessir, and he done took me down to the jailhouse in his car and show it to me."

Will let that lie; he didn't want Roosevelt Watkins to repeat his identification of the truck. "Did the sheriff ask you to look at anybody else?"

"Yessir, he did. A whole line of gentlemen."

"And did you pick one of them out as being Larry Moody?"

"Yessir, I did."

"Roosevelt, how were these fellows standing when you picked them out?"

"They was up against a wall, with a bright light shining on them."

"Did they have their backs to you?"

"Yessir."

"Why did they have their backs to you?"

"Well, I reckon it was because the curtains got in my way a little bit when I was looking out that window, and I only got a good look at him from the back."

"After you picked out Larry Moody in the lineup— from looking at his back—did the men in the lineup turn around?"

"Yessir, they did."

"And was that the first time you ever saw Larry Moody's face?"

"Yessir, it was."

"Roosevelt, how far was Larry Moody from you when you picked him out of the lineup from behind?"

"Oh, 'bout half as far as he is from me right now."

"Roosevelt, do you wear glasses?"

"No, sir," he replied emphatically. "I got the eyes of a hawk."

Will pointed at the courtroom clock, which was hung on the balcony at the back of the room. "Roosevelt, can you tell me what time it is right now by looking at that clock?"

Watkins gazed at the clock for a moment, then squinted. "Well, them little black hands is too little, I reckon."

Will turned to Larry Moody. "Larry, would you remove your jacket, please?"

Larry Moody shucked off his jacket and stood.

"Roosevelt, would you say that Larry Moody is a pretty husky fellow?"

"Yessir, I would."

"Would it surprise you if I told you that Larry is a weightlifter, that he lifts weights every day?"

"No, sir, he look pretty strong to me."

"Thank you, Larry, you can put your jacket back on. Roosevelt, you said the bundle the man dragged out of the truck wasn't too big, that if it was a woman, it would be a small woman, is that right?"

"That's right."

"Well, if I read you from the coroner's report, here"—Will picked up a document from the defense table and read from it—"that Sarah Cole was five feet three inches tall and weighed a hundred and five pounds, would that sound about the size of the bundle?"

"Yessir, I reckon that'd be 'bout right."

"Now, does Larry Moody look to you as if he could pick up a girl weighing a hundred and five pounds?"

"He sure do. He look strong to me."

"But the man you saw take the bundle from the truck dragged it over the mound of garbage. Is that right?"

"That's right," Roosevelt said, scratching his chin and looking curious. "Mr. Moody sure don't look like he'd have to drag her."

Will smiled in spite of himself. Roosevelt was a wonderful witness. "Just one more thing, Roosevelt," Will said. "You ever been down to Milledgeville?"

Roosevelt smiled broadly. "Oh, yessir, I done been to Milledgeville three times. The doctors say—"

Elton Hunter, too late, was on his feet. "Objection!" he cried.

"Withdraw the question," Will said. "No further questions." He returned to his seat with the knowledge that everybody in the courtroom, including the jury, knew that Milledgeville was the site of the Georgia state mental hospital, and that "going to Milledgeville" meant a person was crazy as a coot.

He had won that round, Will reckoned. Tomorrow, though, he would have to take on the state's scientific witnesses, and that was not going to be so clear-cut.

17

The doctor had been right. Mickey Keane shouldn't have left the hospital when he did, and now he knew it. It had taken him two days of rest and slow movement before he could get around at all. Now, while he was far from whole, he could struggle behind the wheel of his new car and drive.

"Just send me the insurance check for your old car when it comes," Manny Pearl had said. "We'll call the difference a bonus for nearly getting killed."

He sat, now, in the car, the smell of the new interior filling his nostrils, and from the mall parking lot next door, he watched the doctor's office. He had been there for an hour when, a little after six, she left. It had been her voice on the phone, he was sure of it.

Through the binoculars, he made a note of her license-plate number, then started his car and swung into traffic behind her red Chevrolet Beretta. Five minutes later, he followed her into a supermarket parking lot and waited while she shopped. She emerged with half a dozen heavy bags of groceries in her cart, a lot for a woman who didn't wear a wedding ring. Suzy Adams, apparently, did not live alone.

He followed her farther along the shopping strip and off into an area of up-market condominiums and rental units, then watched as she turned into the gate of what seemed to be a newly built complex. The gate security guard knew her, waved her through. Keane waited for her to disappear into the complex, then drove to the gate and stopped.

The uniformed guard came out of the gatehouse. "Can I help you?" he asked.

Keane showed him his badge. "You can tell me the name of the lady who just drove through in the red Beretta."

"That's Mrs. Ross."

"She new here?"

"Everybody's new here, pal. The place has only been open for three months or so. There are still some unsold units."

"What does Mr. Ross look like?" Keane asked.

"What's this about?" the guard asked.

"Can you keep your mouth shut?"

"Sure," the guard said, as if his professional standing had been doubted.

"This is a drug investigation. The lady works in a doctor's office where larger-than-usual amounts of opiates and amphetamines have been prescribed for the past few months. I don't know if she's involved, but I've got to find out. I'll clear her, if she's clean."

"Oh, I see," the guard said, suddenly becoming a colleague.

"So, what does Mr. Ross look like?"

"Tell you the truth, I'm not sure which one he is. I only know her because I issued her parking permit when she moved in. Most of the folks here, if they've got a sticker on the windshield, I just wave them through. That's my orders."

"I see. Which unit are the Rosses in?"

"Forty-nine C," the guard said, checking a list. "Ground floor."

"Where is it?"

"Straight ahead, first left, first right, second building on the left. Forty-nine C would be the last unit on the ground floor."

"Thanks," Keane said, driving quickly on. He made the turns and came around the last corner in time to see Suzy Adams do something strange. She rang the doorbell. There was a pause, then someone opened the door from the inside, and she went in. A moment later, she came out, followed by a man.

Keane's pulse quickened. He was tall and skinny, had a mustache, wore sunglasses, even though it was dusk. Keane pulled into a parking spot and got the binoculars out of the glove compartment. The two were unloading groceries from Suzy's car. The man stood still and looked carefully around him. Keane scrunched down in the seat. The man's ears rested flat against his head, and his nose was straight. Apart from his height and weight, he looked nothing at all like Perkerson's photograph, but the hairs were standing up on the back of Keane's neck. Shortly, the two went inside with the groceries and shut the door.

Now Keane had to decide what to do next. It was nearly

dark out now, but he was in no shape to start sneaking around, peeking into windows; not while he was on crutches. He could call the Atlanta PD and demand a raid on the place, but it was outside the city limits and would have to be coordinated with the Marietta police. If he was wrong about this guy, he'd humiliate himself and use up whatever goodwill he might still have in the department. Or he could sit here and wait.

He waited, increasingly hungry and needing a bathroom badly, until after eleven, when the lights went out in the apartment. Tired and sore from sitting in the car so long, Keane drove home. He would come back in the morning and wait the man out. Sooner or later, he'd have to leave the apartment, and then Keane could get a closer look, maybe nail him. Right now, though, he needed a toilet, some food, a drink, and some sleep.

18

At seven A.M. on Tuesday, Will got into a car with Tom Black. He was a little fuzzy, having spoken to two civic clubs and done six telephone interviews with radio stations around the state, all after a full day of the trial. This morning, before court, Tom had scheduled a sausage-and-biscuits breakfast hosted by a Greenville women's club.

"The news is not good this morning," Tom said immediately. "Our most recent poll, taken this past Sunday, shows us stalled at fifty for Calhoun, forty-seven for you, and three percent undecided. The TV stuff has brought us that far. We didn't seem to actually get hurt in the debate, but we didn't help ourselves much, either."

"I don't know what else to do," Will said. "We've put everything we could scrape up into TV; my every moment between now and next Tuesday is scheduled; what haven't we done?"

"I don't know," Tom said. "We've got something new in this poll, though. Moss did an extra layer of questions for all the people who say they're voting for Calhoun. Turns out, eight percent of his voters say they're voting for Calhoun *only* because they suspect you of being a homosexual. That's enough to give him the election."

"Oh, no," Will groaned. "I thought we had put that to rest a long time ago."

"Not when Calhoun keeps harping on it all the time."

"Maybe if *I* were on trial for murdering Sarah Cole instead of Larry Moody, that would convince the doubters."

"Only if you were convicted," Tom said wryly. He pulled into a convenience store. "I want to get a paper," he said. Moments later, he came back, grinning. "Maybe this will help." He tossed the paper to Will.

On the front page was a photograph taken on the courthouse steps, a close-up of Will and Charlene Joiner. She was looking up at him, her chin tucked down, her eyes lifted. The effect was riveting.

"Christ," Will said, "this is all I need." The photograph made him very uncomfortable. Since Katharine Rule's reappearance on the scene, he had been feeling increasingly guilty about his fling with Charlene, and even more worried that it might come to light.

Tom laughed. "Don't knock it; we need it. You know, yesterday Kitty predicted that Charlene was going to become the media star of this trial, and now I believe it. That girl photographs even better than she looks in person, and that ain't bad. Charlene ought to be in the movies. You notice, they managed to get a nice profile of her tits in that shot."

"Well, Charlene is something of a wild card in this trial; she's my best hope for convincing the jury that Larry

Moody would have no desire to rape Sarah Cole, not with
Charlene at home." He stopped speaking and slapped his
forehead with the palm of his hand. "Oh, shit," he moaned,
"I think I've just figured out why Larry is charged only
with murder, not rape."

"Why?"

"Because of Charlene. I think I've underestimated Elton Hunter. He knows Charlene is Larry's alibi, but he
knows I'll try to make her a sort of sexual alibi, too. He's
going to do everything possible to keep rape out of this."

"Then what's he going to use for a motive?"

"I don't know," Will said glumly. "I wish I did."

Elton Hunter called the sheriff and elicited his testimony
on the arrest and identification of Larry Moody and the
removal of the carpeting from his van. Will had no objections to the testimony, and the sheriff stepped down.

"The State calls Dr. Edward Rosenfeld," Elton Hunter
said.

A handsome man in his thirties took the stand and was
sworn.

"Doctor," Hunter began, "how are you employed?"

"I am an associate director of the Georgia State Crime
Laboratory," the doctor replied.

"And, as such, did you conduct the autopsy of Sarah
Cole and supervise the forensic investigation into her
murder?"

"I did."

"How did Sarah Cole meet her death?"

"She was strangled, manually."

Hunter held up his hands. "You mean, someone put

his hands around her throat and choked the life out of her?"

"Yes."

"Doctor, did you and your technicians examine a large piece of automotive carpeting removed from Larry Moody's van?"

"Yes."

Hunter went to the defense table, picked up a plastic bag containing a black sweater, and removed it from the bag. "Is this the sweater Sarah Cole was wearing when her body reached your morgue, one with a label from Rich's department store?"

The doctor examined a tag attached to the sweater. "It is."

"Is there any connection between this sweater and the carpet you examined?"

"Yes, we found fibers on the carpet matching those from the sweater and fibers on the sweater matching those of the carpet."

"A double match?"

"Yes. A double match."

"That increases your certainty that this sweater and the carpet had come into contact?"

"It does."

"What else did you find on the carpet?"

"Well, an attempt—a not very successful one—had been made to clean the carpet, but in addition to the fibers from the sweater, we found samples of blood, of type A positive blood."

"And what was the blood type of Sarah Cole?"

"Type A positive."

"And what do you conclude from all this evidence?"

"I conclude that Sarah Cole was in the back of Larry Moody's van, and that she shed blood there."

"The prosecution enters the carpet and the sweater as exhibits one and two." Hunter turned to Will. "Your witness," he said.

Will stood and walked around the defense table, his mind racing. "Doctor, had Sarah Cole had sexual intercourse shortly before her death?"

"Objection!" Elton Hunter was on his feet. "Irrelevant. The defendant is not charged with rape, only murder."

"Your Honor," Will said, "the prosecution has introduced evidence of blood on the van carpet and implied that it is the blood of Sarah Cole. Since Dr. Rosenfeld has testified that she was strangled, an act not usually associated with the shedding of blood, I think we're entitled to know where the blood came from."

"Then ask the witness where it came from," the Judge said. "Objection sustained. The jury will disregard any reference to rape, since the defendant is not charged with that crime."

"All right, Doctor," Will said resignedly, "why do you believe Sarah Cole bled in the back of the van?"

"Because she had been struck several times in the face, and she had bled from the nose."

At least, Will thought, the word "rape" had been introduced into the courtroom. The jury would not forget it. "Doctor, let me take your points one at a time. You contend that fibers from the carpet in Larry Moody's van were found on the clothing of Sarah Cole. Is that correct?"

"That is correct."

"Doctor, is that carpet in Larry Moody's van unique?"

"I . . . I don't know."

Will picked up a document from the defense table. "Well, let me enlighten you." He handed the document to the doctor.

Rosenfeld looked it over.

"Will you tell the court who signed the document?"

"It appears to be the production manager of the General Motors assembly plant in Doraville, Georgia."

"Thank you. Now, will you read the text?"

Dear Mr. Lee:

In reply to your letter of January 2, I can give you the following information about the van. The model you mention is the most popular van in the Chevrolet line. In the model year you mention, we built 38,000 of these vans, in four colors. The color you mention, Sierra Brown, was the most popular of these colors, being used on 24,200 of the vans manufactured. The same carpet, from the same manufacturer, was used in all the brown vans. Our records indicate that 1,703 of the brown vans were shipped to dealers in the state of Georgia.

"Thank you, Dr. Rosenfeld. Your Honor, we enter the document as defense exhibit one, and a copy of the records of the Meriwether County Tax Commissioner, indicating that thirteen identical vans are registered in Meriwether County, as defense exhibit number two."

Will turned and took a black sweater from the defense table and handed it to the doctor. "Doctor, I show you a black sweater with a Rich's label. Would you say this sweater is identical to the one found on Sarah Cole's body?" He also handed the man the prosecution's sweater.

The doctor examined the two sweaters. "They would appear to be identical."

"Thank you, Doctor." Will handed both sweaters to the clerk. "We enter the sweater as defense exhibit number three, and, as exhibit four, a copy of the business records of Rich's department store, showing that some thirty dozen identical black sweaters were sold in seven Rich's stores in the Southeast as part of a special promotion last fall, more than four dozen of them in the Atlanta store."

"Excuse me, Mr. Lee," the clerk said. "Which is the prosecution sweater, and which is the defense sweater?"

There was a low chuckle from the spectators as Will helped the man sort the sweaters.

Will took a sheet of paper from the defense table. "Now, Doctor, let us deal with the matter of the blood on the carpet. Tell me, is type A positive a rare blood type?"

"No. It is the second most common type, after O positive."

"So, we may assume that thousands of people in Meriwether County, male and female, have type A positive blood?"

"Yes, that would no doubt be the case."

"And are you, Doctor, able to demonstrate that the sample of type A positive blood found on the carpet in Larry Moody's van came from the body of Sarah Cole?"

"No," the doctor sighed, "I cannot."

"Now, Doctor, at the end of your questioning by the prosecuting attorney, you stated, and I quote, 'I conclude that Sarah Cole was in the back of Larry Moody's van and

that she shed blood there.' We have shown that there are
tens of thousands of vans like Larry Moody's in the country, hundreds in the state, and more than a dozen in this
very county, fibers from any one of which might have been
found on Sarah Cole's clothing; we have shown that Rich's
sold hundreds of sweaters identical to that of Sarah Cole;
and you have testified that thousands of people in this very
county have the same blood type. Can you still support
your statement?"

The doctor looked embarrassed. "Perhaps I was too
specific—still, the coincidence . . ."

"Coincidence is not your field, Doctor, science is. Sci-
entifically, you cannot prove that Sarah Cole was ever in
the back of Larry Moody's van, can you?"

"No," the man said.

"No further questions."

Elton Hunter stood up. "Redirect," he said.

The Judge nodded.

"Dr. Rosenfeld, how long have you been in your present position with the Georgia State Crime Laboratory?"

"Seven years, my entire medical practice."

"During those seven years, how many murders have
you investigated forensically?"

"More than four hundred."

"Based on your extensive experience as a forensic scien-
tist in all these murder investigations, do you have any
doubt whatsoever that Sarah Cole was in the back of Larry
Moody's van?"

"No doubt whatsoever."

"That Sarah Cole was *murdered* in the back of Larry
Moody's van?"

"Objection!" Will said.

"Overruled," the Judge replied. "The question is for his opinion. Witness will answer."

"No doubt whatsoever."

Elton Hunter turned to the Judge. "Your Honor, the prosecution rests."

After the lunch break, Will stood in the courtroom. "Your Honor, the defense calls Larry Eugene Moody."

Larry Moody, dressed neatly in a suit, his hair cut, his mustache shaved off, took the stand and was sworn.

"Larry, what work do you do?"

"I repair furnaces and air conditioners for Morgan and Morgan."

"On that Thursday afternoon before Sarah Cole was murdered, did you visit the Meriwether Counseling Center?"

"Yes, sir."

"Why?"

"They called the office and said their furnace wasn't working. I squeezed in the call right before my last call of the day."

"What work did you do there?"

"I replaced the thermostat."

"Did you speak with Sarah Cole that day?"

"Yes, sir. She wasn't very happy about the price of the thermostat, but I explained that it was the only one I had with me, and she paid me for it."

"Larry, did you ogle Sarah Cole?"

"Sir?"

"Did you find her attractive?"

"Well, yes, sir, she was a real attractive lady. I had seen her around town before."

"Did you make any advances to her that day?"

"No, sir."

"When you left the Counseling Center, where did you go?"

"I had one more call scheduled. I went there and serviced a furnace, cleaned the filters, that sort of thing."

"And when you finished there, what time was it?"

"Just before six."

"And what did you do then?"

"I went home."

"Was anyone at home with you?"

"Yes, Charlene Joiner, my girlfriend, got home just after six."

"Did either you or Charlene leave your home at any time that evening?"

"No, sir. We stayed home and had some supper and watched a video."

Will turned toward the defense table, then stopped. "At whose house was your last service call that day, the one you finished just before six?"

"It was at Mr. Elton Hunter's house." Larry pointed at the prosecution table. "The gentleman right over there."

The courtroom burst into laughter.

Will turned serious. "Larry, did you make sexual advances to Sarah Cole?"

"No, sir, I did not."

"Were you at the city dump, unloading Sarah Cole's body from your van?"

"No, sir, I was not."

"Larry, tell us the truth: did you murder Sarah Cole?"

"No, sir, I did not. I never did. I am not a murderer."
And with that, Larry Moody began to cry.

"Your witness, Mr. Prosecutor," Will said, and sat
down.

"I have no questions at this time, Your Honor," Hunter
said. "I reserve the right to recall the witness at a later
time."

You're bluffing, Will thought. You'll never recall him;
you're just trying to save face. He gave Larry his handkerchief as he returned to his seat. "Your Honor, the defense
calls Charlene Joiner."

There was a murmur of curiosity as Charlene entered
the courtroom from the witness holding area, took the
stand, and was sworn. She was wearing a flowered dress,
one slightly more modest than the one she had worn when
she appeared on television in front of the courthouse the
day before.

Will took her through her version of the evening, cor-
roborating Larry's testimony. Then he took her a bit
farther.

"Charlene," Will said, "what did you and Larry do after
dinner?"

"We watched a video, like I said."

"Did you do anything else?"

Charlene lowered her eyes. "We . . . well, we made
love."

Will was amazed at how well she managed being demure. She certainly had not been demure with him the
first time she had described her evening. "Just once?" he
asked.

"No, more than once; two or three times, I think."

"Would you say that you and Larry have a healthy sex life together?"

"Oh, yes," she replied. "I'd say we have a *very* healthy sex life." She managed a shy smile.

"Tell me, do you recall what you did the evening before?"

"Yes, we went to a drive-in movie."

"Did you do anything there besides watch the movie?"

"Well, there was kind of a sexy movie on, and we got, well, excited, so we made love."

"Where did you make love?"

"In the back of Larry's van. On the floor."

Will went to the clerk and retrieved a black sweater. "Do you recognize this sweater?"

"Yes, I bought it on sale at Rich's last fall. See, it has a dry cleaner's mark with my name."

"When was the last time you wore this sweater, Charlene?"

"That night at the drive-in."

"Did you wear it when you were making love in the back of the van?"

"Yes. I didn't take it off."

"Were you lying on your back in the rear of the van?"

"Yes, at least part of the time. We were all over the place."

The courtroom laughed aloud and was hushed by the Judge.

"Did your back rub against the carpet on the floor of the van when you were making love?"

"Yes. For quite a while."

"Charlene, did you bleed at all that night?"

"Yes, quite a bit."

"Did you bleed as a result of having made love?"

"Yes."

"Did you bleed while you were making love in the van?"

"Yes. I tried to clean up the carpet when we got home, but it didn't all come out."

Will went back to the defense table, retrieved a document, and handed it to Charlene. "Charlene, do you recognize this document?"

"Yes, it's a blood-type certificate from the office of Dr. Leonard Allgood, of Marietta, Georgia. You asked me to have my blood typed, so I went to Dr. Allgood, when I was visiting in Marietta."

"And would you read your blood type from the certificate to the court?"

"It says I have type A positive."

"Charlene, you've testified that you and Larry Moody have a *very* healthy sex life together. Would you say that you satisfy all of Larry's wants and needs in that department?"

"Objection!" Elton Hunter said. "Irrelevant."

Charlene smiled a broad smile. The jury had gotten the point, Will reckoned.

"No further questions. Your witness."

Elton Hunter stood. "Miss Joiner, are you aware of the penalty for perjury?"

"Yes, I think so. You can go to jail if you lie under oath."

"Are you aware that, if you testify falsely in order to

give Larry Moody an alibi for a murder, that you become an accessory to that murder and that you become subject to the same penalty as the murderer—in this case, the death penalty?"

"Yes," Charlene said firmly, "I am aware of that, and I would never put myself in that position. Not for anybody."

Elton Hunter sat down, defeated. "No further questions at this time, Your Honor."

The Judge turned to Will. "It's after four o'clock. How much more do you have?"

"I have just two more witnesses, Your Honor, and I do not anticipate that their testimony will take long. I believe we can finish this afternoon."

"Call your witnesses, then."

Will called John Morgan, Larry's employer, who vouched for Larry's sterling character, much as he had at the preliminary hearing. Then Will called Julia McInvale.

The woman was a model of what a high school teacher should look like, Will thought. The first time he had seen her, when she had come to his office to be interviewed, he had thought that Central Casting could not have supplied a better person for the role. She was an ample, motherly woman, sweet-looking.

"Miss McInvale," Will began, "what is your work?"

"I am a retired high school teacher," she said.

"Where did you last teach?"

"At La Grange High School."

"And did you ever have Larry Moody as a student in your classes there?"

"All four years," she said, smiling at Larry. "I taught him two years of algebra and two years of geometry."

"And did you ever have occasion to see Larry outside the classroom?"

"Yes, I was faculty adviser for the automotive club for two years, and Larry was the secretary of the club. Larry also used to come and do odd jobs at my house. He was very handy."

"So you knew Larry better than you knew most students?"

"Oh, yes, much better. I knew Larry very well indeed. He still comes to see me two or three times a year. I bake him cookies."

Will smiled. "And what is your opinion of Larry?" he asked.

"I think Larry is a very fine person," she said.

"Is Larry a truthful person?"

"Oh, yes. Of course, he told the occasional fib, like all boys, but with Larry, he was so embarrassed if he didn't tell the truth that you always knew if he lied. He would all but cry."

"Was Larry Moody ever violent?"

"Oh, no. I mean, he played on the football team, and he was very good, but off the field, he was the sweetest, gentlest boy you ever saw."

"Is Larry Moody the kind of man who would harm a young woman?"

"Certainly not. It's just not possible."

Will pressed on. This woman was wonderful, and he intended to milk her for all she could be worth to his case. He held up his hands as Elton Hunter had done earlier in the trial. "Did Larry Moody ever do anything that would cause you to think that he was the kind of young man who could force a woman to have sex with him, then put his hands around her neck and strangle the life out of her?"

"Oh, no!" Miss McInvale replied.

"Thank you," he said, then turned to Elton Hunter. "Your witness," he said, unable to keep from smiling confidently.

But Miss McInvale had not finished. "And I never believed that he had anything to do with raping that colored girl in high school," she said vehemently.

Will turned and looked at Miss McInvale, stunned. "Thank you, no further questions," he managed to say.

The courtroom burst into excited conversation, and the Judge hammered them into silence.

Elton was on his feet like a panther. "Tell us about that particular incident, Miss McInvale, when Larry Moody was accused of rape."

"Objection!" Will said. "Irrelevant. My client is not charged with rape."

"A defense witness has introduced this statement, Your Honor," Elton Hunter cried. "Surely, I may cross-examine."

"Overruled," the Judge said. "Witness will answer."

Will sat down heavily and stared at the woman. He had made a cardinal mistake: he had asked a witness a question to which he did not know the answer.

"Tell us about that incident in high school, Miss McInvale," Elton Hunter said eagerly.

"Well, it was this little black girl who made the accusation," she replied.

The courtroom gasped. What is happening? Will thought. His case had spun totally out of control.

"Yes, go on," Hunter said, not sure exactly what to ask.

"Well, the girl, her name was Wilson, I think—yes, that was it, Cora Mae Wilson—she said Larry had dragged her into a car after a football game and raped her. Nobody believed her, of course. Nobody could believe a thing like that of Larry."

"No further questions of this witness," Hunter said, then turned to the Judge. "Your Honor, I request a recess until two o'clock tomorrow to give the prosecution time to produce this very important witness, Cora Mae Wilson."

"I object, Your Honor," Will said, rising to his feet. "The prosecution has concluded its case."

"Recess until two o'clock tomorrow," the Judge said. "The court will hear the witness at that time, if she can be found." The Judge brought down his gavel and left the courtroom, where pandemonium had broken out.

Will grabbed Larry Moody by the arm and hustled him out a side door, followed closely by Charlene Joiner. He herded them into an empty office off the corridor and slammed the door. "All right, what the hell is going on here?" he nearly shouted at Larry. "Why didn't you tell me about Cora Mae Wilson?"

"Aw, shoot, that wasn't important," Larry said. "I had forgotten all about that. There never was anything to it."

"Not important?" Will asked, incredulous. "Do you realize that if they find this woman, she might send you to the electric chair?"

"Easy, Will," Charlene said, putting her hand on his arm. "She's got nobody to back up her story. It'll be her word against Larry's."

Will turned and looked at her. "You mean, you knew about this, too?"

Charlene looked away.

Will turned back to Larry, whose features now contorted into a face Will had never seen before—angry, guilty, desperate.

"That's it," Larry said. "It's her word against mine."

In that moment, something passed between Will and Larry, and suddenly Will knew, beyond any doubt, that the story was true. What was more, he knew, for the first time, that Larry Moody had killed Sarah Cole.

Larry saw it in his face. "You wouldn't take a nigger bitch's word against mine, would you? The white people on that jury sure won't."

Will stared at him for a moment, then at Charlene; then he turned and left the room.

19

Will sat in the library of the big house, a bourbon in his hand, and looked at his father.

"So," Billy Lee said, "you've finally lost your virginity."

"I hadn't thought of it that way," Will replied, swigging from his glass.

"You've learned the great truth that clients often lie to their own lawyers."

"It isn't just that," Will said. "I really thought he was innocent."

"His innocence or guilt shouldn't be the point, not when you're defending a man."

"Oh, I know that; I know that everybody is entitled to a defense. But I think he's gotten a better defense so far, because I thought he was innocent."

"Suppose he is guilty? What did you expect him to do, confess everything to you and plead? The fellow's freedom is at stake; it's hardly surprising that he considers it worth lying for."

"You're right, of course. I just don't know how I'm go-ing to stand up tomorrow and plead the man's innocence."

"You'll do what we all have to do every day of our lives—the best you can. Often, it's not good enough, but it'll have to be."

Will stood up and set his empty glass on the bar. "You're right."

Walking back to the cottage in the dark, Will tried to stop feeling sorry for himself. He'd go in there tomorrow and do the best he could. Only, he didn't want to see Larry Moody go free. Feeling as he did, how could he possibly do justice to the man's defense?

As he walked into the cottage, the phone was ringing; he picked it up.

"Hey," a familiar voice said.

"Hello, Charlene," he said listlessly.

"Could you use some company tonight?"

Will was shocked at her boldness. "Are you crazy? Don't you know what we're in the middle of here?"

"Sure I do. What we've been in the middle of all along. What we were in the middle of the last time we slept together."

Will was suddenly wary, suddenly felt that this conver-sation might not be entirely private. "Listen, I have to go now. I have to get some sleep."

"Will, listen," she said, and her voice was serious. "If Larry gets convicted tomorrow, this is going to be out of my hands."

"What do you mean?" he asked.

"I mean, I don't want all this to come out any more

than you do," she said earnestly. "I want it to stay just between you and me."

He didn't know what to say to her, and he had probably already said too much. "Good night, Charlene," he said, and hung up.

Immediately, the telephone rang again.

"Hello?" he said irritably.

"It's Kate," she said. "What's the matter?"

"I'm sorry. What's happening?"

"I just wanted to give you an update. My boss hasn't been able to see the Director yet; their weekend was canceled. You and I can't do anything publicly until he does. I hope you can understand that."

"Sure, I understand," he said, trying to sound sympathetic.

"You really sound awful," she said. "Do you want to talk about it?"

He started to tell her about his situation, about the percentage of the voters in the poll who still thought he was homosexual, but he stopped. It would just put more pressure on her, and he had already done enough of that. There was nothing she could do to help at the moment, anyway. "Not really," he said. "I've just had kind of a bad day, that's all. A real bad day."

20

Will arrived at the Greenville Courthouse; he pulled into a parking place and stopped, but before he could get out of the car, a man he had never seen before opened the passenger door and slid into the front seat beside him.

"Forgive the intrusion, Counselor," the man said smoothly, "but I want to talk with you for just a moment about your case."

The man didn't look like press, and Will was annoyed. "I'm sorry, sir, but I'm not inclined to discuss my case with someone not directly connected with it." He started to get out of the car, but a firm restraining hand was placed on his arm.

"Please," the man said. "I think you could say that I am directly connected with your case, since it was I who paid your fee."

"Oh? What fee was that?" Will said cautiously.

"The twenty-five thousand dollars in cash that was left at your office last December."

"I see," Will said. "And your name?"

"Please understand that it would be better for both your position and mine if I remain anonymous," the man said.

"Perhaps I could understand if I knew exactly what your position is in all this."

"Suffice it to say that I have a deep interest in the welfare of Larry Moody."

Will was growing impatient with all this. "Well, that makes two of us. Now, is that what you wanted to tell me? I really do have to be in court."

"What I want to say to you is that, after the events of yesterday, I am concerned about the depth of your commitment to Larry. I am concerned that your enthusiasm for his innocence may be flagging."

"My level of enthusiasm is my problem, not yours, and—"

"And I want you to know that if Larry Moody is convicted of this crime, the consequences for you could be very serious indeed."

"Now, you listen to me," Will said, his anger rising, "Larry Moody is going to get the best defense I can muster under the circumstances. He's in the position he's in because he lied to me in the beginning. Having said that, I perceive what you have just said to me as some sort of threat, and if I hear another word from you along those lines, there is a very tough old judge in that courthouse who takes a dim view of people meddling in his cases, and who will be happy to show you the inside of the Meriwether County Jail. Do you read me loud and clear?"

The man seemed to be fighting to maintain control of

himself. "I read you, Mr. Lee," he said. "I just hope you read me." He got out of the car and firmly shut the door.

Cora Mae Wilson looked remarkably like Sarah Cole, Will thought. Not so much her face, but her size, her café-au-lait coloring, and her short Afro haircut. She sat erect, her hands folded in her lap, and answered Elton Hunter's questions calmly.

"How are you employed, Miss Wilson?"

"I am a licensed practical nurse," the woman said. "I work at Callaway Hospital, in La Grange."

"Did you attend La Grange High School at the same time as Larry Moody?"

"Yes, I did."

"Did you ever have any sort of encounter with Larry Moody?"

"Yes."

"Will you tell the court about it, please?"

She unfolded her hands and took a deep breath. "It was my freshman year in high school," she said. "I had been to a football game on a Friday night in November, and I was walking home alone from the stadium. We only lived a few blocks from the school. I had to pass through a picnic area—a few tables in some pine woods—and it was near the parking lot at the gym, where the dressing rooms were. The football players were starting to leave, after they had changed after the game, and I was blinded by the lights of a car.

"The car stopped, and I put up my hand to shield my eyes from the lights, then the car pulled into the picnic area, where I was, and the lights were turned off. I thought it must be somebody I knew, and when I heard the car door slam, I turned toward the car. I was having trouble adjusting my eyes to the dark, so I said, 'Who's that?'

"That was when he hit me. He never said a word, he just hit me. I went down, and then he grabbed me by my hair and yanked me up, and he started talking, sort of quiet, saying, 'Hey, baby, look at you. I'm gonna give you something nice.' And all the time, he was dragging me toward the car.

"I tried to scream, but he put his hand over my mouth, then he got an arm—a strong arm—around my neck and he hauled me over to the car and opened the back door. He was tearing at my clothes by this time, and I was struggling. He hit me a couple of times more, then, and said if I didn't shut up, he'd kill me. I stopped trying to scream then, but I was still struggling, while he was tearing at my clothes.

"He tore my blouse, and then he tore my underwear off, right off my body, and then he held me down, and he raped me."

"Were you able to see his face?"

"Yes, cars kept passing by, the players and their girl-friends, and they would whistle or shout—I guess they thought it was some couple parked there, making out, you know."

"And did you know the boy?"

"Yes, I had seen him around the school a lot. He was a football player, and everybody knew who he was."

"Did you know his name?"

"Yes," she said, "his name was Larry Moody."

"What happened next?" Hunter asked.

"When he finished, he sort of slumped down beside me, and I tried to run, but he caught me from behind, and he started choking, strangling me. I was about to pass out, I was desperate, and I grabbed him in the crotch—his pants were down—I grabbed his genitals, his testicles, and I squeezed as hard as I could. He screamed, and he let go of me, and I ran, ran through the woods behind the gym, afraid that he was after me. I got away, though, and I managed to get home before I just collapsed."

"What did you do next?" Hunter asked.

"There was nobody home—my mother worked nights at a restaurant, and my father had left home—so I cleaned myself up as best I could, and I fell asleep."

"Did you call the police?"

"No."

"Why not?"

"The police were . . . white, and I was afraid they wouldn't believe me."

"Did you tell your mother?"

"I told her the next morning, when I woke up, but she said I was right not to call the police, that they wouldn't believe me. So I got dressed and went to school, and on the way, I started to get mad, and when I got to the school, I went to the principal's office and told him what had happened the night before. He seemed to take me seriously, and he asked me to wait while he went out of the room for a few minutes.

"When he came back, the football coach was with him, and I saw Larry Moody sitting outside in the waiting room. Then the principal and the coach started on me, asking questions, trying to shake my story, but I was telling the truth, and I wouldn't change what I was saying."

Tears were running down Cora Mae Wilson's face now, and she struggled to get out the words.

"So then they started saying that it had all been just 'a youthful prank' at worst, and anyway, nobody would ever believe it—not the police, not the kids I went to school with. Larry Moody was real popular, a big football player, and nobody would ever believe that he would have done anything like that to me.

"Then they began to talk like I was the one who had done something wrong, like it was my fault, and I started to get scared. They said that if I kept insisting my story was true, not only would I end up in jail, but that Larry Moody could sue me, take my mother's house that she had worked so hard to pay for.

"Finally, I just wanted to get out of there; I would have done anything to get out of there. They were real stern; they said I would have to apologize to Larry Moody. And they brought him in the principal's office, and I had to say that I was sincerely sorry for any trouble I had caused Larry Moody and for telling lies about him. After I did that, they let me go, but they made me promise I wouldn't mention it to anybody, ever."

"And what happened after that?" Hunter asked.

"After that, whenever Larry Moody saw me in the hall at school, he would wink at me and say nasty things—'You want some more, baby?'—that kind of thing. Sometimes he would pinch me—my behind or my breasts. Pretty soon, some of his friends started to do the same thing."

"Did you go to the school authorities about this?"

She shook her head. "I was afraid to, after what had happened the last time when I went to them for help."

"So what did you do?"

"I left school. My mother sent me over to her sister's in Birmingham to live, and I finished high school there. I didn't come back to La Grange until after I had finished my practical nurse's training, and then my mother got sick, and I came back to take care of her, and I got a job at Callaway Hospital."

"Did you ever see Larry Moody again?"

"No. I heard he'd moved away, but I lived in constant fear of running into him."

"Miss Wilson," Elton Hunter said quietly, "do you see the man who beat you, who raped you, who tried to strangle you, who drove you out of your school and your hometown—do you see him in this courtroom?"

Cora Mae Wilson turned her tear-streaked face toward the defense table and pointed at Larry Moody. "That's him, sitting right there," she said firmly.

"Your witness," Hunter said to Will.

Larry Moody leaned over and whispered to Will. "Go on," he said, "take her apart."

"I have no questions," Will said to the Judge.

"What are you doing?" Larry demanded. "You've got to make her say she's lying!"

"Larry," Will said, "that girl is unassailable. If I attack her testimony, it will only make things worse for you."

Elton Hunter stood up. "The prosecution rests," he said.

Larry had Will by the coat sleeve. "Then put me back on the stand, so I can call her a liar," he said.

"I'm not going to do that," Will said. "If I do, Elton Hunter will cut you into little pieces and feed you to the jury. Except for the summations, it's over. You've still got a chance, on the evidence. That's your best hope."

"You bastard!" Larry whispered. "You're selling me down the river."

"I'm trying to keep you out of the electric chair," Will said to him.

"I can't believe you're doing this to me," Larry said.

Will turned and looked at him. "You've done it to yourself, Larry. Now, just sit quietly while I try to save your life."

21

Elton Hunter, in summation, built his case carefully, block by block, delivering just enough emotion at every step to cement the guilt of Larry Moody into the structure of his case. Finally, with some passion, he reviewed the testimony of Cora Mae Wilson, using it to establish a history of sexual violence for Larry Moody. When he had finished, the jurors looked sober; one or two looked angry. The courtroom was absolutely silent.

Will stood and faced the jury. "Ladies and gentlemen," he said, "I want to thank you for your close attention to these proceedings. The prosecution has attempted to build an overwhelming case against Larry Moody, and the prosecution has failed. At each turn of this trial, we have shown how their evidence is faulty.

"First, they have produced a witness whose identification of Larry is suspect, a witness of poor eyesight and questionable mental state. How can even a sharp-eyed, stable person identify another from behind? Then they have produced evidence of carpet fibers on Sarah Cole's

sweater and sweater fibers on the carpet—but we have
shown that there are thousands of such vans with identical
carpets, more than a dozen of them in this county. We
have also shown that the sweater Sarah Cole wore was
identical to dozens of others sold by the same department
store—and one of those sweaters was owned by the defendant's girlfriend. We have shown that the defendant and
his girlfriend, who was wearing that sweater, made love on
that carpet the night before the murder. We have shown
that Sarah Cole and the defendant's girlfriend have the
same very common blood type, thus accounting for the
blood on the carpet.

"Perhaps you have seen on television, read in the newspapers, that a new type of identification is, today, available
to law-enforcement agencies. This is genetic identification,
where a drop of blood or a single hair can be identified as
belonging to a particular human being. You will, perhaps,
wonder why the prosecution did not avail themselves of
the opportunity to strengthen their case by using such a
technique. Perhaps it is because they believed that such a
test would destroy their case.

"Finally, the prosecution made its last, desperate
move—to call a witness to testify about an alleged incident
which, she says, occurred eight years ago, an alleged incident that was never properly investigated, an alleged incident to which there were no witnesses. Thus, we may
never know what actually occurred on that night so many
years ago; we will never be able to properly assess the
blame for what may or may not have happened. In any
case, Larry Moody is not on trial for that incident, but for
the murder of Sarah Cole.

"You have been called into this court to consider not just allegations, but hard evidence, and I submit to you that the prosecution has not shown you a single unflawed piece of evidence that would prove beyond a reasonable doubt that Larry Moody was in any way connected with the death of Sarah Cole.

"On the other hand, the defense has shown that Larry Moody is a person of good character, who, apart from a few speeding tickets, has never been in any trouble with the law. You have heard Charlene Joiner testify that he was with her at the time the prosecution says the murder was committed. She has testified that she and Larry have a very healthy sex life, that there was no reason for him to seek out Sarah Cole for sex, let alone murder her.

"Finally, the prosecution has failed to establish any motive for this murder. Why would an intelligent young man, leading a happy and productive life, with a beautiful companion, seek to rape and murder a woman he didn't even meet until the day of her murder?

"You all know, I am sure, that in order to convict Larry Moody of this crime, each of you must be *sure,* beyond a reasonable doubt, that he is guilty as charged. It is hard for me to believe that twelve of you could be *sure,* beyond a reasonable doubt, based on the evidence in the case. If, after assessing all you have seen and heard here, any one of you has *any reasonable doubt* that the evidence is insufficient to support a conviction, then you must acquit Larry Moody. Any other vote would be a miscarriage of justice.

"I remind you that Larry Moody's life is at stake here, and that, apart from your duty to the law, each of you has a conscience that he must answer to. I urge you to consider all the doubts in this case, and to reach a verdict that each of you can live with. Thank you."

Will sat down at the defense table.

"Is that it?" Larry Moody asked.

"That's it," Will said. "Now we wait."

22

Will decided to wait at home for the jury's verdict. He returned to the cottage, checked in with campaign headquarters, phoned Kate Rule and chatted for a while, then settled down to wait.

At seven o'clock, he got a call from the bailiff. "Mr. Lee, I just went into the jury room to ask when they wanted to break for dinner, and they said they didn't want to break, that they were close to a verdict. You might want to come on back here."

Will thanked the man and hurried to Greenville. He arrived to find the lawn of the courthouse floodlit and full of demonstrators. Their numbers had grown since the beginning of the trial, and they were still separated into two camps, divided by the front walk to the building. As Will strode up the walkway to the courthouse, both groups fell silent. At the top of the steps, Larry Moody and Charlene Joiner were giving an interview to a television reporter. Will waited for them to finish, and the reporter turned to him.

"Any prediction on a verdict, Mr. Lee?"

"I would never try and predict what a jury will do," Will replied. He waved Larry and Charlene into the building. "I've had word from the bailiff that the jury expects to reach a verdict soon," he said, showing them into a witness room. They all sat down.

"What do you think they'll do?" Larry asked.

"I wasn't kidding that television reporter," Will said. "Juries are unpredictable. There might be one or two strong jurors who will influence them one way or another; they might divide into camps and hold their positions; there might be one holdout against the rest that will result in a hung jury and a mistrial. You just never can tell."

"Does it mean something that they're near a decision now?"

Will looked at his watch. "They've been at it for nearly five hours now. I think that's in our favor. I would have been more worried if they had reached a verdict the first hour. Somebody's on our side in there, I think."

"Listen," Larry said, "I want you to know that I think you did a good job. I know I didn't like some of the things you did, but I've had a chance to think about it, and I think you did the best thing." He looked at the floor. "If I'm convicted, it won't be your fault," he said quietly.

"I agree with that," Charlene said.

"Thank you both," Will said. Nobody said anything for a few moments. "Are you two back together?" Will asked finally, to keep the conversation going.

"Oh, we . . ." Larry began.

"I moved back in a couple of weeks before the trial started," Charlene interrupted.

"Good," Will said, for lack of anything else to say.

They sat in silence, each lost in his own thoughts, for a few more minutes; then the bailiff knocked on the door. "The jury is coming in," he said.

Will, Larry, and Charlene returned to the courtroom. The crowd was noisily filing in from the front lawn, still dividing themselves into camps, one on either side of the aisle. When the courtroom was full, the bailiff called for all to stand, and the Judge entered.

Judge Boggs rapped for order, then turned to the jury. "Ladies and gentlemen, have you reached a verdict?"

The foreman, a white woman, stood. "Yes, we have, Your Honor."

"Please read the verdict," the Judge said.

The woman unfolded a piece of paper and read, "We the jury find the defendant, Larry Eugene Moody, guilty of murder in the first degree . . ."

An uproar broke out in the courtroom. People on one side of the aisle were laughing and cheering, and on the other, there were angry murmurs. The Judge hammered them into silence.

"Please continue," he said to the foreman.

". . . and we recommend a sentence of life imprisonment."

There were cries of "No!" from some of the black people in the courtroom, and the Judge used his gavel again to restore silence. "The defendant will stand."

Larry Moody stood, looking frightened. Will stood with him.

"Do you have anything to say?" the Judge asked.

"No, sir," Larry said.

"Then I hereby sentence you to life imprisonment in the state penitentiary," the Judge said. "I will hear motions."

Will rose. "Your Honor, the defense moves to continue bond pending appeal."

The Judge looked at Elton Hunter.

"The prosecution objects, Your Honor," Hunter said. "This is first-degree murder. Defendant may flee the jurisdiction."

The Judge looked down at his desktop for a moment. "The defendant is employed and established in the community; enough issues have been raised to warrant bail, though this is unusual," he said. "Two hundred fifty thousand dollars is substantial bond; I will continue it pending appeal." There was a noise of outrage from one side of the courtroom, which the Judge ignored. "Court is adjourned pending receipt of notice of appeal." He rapped his gavel sharply, then left the courtroom.

Will stood up and turned to Larry and Charlene. "I'm sorry," he said. "I think it was the best we could have hoped for, under the circumstances. Even if your appeal fails, you could be eligible for parole in as little as seven years."

Larry nodded. "Thanks for your help," he said, offering his hand.

Will shook it, and Charlene's; then he motioned to the group milling behind them in the courtroom. "Larry, do you know these people here? They've been on the courthouse lawn all week."

Larry nodded. "Some of them are members of an organization I belong to."

"What organization?" Will asked.

"We never speak its name."

23

Mickey Keane was bored to stupefaction. He had always prided himself on his patience on stakeouts, but now he was going bananas. He couldn't even get out of the car and stretch, because he didn't want to be seen in this apartment complex—the crutches were too memorable. Not that stretching was much fun these days. His bruises had all turned yellow, making him resemble some species of squash, and he was still sore as a boil all over. His recuperative powers were diminishing with age, he reckoned. He was nearly forty-two, after all.

Then he sat bolt upright. The door to the apartment was open. A moment later, the man left the apartment, closing the door behind him. He walked quickly down to a car, a silver Toyota, opened the door, got in, fiddled with something—maybe the glove compartment—then got out, locked the car, returned to the apartment, and closed the door.

Keane sat there, wide-eyed, his adrenaline pumping. What? The son of a bitch doesn't leave the apartment for three days; then he comes out, gets something out of the car, and goes back in? Christ! The guy ought to have cabin fever by now. Keane certainly did.

Gradually, the adrenaline ebbed away, and Keane sank back into the seat, sick with disappointment. He closed his eyes and sighed. How long, oh, Lord, how long?

Suzy answered the phone, then handed it to Perkerson.

"It's him," she whispered.

"Yes?" he said into the phone.

"I want to see you here," the voice said.

"Right away," Perkerson replied.

"No," the voice said. "We have a problem that must be dealt with first."

"What's that?"

"Your roommate. Deal with her."

"Say that again?" Perkerson replied.

"Kill the girl, and get out of there. Take what you can, but don't bother cleaning up the place; it doesn't matter."

"Half an hour," Perkerson replied. He hung up.

"I want to go with you," Suzy said.

Perkerson looked at her. "All right, why not?"

"Just let me fix my makeup," she said, and disappeared into the bathroom.

Perkerson went to a kitchen drawer, got the 9 mm automatic, and screwed in the silencer. He felt a pang of something he had never before felt when he was about to kill: regret. But he had never questioned an order of the Archon's, and he must not do so for personal reasons. He walked to the bathroom and stopped in the doorway. She was standing, her back to him, applying lipstick in the mirror.

"I'll just be a minute," she said.

"No hurry," Perkerson replied. He raised the pistol.

Her eyes widened in the mirror; she dropped the lipstick. "No . . ."

Perkerson shot her in the back of the head. Simultaneously, the mirror turned red and disintegrated. Her body collapsed over the sink, then slid to the floor.

Perkerson walked into the bedroom and started packing, which didn't take long, because he habitually had everything arranged for a quick departure. Everything went quickly into two canvas suitcases. He had one last look around, then gingerly retrieved his toilet kit from the bathroom, wiped the blood from it, and packed it.

He left the apartment, walked quickly to his car, backed out of the parking spot, and drove toward the front gate. The usual cars, he noted, except for that Ford Taurus. It had been parked in front of 41C for a couple of days now. Nobody in it, though; it didn't look like a problem. He drove on. Inside him there was an unfamiliar hollow feeling.

Mickey Keane stirred and looked around him. Shit, he had dozed off. Might as well call it a day; it was nearing eleven and . . . He looked up. The Toyota was gone. When? How long? I doze off for five minutes, and the guy is gone! He got his new Ford Taurus started and drove quickly toward the gate. The usual guy was on duty.

"Did Ross leave recently?"

"Yeah, maybe two minutes ago," the guard said. "That way."

Keane stomped on the accelerator and spun the car into the road. Maybe he could still catch up. Three minutes later, he reached Georgia Highway 41, the main drag in these parts. Which way? He sped toward the city, looking as far ahead as he could for the silver Toyota.

Ten minutes later, he was at Interstate 75, and there had been no sign of the Toyota. Keane cursed himself for dozing off. He sat at a traffic light until it changed, then drove home. "Fuck him," he said aloud. "I'll start again tomorrow."

24

Will sat with his parents in their library, along with Tom Black and Kitty Conroy, and watched the eleven-o'clock news, a substantial portion of which was devoted to a recap of the trial and conviction of Larry Moody. Interviews with Larry and, especially, Charlene, were replayed, along with interviews with the demonstrators on the courthouse lawn.

"I told you the press was going to love Charlene," Kitty said. "She's the new glamour girl of the state; I hear she's had a couple of movie offers, and an offer of a book contract."

"More power to her," Will said. "I've always thought she was too beautiful and smart to be working at a convenience store. You know, I think she supplied me with some false evidence."

"What evidence?" his father asked, looking alarmed.

"I always thought we were a little too lucky in that Charlene had a sweater identical to Sarah Cole's."

"But how could she have come up with an identical one, if she didn't already have it?"

"I picked her up at her place of work once, in Larry's van, and I had to use the men's room, while she waited in the van. The lab reports, which described the brand and store label of the sweater, were in an envelope on the front seat. It didn't occur to me until after I had had a little shouting match with Larry and Charlene that something like that might have happened. By that time, the sweater was already in evidence."

"You really think she's that bright?" Tom asked.

"I do," Will said. "And now I wonder about her blood type, too. She gave me this certificate from a doctor in Marietta, said she was up there visiting, and he was an old family friend. She could have learned Sarah Cole's blood type from that lab report. I should have chosen the doctor myself and had the certificate sent directly to me. Sloppy lawyering."

Martin Washington, head of Attorneys for Racial Equality, was being interviewed in front of the courthouse.

"Mr. Washington, Will Lee is a candidate for the U.S. Senate. Do you think black people are going to resent his defending Larry Moody, and, perhaps, not vote for him because of it?"

"I hope not," Washington replied. "This was not a case Will Lee sought out; the Judge got him to agree to it, along with Mr. Hunter, and then tossed a coin to see who prosecuted and who defended. The Judge told me that himself. I think Mr. Lee performed a public service in taking the case, and he acquitted himself well in the trial, even if his client was not acquitted."

The anchorman came back on the screen. "That opinion of Will Lee's performance in the trial was backed up by

the foreman of the jury, Mrs. Evelyn Everett, in an interview taped only a few minutes ago." He turned and looked
at a monitor.

Mrs. Everett appeared on-screen. "I think that, up until
the point of the testimony of the schoolteacher, Miss Mc-
Invale, most of us on the jury were leaning in favor of acquittal. Mr. Lee had poked a lot of holes in the other
evidence in the case. Her testimony, however, turned the
tide in favor of conviction, and I think that testimony surprised Mr. Lee as much as it did us."

"Was there much argument about the life sentence
among the jurors?" the reporter asked.

"Yes, some of us were in favor of the death penalty. It
was Mr. Lee's summation, though, that kept us from going that route. I think that, although we all felt that Larry
Moody was guilty beyond a reasonable doubt, Mr. Lee
made some of us feel that there was, at least, *some* doubt,
and that made us reluctant to take the man's life."

"That's a pretty good review," Tom Black said. "We
may come out of this well, after all."

The camera returned to the anchorman. "All during
the trial, members of a white supremacist group kept a
vigil on the courthouse lawn. Our reporter interviewed
one of their leaders."

The camera switched to a young man, severely dressed
in a dark suit and black tie, being interviewed by a
reporter.

"Mr. Johnson," she asked, "what is the feeling of your
people about the verdict in this trial?"

The young man's brow furrowed. "We think this is a
major miscarriage of justice, brought on by racist attitudes

favoring blacks in our society," he said, "and by a particularly poor performance by the defense lawyer, Mr. Will Lee."

"Thank you, God," Will said, bringing his hands together.

"We feel," continued the man, "that a good attorney would have destroyed the credibility of the Wilson woman when she took the stand. We don't think we got our money's worth from Lee."

"Are you saying that your organization hired Mr. Lee and paid his fees?"

"Oh my God," Tom Black said. "Is that true?"

"While we didn't choose him, we certainly paid his fee—twenty-five thousand dollars," the young man said.

The reporter came on camera. "I asked Will Lee about this only moments later," she said.

Will's face appeared on camera, looking serious.

"Mr. Lee," the reporter asked, "were you aware that your fee was being paid by a white supremacist group?"

"I was completely unaware of that until five minutes ago," Will replied. "Shortly after Judge Boggs assigned me to the case, my office received a plain brown envelope containing twenty-five thousand dollars in cash and an unsigned note saying it was for the defense of Larry Moody. That same day, I reported to Judge Boggs that someone, who wished to remain anonymous, had paid a retainer for the defense of Larry Moody, and I asked that Larry be removed from the indigent defendants' list and that I not be paid a fee from public funds."

"So you were well paid for your defense work?" she asked.

"The envelope containing the money is still in my safe, and I have not spent a dime of it. In light of today's discovery of where it came from, I have decided to donate the entire amount to ARE, Attorneys for Racial Equality, where I hope it will be used in the defense of indigent black defendants. I myself want no part of it."

"Whew!" Tom Black sighed.

"That was scary," Kitty said, holding a hand to her breast.

"You never mentioned the money," Billy Lee said.

"To tell you the truth, I just forgot about it," Will said, "and a good thing, too, or I would probably have dumped it into the campaign. It's still sitting in my safe in the cottage."

"You know," Tom Black said, "I'm beginning to think I may not be cut out for politics; I'm not sure my heart is strong enough."

"So what's the next step in the campaign, Will?" his mother asked.

"I'm flying back to Atlanta with Tom and Kitty tomorrow morning. We're going to spend the rest of our time in the Atlanta suburbs, where we badly need votes. My only scheduled appearance is Sunday morning at Dr. Don's church."

"Have you figured out what you're going to say to those people?" Patricia Lee asked.

Will shook his head. "I haven't a clue."

25

Perkerson had never seen the Archon in this sort of mood. The man seemed both depressed and agitated. He ranged nervously about his study, pouring drinks, fiddling with things on his desk, warming his hands at the fire.

"The girl was an FBI informer," Willingham said, taking a large sip of his bourbon. "I got some inside information. She was arrested last year on a drug charge, and she dealt with them in order not to be prosecuted. Apparently, they sent her to Leonard Allgood's office, where she was hired."

Perkerson was shaken. "That means the FBI must know about me," he said. "Why haven't they tried to arrest me?"

"Perhaps they were hoping you'd lead them to me. Are you sure you weren't followed here tonight?"

"Absolutely positive."

"Well, you're out of the net, then, since the girl and I are the only ones who knew where you were, right?"

"That's right."

"Did the girl know about me?"

"No," Perkerson lied. How long had it been since he had told her who the Archon was? Had she had time to report the information?

"Good. Apparently, I'm in the clear, too. I've had the house and my telephones swept. No devices." He went to the safe behind the liquor cabinet and took out an envelope. "Here is a new set of identification," he said. "Burn your old license and cards in the fireplace now. Your new name is Howard James."

Perkerson did as he was told. The plastic cards melted away in the fire.

The Archon tossed him some keys. "There is a Volvo station wagon parked in the northeast corner of the Lenox Square shopping mall. Take the Volvo and leave your car there with the keys in the glove compartment. It will be disposed of."

Perkerson nodded.

The Archon still looked worried.

"Is something else wrong, sir?"

"We have a situation," Willingham said.

"How can I help?" Perkerson asked, leaning forward and resting his elbows on his knees.

"I'll come to that in a minute. Harry, I've never for a moment questioned your loyalty, but I have to now. I want to know if you're ready to die, if necessary."

"Yessir, I am," Perkerson answered without hesitation.

Willingham sat down heavily in the chair across from Perkerson. "It may come to that," he said. "I hope not, but it may."

"I understand, sir."

"You're like a brother to me, Harry. You know I wouldn't give the order unless I absolutely had to."

"I know that, sir."

"There's something else. I'm beginning to feel the strain of leadership; I have to question my own resolve."

"Not you, sir."

"You have to help me, Harry."

"Of course I will, sir."

"I'm going to give you an irrevocable order."

"I would never allow anyone to revoke your orders, sir."

"I mean irrevocable, even by me. If I should weaken, you must be strong and carry out this assignment, regardless of anything further I have to say about it."

"If that's what you want, sir."

"We have a situation," Willingham said again.

Perkerson waited for him to get to the point.

"This fellow Lee has turned out to be a problem. He failed us in Larry Moody's trial. I had high hopes for Larry. I had hoped that, one day, he might be as good as you. It was only chance that tripped him up on his maiden assignment. Lee allowed Larry to be convicted, I think, because after he heard the schoolteacher's testimony, he began to think that Larry was guilty. I tried to reason with him, but he ignored me, even insulted me."

"Sir, as far as I'm concerned, that's reason enough to kill him."

"Perhaps, but there's the election, too. I thought Lee would be a weaker candidate than Mack Dean, but I was wrong. Calhoun's pollsters are showing the two nearly even. I can't take a chance on Lee's getting any luckier;

there's too much riding on it. You realize that, with Calhoun elected, we would have our own man in the United States Senate?"

"Yessir."

"My plan is twofold: First, I want his death to look accidental, if at all possible. I believe I know how to accomplish that. Second, I have a way to simultaneously destroy his reputation. This is important to me. It's because of the way he spoke to me this morning at the courthouse."

Willingham reached into his pocket and produced a handful of plastic bags. He smiled slightly. "This is something I came up with in Vietnam, but I've never had a chance to use it until now. These bags can be bought at any grocery store. They are of two thicknesses of weight: one will dissolve in gasoline in a little over an hour; the other will take something between two and three hours."

Willingham went on explaining exactly how his plan would work. Perkerson had to admit it was brilliant.

"If this doesn't work," Willingham said, "then I will leave his demise in your hands. I realize that on such short notice it may not be possible to make his death look like an accident. In that event, you may use whatever means are necessary, and I realize that may mean the sniper's rifle."

Perkerson nodded. "I'll use it if I have to."

"If you have to kill him openly, you must never be taken alive, do you understand?"

"I understand, sir. In that event, I know what I have to do."

"If my plan works, he will be dead before his appearance at the church on Sunday. If not, stay away from the church. We can't have it seem that his death has anything to do with his appearance there. It would be best if he died before the polls open on Tuesday, but he absolutely *must* be dead before the polls close on Tuesday, at seven P.M. A dead man can't be elected; the man with the second-largest number of votes will be declared the winner. Do you have it all straight?"

Perkerson nodded. "Yessir, I do. I promise you he will not live to see the polls close."

"This order is irrevocable; not even I may change it."

"I understand, sir."

They walked to the door together. "Wait until just before daylight to plant the plastic bags," Willingham said. "He has to be back in Atlanta early tomorrow morning; he's advertised to be speaking at nine."

"Yessir."

Willingham put his hands on Perkerson's shoulders. "I know I can count on you, my boy," he said. "If we don't meet again, I want you to know how grateful I am for your loyalty."

Perkerson's eyes brimmed over with tears. "Yes, sir."

Willingham embraced him, then sent him on his way.

26

Will, Tom, and Kitty left the Delano farm at six-thirty, in the dark of the November morning. It was Friday, and he had a nine-o'clock appearance at a businessmen's breakfast in Lawrenceville, in the northern Atlanta suburbs. Tom and Kitty tried to doze in the car, to catch a few moments more of sleep before truly greeting the day. Will was working on waking up, because he had to fly.

As he pulled into the entrance of Roosevelt Memorial Field, the Meriwether County airport, a predawn light was in the sky, and he was surprised to be met by a station wagon, on its way out of the airport. He got a glimpse of the driver, but he didn't know him. Could some visitor have arrived at this hour? Will looked at the pilot-operated runway lights, which turned themselves off automatically after fifteen minutes of use. They were off. He wondered if someone had perhaps been trying to steal gear from the airplanes parked there.

As he pulled the car up to the Cessna, he could see

nothing amiss, with his airplane or the others, nor were there any airplanes he didn't know. He roused his companions, and they got their bags into the luggage compartment. Tom and Kitty climbed aboard while Will did his normal pre-flight inspection and checked the fuel for water, which sometimes condensed in the tanks during the cool evening hours, or arrived in contaminated fuel. Then he climbed into the airplane and began working through his checklist.

Tom was already snoring softly.

Will started the engine, taxied into the runway, performed his usual run-up procedure, then centered the airplane on the runway, put in ten degrees of flaps, and shoved the throttle in. The airplane began to roll; at sixty knots, he pulled back on the yoke, and the Cessna rose into the air. The sun was just coming up.

They climbed through the morning haze, over the green fields and woods, and Will set the autopilot to take them to a point southeast of Hartsfield International Airport, so as to avoid the Terminal Control Area around the huge facility. He never filed a flight plan on this forty-minute hop, and at this time of day, there would be few planes at his altitude, so he didn't check in with air-traffic control and ask for traffic advisories. He leveled off at three thousand feet, and the little airplane drummed its way smoothly through the still morning air.

Thirty-five minutes later, they were over Stone Mountain, the huge lump of granite in the northeast Atlanta suburbs, and descending into Peachtree De Kalb Airport, to the traffic pattern of two thousand feet above mean sea level, which was a thousand feet above ground level. Will listened to the Automated Traffic Information Service on the radio, then switched to the frequency of Peachtree De Kalb Tower. "Good morning, Peachtree Tower, this is November One Two Three Tango, six miles to the southeast, with information Alpha, for landing."

Then the airplane's engine stopped.

"Good morning, One Two Three Tango," the controller answered. "Enter a left downwind for runway two zero left; cleared to land; no traffic in the pattern."

One moment the engine had been running smoothly, now there was only the sound of the wind rushing past the airplane.

Will couldn't believe it. Quickly, he ran through the procedure for a restart, while pulling the nose of the aircraft up to establish its best glide speed of eighty knots. The engine did not restart.

"Will, what's wrong?" Kitty asked, panic in her voice.

Tom woke up. "What's going on?"

"Engine failure," Will said, trying to keep his voice calm. "Both of you tighten your seat belts and be quiet. I'll talk to you when I have time. Right now, I've got to find a place to set this thing down."

Will fought his memory for what to do next. Fly the airplane; airspeed eighty knots. He looked at the altimeter: 2,700 feet MSL, 1,700 feet above the ground. The airplane had a glide range of about two miles for every thousand feet of altitude; that meant he could fly for only three miles or so before he met the earth. He glanced at the distance-measuring equipment: five and a half miles to the airport. He tried to remember where the wind was: from the northwest at four knots. His direction was good to get the best out of the wind, but there wasn't much of it. He began looking desperately at the ground.

The airplane was descending at a rate of five hundred feet per minute over a densely packed suburban neighborhood of houses, shopping strips, and office parks. To make matters worse, the area was, like most of Greater Atlanta, thickly forested. He saw the northeast expressway pass under him; rush-hour traffic was heavy—no landing on the highway. The meridian, he thought, but then they were already past it, and there were too many bridges across it anyway. He continued straight ahead, in the direction of the airport.

His mind, past the first panic, began to work better. He pressed the push-to-talk button on the yoke. "Mayday, Mayday, Mayday," he said, "Cessna One Two Three Tango has engine failure four and a half miles southeast of Peachtree Airport. Restart has failed; I'm going in."

"Roger, One Two Three Tango," the tower replied. "I have you in sight; I'll follow your progress and alert emergency services."

"Can you suggest a landing place?" Will asked.

"Negative," the controller replied. "You are over a heavily populated area; you'll just have to do the best you can. Watch out for WSB radio tower, eleven o'clock and two miles."

Will found the flashing lights of the tower. He saw a high school football field, but rejected it; it was only a little over three hundred feet long, and there was what appeared to be a marching band practicing on it. He needed a thousand feet of space to land—seven hundred and fifty was the absolute minimum. He kept looking. He was down to seven hundred feet. He had to commit.

To his right, he saw a long, low building with a white roof, and immediately next to it, a large parking lot. The parking lot was his only chance; he turned toward it and began to think about when to put the landing gear down and whether to use flaps. He judged himself a little high and fast for the approach, but if he put the gear down, that would alter his glide path radically. Instead, he put in ten degrees of flaps. Immediately, the airplane began to rise and slow, and he adjusted trim to compensate. The lot was getting closer now, and he would clear the tall pine trees at its edge, he felt sure. Then he could see the lot better, and his heart sank. It was rapidly filling with cars, streaming in from the street, going in unpredictable directions. There were people walking from their cars to work in the building. He could not land there without killing himself and his passengers and people on the ground, too. With no engine, they would never hear him coming.

Suddenly, he realized the roof of the building was flat. How long was it? No time to figure it out. He turned left twenty degrees and pointed at the building. It was his only hope. He pulled the mixture knob all the way out, and switched off the ignition and the master switch. He didn't want the engine coming to life while he was landing.

He was no more than two hundred yards out and a hundred feet high when he lowered the gear and flicked in a full forty degrees of flaps. The nose came up a bit, and his airspeed dropped under sixty knots, too slow. He pushed the nose down, picked up five knots and aimed at a point ten yards before the edge of the roof, knowing from experience that the high-winged aircraft had a tendency to float.

"Brace yourselves!" he said to Tom and Kitty.

For a moment he seemed to be below the edge of the roof. Realizing his error, he yanked back on the yoke and the airplane came up a few feet, then settled quickly. Then there was a thump, and the nose dropped, and the airplane was on the roof. Gravel from the roof spewed up from the wheels and drummed against the bottom of the fuselage, and the opposite end of the long roof seemed to race toward the airplane. Will reached over and flipped up the flap switch.

The airplane sank more and slowed. Will hit the brakes as hard as he could.

The Cessna came to a halt. Will put his face in his hands and breathed as deeply as he could; he was shaking violently, and he felt as if he might throw up. With a trembling hand, he undid his seat belt, opened the door, and got out of the airplane; he took a few steps, then sank into a sitting position. The gravel under him was six or eight inches deep; that was what had stopped them so quickly. He looked at the airplane; the wheels were sunk in the gravel almost to the hubs.

"Is everybody okay in there?" he shouted weakly.

"I think so," Tom said. "Kitty looks all right, but she won't say anything."

"Go to hell, both of you!" Kitty suddenly shouted; then she hopped out of the airplane on Will's side. "Are you crazy?" she demanded. "Why did you do that?"

Will didn't feel that he could stand up yet. "Kitty, I didn't do it on purpose. The engine failed."

"Oh," she said. She was breathing rapidly.

Tom got out of the airplane and joined them. "What a hell of a way to wake up in the morning!"

From a distance, ambulances and police cars could be heard approaching. Then a panel in the building's roof opened and a man stuck his head up.

"Jesus Christ!" he blurted. "Are you people okay? Do you need any help?"

Will looked at his wristwatch: eight-twenty. "Do you think you could call us a taxi?" he asked. "We have to be in Lawrenceville by nine o'clock."

27

Keane was back at the apartment complex in Marietta at eight sharp, determined to wait out his man, no matter how long it took. The Toyota was not in its usual place; Suzy's Beretta was.

Shit, Keane thought. The guy wasn't even back yet. He settled in for the wait. Suzy usually left for work at eight-thirty sharp, but at eight-fifty, she had not appeared. Just after nine o'clock, a van appeared bearing the name of the complex, and the driver, carrying a toolbox, went to the front door of the apartment and rang. When no one appeared, he rang again, then opened the door with his pass-key, closing it behind him. Less than a minute later, he burst out of the apartment and headed for the main gate at a dead run, ignoring his van.

Keane, alarmed, got out of his car and, using a single crutch, hobbled toward the apartment. The door was still open, and he walked straight in. The living room was very neat; so was the kitchen. He started toward the bedroom, then stopped at the bathroom door. Suzy Adams's brains were spread all over a mirror that had many cracks radiating from a single bullet hole. Suzy was on the floor, face up—what little was left of her face.

Keane looked at his watch. He had, maybe, two minutes before the cops arrived. He went to the bedroom and began methodically searching it. One of the two closets was empty, also one of the two chests of drawers. He went over the room as well as he could without disturbing anything, then did the same to the living room.

"Freeze!" somebody shouted, and Keane looked into the barrel of a uniformed policeman's pistol.

"I've got ID, okay?" Keane said, moving his hand slowly to his pocket.

The patrolman relaxed a little at the sight of the badge; then he was brushed aside by a detective.

"Who the hell are you?" the detective demanded of Keane.

Keane showed his ID and explained what he was doing there. "The guard at the gate can confirm my story," he said. "This guy, Ross, must have shot her last night. Either that, or he came back late and left early. My guess is last night."

"Okay, thanks for your theory," the detective said, making a note of Keane's address and phone number. "Now get off my crime scene."

Mickey left, and as he was about to get into his car, a brown sedan pulled up behind him. He recognized the FBI agent who had visited him in the hospital.

"I should have known you'd be here," the agent said.

"Yeah? Well, you can chalk up another killing for the FBI—a nurse called Suzy Adams. How many more you going to let him knock off before you pull him?"

The agent reddened. "Adams was ours; we've had her on a string for a year. I swear to God we didn't know she had helped Perkerson set you up until after it was over. She didn't know herself exactly what was going on until he told her, later."

"If you say so," Keane replied. He believed the agent really felt bad about it.

"She went a long way toward breaking this thing," the agent said.

"Breaking what thing?" Keane asked.

"You'll hear about it soon enough. We're just tracking down loose ends now."

"Well," Keane said, "go take a look in the bathroom of that apartment; one of your loose ends is lying in there with no face. Now move the fucking car so I can get out of here."

The agent looked at him for a moment without saying anything. "Hang on a minute." He rummaged on the front seat of the car and came up with a photograph. "This was taken last week. It may be too little, too late, but maybe it'll help. I owe you one, I guess."

Keane looked at the photograph; Perkerson was wearing his usual dark glasses, but finally Keane had a face to look for.

"I know it's not much, but it's all I've got at the moment. We lost him last night, and the Cobb County Sheriff's Department found the Toyota in the Chattahoochee River this morning. I don't believe for a minute Perkerson was in it."

"Neither do I," Keane said. "Thanks for the picture, anyway."

"You didn't get it from me," the agent said, then drove away.

Keane sat in his car and memorized the photograph. What would Perkerson look like without the mustache and dark glasses? Now he had a complete picture of the man in his mind—size, gait, the way he held himself, a face. What should be his next move?

A moment's reflection told him what he had to do if he was to live with himself.

Keane found a pay phone and called Dave Haynes at Atlanta PD Homicide. "Dave? I've got a new picture of my man."

"Yeah? How'd you get that?"

"Never mind, but it's the real thing. He's had his face rearranged. I want an APB on him right now."

"Where are you?"

Keane told him.

"Then drive down here right away with your picture, and I'll take it to the captain."

"Will he do it?"

"I don't know."

Three hours later, Keane sat in his old captain's office.

"Where'd you get this, Mickey?" the captain said, looking at the photograph.

"I can't tell you."

"Well, I've no way of knowing if it's the real thing, do I?" The captain seemed to be making an effort to look concerned.

"You're not going to order the APB, then?" Keane asked.

"I don't see how I can, under the circumstances."

Keane struggled to his feet and got the crutch under his arm. "In that case, Captain," he said, "everybody in Atlanta's going to be looking for Perkerson except Atlanta PD."

"What do you mean by that?" the captain asked, his features darkening.

"I mean that before I came here, I stopped at a photo shop and had a whole lot of copies made of that picture. Then I delivered them to the newspapers, the TV stations, and the network news bureaus. So, you just turn on the six-o'clock news, and you'll see a Mickey Keane APB in action."

28

Will got back to campaign headquarters at noon, after a midmorning stop at a shopping mall. There was a message from the Federal Aviation Administration waiting for him. Will dialed the number; the man's name was Barran.

"This is Will Lee, returning your call."

"Glad to hear from you, Mr. Lee," Barran said. "I'm talking on a transportable phone from the site of your, er, incident this morning. You've got at least half a gallon of water in each fuel tank."

"That's impossible," Will said. He explained how he had checked for water in the fuel that morning.

"I'm surprised you don't know there's an airworthiness directive out on the rubber fuel bladders in Cessnas. They tend to wrinkle when they're old, and water collects in the wrinkles. I'm going to have to cite you for improper preflight procedure."

"Hang on, Mr. Barran," Will said. "I'm perfectly aware of the wrinkling problem; that's why I installed new bladders last year. They couldn't possibly have wrinkled in this short a time." He didn't want to be cited this close to the election, and he wanted to know what was going on. "I'll send a mechanic out there right now to pull the wings off the airplane and get to the bladders. I think you ought to inspect them before you go citing me."

"Fair enough," Barran replied. "You'll have to take the wings off to transport the airplane to the airport anyway. And you might as well order a crane, while you're at it. Check back with me this afternoon. I'll be at this number."

Late in the afternoon, on the way to a campaign appearance, Will stopped by the building where he had landed. There was a crane being set up, and he could see half a dozen people on the roof, milling around the airplane, which was now without wings.

When he emerged onto the roof, Barran introduced himself and walked him over to the airplane, where Will's mechanic was draining the fuel bladders through a filter into jerry cans.

"Nice piece of flying, Mr. Lee," the mechanic said. "I paced off the roof; I make it about six hundred feet."

"I was lucky," Will replied, "and the gravel slowed me down."

"These bladders are in very good shape," the mechanic said. "No wrinkles at all."

"In that case," Will said, "any water in the tanks should have shown up in the fuel when I checked them during my pre-flight."

"Should have," Barran said. He bent over and picked something out of the fuel filter. "What's this?"

"It looks like the top of one of those plastic bags that zip shut," the mechanic said. "I've found two of them in each tank."

"That's very odd," Barran said. "Unless . . ."

"Unless what?" Will said.

"These things dissolve in gasoline," Barran said. "Almost, anyway. You could fill them with water, put them in the tank, and they would slowly dissolve. Then, even if you'd checked thoroughly for water, as you say you did, as soon as the bag dissolved, you'd have water in your fuel again."

"Funny," Will said. "When I arrived at the airport in Meriwether County this morning, there was a station wagon leaving. This was at dawn. One man in the car. He apparently had not just landed, either."

"Mr. Lee," Barran said, "I'm not going to cite you; but I'm sure as hell going to call the FBI. It's a federal crime to tamper with an airplane."

29

Will and Tom were watching the six-o'clock news coverage of his campaign day, most of which was devoted to his forced landing that morning. There was no mention of the possibility of sabotage.

Kitty Conroy brought a man into the room. "Will, this is Special Agent Davidson, of the FBI."

Will shook the man's hand. "You heard from the FAA, did you?"

"Yes," Davidson replied, "Barran seemed convinced that the airplane had been tampered with, and we agree. It's hard to think of any other reason for finding the remains of two plastic bags in each fuel tank."

"It's funny," Will said, "if the bladders hadn't been so recently overhauled, then I would have attributed the water Barran found in the tanks to wrinkled fuel bladders and figured it was my own fault for not checking more thoroughly."

"Can you think of anybody who might want to kill you?" the agent asked.

"No one person," Will replied, "but I've just finished a

pretty controversial trial, and it may have had something to do with that. There were some members of a white supremacist organization at the trial all week. They were pretty unhappy with the verdict."

"We're familiar with them," Davidson said.

Will glanced at the television set and froze. A photograph of a man in dark glasses filled the screen.

"This man, Harold Perkerson, is the subject of an all-points bulletin issued this afternoon by the Atlanta Police Department," a reporter was saying. "Perkerson is wanted in connection with the murder of three adult-bookstore employees and the attempted murder of the store's owner, Manfred Pearl."

An old photograph of Perkerson came on-screen side by side with the new one.

"Perkerson is said to have undergone plastic surgery to change his appearance. The photograph on the left is how he originally looked, and the more recent photograph, on the right, shows how he probably looks today. The police caution that Perkerson is armed and very dangerous."

"Pretty big difference in appearance, isn't it?" the FBI man said.

"Mr. Davidson," Will said, "I saw that man leaving Roosevelt Memorial Field in a station wagon about a quarter to seven this morning, just as I was arriving."

"You're sure?"

"Yes. His face was in my headlights for a second or two. I'm sure it's the same man."

"What kind of station wagon?"

"Dark—black or dark blue, something foreign, I think. Name some foreign station wagons."

"Peugeot?"

"No."

"Volvo?"

"Yes! I'm sure it was a Volvo station wagon."

"May I use your phone?" Davidson asked.

Harold Perkerson was sitting at the Varsity Restaurant in downtown Atlanta, enjoying a chili dog and watching the news on television. The Archon's plan had worked perfectly, but Lee had survived anyway. No matter, he thought. I'll get him. Then Perkerson's picture appeared on the screen. He listened for only a moment, then abandoned his meal and left the restaurant, hoping that nobody would recognize him before he could get to his car. On the way out, he stopped and bought the afternoon *Atlanta Journal* from a dispensing machine. His picture adorned the front page. How the hell had they gotten that photograph?

He sat quietly in the Varsity's parking garage, trying to think what to do next. The first thing was the mustache. He reached into his bag in the backseat and got an electric razor. It was hard going, but soon he was clean-shaven again. A big difference, he hoped.

He read the newspaper story carefully. There was no mention of his connection with Will Lee's engine failure, nor of his newly assumed identity, nor of the Volvo. Then, at the bottom of the front page, he saw another story.

"Candidates' Plans for Election Day," the headline read. Perkerson read the story carefully. Don Beverly Calhoun would be celebrating in the grand ballroom of the

Atlanta Hilton, while Will Lee's base for the day would be a suite at the Omni Hotel, next door to the World Congress Center. An election-evening party would be held for Lee's campaign workers at the Omni on the mezzanine level. The candidate would make an appearance at six o'clock, then return to his suite until the results were known.

Perkerson knew the mezzanine level at the Omni. He had once visited there when the level had been an amusement park, some years before. The Omni boasted a huge atrium, many stories high; the mezzanine level was under that, and many of the hotel's rooms overlooked it.

Perkerson thought hard. He could no longer be absolutely sure of being safe on the streets, and that made a hunt for Lee a bad idea; the Archon had told him not to hit the man at the church on Sunday. Perkerson started the car and drove out of the parking lot; he found a pay phone and called the Omni Hotel.

"I'd like to book a room, please."

"When for, sir?"

"I'll be checking in shortly, and checking out on Wednesday morning."

"That's five nights, sir. What sort of accommodation would you like?"

"I'd like something comfortable overlooking the atrium," Perkerson said. "Not too high up."

"Let's see, I have a very nice suite on the fifth floor, right in the middle of the atrium, sir. The rate is two hundred fifty dollars a day."

"That sounds ideal," Perkerson said. "I'll give you a

credit-card number to hold the room. I should be there in less than half an hour."

Perkerson got back into the Volvo and drove to International Boulevard, then straight to the Omni. He turned into the garage and gave his bags, except the briefcase containing the sniper's rifle, to a bellboy. "I'll park it myself," he said to the garage attendant, handing him a couple of dollars. "It's new."

He drove up the ramp to the very top of the garage and found a half-concealed spot in a corner. If they knew about the car, they wouldn't be looking for it in the Omni garage, he reckoned.

He found a drugstore in the building and bought a pair of nonprescription glasses with heavy horn-rims. Good camouflage. At the front desk he registered as Howard James, gave them one of his new credit cards, and signed a chit. When they checked it with the credit-card company, it would be good. He followed a bellboy to the fifth floor and was let into the suite; it was roomy, well furnished, and the view was outstanding.

Perkerson held up a fifty-dollar bill. "Do you think you could arrange for me to have some female companionship this evening?"

"I think so," the bellboy said, smiling. "What time?"

"Around nine, I think. I'll want her for the rest of the evening. If she's really nice, there's another fifty in it for you."

"You leave it to me, sir," the bellboy said, backing out the door.

Perkerson crossed the room, opened a window, and looked out into the atrium, down onto the mezzanine level, which was less than fifty yards away. Just perfect, he thought. And I'm off the street. The last place they'd look for me would be a suite at the Omni.

He glanced at his watch. He'd better phone the Archon and check in.

30

Will sat at the front of the Holy Hill Pentecostal Baptist Church and listened to a man with a bouffant hairdo sing a "sacred" song Will had never heard before. Behind him a choir of a hundred voices swelled in song, and a seven-piece orchestra accompanied them. Will had never before seen a set of spangled drums in a church.

The place was a riot of color, from the gold robes of the choir to the electric blue of the carpet, which ran, from where he sat, right up both aisles. The place was only slightly smaller than the Fox Theater, the 1920s movie palace in downtown Atlanta, and the decor was nearly as flamboyant.

Will found it disconcerting, too, that half a dozen television cameras were dotted around the auditorium, and a floor manager in a headset was giving everybody cues from off-camera. The electronic church, Will thought.

The singer ended his song with a flourish, and the congregation burst into applause. Will's experience with church was mostly confined to the First Baptist Church of

Delano and the Church of Ireland outpost near his grandfather's house in County Cork; neither tolerated applause
from its worshipers, let alone a set of spangled drums.

The Reverend Ralph Beverly Calhoun, Don's pimply
son, stepped to the pulpit and talked for ten minutes about
the importance of giving, while the collection plate was
passed. He did not exclude the television audience, ex-
horting them to keep those little envelopes coming in, and
offering a toll-free telephone number for those who preferred to give by credit card. Then he introduced his
father.

The Reverend Don Beverly Calhoun stepped into his
former pulpit as if slipping into an old glove. "My friends,
as you know, I have resigned the pulpit of this church,
because God has told me to pursue, for the time being, a
secular goal. But today, I return to introduce you to a
young man who is pursuing that same goal." He half
turned toward where Will sat. "And I think I may say he is
pursuing it with considerable zeal."

Will smiled slightly, and nodded.

"During this campaign," Dr. Don continued, "Will Lee
has often complained that I keep bringing religion into my
politics." He smiled broadly. "Well, friends, I have been
bringing my religion into everything I do for so long that
I cannot and will not keep my faith out of anything."

There was warm applause, and Calhoun basked in it for
a moment.

"Mr. Lee has not been quite so willing to share his own
faith with the people whose support he asks, and I have so
often taken him to task for it that he has complained of not
having a pulpit from which to do so. And that is why, to-

day, with your indulgence, I have offered him this pulpit, so that he may tell the world what he believes." Calhoun turned toward Will and offered his hand, and when Will took it, he was propelled into the pulpit.

Will laid his grandfather's Bible on the podium, placed his watch next to it, and smiled at the congregation. "Good morning," he said. To his surprise, they answered him.

"Good morning," they said in unison, all three thousand of them.

"I would like to express my gratitude to Don Calhoun, as he likes to be known these days, for the opportunity to address you and all those who are watching and listening from their homes this morning.

"I bring you greetings from the members of the First Baptist Church of Delano, my home church. And if my Meriwether County ancestors—a long line of Baptist preachers, lay preachers, and public servants—are looking down on us today, I am sure they send you their greetings, too.

"I have been asked, this morning, to tell you what I believe. I believe, above anything else, in a just God. I believe that at the end of our lives, or perhaps before, each of us will be dealt with justly.

"I believe, as you do, that the Holy Bible is God's law. But I believe that God's law may also be written in other books—in the Talmud, in the Koran, and in others. I believe that God's law is also written in the stars, and in the stones of the earth, and in the hearts of men.

"I believe that God gave each of us a mind, and that he expects us to use it. When I was growing up as a Baptist I was taught that each human being has a right to interpret the Scriptures according to his own conscience, but that he could expect to be judged on his interpretation.

"I believe that God expects us to question each of the teachings of the Bible, and to decide for ourselves how they apply to us. And that, perhaps, is where we differ, for if I am to believe your former pastor, you are all fundamentalists, bound to take every word of the Bible literally, without question.

"That is a position that puzzles me, especially when I look around and see that so many of those who describe themselves as fundamentalists are very selective about which passages of the Bible they take literally. The Bible says, 'Thou shalt not kill.' And yet large numbers of fundamentalists profess their strong support for capital punishment. Even more puzzling is that when a man takes literally the Bible's injunction not to kill he is often called godless; or a pacifist; or a coward; or, sometimes, a liberal. God help the political candidate who takes that injunction literally.

"I find it difficult to reconcile the fundamentalist's support of capital punishment with his opposition to abortion. Can it be true, as someone has said, that the fundamentalist's concern for human life 'begins with conception and ends with birth'?

"It puzzles me why so many people who stoutly profess their unerring Christianity adopt political and economic views that seem so often at odds with the teachings of Jesus Christ. Christianity is a religion of love, of sharing, of concern for one's neighbors; and yet so many of the politicians who have the support of fundamentalists preach a philosophy of greed and vote against any program designed to help human beings. Christianity damns pride and reveres meekness; and yet these same politicians thump their breasts and boast of their patriotism and question that of anyone who points out that patriotism is more than empty pledges and the waving of flags. This puzzles me.

"Fundamentalism of any kind worries me. The Ayatollah Khomeini is a religious fundamentalist; the most ardent Communist is a political fundamentalist; Soviet generals are military fundamentalists, and we have a few in this country, too. I am always worried by any man who *knows* he has the absolute, unchangeable truth grasped tightly in his hands, and, because others disagree with him, they must be wrong.

"A little over two hundred years ago, our founding fathers conceived a political system that would guarantee the free exchange of ideas, one that almost demanded dissent from its constituents. And that system was secular, an invention of man. Should we accept anything less from a religious faith?"

Will glanced at a man standing next to a television camera. He was making a winding motion with his hand; wind it up, he was saying. Will stole a look at his watch. He was already past his time allowance, but he was not through; he did not want Calhoun to follow him with time for a rebuttal.

"I know that my time is short," he said, "and I want to close with a passage from the New Testament. The best Christian I ever knew was my step-grandfather, my widowed grandmother's second husband, who was a real grandfather to me. He was a quiet man, shy, reticent, and yet he did more Christian good in his community than anybody I knew. When he died, we found among his possessions a letter outlining how his funeral should be conducted, and it included his instruction that the only Scripture to be read at the service was the sixth chapter of Matthew, the first six verses."

Will opened the old Bible to the marked passage and looked around the gaudy auditorium. "He specified that the first verse be read from the translation of the New English Bible, the rest from the King James Version; that is how I shall read it to you. These are the words of Jesus Christ." He read first from a sheet of paper.

"Be careful not to make a show of your religion before men; if you do, no reward awaits you in your Father's house in heaven."

Then he read from the old Bible.

"Therefore when thou doest thine alms, do not sound a trumpet before thee, as the hypocrites do in the synagogues and in the streets, that they may have glory of men. Verily I say unto you, They have their reward.

"But when thou doest alms, let not thy left hand know what thy right hand doeth:

"That thine alms may be in secret: and thy Father which seeth in secret himself shall reward thee openly."

Now Will slowed his delivery for emphasis.

"And when thou prayest, thou shalt not be as the hypocrites are: for they love to pray standing in the synagogues and in the corners of the streets, that they may be seen of men. Verily I say unto you, They have their reward.

"But thou, when thou prayest, enter into thy closet, and when thou hast shut thy door, pray to thy Father which is in secret; and thy Father which seeth in secret shall reward thee openly."

The television floor manager was going berserk with his sign language. Will closed his Bible. "The last thing my grandfather said to me before he died was, 'Will, when you see a fellow coming, telling you what a good Christian he is, you keep your hand on your wallet.'

"Thank you for your attention." Will stepped back from the pulpit, glancing at his watch. Right on time. The audience regarded him with an intense, curious silence, as if they were not sure what he had said to them.

Calhoun came charging toward the pulpit, but the floor manager waved him back, desperately cuing the choir, who stood and burst into song.

The television lights went off. Will was shown out by a side door.

31

Keane answered the phone.

"It's your favorite federal fairy," a voice said.

"Nothing I'd rather do than talk to a federal fairy," Keane replied, grinning.

"You know that guy Lee, who's running for the Senate?"

"The glider pilot? Yeah."

"I thought you might like to know that he made Perkerson as the guy who sabotaged his airplane."

"No shit! I'll bet it's got something to do with Dr. Don, hasn't it? Calhoun and Willingham are in bed together, and Willingham knows Perkerson."

"I wouldn't say that out loud, if I were you."

"Come on, you guys must've known that for a long time."

"Listen, Calhoun and Willingham have got political clout. We have to tread lightly there. I doubt we'll ever lay a glove on Calhoun, but if we can tie Perkerson to Willingham, we'll nail Willingham."

I can do that, Keane thought. "You have nothing on Willingham now?"

"We know that he's the leader of this bunch—the Archon, they call him; Suzy Adams got that out of Perkerson; but Suzy's dead, and we can't prove it. Willingham's too careful."

"What else can you tell me?"

"You know as much as I do now. We think Perkerson might have another run at Lee. The Omni Hotel is going to be lousy with our people and Atlanta PD tonight. Perkerson is now a federal fugitive because of the airplane tampering."

"Maybe I'll have a look around the Omni myself," Keane said.

Will met Kate Rule at the door of the suite and hustled her into the bedroom. There was a long embrace, and when they broke, Kate asked, "Who are all those people in the living room?"

He sat her down on a bed. "Some of them are my campaign people; you'll meet them in a minute. The others are FBI men and cops."

"How come?"

"I don't want you to get upset about this, but on Friday, somebody sabotaged my airplane, and I had to make a forced landing. They know who the guy is, and he seems to be linked up with some far-right-wing outfit. They also think he might try again."

"Sounds like it's going to be a swell evening."

"Don't worry, there are cops all over the place; they know what he looks like, and he'll never get into the hotel."

"I wish you'd told me. I would have brought a gun."

"I'm glad I didn't tell you."

"I saw your sermon on TV Sunday. Don's show is seen in Washington, too. I stood up and cheered. I really did."

Will grinned. "Thanks. I got a lot off my chest in that pulpit. I figured that nothing I said to Calhoun's followers was going to make a dent, so I decided to direct my remarks to anybody watching who was not a follower. We tried to boost that part of the audience with some of our advertising, but we have no way of knowing how many we attracted. The press was good, though."

Will paused and took a deep breath. "Listen, there are some things I've got to tell you, and I know this isn't a very good time or place to do it, but I don't have a choice."

She looked at him suspiciously. "You look guilty."

He nodded. "I have a confession, I'm afraid."

"All right," she sighed, "get it off your chest."

Will gulped. "During all those months that we were apart, I wasn't as chaste as you were."

There was a flicker of hurt in her face. "Was it somebody important?" she asked softly. Her eyes were suddenly moist.

"No. She was never important for a moment. It was nothing more than a roll in the hay."

She sighed. "All right, I can handle that. Maybe I even asked for it, a little bit."

"There's more," he said. "It's why I asked you not to read an Atlanta paper on the way down here."

"Jesus Christ!" she said, exasperated. "All right, I'm braced."

"The girl was a witness in the murder trial; she was the

girlfriend of my client." He held up a hand. "But not on the day this happened." He recounted the incident, leaving out a great deal of detail.

"Well, I guess it doesn't matter who she was, as long as it wasn't important, and as long as I never get a chance to lay my hands on her."

"You won't, not if I have anything to say about it."

"I'm acquainted with the sort of people who could arrange a hit, you know."

"I know. Now, let me tell you the rest. My client was convicted—you know that."

"Yes, you told me. You sounded awfully happy about it."

"Well, yesterday, he filed an appeal. The grounds of his appeal are that he didn't get a fair trial, because he wasn't properly represented, because his lawyer wanted his girlfriend and wanted him to get convicted."

"I love it," she said. "I could get a novel out of this story."

"Please," he whimpered, "I've been punished enough."

"So the whole world knows about your little roll in the hay with . . . what's her name?"

"Charlene. Yes, the whole world knows, or at least the whole state. Charlene went on the six-o'clock news last night and explained it to them."

Kate's face fell. "Jesus, what is that going to do to you in the election?"

Will laughed. "Oddly enough, my people think it may not hurt—in fact, they think it might even help. You see, something like eight percent of the people polled who said they were going to vote for Calhoun said they were voting for him only because they thought I was gay."

"And now you're a stud, right?"

"Well, to some people, anyway."

"How have you handled this with the press?"

"What could I do? I had a press conference last night and told all. I said we were both unmarried, consenting adults, and our sex lives were nobody's business but ours."

"Have you been disbarred yet?"

"Nope. I released Charlene's pre-trial deposition and suggested that it be compared with her actual testimony."

"When caught, tell the truth. I like it."

Will looked embarrassed. "Will you ever be able to forgive me for all this?"

She took his face in her hands and smiled. "Listen, the entertainment value alone makes up for most of it."

He kissed her. "Now come on and meet my people."

He led her into the living room. "Kate, this is Tom Black and Kitty Conroy, who have done all the work in this campaign. Tom and Kitty, Katharine Rule, known as Kate."

Everybody shook hands.

Tom looked at Kate, then at Will. "Is there something you haven't told us?"

"Well, yeah," Will said. "Kate and I are getting married next week."

"*Now* you tell me," Tom said.

"Yeah," Kitty chipped in, "couldn't you have mentioned this a couple of weeks ago, when it might have gotten you elected?"

Two floors down, Harold Perkerson gave a prostitute two hundred dollars and dismissed her. He walked to the

window, parted the curtains slightly, and had a look at
the mezzanine level. Staffers were setting up TV sets and
moving furniture around. Caterers were bringing in boxes.

Almost four. Two hours until Lee's appearance at six
o'clock. Perkerson switched on the TV and looked for a
movie. He was bored.

Mickey Keane arrived at the Omni and got out of his car.
Immediately, he could see that the hotel was sealed. He
could waste time walking around to the other entrances,
but this was big-time stuff, bordering on what they would
do for a visiting President. Perkerson would never get into
the hotel today.

He spoke to a couple of cops he knew who were watching the elevators, passed the time for a minute. What the
hell, he thought, He'd have a look around the hotel.

Willingham picked up the phone. He recognized the voice
immediately as one of his sources.

"You've got a problem," the man said.

"What's that?"

"You know the ex-cop that your friend helped have an
automobile accident?"

"Yes, he's in an irreversible coma, I hear."

"Wrong. I heard in the office today that he's out there
walking around."

Willingham sat up. *"What?"*

"He wasn't even hurt badly. The coma was a cover."

Willingham tried to think what this meant.

"He followed you for days," the man said. "He can tie
you to Perkerson."

"Thank you," Willingham said, trying to keep his voice steady.

"They know about Perkerson's sabotaging the airplane, too, and they're expecting another attempt on Lee. But don't worry, the hotel is crawling with cops; there's no way your man can get in without being seen. Or if there is, you'd better call him off; if he succeeds, they'll come after you on a conspiracy charge."

Willingham hung up the phone. He sat frozen for several minutes; then he picked up the phone again.

"Omni Hotel."

"Mr. Howard James, please."

"Ringing."

"Yes?" Perkerson said.

"Harry?"

"Yessir."

"Are you in position?"

"Yessir. It's perfect."

"What room are you in?"

"Room 518. Don't worry, sir. I'll carry out your irrevocable order. And I won't be taken alive."

"Thank you, Harry. Good luck."

Willingham hung up. That miserable little cop was still alive. A man he had never even seen could tie him to Perkerson, and Perkerson could not be called off. Jesus God!

Willingham went to his arms locker and looked at the array of weapons there. This would be close work, with soft-nosed ammunition. He chose a .25-caliber automatic, easily concealed, and a matching silencer.

"Now, where did I put my car keys?" he asked himself absently.

*   *   *

It was five-forty P.M., and Mickey Keane was tired. He slumped into a large sofa in the Omni lobby. He had shown Perkerson's photograph to a couple of people, but apparently, the FBI had already shown it to every employee in the hotel, with no success. Somebody sat down on the other end of the sofa.

"Hey, Mickey," she said.

Keane turned and looked at her. "Hey, Margie, how's tricks? I haven't seen you since I worked vice."

Margie crossed her legs. "Tricks ain't bad. I've made three house calls since Friday to a john upstairs. He's had two other girls, too. A horny gentleman."

Keane showed her Perkerson's photograph. "Is that, by any chance, the guy?"

She glanced at the picture. "Nah. He don't have a mustache, and he wears horn-rims. You're the third one who's showed me that picture. He must be some bad guy."

"Yeah, he is." Keane looked up to see a gaggle of people crossing the lobby, headed for the atrium. It was that guy Lee, and he was hemmed in on all sides by men who looked at everybody but him. Their coats were open, and they all wore the same lapel pins.

Keane glanced at his watch. Ten to six. Lee was supposed to appear on the mezzanine at six. What the hell, Keane thought, I'm not doing any good here. I might as well go up there. He struggled to his good foot and got the crutch under his arm.

Then he turned and saw somebody else he knew striding purposefully across the lobby, ignoring everyone.

*   *   *

Perkerson set up his tripod and opened the briefcase. This was going to be something like the shot at the abortion clinic, he reflected, but easier. The distance was shorter, and since the mezzanine was indoors, there was no chance of a gust of wind to ruin his shot. He locked the rifle barrel into the stock and began screwing on the large scope.

Keane swung along as fast as he could, taking an extra hop on his good leg at every step. Willingham was headed for the elevators. The colonel disappeared around a corner of the elevator bank, and Keane began praying, "Don't let me lose him, please, God." At the corner of the elevator bank, he stopped, took a deep breath, and limped slowly around the corner. Willingham was entering the last elevator down the line.

"Going up, please!" Keane called out, trying to keep the desperation out of his voice. "Going up!" He reached the door to find Willingham holding it for him and looking at his watch.

"Floor?" Willingham asked.

Keane looked at the buttons. Willingham had punched five. "Six," he replied, mopping his brow. "Thanks very much."

The two men rode up in silence. Willingham looked at his watch again; the muscles in his face were flexing as he continually clenched and unclenched his jaw. The elevator reached five, and Willingham stepped out. Keane was going to follow, but Willingham had stopped and was reading the sign pointing to various room numbers. The elevator closed.

Keane banged on the side of the car in frustration and

looked at his watch. Four minutes to six. The door opened on the sixth floor and Keane hustled out of the car and toward the door to the fire stairs. Steps were a goddamned nuisance with a crutch, and he grabbed the handrail and swung down them two at a time, the crutch in his other hand. As he turned the corner at the landing, he missed a step and pitched headlong down the last half dozen of the steel steps.

Whimpering in pain, Keane struggled to his good foot and hopped toward the door. Locked. It would open only from the other side. He hammered on it. "Open up!" he yelled. "Emergency!" He put his ear to the door and heard nothing on the other side.

Keane dropped to his knees and went into his inside pocket for his tools. He began trying to pick the lock.

Perkerson had the rifle set up, locked, and loaded. He saw Lee start up the long escalator to the mezzanine and brought his eye to the sight and his finger to the trigger. He'd get him before he made the mezzanine. He got the crosshairs centered and began squeezing the trigger. There was a loud knock on the door.

Perkerson swung around, grabbing for the pistol in the shoulder holster.

"Harry, it's me, Willingham!"

What the hell? Perkerson thought. "Say that again?" he shouted.

"It's Colonel Willingham! Let me in, quickly!"

Perkerson glanced out the window. Lee had reached the mezzanine and was headed for a raised platform at one end of it, making his way through a crowd, shaking hands. He'd shoot when Lee was on the platform, speaking.

Perkerson crossed the room and opened the door. Willingham was standing there, looking worried.

"I want to watch you shoot," Willingham said.

"All right, sir," Perkerson replied, "come on in. He's just about to speak." As he turned away, he wondered what the Archon was doing there. And then a terrible thought crossed his mind; he heard the door close behind him; he turned and saw the gun in Willingham's hand. "You're weak," he said, as he dropped and brought up his own pistol.

Keane got the fire door opened and hopped through it, abandoning the crutch. He came to the hallway and looked up and down it; empty, except for a maid's cart. He began to run, on both his good foot and the cast, from door to door, putting an ear to each one, listening for an instant. As he moved down the hallway, the maid came out of a room ten yards away, and then a very odd thing happened. A fist-sized hole appeared in the door just ahead of him, and a little cloud of splinters and dust exploded outward. There had been no other sound.

Keane dived past the door, and when he regained his feet, he had his pistol in one hand and his badge in the other, holding it out to the maid. "Police!" he half whispered, half shouted. "Give me your passkey, now!"

Perkerson sat on the floor of the suite's living room, holding his belly, which was wet and sticky. He was having trouble getting his breath. Willingham was sitting, too, leaning against the door, a bloody hole in his cheek and another in his forehead, over his right eye. His eyes stared blankly at Perkerson, and there was a streak of gore down the door where the Archon's head had left its trail. One of Perkerson's three shots had missed, and there was a hole in the door, next to the peephole.

Perkerson grabbed a chair and hauled himself to his feet. The pain was starting now, and it was more terrible than any he had ever known. He staggered toward the rifle on its tripod, the pistol still in his hand, and dropped to one knee, his firing position. Lee was on the platform, holding up his hands for quiet. Perkerson sighted.

"I just want to say a few words to you before the evening starts," Will said. "The polls don't close for another hour, and, of course, we don't know anything yet, but I want to tell you that no matter what happens tonight, each of you will have my deepest gratitude for a long time to come. I'll tell you the truth, I didn't know people could work as hard as you have for no money at all." He paused as the sound of breaking glass came from somewhere.

Keane got the key into the lock, turned it, and pushed. There was a dead weight on the other side. He dug in his good foot, put his shoulder to the door, and pushed. Slowly, it slid open. Perkerson was on one knee at the window, crouched over a rifle fixed to a tripod. Keane brought his weapon up with both hands.

"Nooo!" he screamed as he fired.

* * *

Will turned to his right to take in a television camera, and as he did, the fabric on the shoulder of the FBI man standing next to him exploded, and the man sat down hard. Will bent to help him, wondering what had happened, and as he did, a pitcher of water on a table behind where he stood blew into a thousand pieces, showering everyone with water and ice. While Will was still trying to figure that out, he was hit, hard, in the back, and he collapsed onto the floor of the platform. People began screaming and diving to the floor.

Keane's first shot had gone wide, through the window, but his second caught Perkerson in the shoulder and spun him around. Keane advanced toward him, hobbling on his cast, firing as he went. It was still a better than twenty-foot shot, and he was taking no chances. He wasn't sure where the fourth shot went. Before he could fire a fifth, something hit him, hard, in the groin, and he went down. Perkerson had produced a pistol from somewhere.

From the floor, Keane kept firing.

The noise had stopped. The maid was afraid to put her head through the doorway, but, flattened against the wall, she called out, "What's going on in there?"

"I need help," a man's voice replied weakly. "Call police, tell them an officer is down; need an ambulance."

Another noise came from the room, a sharp report. The maid heard a sigh on the other side of the door.

Will was having trouble breathing, but still, they were moving fast. He had been half carried to a freight elevator at the back of the mezzanine, and now they were going down.

"How are you feeling?" an FBI man asked.

"Just a little winded," Will panted.

"I'm sorry I hit you so hard," the man said. "When I saw Wilkins go down, I just threw a block into your back and fell on you."

Will looked at the man. He was maybe six-four, two hundred and twenty pounds. "Where did you play?" he asked.

"I played for Bear Bryant at Alabama," the agent replied. "About two hundred years ago."

Will managed to get some air into his lungs. "I'm not surprised. Where are we going?"

"Just out of here, until we find out what's going on," the agent said.

They stepped out onto a loading platform, and the agent looked around. The Atlanta detective with them had a handheld radio to his ear.

"This ought to do for the moment," the agent said. "We should know something soon. Are you cold?"

"I'm enjoying the fresh air," Will said, breathing deeply for the first time in several minutes.

The detective spoke into the radio. "Roger, I got it. How's Keane?" He listened for a moment. "Oh," he said.

"What's happened?" Will asked.

"Perkerson's dead. There were three of them in a suite on the fifth floor. An ex-cop named Mickey Keane, a friend of mine who's been hunting Perkerson, was one of them. A maid saw him go into the room, and there was lots of shooting. A guy named Willingham is dead. That mean anything to you?"

"No," Will said.

"No. Anyway, Mickey apparently got Perkerson, but he took at least one himself. They're on the way down now."

Will noticed for the first time that an ambulance was parked at the loading platform. "That got here fast," he said.

"It's been here all afternoon," the detective replied dryly. "We thought we might need it for you."

A stretcher on wheels came through a pair of swinging doors, propelled by a paramedic, while another carried a bottle of clear liquid attached to the man on the stretcher. They paused at the back of the ambulance while the rear doors were opened.

The detective walked over to the stretcher, and Will followed. "How is he?" the detective asked the paramedic.

"Ask me," Keane said.

"Shit, I knew that bastard couldn't kill you."

Will leaned over the stretcher. "Mr. Keane, I'm Will Lee. They tell me you just saved my ass. Thank you."

"Ah, I didn't do it for you," Keane said. "I did it for a buddy of mine, a cop. He's dead now."

"The effect was the same. I'm indebted to you."

"Another friend of mine, named Manny Pearl, is pulling for you in the election," Keane said.

"The guy with the stripper demonstrators? Tell him I love his bumper sticker, 'A.B.D.D., Anybody But Dr. Don.' I've seen them all over the place."

"I'll tell him," Keane said. "He'll be pleased."

"We gotta go," the paramedic said, and Keane was rolled into the ambulance.

"Well," Will said to the agent and the detective, "I think I'd better get back upstairs and show them I'm not dead. The polls are still open, and I wouldn't want anybody to stay home."

32

Kate opened the door to the suite and grabbed him. "We saw the whole thing on television," she said, hugging him tightly. "Don't ever scare me like that again."

"I'll try not to," he said, kissing her on the neck. They stood, holding each other, for a moment.

"There's a surprise waiting for you," Kate said, leading him toward the living room.

Will turned a corner to find Senator Benjamin Carr, sitting in a wheelchair, something like a grin on his face. Jasper was with him, and a uniformed nurse hovered nearby.

Will knelt by the wheelchair and took the Senator's hand. "I'm awful glad to see you, Senator," he said. "I'm sorry it's been so long, but they've been keeping me busy."

The Senator tilted his head, and his jaw worked, but no words came.

Jasper stepped over to the wheelchair. "Now don't you worry none, Senator, it'll come." He turned to Will. "The Senator's been trying to talk."

*　　*　　*

It was eleven o'clock, and the results still weren't in. Will, his parents, his aunt Eloise, Kate, the Senator, his nurse, Jasper, Tom Black, and Kitty Conroy all sat around the huge television set. The FBI agent was on the phone, and the detective was pouring himself a bourbon.

"It's all going to depend on the ruburbs," Tom said. "We've taken the places our polling said we would, but Moss Mallet couldn't say about the ruburbs."

The FBI agent hung up the phone. "My people went into Willingham's house with a federal warrant," he said. "It took them two hours, but they found a concealed safe, a big one, with a lot of records in it—membership lists, contributors, paramilitary teams—hundreds of names." He turned to Detective Dave Haynes. "There was a clerk in our Atlanta bureau on the list, and also the name of an Atlanta police captain."

"You don't have to tell me who," Haynes said, rising. "I gotta get out to the hospital and tell Mickey."

"Calhoun's going to have a hard time explaining his connection with Willingham. The guy was the chairman of his board of deacons," the agent said.

"He'll find a way," Will said.

"Maybe," the agent said. "But what my people found in the safe is going to make it tough for him."

"Listen up," Tom said, pointing at the television set.

The anchorman turned to the camera, a sheet of paper in his hand. "We finally have a projection to make in the race for the United States Senate," he said. "Results just in from the north Atlanta suburbs have tipped the scales, and our projected winner is Will Lee."

A rush of air went out of Will. Kate came and put her arms around him. There was much hugging and shaking of hands in the room.

"Our projected final result is fifty-one point six percent for Lee and forty-eight point two for Calhoun, with two-tenths of one percent write-ins for other candidates," the anchorman said.

"I'm glad we didn't need that two-tenths of a point," Tom Black said.

"And now," the anchorman said, "I'm told that the Reverend Don Beverly Calhoun is entering the grand ball-room at the Atlanta Hilton, and we'll take you there, live, for his statement."

The camera followed Calhoun through a crowd of teary supporters. He mounted the platform and called for quiet. "Before I make my statement," he said, "I have to announce that a close friend of our campaign and our church has died this evening under tragic circumstances. I will have more to say about this tomorrow, but now I would like us all to have a moment of silent prayer for the soul of Colonel J. E. B. Stuart Willingham."

"His soul is going to need it," Will said. "Come on, I don't want to see the rest of this. Let's all get downstairs."

The group gathered itself to go. Patricia Lee gave her son a huge hug, and Billy Lee shook his hand. Aunt Eloise hugged him, too, and Tom Black was pounding him on the back while Kitty Conroy kissed him. Then Jasper came and put a detaining hand on Will's arm. "The Senator wants to see you, Mr. Will."

Will crossed the room and knelt beside the wheelchair. The Senator managed a smile, and Will could tell he was struggling. The old man gripped Will's hand tightly, and his lips moved. Finally, the words came haltingly out.

"Congratulations . . . Senator," he said.

ACKNOWLEDGMENTS

I am most grateful to Tom Susman, once again, for his knowledge of Washington and his personal contacts; to Melody Miller, deputy press secretary to Senator Edward Kennedy, for a superb tour of the United States Capitol and many insights into the workings of the Senate; to Bill Johnston, chief assistant to Senator Wyche Fowler of Georgia, for his detailed reminiscences of the senator's 1986 race; to Carter Smith, Jr., M.D., for advice about the effects of strokes; to former congressman Elliott Levitas, for his comments; and to Ed Garland, ace trial attorney, for his suggestions on the conduct of murder trials.

If I got any of this wrong, it is my fault and not theirs.

I am also very grateful to my agent, Morton Janklow, his associate, Anne Sibbald, and all the people at Janklow, Nesbit Associates, who continue to exercise the greatest care and concern for my career as a writer.

I am particularly indebted to the enthusiasm of my new editor, Trish Lande, who, at a difficult time, took charge of this book and devoted nights and weekends to its prompt and successful completion.

AUTHOR'S NOTE

I am happy to hear from readers, but you should know that if you write to me in care of my publisher, three to six months will pass before I receive your letter, and when it finally arrives it will be one among many, and I will not be able to reply.

However, if you have access to the Internet, you may visit my website at www.stuartwoods.com, where there is a button for sending me e-mail. So far, I have been able to reply to all my e-mail, and I will continue to try to do so.

If you send me an e-mail and do not receive a reply, it is probably because you are among an alarming number of people who have entered their e-mail address incorrectly in their mail software. I have many of my replies returned as undeliverable.

Remember: e-mail, reply; snail mail, no reply.

When you e-mail, please do not send attachments, as I never open these. They can take twenty minutes to download, and they often contain viruses.

Please do not place me on your mailing lists for funny stories, prayers, political causes, charitable fund-raising, petitions, or sentimental claptrap. I get enough of that from people I already know. Generally speaking, when I get e-mail addressed to a large number of people, I immediately delete it without reading it.

Please do not send me your ideas for a book, as I have a policy of writing only what I myself invent. If you send me story ideas, I will immediately delete them without reading them. If you have a good idea for a book, write it yourself, but I will not be able to advise you on how to get it published. Buy a copy of *Writer's Market* at any bookstore; that will tell you how.

Anyone with a request concerning events or appearances may e-mail it to me or send it to: Publicity Department, Penguin Group (USA) LLC, 375 Hudson Street, New York, NY 10014.

Those ambitious folk who wish to buy film, dramatic, or television rights to my books should contact Matthew Snyder, Creative Artists Agency, 9830 Wilshire Boulevard, Beverly Hills, CA 98212 1825.

Those who wish to make offers for rights of a literary nature should contact Anne Sibbald, Janklow & Nesbit, 445 Park Avenue, New York, NY 10022. (Note: This is not an invitation for you to send her your manuscript or to solicit her to be your agent.)

If you want to know if I will be signing books in your city, please visit my website, www.stuartwoods.com, where the tour schedule will be published a month or so in advance. If you wish me to do a book signing in your locality, ask your favorite bookseller to contact his Penguin representative or the Penguin publicity department with the request.

If you find typographical or editorial errors in my book

and feel an irresistible urge to tell someone, please write to Sara Minnich at Penguin's address above. Do not e-mail your discoveries to me, as I will already have learned about them from others.

A list of my published works appears in the front of this book and on my website. All the novels are still in print in paperback and can be found at or ordered from any bookstore. If you wish to obtain hardcover copies of earlier novels or of the two nonfiction books, a good used-book store or one of the online bookstores can help you find them. Otherwise, you will have to go to a great many garage sales.

Read on for an excerpt from another
thrilling novel by Stuart Woods

SON OF STONE

A Stone Barrington Novel

E laine's, late.

Stone Barrington and Dino Bacchetti sat, sipping what each of them usually sipped, gazing desultorily at the menu. Elaine came and sat down.

"Having problems deciding?" she asked.

"Always," Dino said.

"Are you being a smart-ass?" she asked.

"I'm torn between the pasta special and the osso buco," Dino said.

"Yeah," Stone said, "Dino is always torn."

"Are you being a smart-ass?" Dino asked.

"I'm just backing you up, pal," Stone said.

"Oh."

"Have the pasta," Elaine said. "It's terrific."

"How can I pass that up?" Dino asked, closing his menu.

"Dino," Stone said, "you're veering toward the ironic again. Watch yourself."

Elaine looked at Dino. "You're lucky there isn't a steak

knife on the table." She flagged down a passing waiter. "Two pasta specials," she said, her finger wagging between Stone and Dino.

"I'll have the osso buco," Stone said.

"I just sold the last one," the waiter replied.

"Tell you what," Stone said, "I'll have the pasta special, with a chopped spinach salad to start."

"Me, too, on the salad," Dino said.

"And a bottle of the Mondavi Napa Cabernet," Stone added.

"Good," Elaine said; then she got up and wandered a couple of tables away and sat down there.

"That was close," Stone said. "You could have gotten a fork in the chest."

"I didn't want the pasta," Dino replied.

"Then why didn't you order the osso buco to begin with?"

"They were out."

"You didn't know that."

"Does it matter? They wouldn't have had it anyway."

They sat in silence for a moment, Stone sipping his Knob Creek, Dino sipping his Johnnie Walker Black.

"When does Ben get home for the holidays?" Stone asked. Benito was Dino's teenaged son.

"Tomorrow," Dino replied. "I get him first. Mary Ann will have him for Christmas dinner at her father's."

"Could you bring him to dinner tomorrow night?"

Dino looked at him oddly. "Since when did you especially want to have dinner with Benito?"

"Since Arrington decided to come to New York for Christmas and bring Peter."

"You didn't tell me."

"I didn't know until tonight. I was just leaving the house when she called. They're due in early tomorrow afternoon." Stone showed Dino the photo of the boy that Arrington had given him. "This was over a year ago," he said. "I guess he's bigger now."

Dino gazed at the photograph. "Amazingly like your father," he said.

"How would you know? You never met my father."

"I've met the photograph of him in your study about a thousand times," Dino replied.

"Oh, yeah."

"Does he know?"

"Who?"

"Peter."

"Don't start that again," Stone said.

"I didn't start it—you did, some years back."

Stone's shoulders sagged. "All right, all right."

"When, exactly, was it? I know you know."

Stone cast his thoughts back. "Right before we were going to the islands for the holidays, to St. Marks. The night before, actually. I had bought her a ring."

"You never told me that. You were really going to ask her?"

"Yes, I was. That morning it started snowing. I got to the airport and got a call from her, saying that she was stuck in a meeting at *The New Yorker*. She had written a piece for them, and she was working with the editor. She said she'd get the same flight the next day. I was pissed off, but my bags were already on the airplane, and I didn't want to go through *that* a day later, so I left. As it turned out, while she was at *The New Yorker*, they assigned her to write a profile of Vance Calder."

"Uh-oh."

"Exactly. Turns out I got the last flight out of the airport before they closed it because of the snowstorm. She was stuck in the city for another day. Then Vance arrived in town and they had dinner. I met the flight the following day, and she wasn't on it, and I couldn't get her on the phone. Finally, a few days later, I got a fax at my hotel."

"A Dear Stone letter?"

"Right. She was marrying Vance."

"And when did she find out she was pregnant?"

"I'm not sure. I was out in L.A. four or five months later, and—"

"I was there, too, remember?"

"Yes, I remember. And when I saw her there, she was obviously pregnant."

"Did she say whose it was?"

"No, because she didn't know."

"The two . . . events were too close together, huh?"

"Right."

"When did she know?"

"Not until after Vance's death, I think."

They were quiet again. "Had she seen the photograph of your father?"

"Sure, she was in the house a lot when we first met."

"So she knew sooner than Vance's death?"

"I don't know; she may have been in denial."

"Did Vance know?"

Stone shook his head. "She told me the subject never came up."

"When did she finally admit it to you?"

"When we were in Maine a few years back, remember? Then, when you and I were staying at her house in Bel-Air last year, we had a frank talk about it. She said she had had a brush with ovarian cancer and had surgery, and that seemed to get her thinking about Peter's future. She wanted me to spend some time with Peter, but it hasn't happened until now. He's been in boarding school in Virginia for more than a year."

"So we're looking at a family reunion, huh?"

Stone grinned ruefully. "I never thought of it that way. Arrington and I have spent so little time together over the years."

"So how are you feeling about this?" Dino asked.

"Scared stiff," Stone said.

FROM #1 *NEW YORK TIMES*–BESTSELLING AUTHOR

STUART WOODS

STUARTWOODS.COM
StuartWoodsAuthor

PUTNAM | Penguin Random House